THE
TREE OF LIFE

*Second book of
the Cup of Christ and the Forgotten Disciple Trilogy*

A Mystery-Thriller

JACK HOLT

Holt Publishing™

For information, questions, or comments, contact
jackmholt.com
jackmholt21@gmail.com

ISBN: 978-1-7355283-3-5 (hard cover)
ISBN: 978-1-7355283-5-9 (paperback)
ISBN: 978-1-7355283-4-2 (e-book)

Cover and interior design
Deborah Perdue, Illumination Graphics

Introduction

The high history of *le Sangraal* has never been
told by any mortal man since Saint Joseph de
Arimathea wrote these sacred words about our
Lord and Savior. However, I declare to all men
and women who wish to own this book,
if God allows me to live in good health, it
is certainly my intention to bring his story
together. If God blesses my holy quest, these
parchments will be found.

—Lord Robert de Borron
Anno Domini 1190

Anno Domini 1190

Jesus Christ Map of Life Events

Jerusalem in Roman Times

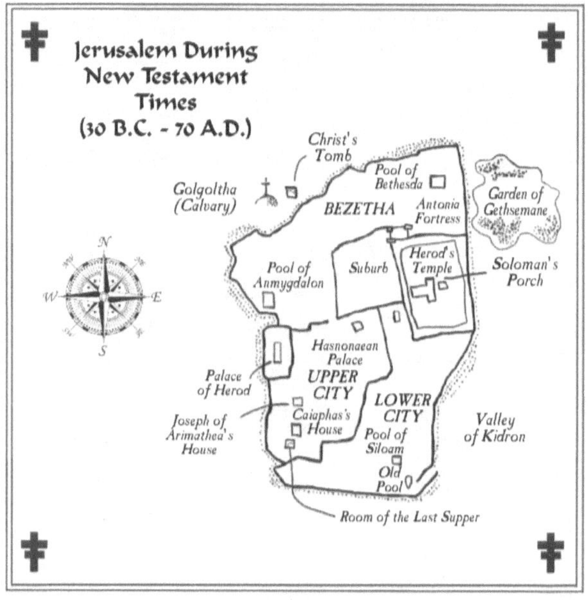

Tree of Life

Indeed, to them the books will be given,
and they will believe in them, and in them
all the righteous will rejoice and be glad,
to learn from them all the paths of truth.

1st Book of Enoch
Epistle 104:13

The High History
of *le Sangraal* and the Forgotten Disciple
is Dedicated to My Patron and
Brother-in-Law
Comte Gautiér de Montbéliard

—Lord Robert de Borron

Dedication

To my loving wife, Carol, who had patience for the last twelve years listening to me speak about my book. Also, to my late mother, Charlotte, who gave me the interest to write, and my late dad, Jack, who had a great thirst for history.

Acknowledgments

I would like to acknowledge author Stephen Lawhead, for inspiring me to write my first book in the Cup of Christ trilogy. His tireless research in Celtic lore and the legends of King Arthur motivated me to create my own ideas.

Dan Brown, author of *The Da Vinci Code*, provided the inspiration for me to use symbols, codes, and arcane terminology.

I am grateful for Joanna Penn whose success as an independent author contributed to me taking the same route.

Thank you to my indefatigable graphic designer, Deborah Perdue, from Illumination Graphics, who used her artistic abilities to capture my book's vision. My sincerest gratitude to Reverend C. Allen Colwell for his counsel.

I offer my humble thanks to my great taskmaster, Pam Johnson of Pam the Editor. Without her helpful advice and developmental editing, I would not have accomplished this writing journey. Also, to my copyeditor Joni Wilson who kept me in the proper boundaries of literary grammar.

My printing company IngramSpark that offered great advice about getting my book published for all those who love historical fiction and mystery thrillers.

Jack Holt

The Principal Characters of Frankish Gaul and the Levant

Anno Domini 1190

Baroness Marie de Borron—wife of Lord Robert de Borron; mother to Robert's sons, Brian and Henri; sister to Count Gautiér de Montbéliard

Cardinal Folquet de Marseille—archbishop of Toulouse, former troubadour, head of the Roman curia

Chevalier **Marcel de Tournay**—seneschal to Cardinal Folquet, archbishop of Toulouse

Commander Armound de Polignac—Templar leader at the commandery of Carcassonne, old friend of Grand Master Gilbért de Érail

Comte **Gautiér de Montbéliard**—former Crusader, writing benefactor to Lord Robert de Borron, brother-in-law to Robert de Borron

Grand Master Gilbért de Érail—Iberian grand master of the Poor Fellow-Soldiers of Christ (Knights Templar)

Hughes de Montbard—Templar squire, great-nephew to Saint Bernard de Clairvaux, under the command of Grand Master Gilbért de Érail

Muhammad Nur Adin—former emir from the Levant, constable of the Templar horses in Gaul, scout

Richard I, le coeur de lion—king of England; duke of Normandy, Aquitaine, and Gascony; lord of Cyprus; *comte* of Poitiers, Anjou, Maine, and Nantes; overlord of Brittany; reign 1189–1199

Robert de Borron—Lord of *Château* Borron, poet, writer, troubadour, swordsman, from Northern Burgundy

Robert de Sablé—grand master of the Templar's entire order, reign 1190–1193

Saladin (Salāh ad-Din Yūsuf ibn Ayyūb)—Muslim Kurdish Suni sultan of Egypt, Syria, and part of Palestine; led a great army against Christian crusaders; reigned from 1174–1193

Sergeant Guy de Béziers—Templar scout, former seaman, under the command of Grand Master Gilbért de Érail

Sergeant Jacque de Hoult—Templar scout, under the command of Grand Master Gilbért de Érail

The Principal Characters of Iberia (Spain)

Anno Domini 1190

Alfonso II (The Chaste)—king of Aragón; conde de Barcelona, Catalonia, Provence, Cerdanya, Y Roussillon; husband to Queen Sacha; brother-in-law to Princess Helena

Andreas—king of Iberian Romany (Gypsies); spouse of Queen Esmerelda

Benjamin and Esther—Jewish father and mother of Deborah, maternal grandparents of Chaplain Jeremiah Santiago de Compostela, son of Grand Master Gilbért de Érail

Commander Hugo de Joffre—Hospitaller monk commander of Zaragozza

Deborah—Jewish lover of Gilbért de Érail; mother of Jeremiah Santiago de Compostela

Diego—deceased infant son of Princess Helena of Aragón; lived just one day

Esmerelda—queen of the Iberia Romany (Gypsies) and seer

Esperanza—lady-in-waiting to Princess Helena of Aragón

Frère **Chaplain Jeremiah Santiago de Compostela**—Templar chaplain, scholar, and son to Grand Master Gilbért de Érail

Gerard de Ridefort—infamous tenth grand master of the entire Templar order (1184–1189) who lost the battle of the Horns of Hattin in Levant

Helena—princess de Aragón; marquésa de Barcelona, Castile, y Provence; widow of the martyred principe Pedro, late brother to King Alfonso II of Aragón

Holy Roman Emperor Fredrick Barbarossa—emperor of central Europe and commanding 150,000, army on the third crusade; drowned in a Turkish river on the way to the Levant. Lore says he dropped the spear that pierced the side of Christ and the emperor then drowned.

King Alfonso I (The Battler)—Iberian king who reconquered more than half of Moorish Iberia; great uncle to King Alfonso II (The Chaste)

Marshal Poncho Diaz de Vivar—Templar ancestor of El Cid and carried El Cid's sword, Tizona

Miguel—hermano, frère abbe, abad, abbot of San Pedro el Viejo in Huesca, Iberia; traveling companion of Lord Robert de Borron

Pedro Bernardo Ramón—principe de Aragón; marqués de Barcelona, Provence; martyr of the Battle of the Horns of Hattin in the Levant; late brother to Alfonso II (The Chaste); late husband to Princess Helena

Pope Clement III—papacy reign 1187–1191

Ramiro II—late monk, abbot, and king of Aragón (1134–1137); married Agnes of Aquitaine; sired the child Petronilla, future mother of King Alfonso II (The Chaste)

Reccared—Visigoth king of Southern Iberia, reign 586–601

Rodrigo de Balaguer—double agent working for Cardinal Folquet

Alfonso VII—king of Castile, late brother to Princess Helena

Sancha—reina de Aragón; Condesa de Barcelona, Catalonia, Provence, Cerdanya, y Roussillon; also spouse and queen of Alfonso II (The Chaste)

Shandar—son of Romany (Gypsy) King Andreas and Queen Esmerelda

Suleiman—one of the assassins

The Principal Characters of the City of Jerusalem and Palestine
Anno Domini 37

Alein Yosephe—son to Yoseph of Arimathea, partner in his father's business

Barabbas—the murderer set free by Jewish Sanhedrin, instead of Jesus the Christ, and released by Pontius Pilate

Cephus—fisherman, "the Rock," disciple of Rabbi Yeshua ben Yoseph, brother to another disciple called Andrew

Clotho—Greek woman and early follower of Yoseph of Arimathea living in Palestine with new baby and wife to Georgeus

Eli of Yerushalayim (Jerusalem)—camel and cloth merchant; with two sons, Eliyah and Isaiah

Eliyah—son of Eli, the camel and cloth merchant

Enoch—infant son of Hebron and Enygeus; also name of Old Testament prophet who walked with God and didn't die

Enygeus—sister to Yoseph of Arimathea, husband to Hebron

Gaius Cassius Longinus—Roman Centurion guard, at the cross

Gaius Sertonius—centurion

Georgeus—Greek man and early follower of Yoseph of Arimathea living in Palestine with new baby and husband to Clotho

Hebron—brother-in-law to Yoseph of Arimathea, overseer to Yoseph's merchant business, husband to Enygeus

Herod Antipas—tetrarch of Galilee-Perea; one of the sons of Herod the Great

Isaiah—Eli's son

King Arviragus—ruler of the Celtic Silures

Lazarus—resurrected from the dead by Yeshua ben Yoseph (Jesus the Christ), brother to Miriam and

Martha, later follower of Yoseph of Arimathea

Martha from Bethany—sister to Lazarus; sister to Miriam

Miriam of Magdala—landowner, mystic, student of Rabbi Yeshua ben Yoseph, a new friend to Yoseph of Arimathea

Miriam of Nazareth—niece to Yoseph of Arimathea, mother to Rabbi Yeshua ben Yoseph, widow to the late mason and carpenter Yoseph of Nazareth

Nathaniel—friend to Philip; from Cana; early follower of Rabbi Yeshua ben Yoseph

Nicodemus—member of the Jewish Sanhedrin ruling council, scholar, lawyer, old friend of Yoseph of Arimathea

Philip—one of the twelve disciples chosen by Rabbi Yeshua ben Yoseph; also good friend to Yoseph of Arimathea

Pontius Pilate—Roman *procurator* of Yehudah (Judea)

Rabbi Yeshua ben Yoseph—itinerate preacher, mystic, biblical scholar, son of Miriam of Nazareth, rumored to be the foretold *Maishiach* (Messiah)

Saul of Tarsus—later called Paul, before Christian conversion was a tent merchant and member of the Jewish Sanhedrin and a persecutor of Christians

Shimon bar Yona—also known as Cephas or Peter; brother to Andrew, fishing merchant

Shimon the Zealot—half-brother of Rabbi Yeshua ben Yoseph and apostle; also later follower of Yoseph of Arimathea

Stephanos—first martyred Christian deacon in Jerusalem; later scholars say Saul of Tarsus (Paul) had Stephanos stoned to death

Thomas Didymus—apostle of Rabbi Yeshua ben Yoseph; also a later member who joined Yoseph of Arimathea

Yohanan bar Zebedee, the Writer—disciple of Rabbi Yeshua ben Yoseph, biographer, a close friend to Rabbi Yeshua

Yohanan Marcus—writer, student of Rabbi Yeshua, his two-story home used for the Seder (Passover meal)

Yohanan the Baptizer—cousin to Rabbi Yeshua ben Yoseph. He foretold Rabbi Yeshua as the Messiah and he would baptize his disciples with the Holy Spirit. Yohanan was possibly Essene trained. He had a son named Zechariah and, after Yohanan's beheading, his son was raised by Yoseph of Arimathea's family.

Yosa—daughter to Yoseph of Arimathea

Yoseph ben Caiaphas—high priest of the Jews; head of the Sanhedrin

Yoseph of Arimathea—richest merchant in the Mediterranean region, member of the Jewish Sanhedrin ruling council, uncle to Miriam of Nazareth, great uncle to Yeshua ben Yoseph of Nazareth

Yudas Iscariot—treasurer, disciple for Rabbi Yeshua ben Yoseph, rumored to be a member of the Sicarii (daggermen), a group who assassinates Roman officials

Zechariah—orphan son of Yohanan the Baptizer, toddler second cousin to Rabbi Yeshua ben Yoseph

PART I

The Wolf

CHAPTER I

Anno Domini 1190
Late Fall
Pyrénées Mountains

The steep descent down the frozen mountain range, while following my fellow *frères* was circumspect, but uneventful. We encountered several thundering waterfalls along the winding rocky path toward the valley floor and decided to stop at one before nightfall and make camp. Marcel de Tournay and his men were now dead from the Pyrénées *montagne* snow avalanche and not pursuing us. This gave me some emotional relief along with my physical wounds, which now seemed healed. This gave me more strength to do strenuous chores. However, before dismounting, I sensed someone or something stalking us, forcing the hair on the back of my neck to tingle and the palms of my hand to sweat.

The pine-scented forest, on both sides of the trail, divulged nothing, other than a misty dark green color from the evergreen trees. None of the other four men seemed agitated, with both sergeants' bobbing heads starting to drift with sleep. Once we stopped, Muhammad gathered some wood to start our campfire, and I thought it best to try to find something to eat for my companions. They were gaining their strength, but we had just a little food left. Drinking water wasn't a problem, for there was an abundance of melting snow scattered about the rocky cliffs, and the large waterfall nearby provided more than sufficient water for our needs.

"Commander de Érail, do you have any suggestions as to where I could forage for some food?" I queried, for I knew he was familiar with the terrain.

"Lord Robert, there is a large trout stream on the other side of these cliff rocks. Travel upstream about half a league. If my memory is correct, there's a small offshoot of the stream where the trout feed. Search for a large grove of white birch trees, which should mark the spot. I will tell Muhammad to fix you a fishing line with some down bait. Retrieve my battle-ax from my horse and use it to cut a pole for the line."

I felt quite reluctant to do this for two reasons. One, I didn't know how to fish, and the other, I thought I saw dark shadows of movement in the dense evergreen forest to my right.

"Commander de Érail, I must confess I have never fished before, and what if I become lost?"

"I would do it, but my strength hasn't returned from our battle at Gavarnie and my cabin surgery. Don't worry about that, Lord Robert de Borron, use my ax to mark the tree trunks, every third tree. Also, stay along the streambank, which will lead you there and back. As far as not being able to fish, Muhammad guarantees his bait of down always works. Just don't make a lot of noise when you wade out into the cove. Now hurry and leave. We are all starving for some hot grilled trout."

I proceeded to chop a young river birch sapling and used my boot dagger to remove the small limbs and leaves. By now, Muhammad had finished the lure and I attached the twine to the end of the pole. The bait color was a bright blue and resembled a small dragonfly. I was thankful he attached the bait lure first to the twine; thus, I was reassured it wouldn't come off if the fish bit the hook. Before leaving, Muhammad placed several small drops of a liquid that made the lure shine. I examined the bait as I started on my fishing trip. At the far end of the bait was a sharp broken piece of chain mail made into a hook and secured with colored thread. The curved nose of the lure had some twine attached, well-knotted.

"Lord Robert de Borron."

I heard my name as I started through the thick forest of trees. It sounded strange, and then I realized it was Muhammad trying to gain my attention. He motioned for me to come back.

When I turned to him, he gave me a large cloth sack to carry any fish I might catch and grinned. He said something in his Saracen language and motioned for me to leave.

The day started to warm up after I had trudged a quarter of a league, yet I couldn't shake the sense of being followed. Before reaching a rocky stream, a low guttural growl came from the misty wood, just as I stopped and marked a tree with my shaky ax. My heart started beating louder. It sounded familiar, like the wolves that had attacked us at the *montagne* cabin, but a creepy deeper throaty sound.

After some time, I approached a large row of cliffs that enclosed both sides of the rushing stream, stopping only to rest before proceeding any farther. A cool breeze rose from the stream, which dried the sweat from my face as I sat down to reflect on how far I had come on my journey for *le Sangraal* parchments.

Momentarily, my thoughts went astray when a large brown eagle flew overhead and gave out a piercing cry for its circling mate. My thoughts drifted back to young Squire Hughes de Montbard and his heroic act of throwing his body in front of Marcel de Tournay's crossbow arrow to save his fellow *frère moines*. I so missed his aid and companionship, which left a dull ache in my stomach that wasn't hunger. It was a gnawing ache like losing a loved family member.

After gazing at the sky, my ears heard heavy footfalls running through the forest on the other side of the stream. Faintly, four huge, gray-colored legs appeared, but not the animal's body or head. An enormous sounding howl erupted at once from the other bank, followed by a rapid crunching noise of forest debris. For just a brief movement, I caught sight of two large round-shaped orange eyes. Without thinking, my sword came out of its scabbard, after which I tightly brandished it with my right hand, while holding the battle-ax with my left. The undetermined animal or thing wasn't showing itself but seemed to gaze at me through the dense woods with its fiery, orange-colored eyes. The eyes didn't move but waited for me to react, which I did, by shouting at the beast, while striking the flat part of my ax against the blade of my sword. Immediately, the creature crept out of the woods.

To my horror, the wolf was gigantic in size, which I estimated to be the size of a small grown cow. It didn't seem mortal in nature, for its head and shoulders were twice the size of an average wolf. Especially, its large pointed canine teeth, which dripped with hungry saliva. Quickly, the beast raised its head toward the sky and gave out another blood-curdling howl, then afterward raced toward me. At once, I said a prayer to my Lord, Marie Magdalene, and the Almighty asking for protection from this devilish creature. Just as the enormous animal lunged toward my throat, a bright beam of light appeared between us.

"Lord Robert de Borron, fear not, for the beast is an apparition from Satan," came a familiar female voice. "You are now protected from his evil snare, have strength and faith, my *frère*, for you're safe from harm." Her golden-colored beam of light covered my entire body and warmed me like a blanket, making me experience a safe sensation from any adversary, imaginable or not. Once he collided with the yellow beam of light, the wolf's gigantic body dissolved into a thousand miniature sparkling stars.

The light beam drew me to two large cliffs with a talus that jutted out into the large stream. It seemed difficult to climb, but Marie Magdalene's soothing voice made it easy to reach the other side. There in front of me appeared a grove of snow white-colored birch tree trunks surrounding the perimeter of the cove. Suddenly, the wind increased in speed and the white birch trees started swaying from the gusts, causing their small, yellow-colored leaves to issue forth an eerie rustling sound.

Once more, in the shadows of the birch grove, appeared a white radiating light, different from the yellow one radiating above me. It appeared similar to the one I had seen several months ago at the priory in Montpellier. At once, the white light turned a reddish-tinged color and began to form a human shape just as I reached the bank of the stream. The light's pinnacle radiated out several colors of yellow, red, and white, in what appeared to be a woman's head. Indeed, it was the Holy Marie Magdalene who appeared in front of me.

"Robert de Borron, I come again to give you my counsel," the now fully formed body said. "You have done quite well in our Lord's work. So far, what you have written, accurately tells of my friend Joseph and his trials. The search for the second set of *Sangraal* parchments will be fraught with intrigues, enigmas, and betrayal. However, Robert, beware of the third of these three, for Satan hides in many disguises. In addition, seek the truth in the building blocks of our God's universe; these will protect you from evil."

"But Holy Marie," I beseeched her on my knees. "Where and when will I know these things?"

"Some of these things will be revealed sooner than you might want, Robert de Borron. Remember my last words before I leave. We are all God's people no matter where we were born. Learn to be open in thought and have patience with others not similar to you. Now, I must leave, so you can continue to write about the forgotten disciple and our Lord's work."

She faded and with one last ray disappeared. By now, Holy Mary had given me a renewed sense of euphoria as I crossed myself and then reached for my fishing pole.

At once, I waded out into the cove of cool water and cast my line. After a short period, I felt a sharp tug on my line and a large iridescent fish leaped out of the water. He struggled for a short time trying to hide under a rock in the cove, but it was to no avail. I gently grabbed hold of the trout and placed it in my sack. I pulled the drawstring to secure the fish and then put it into the water.

Some time had passed, for the sun hung high over my head and a large set of what seemed fish-shaped clouds drifted across my view. I estimated by now, I had caught enough fish to feed all my fellow disabled companions. The capture sack was writhing with activity as the trout fruitlessly tried to escape. My pride and confidence now surged, and I felt more essential to my *frère moines*.

The trail back to camp was easy to find, for I had marked the trees well. As I approached the campfire, I could see all of my fellow *frères* had large smiles of surprise as I held up a large sack of fish. *Frère* Jacque de Hoult insisted he wanted to count the number of fish I had caught. I gave him the sack followed by Muhammad storing my fishing pole for later use. I sat down near the fire and gazed into its flames. Everyone was in a jovial mood as our abundant evening meal was being prepared. I didn't say a word until Commander de Érail spoke to me.

"Was your fishing expedition uneventful, Lord de Borron?"

"Yes," I replied, sensing a crooked smile on my face. "The fishing part was quiet and fruitful, but I had another encounter with a wolf. This time the creature appeared to be the size of a cow and not of this world. It attacked me, lunging for my throat, but a yellow beam of light slew the phantom demon." The rest of my compatriots stopped what they were doing and stared at me.

"Quite frightening, indeed. Please, tell us more." Commander Gilbért queried.

"Shortly thereafter, a human apparition appeared in the white birch grove that you mentioned. It was our Saint Marie Magdalene who appeared to me, and I know it was her intercession that saved my life. Holy Marie imparted several warnings to me. She said to remember three words: intrigues, enigmas, and betrayal. These were her pertinent didactic clues to what lies ahead for us. Saint Marie wouldn't say anymore, but her holy parting words were to be patient of others not similar to ourselves and to be alert to the powers of darkness. Satan hides in many disguises, she said. Oh, and Commander, she mentioned a vexing sentence that maybe you can interpret. She said to seek the truth in the building blocks of God's universe. She spoke of this as being our protection from evil. Can any of you explain what she meant by the building blocks of the universe?"

"*Non,*" both sergeants replied, but Sergeant Jacque de Hoult spoke with wide eyes.

"You were with Marie Magdalene? The beloved student of our Lord and Savior?" At once Sergeant Jacque crossed himself and said a silent prayer.

"*Oui*, but this wasn't my first visit. She spoke to me at the *iglesia* at Vézaley and then appeared to me at the fortress of Montpellier. Commander Gilbért knows of her appearances too. That is how he recognized me at your fortress."

Commander de Érail waited in silent thought before he gave me a reply.

"*Oui*, that is true, my fellow *frères*. I failed to mention it until our quest led us to more truths. I don't know what her cryptic message means, but my chaplain at our fortress at Zaragozza should know. *Frère* Jeremiah Santiago de Compostela is an antiquarian and a learned man of mathematics and philosophy. If anyone should know, he's the person who can answer our Holy Marie Magdalene's conundrum. Let's hope the weather stays pleasant, we should be at my home commandery in less than a fortnight. In addition, *Frère* Jeremiah is aiding me in our search for the second set of *Sangraal* parchments."

Sergeant de Hoult approached me with a broad smile on his face as Commander de Érail and I were finishing our conversation. His wound seemed to be healing fast, for his limp was just a small shuffle.

"Lord de Borron, you had seventeen fine fish in your capture sack, and you caught them in less than half a day. This should give you the confidence you need to return eight more times."

"Why eight more times, *mon bon frère*?" I asked.

"Our Saint Peter caught one hundred and fifty-three fish when our Lord told him to throw out his net on Lake Tiberias. I estimate this amount should feed us until we reach our home commandery. I have already started smoking nine of them. The remaining eight we will eat tonight."

"I lost count of the number I caught. My mind was still pondering what our holy lady said. I am still amazed at the holy clues we are receiving. This is an affirmation that God is leading us in the right direction."

The evening meal was quite tasty and gave each one of us the strength we needed. Furthermore, Muhammad and Sergeant de Béziers picked some winter berries to augment our fish dinner. Commander de Érail told us that we would now remain at this camp for several days before proceeding down the mountain. He said we would obtain some additional supplies when we reached the village of Huesca and the local commandery there. He estimated Huesca would be about twenty to twenty-five leagues from here. The commander further stated he would be pleased to see his old commandery at Zaragozza too.

Then Commander Gilbért revealed the *abbé* at Huesca, who was a *bon ami* and confidant, would meet us there.

I must have dozed off after completing our evening meal, for the next thing I remembered was the nickering of our horses as dawn broke through the evergreen trees.

The remaining few days kept me busy with fishing trips, after which Sergeant de Hoult meticulously counted my fish after each trip. When I had reached one hundred and fifty-three, he said it was time for us to leave the mountainside. The next day we broke camp after the fish were smoked.

I could see that my companions were gaining strength each day, for they started riding their horses on the remaining descent down into the valley floor.

On the final part of the steep rocky trail down the Monte Perdido pass, our horses' hooves *clicked* and *clacked* on the moist rocks, but not one of them stumbled. Sometimes, we would see large venues of winged bearded vultures gliding on the warm air currents. We made our night camp next to a fen at the base of the canyon pass. Nearby beside a swampy lake, I viewed several families of geese who were conversing with one another over their evening meals. This serene scene melted some of my trepidations and the beautiful snow-capped *montagne* landscape gave me a sense of peace and confidence in what unknown we might face.

CHAPTER II

During our descent, my mind conjured up numerous questions to ask Commander de Érail about the *Sangraal* book. After Muhammad and I finished preparing our camp for the night, we sat down to eat. Our commander was moving about quicker than usual as he finished feeding his horses. I could see Commander de Érail's former cat-like moves were almost back to normal despite a slight moan as he sat down beside me.

"Commander, I have waited until you regained your strength before asking you some questions that have vexed me. Whatever became of the blood cups and vials? Especially the one used during the Last Supper." There was a moment of silence as Gilbért de Érail stared into the crackling campfire to recall an answer to my question. He shifted back and forth on his rock before answering.

"Lord Borron, the majority were lost in time. Supposedly Saint Lawrence sent one of the cups to Huesca hundreds of years ago where it once resided. Another one turned up at Aleppo during the first 'taking of the cross.' Later, it found its way to Genoa by the merchants who sailed from the Levant. I have no idea of the whereabouts of the alabaster jar of our Holy Marie Magdalene. As for the vials and the Last Supper chalice that Saint Joseph received, I am hoping the next *Sangraal* parchments will tell us more."

"I didn't know that. How factual are these other reports?"

"It is just as factual as our faith wants us to believe. You must trust in our Lord and Savior's divine words. He gives us the ability to think and see past his holy words. Lord Borron, I have been thinking a lot about why we have been murderously pursued by the cardinal's men and the evil de Tournay. It's obvious there's more at stake than the parchments. As I have mentioned, the church is aware of several blessed cups and their locations. Yet, there must be more in the *Sangraal* stories that we haven't found. Are you positive you didn't ignore any clues, symbols, or parables before we left Montpellier?"

"I have always prided myself on my memory and I am thankful for the gift the Holy Marie Magdalene has given me. I didn't detect any other hidden meanings or knowledge in the *Sangraal* parchments."

"What I am alluding to is the *Sangraal* parchments are quite important, but they're part of what the evil cardinal desires. Our Savior and Saint Joseph of Arimathea wants us to lift our veil of ignorance. It's quite apparent that the cardinal's men have some information we don't have. I suspect before Gérard de Ridefort died, he forced my loyal chaplain to divulge what he translated, but this information is the same as you have read and copied."

"It appears this way, but our travels are starting to fill with hidden words, esoteric symbols, and parables that may have several connotations. Commander Gilbért, it requires time, prayer, and study for the parchments to speak to us and reveal their secrets."

I knew the cardinal coveted my holy gifts and me. He and his men were aware I could quickly chronicle the words of these *Sangraal* parchments. It appeared there were more hidden secrets in the next set of parchments. Yet, the second set seemed as a dream to me.

We both sat there at the campfire eating our smoked fish and contemplating what clues we may have missed. I felt certain I hadn't missed anything in my transcribing, but I told myself tomorrow I would again review our parchments. Oh, how I missed *mon bon* aide, Squire Hughes our martyred *chevalier*, and *bon ami*. May he rest in everlasting peace, I prayed.

As we prepared to retire, grayish-black clouds crept over the stars, followed by the wind whistling through the trees. In the distance in front of us appeared jagged bolts of lightning approaching from the west. We were still at a high altitude, where a storm could become quite dangerous. Muhammad with celerity gathered our swords, chain mail, and axes and placed them some distance from our camp to prevent attracting the lightning to the metal implements. Commander de Érail told me to help Muhammad pick up some large rocks and place them as a shelter around us. On each of our horses' loose bridles, we placed a large gritty rock. I surmised this would prevent them from running to the nearby trees for shelter, which would further attract more lightning. We had to see that they weren't killed by the storm.

I was apprehensive at first to lift these large stones because of my broken ribs, but to my amazement, I felt no pain. Either the strips of bandages were holding tight, or I was healing. It didn't matter, I told myself, and completed my job.

Commander de Érail positioned each horse at different intervals so if lightning did strike our camp, not all would perish. Muhammad forced each of our horses to lie down next to each of us as the thunderstorm struck. The thunder echoed all around us until almost dawn. During the night, lightning ignited some trees next to the fen and they caught fire. The axes, swords, and chain mail that Muhammad had placed some distance from our camp, erupted with large dancing sparks. It was an eerie sight to see our swords glowing from the lightning strikes. Each sword gave off a bluish-red color that stayed with the blades for a moment. As I lay under my mound of rocks, I thought dawn would never arrive. As the sun rose, the storm disappeared, and our horses were miraculously still lying tethered to their rocks. I said a quick prayer of thanks to God for our horses not running off.

That morning we packed our equipment, mounted our horses, and left for the grassy plains below the mountains. I marveled at the difference in terrain as we reached the base of the mountains. Stretched out before us were open fields of tall green grass that waved with each breeze that passed ahead of us. There were some stunted pine trees scattered about, but the majority of the trees followed the streams and rivers that came down the Pyrénées *Montagnes.* The dense grass touched the barrel level of our horses but didn't make traveling difficult. We made excellent time and expected to reach the next major town in two to three days.

"Commander, how many leagues left to Huesca?" I asked.

"Lord Borron, it will be another twenty leagues before we reach our commandery at Huesca. It will require us to cross another *montagne* range; however, it won't be as treacherous as the Pyrénées. If all goes well, we will reach Huesca in three days. I'll ask Muhammad to scout ahead for unexpected visitors, but we'll still need to be vigilant. We need to be on guard for any suspicious occurrences and won't be out of danger until we reach Huesca." His words jangled my nerves, and my heart started to race.

The sun was beaming high overhead causing me to sweat. We stopped at a nearby shady stream and rested both our horses and ourselves. After sitting down, the only noises we heard were a gurgling stream and the ever-present wind. Oh, how peaceful it was here, thinking I never wanted to leave this small piece of heaven. Then I remembered I was to review my manuscript for clues. While the others were eating fish and sharpening their swords, I proceeded to my horse. There I grabbed my parchment pages out of the saddlebags and started to review them under a large unfamiliar tree. The buffeting wind made it difficult to hold my pages. Several of the parchment sheets flew from my hands and I raced to retrieve them in the tall grass. After recovering several, as I returned to the tree, I heard Sergeant Jacque de Hoult's shout.

"A rider is coming fast over the next hill!"

Unbeknownst to me, Sergeant de Hoult had climbed up to the top of the tree I was sitting under. Now I heard the heavy thumping of the horse's hooves and the loud snorting of its strained breathing. Sergeant de Hoult shouted again.

"It's Muhammad!"

He scrambled down the tree and nearly jumped on top of me before tumbling to the ground. We raced out to hear what possible urgent message Muhammad had to say. Sergeant de Béziers was the first to greet Muhammad. They conversed quickly and then Guy de Béziers turned and shouted, "Thirty to forty heavily armed riders are approaching from the northwest. We must leave now!"

We jumped on our horses, spurred them, and then swiftly departed. I had left my parchment satchel lying under the tree, but Commander de Érail shouted at me to grab it.

"Damn it, Lord Robert, grab your satchel!"

I could tell his wounds were healing because his old truculent manner had returned. I reached down from my saddle, grabbed the writing satchel, and spurred my horse to leave. Sergeant de Hoult grabbed the smoked fish and berries and followed right behind me.

As I glanced back, Muhammad had mounted a fresh horse. He moved with the quickness of a cat and was almost alongside the commander. Muhammad said something to the commander, which I couldn't hear because of our horses' pounding hooves.

Commander de Érail replied to Muhammad, which caused him to split off from us with the packhorses. He motioned to the remaining three of us to head for the large river some distance away. It appeared as if it was more than half a league away, but on the open plains, the distance was deceiving.

After some hard riding, our lathered horses approached the riverbank. The river appeared wide and deep and, if this wasn't a problem enough, the bank was too steep to navigate down. No horse or man could travel down this drop off to the river.

"Lord Borron, I know a place where we can ford this river, but we must hurry. Muhammad is to meet us there."

We again spurred our tired horses and galloped off for this unknown rendezvous.

"The ride will be long, but there is a hiding place near the path down to the river!" yelled Commander de Érail over the labored snorting of our horses. I wondered if our already exhausted steeds would make it to this hiding place. Muhammad wasn't here to coax them on to greater speed and it seemed we would never arrive at our meeting place. I turned around, and I observed a large fast-moving dust cloud surrounding us.

Our labored horses now gave forth desperate wheezes, as I spied a copse of trees that lined the riverbank and heard the din of a waterfall. The edge of the riverbank fell off to a path that abruptly dropped to the river. Commander Gilbért de Érail pointed at the trail that snaked parallel to the falls and motioned for us to follow him.

The river in front of the falls was foamy from the steep height of the tumbling water, yet the river didn't appear deep as we trotted down the narrow path. Then I remembered where the river had separated upstream, which now left the river shallow. Commander de Érail shouted to us to leave the path.

"We must now ride a short distance down this path and double back through the river on my command. Don't waste any time returning to the falls. There is a flat rock path on the left of the falls that enters into a cave behind the falls."

We continued down the dirt trail a short distance and then the commander gave the order to enter the shallow river. Our racing horses refreshed themselves in the cool water and then we picked up speed. However, their galloping didn't seem fast enough. We approached the falls drenched from the splashing water. The roar of the falls precluded conversation, so Commander de Érail pointed at the hidden pathway that led behind the falls.

It was quite slippery trying to navigate the wet stones, and my horse slipped once, but she regained her footing on the wet slate rock. My luck held as we entered the large dark cavern, where my eyes quickly adjusted to the lack of light.

At once, I smelled something burning the farther we traveled into the interior and then appeared a flickering light that gave off shadows of horses on the cavern wall. I drew my sword thinking this could be the cardinal's men. Commander de Érail dismounted and then crawled forward by himself whispering Arabic and to my relief it was Muhammad. The commander pointed past Muhammad, forcing me to stare forward that revealed a partially hidden exit.

"It is quite important," he whispered, "that we remain quiet and that any sound made will echo through the rear of the cave, out the exit."

We cautiously dismounted and sat down against the cool walls. Muhammad crept back toward the fall's entrance to observe for the pursuing riders. Quietly, I rose, approached Commander de Érail, and asked in a whisper for a favor.

"Commander, I request you to let me stand sentry duty for the rear entrance this evening and tonight. I could contribute something other than my writing skills to our quest efforts." There was a momentary silence as he pondered my request.

"Lord Robert, I will grant your request, but you must use some of this time now to search for the *Sangraal* book cipher. You can relieve me when the moon has started to rise."

"Thank you, Commander. I will be quite vigilant tonight and not disappoint you."

I reached for my completed manuscript from my saddlebags, and I quietly sat down to review what I had written. There was just enough light coming from the exit of the cave to allow me to read the parchments. Again, several passages struck me as odd. "Remember the secret words and numbers," Jesus said. "Also, you will be the first apostle to speak in my First Temple and, Joseph, remember the words of Solomon." These sayings of our Lord were still an enigma to me. What was he trying to tell me? I must note these lines and discuss them with the commander later tonight.

I continued pondering over the remaining sections, and then it struck me like a great gust of wind. It was Saint Joseph of Arimathea who founded the first church or tabernacle, not Saint Peter! I couldn't believe what the words revealed. My Roman faith and church had drummed into my head about Jesus the Christ and how his church was built upon a rock and overseen by Peter; his name meant a rock. However, from Saint Joseph de Arimathea's scrolls, I knew Jesus taught some of his disciples differently. The diverse ones were Saint John the writer, Saint Thomas, and his closet student, Saint Marie Magdalene. At that moment, my heart raced, and cold beads of sweat broke out on my forehead. Nevertheless, how could this be? Where was this church, and what did the secret numbers and words mean?

My epiphany left me with numerous questions racing in my mind. It seemed there were more questions at this point in the *Sangraal* story than answers.

The steady roar from the falls helped calm my mind and prompted me to start organizing my clues. I reached for a blank parchment and started writing down what I had discovered. The first conundrum was the meaning of King Solomon's words to Saint Joseph. Why did Jesus want Saint Joseph to study about King Solomon's passages? What secret words did Jesus reveal to Saint Joseph? I reread the sections in my manuscripts several times in which our Lord and Savior spoke to Saint Joseph. The passages disclosed nothing else before it was time to relieve the commander.

"Commander, I would like to discuss an extraordinary revelation I have discovered in my writings. In addition, several puzzling things our Lord said to Saint Joseph. I would appreciate any thoughts you may have on what I have found."

I elucidated my great epiphany to him and its arcane words, but no information on the old church's location. He seemed quite excited and intrigued by my discovery about the secret words of our Lord and Savior, Jesus the Christ.

"*Seigneur* Robert, if you remember previously, I believed my chaplain in the Levant may have divulged this information under torture.

"I think this explains why the cardinal and his men want these *Sangraal* books. They know that each parchment sheet links another piece of the puzzle to whoever should be the head of the church and its founding whereabouts. The cardinal and his *chevaliers* want these books, after which they will destroy us. They keep you alive until last. It's paramount that we reach Zaragozza as soon as possible. We can strengthen our fighting force and I can speak to Chaplain Jeremiah about what you've told me.

"I knew there had to be more to our quest than the spiritual nature of the cup of our Lord's Last Supper. The *Sangraal* and Saint Joseph are leading us to several truths. These truths will remove authority away from the powerful few, thus transferring these revelations to the many people of Christendom and a new authority. The cardinal will use this epiphany of new information to blackmail numerous people, including the current Holy *Père*. He wants the divine office of Holy *Père*. We are now in more danger than I first thought. Be most vigilant tonight while you guard us. I will retire now and contemplate what you have told me. We will leave at first light if all is well."

I was now all alone on my sentry duty and my sole company was a crescent-shaped moon. The ever-present sound of the falls kept me from hearing anything but the movement of my cohorts. My mind kept wandering from one passage to another from the *Sangraal* book. The singular beneficial thing about my restless mind was that

I didn't want to sleep. What was in the meaning of the glory of King Solomon? This sentence kept repeating itself in my mind.

All of a sudden, I observed movement on a small hill some distance away. My heart raced faster as the riders approached. Two of them carried torches, but I could not detect how many men the riders encompassed. They stopped a short distance from the concealed exit of the cave, and then the riders dismounted and proceeded to build a campfire.

Without warning, Muhammad grabbed my arm and made a sign not to speak and then crept back to Commander de Érail, who was sound asleep. In silence he woke the commander and the three of us observed the strangers for some time.

"Lord Borron," whispered the commander, "I don't think they have detected our presence. The cardinal's men began with forty *chevaliers*. If these are the cardinal's men, where are the remaining twenty men?"

As soon as Commander de Érail whispered his question, their just-built campfire gave us the answer. I pointed at the cardinal's crest on the saddle blankets as twenty additional *chevaliers* rode into their camp.

"Muhammad, hurry back to your sentry duty at the entrance by the falls," Commander de Érail whispered. After which, Muhammad ran to his former sentry post.

"*Seigneur* Robert, if they move in this direction, use these crossbows to kill them and sound the alarm. I'll awaken the others and alert them of our visitors."

Now there were three crossbows at my disposal, and I had already started spanning them for any threatening movements. I prayed my aim would be true.

It was difficult to listen for danger because of the din of the falls. My palms sweated from tension while observing for any sudden movement in my direction.

My fears were realized when a man soon walked in front of me and then relieved himself. I felt a lump in my throat with the fear of being detected. How had he approached me without having his presence known?

The man finished urinating and started to turn but spied my ever-so-slight movement back into the cave. He pulled the heavy brush apart and stuck his head into the cave opening. At that moment, my survival instincts came forth and I reached for my mercy dagger and plunged it into his throat. He grabbed his neck, gasped with a gurgling sound, and fell forward, headfirst. When he struck the ground, my dagger lodged farther into his neck. I stood there, stunned, realizing that I had killed him cheek to cheek.

Then I heard a voice, which brought me back to reality. "Lord de Borron that was a job well done," said *Frère* Jacque, "you prevented him from sounding an alarm and killed him too. God has guided your effort. He would have killed you in a heartbeat. Notice, his hand is on his dagger. It's out of its sheath and pointed to kill you."

Jacque de Hoult was right, but remorse had overcome me. Commander de Érail agreed with *Frère* Jacque and signaled for Muhammad to leave his post. We stood there wondering what to do with the body.

Guy de Béziers spoke first.

"I think we should remove the body and throw it off a cliff near the camp. The cardinal's men will search for their fellow *chevalier* and see that he fell to his death in the black of night. By that time, we will have left, and they will be none the wiser. It will be told as an accident, and this should give us a sufficient lead to reach Huesca."

"Lord de Borron, have *Frère* Guy and *Frère* Jacque find a suitable cliff to dispose of the body. Make sure you leave no foot tracks other than a single set to the edge of the cliff," Commander de Érail said with a whisper. "Muhammad will saddle your horses, while I guard the camp. Now leave at once. Oh, but first, let me search the body." The commander made a hurried search of the chain mail and surcoat and found a parchment, which he read.

"That damn son-of-a-bitch cardinal! There's a writ for my arrest by him. I am to go to Montpellier in chains for imprisonment. Damn him again and curse the day he was born. This also goes for his men!" Commander Gilbért slammed his fist, covered with chain mail, against the cave wall. "When we arrive at Huesca, I must send an urgent message to our order's grand master."

Commander de Érail stuck the parchment back into the *chevalier*'s surcoat belt and told us to leave now. The *chevalier* wasn't a big man, for we managed to drag the body out of the cave with little effort. The path alongside the cave entrance made it easy for us to climb the short distance to the top of the ravine. After I removed my dagger from his neck, we said a quick prayer for this misguided soul and threw him off the top of the ravine.

The roar from the falls muted any sound of him striking the rocks below. Jacque de Hoult started creeping backward as we traveled back down the path. *Frère* Guy cut a small cedar tree and used it to remove any footsteps we had made. A short time later, we reached the rear of the cave undetected and entered. At once, we left the cave by exiting through the falls. My fellow *chevaliers* continued up the river for about three leagues before crossing over a low section of the ravine. Up ahead was a low mountain range that was visible in the approaching sunrise. The commander said we must cross this range before reaching the commandery at Huesca. The *montagnes* weren't as tall and difficult to traverse as the Pyrénées, which was some relief to me, but we still had to travel over them. I was quite anxious to clean myself and sleep in a normal bed again. My days were confused, and I had to refer to my manuscripts each day to know the correct date.

We must have ridden another three leagues before resting our horses in a thick copse of birch trees at the base of the *montagnes*. Next, to the woods, a large lake gurgled with foam from a wide river rushing out of the mountains. Commander de Érail said we would rest half a day and then continue up the mountain river path until dusk.

"Lord Robert, we should be in Huesca in two days if the weather holds. I think we have out-smarted the cardinal's men for now. Yet, I have plan to thwart them if they happen to find us. However, I'll consider it a lot safer for you and my men when we reach Zaragozza. The king of Aragón, Alfonso II, resides there and he's a trustworthy friend of mine. He is a noted poet and *chanson* singer, and both of you should do well at court.

"*Roi* Alfonso II is also the *roi* of Barcelona and *comte* of Provence and I hear tell he's a cousin to *Roi* Richard I, *le Coeur de* Lion of England. I think you will enjoy being at his court and seeing his charming wife, *Reine* Sancha. The *roi i*s a great supporter of our Templar order and his influence is strong with the clergy. His wealth has increased to a great extent, and he has donated considerable sums to the next crusade, led by Richard I, *le Coeur de* Lion. *Roi* Alfonso realizes that with *Roi*

Richard's military skills, his great *chevaliers*, our Templar *frères*, and God's will, he can recapture the holy city of Jerusalem. Then we will regain our glorious Temple headquarters. I pray that he's successful. The *roi* should have current news about this matter when we are presented at court. Once reaching his demesne, he will hide or shelter us from the cardinal's *chevalier*."

I used the daylight hours to rest, clean my equipment, and sharpen my sword, after which we mounted our horses and continued up the mountain trail into another dense forest of evergreen trees. Once entering, little daylight penetrated to the forest floor. The several sounds we heard were the crushing of the thick carpet of evergreen needles by our horses' hooves. In addition, we heard the occasional chattering of squirrels and their gnawing of pinecones.

It must have been a league before the forest thinned out and large boulders started appearing. We were approaching a higher elevation, but not yet at the summit. A dark slate-gray sky appeared above, and a light fog settled in the valleys that we approached. Commander de Érail decided it was time to make camp for the night, for traveling any farther was risky.

After we finished unpacking our horses, we had our holy office of Compline. I sat there and said thirty *Pater Nosters* for our departed *frère*, Hughes de Montbard, after which I repeated the same for my mother and my father. My back and shoulders ached from riding all day. I had been in the saddle a month or better since we had left Montpellier, and I wondered if I had the strength to arrive at Huesca.

My mind started obsessing with thoughts of a warm bed and hot food. By now the smoked trout was tough to eat and hard to swallow as I started consuming my evening meal. Though, we did have some oats to boil to break our fast, yet we needed a goodly portion of it to feed our horses. The small remaining amount of wine was the sole consolation to a dull and tasteless meal. We couldn't make a campfire because of the imminent danger of the cardinal's scouts. There wasn't much to do around the dark camp other than make general conversation while the cold night wind penetrated my aketon. Muhammad had departed to scout around our campsite and Sergeants de Béziers and de Hoult had finished their meals and were preparing for sleep. Commander de Érail approached me after removing the saddle from his horse.

"Lord Borron, have you thought of any more clues in our Lord's words and what he had in store for Saint Joseph of Arimathea?"

"No, I have not," I replied, knowing I sounded exhausted. "I am still ruminating over the numbers one hundred fifty-three, eight, and King Solomon's glory. I hope your chaplain can help us solve these mysteries. How big is the commandery at Zaragozza?" I thought of my stomach and the welcome taste of hot food.

"It's not in Zaragozza, but a short distance from there. It's the largest commandery fortress outside of *Castillo y Léon at Ponferrada*. You will enjoy the accommodations there; it even has a decent library started by my chaplain. However, there's a small preceptory at Zaragozza."

He sat down and asked me to join him.

"Tell me about your family, *Seigneur* Robert. How many children do you have and what is your wife's name?"

"My wife's name is Marie and I have two sons; one is called Brian and the other is Henri. Brian is the oldest at six years and Henri is two. I miss them all so much." My voice cracked with sadness.

"Who is seeing after your estate while you are gone?"

"My brother-in-law," I replied. "When we left Montpellier, I wrote to my sister to travel to my *château* at Borron. From there she and *mon épouse* and two *fils* would travel with the *comte* to Montbéliard.

"Again, I apologize for taking you away from your family. I am forever indebted to you and after our *chevauchées* are over, don't hesitate to call on me for anything. You are a true *ami* of mine and have proved yourself to be a great Templar *chevalier*."

"You're too kind, Commander, in your praise, but I do ask one boon now. When we arrive at Zaragozza, I would like a letter sent to my family at *Château* Montbéliard. This would ease my mind and that of *mon épouse*. Can this be arranged when we arrive there?"

"*Oui*, I will send a courier with your letter as soon as we arrive. Also, I need to send one to our order's grand master concerning my arrest."

This for a moment uplifted my spirits, until Sergeant de Béziers said there was a rider approaching. We grabbed our swords and prepared for the intruder. At once the horse hooves stopped and there was silence. Each of us pushed our backs together with our swords pointed in different directions around the perimeter of our small camp. I was the first to see a slight dark movement.

"Who goes there?" I shouted.

No one replied, but out of the woods stepped Muhammad with a finger pointed straight up across his lips. He whispered, "*Mudéjar, Mudéjar.*" Commander de Érail replied in Muhammad's Saracen language and then told us to mount at once and leave.

"Muhammad said that Cardinal Folquet has hired local Moors to track us, and they are just half a league away. Also, the cardinal's men are at the base of the Sierra de Guara. We don't have much time; we must reach Huesca before noon tomorrow." Commander de Érail leaped on his horse.

When will this trial end? I felt my remaining physical strength ebbing fast from my body. I said a quick prayer, crossed myself, and spurred my horse right away to exit our camp. Muhammad stayed behind to douse our fire and hide our campsite remains. A moment thereafter, he caught up with us. We continued down the river path toward Huesca. The trail downward was rocky, with just a crescent moon to guide us. The rocks glistened with a dark wet shadowy sheen.

I knew the horses were quite anxious, for they kept whinnying throughout the night. We reached the plains on the north side of the mountains about daybreak. Muhammad proceeded to scout our left flank and Sergeant de Hoult was at our right flank. After traveling half a league, I could see a lone rider's dust in the distance. Commander de Érail raised his spyglass and focused on the dust cloud.

"It's Jacque de Hoult and he's galloping in our direction."

I spurred my horse and raced out to meet him. I could hear the sergeant shouting something as I galloped toward him. The dust cloud and noise of horse hooves blunted some of what he was saying, but I did hear him say that thirty riders and the Moors were approaching. I spurred my horse and raced to warn the others.

"Commander, Commander!" I shouted, "there are thirty riders and the Moor scouts heading in our direction."

Commander de Érail, Sergeant de Béziers, and Muhammad Nur Adin spurred their horses toward a small ravine path that crossed a narrow muddy stream. We fell into a single line behind each other racing for the ravine and the stream. I thought this must be where we would make our final stand against the cardinal's men. However, to my surprise, the commander and Muhammad dismounted and reached into their saddlebags.

It was hard to tell what they were placing along the road before the ravine. They jumped back on their horses and then raced farther up the road and stopped again. The same objects were scattered on both sides of the route. Again, they remounted and galloped toward the stream, which was quite shallow and muddy. For a third time, they stopped, placed the same objects in the muddy water, and raced to catch up with us. They stopped a final time and placed the remaining objects on the path that left the stream.

The large dust cloud sped closer and closer. The riders then broke into two groups and raced for different sections of the ravine. Without warning, there were high-pitched whinnying sounds of horses in pain, which then followed with sounds of men cursing and screaming in agony. The first large dust cloud of riders had stopped following us and were heaped in a horrific pile of men and flailing horses. The second set crossed the stream to the right of the path. After a short distance, the same agonizing sound came from this group of the cardinal's men. They too ceased following us.

I was both dumbfounded and thankful to our Lord and Savior, but what had caused these men to fall and their horses to be in such pain? We kept riding for another league and came upon a large valley in which the town of Huesca lay. I could see the outcroppings of several tall buildings on the skyline. One was a dome-shaped building of an architecture that wasn't familiar to me. Commander de Érail led the way toward the city gate. Before we entered the town, I had to know what stopped all those horses and men who were following us.

"Commander de Érail, what did you and Muhammad place on the path in front of the cardinal's men and the Moors?"

"They are called caltrops. It's four sharpened spikes forged together that always point up no matter how it's placed. We used them in the Levant against the great Sultan Saladin and his army until they learned a painful lesson."

There were momentary smiles on my companions' faces, however, this enthusiasm vanished, replaced with downtrodden heads of exasperation as we continued our quest. The cardinal seemed to create an endless supply of *chevaliers* to kill or capture us. *When would it stop?*

CHAPTER III

oming up the road toward us were several *chevaliers* dressed in white surcoats and heavy chain mail. I detected that each had flails, maces, crossbows, and battle-axes. Each of their horses was wearing white cloaks covering them from their withers to the docks of their tails.

One *chevalier* held a piebald-colored banner pole with the Templar red cross sewed in the center of the stiff banner flag. It was quite an impressive sight as the *chevaliers* cantered toward us from the raised portcullis. In addition, it was a relief to see the safe harbor of the town of Huesca.

The first *chevalier* who approached us acknowledged Commander Gilbért in the Templar's coded greeting, which he spoke in Latin. "*Non nobis Domine, non nobis.*"

Gilbért de Érail then gave a satisfactory reply of "*Sed nomini tuo da gloriam.*" It was from Psalm 115.

I heard him say he was Commander Ramáirez Sancho del Zaragozza. Half of his men fell in behind us and the remaining five were in front leading us through the village gate. It wasn't a large fortification, like the Montpellier Templar fortress or Carcassonne, but the city walls were thick enough minus any bartizans I could see.

The heavy gate doors were closed, and the portcullis lowered as the last *chevalier* passed through. We dismounted in front of a square-shaped chapel, alongside their commandery. Two young men, who were squires, ran out and grabbed our horses' reins. They stared at Muhammad as he strolled toward the commandery. Both men knew Muhammad was an unknown Saracen and not a Moor, by his darker complexion and a black turban. They kept a wary eye as Muhammad entered inside with Commander de Érail.

As I gathered my writing satchel, I could see several villagers who must have been Moors. Now I could see the difference. The women townsfolk were wearing face-covering hooded scarves and their clothing was dark with faint stripes that gave little contrast in design. Most of the women were strolling from the market square, holding large geometric-designed baskets. It amazed me seeing several women balancing their large baskets on their heads as they ambled along the dusty thoroughfare.

At one end of the town was an "old Roman ruin." To my left, some distance away, appeared a Romanesque-designed monastery and church. To my right were the remains of a building, which appeared to be a cathedral, but the remaining parts were unique in design, which I didn't recognize. Now I knew I was in a foreign land.

Sergeant Guy de Béziers finished overseeing the young squires and interrupted my visual survey of the new town.

"Lord Robert de Borron, my commander requests that you be present when he's briefed by the commander of Huesca. Don't worry about unpacking your horse. The young squires will carry your possessions to your cell."

I climbed up the steps, which faced a large ornate opening that led into the interior of the commandery. On each side of the entrance were statues of Saint John the Baptizer and the archangel Saint Michael holding a large spear and a globe. The interior stone hallway had many figures of heads carved into each column. Above me, in the ceiling arches were more carved heads that formed bosses at the ceiling rib intersections. Below each of the heads were additional carved pattée crosses.

As we approached the end of the stone corridor, there was a flight of steps. Sergeant Guy motioned for me to follow. We climbed up three flights and turned to travel down another stone-covered passageway. A short distance later, we faced a large oak door with another pattée cross carved into the wood. Sergeant Guy opened the door for me, revealing Commander Érail. In front of him was the commander of Huesca.

"Lord Robert de Borron, let me introduce you to Commander Ramáirez Sancho del Zaragozza. Commander Ramáirez, this is Lord Robert from Northern Burgundy."

"*Bienvenido*, Lord de Borron. I hope your stay here is comfortable. You have arrived just in time for the feast of Saint Michael, which our *frères* will be celebrating tomorrow with much fervor. The celebration should be quite inspiring."

"*Merci beaucoup*, Commander Ramáirez for your invitation. I will be present for the mass."

"Commander Érail was just telling me that he lost one of his squires to Cardinal Folquet's men on your journey."

"*Oui*, he was a pious young man and a brave *chevalier*. I miss his companionship each day. The rest of my *frères* agree as I do. I would like your priest to say a special mass for this courageous young man."

"*Si*, I will ask our chaplain to honor your wishes tomorrow morning. Also, I spoke to Commander Gilbért about sending my men out to further retard the cardinal's men. I will make all my services available to you, so you can complete your quest. Commander Gilbért has shown me the letter from the grand master of our order. It mentions your name and your great reputation. It will be an honor to serve you while you stay here in Huesca. Let me have one of my squires prepare your quarters, but first, let's have some refreshments. I think you will like our Iberian wine. It's quite different from your Burgundian wine."

Commander Ramáirez poured wine into three wooden goblets and handed one each to Commander de Érail and me. The *vin* was quite different from my homegrown *vins*. It had a sweet flowery bouquet and was full-bodied. The ruby-red liquid right away relaxed me.

"Lord Borron, I see you are wearing a hamsa necklace. It appears you have visited my fellow sword *frère*, Commander Armound de Polignac of Carcassonne," stated the commander of Huesca.

"*Oui*, you're correct. Did Commander de Érail mention that we refreshed our provisions while we were there?"

"No, he didn't mention it. I see that Commander de Polignac is letting you wear his hamsa. When we fought together in the Holy Land, he was never without it. Commander Armound must have trusted you to part with his sacred amulet. He was our *gonfanier* and the *beauséant* flag never fell in battle against the Saracens. We both left for new duties in the west before the Battle of Hattin. May the Lord bless our martyred *frères* who fell on that fateful day. Moreover, I curse the day Gérard de Ridefort became our grand master. May Saint Peter and Saint Michael give him his proper judgment."

The Huesca commander then crossed himself and said a stern amen. "Enough of past sad days. We must concentrate on our new enemy, Cardinal Folquet. I promise your stay here will be safe. You should be able to obtain some rest for your next destination of Zaragozza.

"Oh, by the way, Commander Gilbért de Érail is now the grand master of Aragón, Catalonia, Provence, and part of New Castile. You need to congratulate him."

I was quite surprised by this pleasant news. I shook his hand and we both embraced. He expressed a large scar-faced grin and then we both sat down. This new promotion I knew was long overdue. The commander continued smiling as Commander Ramáirez poured him another goblet of *vin* filled to the brim.

"You can give thanks to *Rey* Alfonso. He was the one who influenced your promotion. He must carry enormous power with the Papal Curia. We know that Cardinal Folquet believes Robert de Sablé, our beloved current grand master of all the Poor-Soldiers of Christ, as well as all of our *frères* and nuns are a threat to his power."

Commander Ramáirez then changed thoughts and asked Grand Master de Érail an odd question.

"What new territories will you conquer as our new grand master of Iberia? Just say where and my men will follow."

"I appreciate your loyal support, Ramáirez, but all I ask of you is to delay the cardinal and his men. I know he has become quite dangerous since many of his *chevaliers* have died by our swords. This has made him even more treacherous and vindictive. We must stay vigilant and observe anything that appears out of the ordinary. Our holy quest we now seek is why the cardinal *chevaliers* are pursuing us. That is all I can say at this time. Most people know how ambitious he is and quite controlling."

"I agree. It was premature of me to think of new conquests. I have been a fighter so long, the response came without thought. Please forgive me. I know your quest is quite important. Let me escort both of you to your rooms, for you must be tired. By now my squires have readied your rooms."

I detected disappointment on Commander Ramáirez's face, for his demeanor changed with a quiet slack expression.

We rose and the commander of Huesca led the way out of his cell. Just as we entered the stone-covered hallway, there came a high-pitched mournful sound from the arched window in front of us.

"What is that sound?" I asked.

"Lord Borron, that's the local *muezzin* calling the *Mudéjars* to prayer, but you know them as the Moors. You must become familiar with this sound. It's their call to prayer five times a day. Expect this same noisy sound starting at sunrise each day, yet it will become a common occurrence after several days," Commander Ramáirez informed me.

"Here are your rooms. Our new grand master will be right next to you. I hope you catch up on some well-deserved rest. I will see you at Vespers and Compline. Now I bid you *adieu*."

As Commander Ramáirez strolled back to his cell, I noticed he had a slight limp in his right leg. He must have sustained a wound in the Levant, I surmised.

My cell was about the same as the one back at Montpellier, but this one had more window openings. One of the openings was in the shape of a pattée cross; the other opening arched with two stone-carved statues. Their heads were facing the opposite of each other, and they appeared to be saints, but I couldn't distinguish which ones, because their bodies were weathered.

The stone ceiling had numerous carved doves as ceiling bosses. The bed mattress was large with plenty of straw ticking. My nose detected sweet-smelling herbs, which I gazed down and observed small broken leaves scattered about on the stone floor. It was a great temptation to lie down and sleep, but my conscience told me otherwise. I thought it best to start a personal journal of my travels. After some time, my eyes and body succumbed to the temptation of sleep. I fell into the bed with a sweet sigh of relief and fell fast asleep.

I woke up sometime later, quite refreshed but disturbed by the eerie sound of the *muezzin's* call to prayer. After a short time, his chant stopped, and I could hear whispering voices outside my door. The voices were in the local language, which continued for a while, and then I heard footsteps leaving. At once, I recognized the shuffling sound on the stone hallway floor as that of Commander Ramáirez. Just then, the commandery bells started ringing for Vespers as the sun just now sliced the western horizon. I opened my door and there was Commander de Érail in the hallway leaving his cell.

"Did you sleep well, Lord de Borron? I slept great! This was the first time since Montpellier I haven't slept on the ground."

"*Oui*, I did obtain some rest like you, yet it's amazing how refreshing a fine bed can make a person."

We continued down the hallway until an unknown sergeant stopped us.

"Your Excellency, our draper has requested me to give you and Lord Robert de Borron new mantles, surcoats, and chain mail. You can use the sacristy next to the chapel to change."

He led us to a side hallway and directed us to a large room. The sergeant laid our clothing on a large stone table and left. The room held priest chasubles, chapel crosses, and an unusual square wooden box. The sides of the square box revealed two symbols. One was in the shape of an eagle and the other was a long-shanked, single-barreled cross. The box was plated with gold and jewels encrusted into the gold. I wasn't familiar with this type of church display. It appeared like a reliquary but left me puzzled.

A fresh change of clothes felt decent as we proceeded down the stone passageway. The chapel filled up fast as we continued to our stalls. Commander de Érail moved to a large carved wooden seat as the new grand master in the chancel. This was on the other side of the choir and opposite to where I stood. Next to him was Commander Ramáirez. There at the high altar, a Templar chaplain rose from his seat. From the back entrance of the chapel, I heard the large oak doors bolted with a *clanking* sound.

The priest proceeded to the front of the altar. To my surprise, he picked up the ornate wooden box that I had seen earlier in the sacristy. A *frère chevalier* had brought it in unnoticed after we had marched down the chapel aisle. The chaplain grabbed the box and raised it high over his head. He chanted the Latin words "*Templi omnium hominum pacis abbas*" and then laid it on the high altar. Then all the *frères* present started a low chant that rumbled like distant thunder. They kept repeating the word "Baphomet" over and over in a steady droning sound. This lasted a while until the priest crossed himself, followed by all the *frères* present. He then knelt before the box, said several *Pater Nosters*, then rose, and eased open the box.

From where I was standing, his vestments obscured the box opening. The priest then reached for the opened box and raised it overhead for all to see. The contents glowed from the many candles placed at the altar. The chaplain then faced toward me with the box so I could see. Inside were two detailed sculpted gold heads. They were similar to the stone-carved heads in my cell and like the ones throughout the commandery.

He stepped down several steps and stood at the communion rail. Each *frère* ambled forth and knelt before the golden heads. This included Sergeants Jacque and Guy, who stood a short distance from me. The priest let each Templar *frère* kiss the heads while he held it, after which each *moine* crossed himself and strolled back to his stall.

It was now my turn to come forth and pay homage to this strange reliquary. Both heads appeared to be that of saints, but I wasn't sure who they were. I too kissed the heads, crossed myself, and strolled back to my stall.

The rest of the mass proceeded as usual. When it was over, we proceeded out of the chapel, with the bejeweled wooden box raised overhead as the chaplain carried it forth, and then he disappeared into one of the stone passageways. The rest of the *frères* marched to the refectory under a vow of silence, including Grand Master Gilbért and his two sergeants. Muhammad stayed with the horses, and we were to bring him some food. I had the honor to sit at the head of the table with our appointed new grand master and Commander Ramáirez.

We were all sitting in stillness as the young squires poured our wine. My overwhelming curiosity was still strong with what had just transpired in the chapel. I didn't know if I could keep my vow of silence during the meal. My urge to speak became tormenting as the chaplain arrived and seated himself. He sat across from Commander Ramáirez. Both Grand Master Gilbért and the chaplain rose for the blessing. The rest of the warrior *moines* followed suit. The chaplain mumbled a blessing over the food and then we sat back down.

I didn't drink too much wine for fear my tongue might slip. The Iberian wine was excellent and made it even more difficult to refrain from speaking. The meat and bread were delicious, which distracted me from my never-before-seen strange ceremony.

The young bull we were served had been roasted to perfection. The meat was tender and had a hot peppery flavor. I tore off a large piece of bread and topped it with fresh butter. The crust was flaky, but not hard.

One of the *chevaliers* was reading from Psalm sixty-four, which further kept my mind off the unusual ceremony I had just witnessed. This Psalm was a favorite of mine about a prayer for the protection from your enemies.

By this time, we had our fill of wine and food, and when the Psalms were completed, we stood with the chaplain and said thirty-three *Pater Nosters* and then proceeded out of the refectory to return to our cells.

I whispered to Grand Master de Érail and asked if he would come into my cell and explain what I had seen earlier in the chapel. He agreed with a nod and a short time later we both sat down on two of the wooden benches in my room.

CHAPTER IV

"Grand Master Gilbért, what was that observance with the two golden heads? I haven't seen anything like it at any of the masses I have attended."

"Lord Borron, we Templars are guardians of many sacred relics from the Holy Land. We protect these in secret and few people know about them. What you witnessed was the image of Saint John the Baptizer and Saint John the Evangelist. If you noticed, the outside of the box had the symbols for both saints. First, Saint John the Evangelist is represented by an eagle and the Baptizer by the long-shanked cross.

"But more important was what each golden head reliquary contained. One had the jawbone of Saint John the Baptizer, which our order obtained in the Levant. The other golden head contains the partial skull of Saint John the Evangelist. This was fought for on the island of Patmos. The word Baphomet is the arcane name for this sacred relic. That was the chant you heard in the church.

"Some of our other chapels and churches have relics of saints, which the secular world is unaware that we have obtained. I know I can trust you not to divulge what you have just witnessed. Some of our other holy relics were obtained by loans to *comtes*, *ducs*, and *rois*. They pledged them as collateral for loans and never paid back their debts. Our banking interests have helped to protect these precious relics. This is what you are now a part of on our quest. You have become a guardian of the *Sangraal* words and the secrets they impart.

"There are many people who would like to see us fail. In the coming months, we will be confronted with many obstacles as we have already faced in the last month."

"Oh, I have one other question to ask before you leave, Grand Master de Érail. How long will we be staying in Huesca before we arrive at your home commandery near Zaragozza?"

"It's hard to say." He pulled on his curly beard in deep thought. "Maybe less than a fortnight; this depends on two things. I pray the cardinal's men will be led astray by Commander Ramáirez and our *frère* Templars. Moreover, it will be dependent on the weather and our health. I will decide in several days. For now, rest up, gain your strength, and pray upon the words you have written. This extra time should allow you to write a lengthy letter to your wife. Now I bid you good night and will see you again at Matins tomorrow morning."

Gilbért de Érail rose and then left to complete his commandery duties. He was right, for I needed to write to my wife and family and tell them I was fine. My ribs were still sore, but mending well, so I felt there was no need to mention my injury.

I sat there some time contemplating what I might say in my letter but decided some fresh air would help my thought process. I left my cell and proceeded down the torchlit passageway and stone steps into the cool autumn air. The sky was clear, and the stars' brilliance radiated the ink-black heavens. To my north, I could see the black silhouettes of the Cañones de Guara mountains in the distance.

The dirt street led in several directions. With few people on the thoroughfares, I decided for a stroll in the night air. There was a *Mudéjar* church or mosque as I heard Sergeant de Hoult call it when we first arrived. My curiosity grabbed hold of me, and I strolled in that direction. As I approached the front entrance, three things struck me as odd: One was several tall narrow towers in front of it, the blue tiles on the facing entrance, and its unusual mushroom-shaped arches. I stood there gazing in the torchlit light at the designs of the geometric entrance when at once my curiosity ceased.

I heard the sounds of whinnying horses. I moved closer to see and heard whispering voices. One sounded familiar. They were coming from a small vestibule that led into the mosque proper. Sliding my back against the outside wall of the mosque, I crept closer to see. One voice was Commander Ramáirez, but the other I could not distinguish. It sounded like the local *Mudéjars*. By now, I had reached a small opening where I could see unobserved.

A large torch next to them made it easy to see. It was Commander Ramáirez, who spoke to an oddly dressed man. This man wore a red cloth turban, red waistband, a white robe, and red-colored boots. They conversed for a while in the native *Mudéjar* tongue. Their conversation was meaningless to me until Commander Ramáirez produced a sack of coins out of the dark shadows. The *Mudéjar* stranger then grabbed it. It seemed a payment of some sort for services rendered or something just consummated.

I moved forward to obtain a better view and stepped on a twig. The cracking sound made them stare in my direction. They both paused for a moment in their conversation, but to my surprise didn't come to investigate. Instead, both men mounted their horses and rode out into a dark side street next to the mosque. It was obvious they were hiding something as both men glanced around searching for some unknown observer, while trotting into the darkness of the night. I exited parallel to the mosque entrance and crept toward the center of the town.

I hugged the house walls for some distance while ruminating on what I had just seen. My sole distraction was that of a few stray dogs barking in the distance. Skulking between the dark houses, I approached a church and monastery. It had a red-tiled roof on both the church and the monastery buildings. This gave the roofing an appearance of giant turtles back-to-back with rust-colored shells. The church entrance arch was replete with many carved biblical scenes from the life of our Savior.

I approached the stone steps and decided to enter, thinking I must light some candles for our departed *frère*, Hughes de Montbard, and pray that I would see my épouse and *fils* again. My motive this time wasn't to investigate, but spiritual in nature. My nose first detected the burning smell of sandalwood. The nave was large, yet not to the extent of the churches in Burgundy. I noticed there were several statues of Saint Peter as I proceeded farther into the nave. There I noticed several chapels off to each side of the chancel. I felt it agreeable for me to enter the one closest to me. It was quiet and peaceful there praying. I lit four candles, knelt, and prayed some more.

To my right side, I heard a sound. It was someone's footfalls coming toward me as I knelt. The footsteps weren't that of a *chevalier*. Whoever made it, a quiet thumping sound came from their sandals. As I ended my prayer, I arose and a black-robed Benedictine *moine* greeted me.

"Don't let me disturb your prayer, *hermano caballero*. Please continue."

"I was finished," I replied gazing into the *moine's* cowl-covered head. His eyes were an unusual shade of green with a golden tint to them. To my surprise he could speak my language.

"I am *Hermano* Miguel, *abad* of our monastery. It's not often we see a Soldier of Christ in our church. What brings you here to pray, my *amigo*?"

"I was praying for a *bon ami* who died not long ago while trying to save another fellow *frère*. In addition, I was praying for my épouse and our holy quest."

There was a wide-eyed expression on his face after I told him I was praying for my épouse.

"Has your *esposa* entered into your holy order as a nun, my *hermano*?"

"*Non*, I must apologize for not introducing myself. I am Lord Robert de Borron from Burgundy. I have been traveling with my fellow Poor-Soldiers of Christ for several weeks. They have selected me as a tertiary member of their order."

I felt reluctant to say anymore, even if he was an *abbé*, but he kept inquiring about my travels.

"Lord Borron, you mentioned that you were on a holy quest. Is this a pilgrimage to our beloved

Santiago de Compostela?"

I didn't know what to say and was hoping not to lie to this holy man, but whom could I trust? Instead, I strode the middle ground and didn't lie, but evaded his question.

"We are on our way there soon, but we thought it was best to rest here first. My fellow *frères* have traveled through the Pyrénées Mountains and are in much need of succor."

"I think you will enjoy our quiet town. Quite soon, you'll adjust to our customs. Let's stroll to the cloisters, where we can sit down and discuss the further peaceful merits of Huesca."

I agreed with *Frère* Miguel and followed him to the cloister area of the monastery. As we stepped out into the night air, I could still smell the heady incense from the church. He picked a spot where there was some moonlight for us to see. The stone benches were hard, but I could rest my back against the ashlar masonry. The stone supported my sore back and still had the warmth of today's sun. In addition, it helped stifle the cool night air and relieved the soreness in my ribs.

"Lord Borron, how is the weather where you live? Is it like ours here?"

"*Non*, where I come from, there is more rain and a cooler climate; yet, how do you know to speak my native language, *Frère* Miguel?"

"I was raised in a small village in southern Burgundy as a child. My parents gave me over to the order of Saint Benedict when I became ten. I studied at the Cluny *abbaye* until I was a young man. My parents were of poor means and wanted me to be educated. When I became of age, I was to use my education to help others. I requested a transfer here to help start a new *abbaye*. This place has been part of my life for almost forty years. Our Lord has been kind to me, for I still have a natural *soeur* and two natural *frères*. Besides, my blood *frère* is a *moine* here at our monastery and plans to leave in several days for our motherhouse in southwest Gaul at Cluny. Would you like him to deliver a message to your family? I am sure he won't be too far from your *château*."

"Bless you, *Frère* Miguel. I was planning to write a letter to my épouse tomorrow. Can I meet you at the same time here tomorrow evening?"

"*Si,* you may, and I know my *frère* will be quite happy to deliver it to your épouse. I will see you tomorrow and we'll speak some more."

"*Merci beaucoup, Frère* Miguel."

As I rose, he said a short blessing, and before I left, he made the sign of the cross in front of me. We parted with the words, "*Pax vobiscum,*" and we left in different directions. I traced my steps back out through the chapel, the nave, and at last onto the dusty plaza. It was late and my curiosity had turned into a weariness beckoning me to bed.

I strolled by the mosque on my way back to the commandery. There wasn't any sound of voices this time, but only the flapping and hissing sounds from the blowing pitch torches outside the mosque entrance. Thereafter, I approached the commandery door entrance steps and noticed two sergeants posted outside as sentries. Right away they shouted to ask for my identity. "Who goes there?" When I gave them my name, they opened the door for me to pass.

Upon entering, my eyes tried to focus on the many torches that lit the hallway corridor. I stumbled when I saw a moving shadow. I tip-toed up the stone steps that led to my cell, while hearing muffled voices coming from Commander Ramáirez's cell. One of the voices resembled what I just heard from the red-turbaned stranger. The other was the commander's voice. Neither spoke my language and I thought it best to enter my cell.

The refreshing night air, my curiosity, and *Frère* Miguel's conversation kept me awake. I thought I would use this time to write to my épouse and update my journal. My writing satchel was lying next to my bed where I left it. Nothing seemed to be disturbed. I lit several new candles and commenced to tell my dearest Marie what had transpired with my many adventures. I felt it was prudent to leave out the terrible confrontation we faced at Gavarnie. I spoke of Commander Armound de Polignac and his knowledge of her *frère*, *Comte* Gautiér de Montbéliard. Moreover,

I mentioned the mysterious Cathar *moine* I met in the cave and my newfound friendship of a Saracen lord.

Marie, my dearest, you won't believe the quest that I have been asked to undertake. The Poor-Soldiers of Christ have enlisted me to find and translate the holy words written by Saint Joseph of Arimathea and the teachings of our Lord, Jesus the Christ. I had in my hands the actual pages written almost twelve hundred years ago. I was mysteriously blessed with the ability to cipher the ancient words. We're now in the peninsula of Iberia resting from our arduous trip over the Pyrénées Mountains. We are staying in a small village called Huesca in the royaume of Aragón. The accommodations are at a Templar commandery here and, according to Grand Master Gilbért de Érail, we'll be spending a fortnight or less here. From Huesca, we will travel to the royaume capital called Zaragozza, where the roi resides. Our final destination will be the city of Toledo. This is the city where we expect to find the next clue in our search for the second set of Sangraal parchments, which I suspect may not be there.

I am glad I wrote to you now instead of waiting until we arrived at Zaragozza.

*I miss you and the children so much. Please
pray for my safe return and light a candle
every day for the salvation of my soul.
Your affectionate husband,
Robert*

I sealed the letter with red sealing wax, affixed my ring crest in the wax, put it in a folded envelope, and sealed it again. I placed it aside to give to *Hermano* Miguel tomorrow. I felt I could trust the *abbé* to deliver my precious message. However, the sensitive information about our trip's purpose left me with some anxiety what Grand Master Gilbért would say. In addition, I must tell him about Commander Ramáirez and the red-turbaned stranger he gave money to.

Then, I picked up my journal pages and continued from where I last left off. I wrote until I could write no more. My eyes fluttered and my mouth yawned, telling me it was time for slumber. However, it was hard to believe I would realize a full night's sleep in a bed and not on the ground. I ambled toward the bed, undressed, and then slipped under the comforter. How many days had it been since I last slept in a bed? I could not answer that thought in time, for I fell fast asleep.

The office of Matins came too soon for me, but once I stirred about, I was fine. The ringing bells livened my step as all the *frères* and *chevaliers* proceeded to the chapel. We proceeded in as before and stood in our stalls saying our *Pater Nosters*. After the other Templar *frères* had finished, I continued with prayers for young Hughes, then I ambled back toward my cell and in the dim light of the early morning started writing in my journal.

Without warning, I was distracted by the same eerie wailing sound emanating from the tall stone columns in front of the mosque. The call to prayer at first frightened me, then I recalled what Commander Ramáirez said. However, I don't think I would become accustomed to the eerie sound.

I proceeded to write in my travel log until the office of Prime. After Prime, I would tell Gilbért de Érail about my meeting with *Frère* Miguel. I suspected he already knew about the *abbé* of San Pedro el Viejo.

We proceeded into the chapel again and said another set of *Pater Nosters*. The altar had been prepared for Saint Michael's day mass. There were numerous altar candles about the chancel in readiness for the mass. Instead of returning to our cells, we left the chapel, and I followed the rest of the *chevaliers* to the refectory. Once arriving, we stood for the blessing and then sat down to break our fast.

Placed at each table were large wedges of cheese, along with fresh baked dark bread and roasted capon. The smell of hot fresh rye bread was irresistible. It permeated the whole refectory. My mouth watered with anticipation, and it amazed me how well the Templar *frères* ate and drank. I was sure these hearty meals contributed to their fighting prowess, while the other monastic orders I had visited were proud of their fasting before God. I knew my physical strength would return by eating such delicious meals. The food never seemed to end; there were continuous trays of food during our breaking of the fast. There were vegetables of cabbage, lentils, and peppers served with the capon. All the food consumed had with it a *bon* Iberian *vin* to drink.

After our silent meal, we returned to the chapel for Terce and the special mass for Saint Michael and then the requiem mass for the death of *mon bon ami Chevalier* Hughes. It saddened me to be there so long while the chaplain chanted both rituals. I knew one of the masses was in honor of Hughes's memory and the salvation of his soul, still it wouldn't remove the emptiness I felt. I said more *Pater Nosters* and prayed Hughes was now in paradise.

The droning sound of the masses seemed to last forever. It left me in a state of mental numbness until I heard the words "The sword and spear of Saint Michael's judgment." Then my mind refocused on what the chaplain was saying. At once, I had a mental image of the evil *bâtard* Marcel de Tournay. His sneering face, in my mind's eye caused my blood to warm my face with rage. I prayed that Saints Michael and Peter had sent him to hell and the devil made it extra hot for him.

In much haste, I left the service and proceeded to the market square. There the morning air helped cool my cheeks, along with an enjoyable breeze coming out of the west as I turned my face into it. My hot rage cooled as I saw Muhammad coming out of the mosque along with the local *Mudéjars.* He approached me and spoke, "*Salaam alaikum,* Lord Borron," to which I replied, "*Alaikum al salaam,* Muhammad Nur Adin."

We both stood there with awkwardness trying to converse with each other. He spoke to me in my native language mentioning *Chevalier* Hughes. He seemed concerned about whether or not my fellow Christians had prayed for Hughes. He mentioned the word "*salat*" several times, which I understood to mean prayer. I answered with a positive *oui.* He seemed quite satisfied with my response and then I bowed. Afterward, he excused himself.

With less irritation, I continued through the market square toward San Pedro el Viejo. The town plaza bustled with people milling about to purchase strange, orange-colored fruit and nuts, accompanied by the plinking sound of coins, which reflected the many business transactions. The two busiest stalls were the bakery ovens and the blacksmith shop. The continuous pinging sounds from his hammer irritated my ears. The acrid smell from his charcoal furnace created a haze of blue smoke that lingered over his red clay-tiled roof. The blue haze drifted toward me, causing my eyes to tear as I ambled toward the monastery.

The church and *abbaye* appeared different in the morning daylight than I realized last night. Now I could see more stone-carved detail in the archivolt to the entrance of the monastery, with my eyes focusing on the labarum cross and the ornate columns on each side of the door opening. The stone cross itself appeared similar to a Chi-Rho cross but was enclosed in a circle. It displayed a large carving on the tympanum above the door and it appeared to glow. Two angels held each side of the wheel-inserted cross. Without warning their heads turned toward me and to my further disbelief, they pointed their free hand in my direction. They were now conveying some hidden symbolism here, but it escaped me at that moment.

I concentrated harder and saw that one of the angels pointed toward a serpent-shaped design at the bottom of the Chi-Rho. It must be telling me to seek the cross's knowledge and where to find it. I could just perceive a stone-carved, letter-shaped cross on the snake's stone body.

I moved closer and saw it was quite assuredly tee-shaped. Right away it came over me what the symbols were saying. The tee-shaped design represented several things. It was a tau cross and the Greek letter tau, but more important, the beginning letter in Toledo and a symbol that came from ancient Egypt.

I knew the Greeks gave numerical values to each of their letters, but I wasn't well-versed in their numerical knowledge. Did the coiled snake around the bottom of the cross symbolize evil? Could the stone letters—the Greek letters alpha and omega—that were carved between the spokes, represent the beginning and end of our quest? All of these symbols started glowing and seemed to come out of the wall. The doorway entrance was telling me many things. However, I hoped *Abbé* Miguel would reveal who the unknown angels were and the interior circle designs.

By now, I was quite warm, standing out in the sun as it drew nearer to noon. The tympanum and the archivolt held me both excited and in a trance. The stone's designs were giving me verbal clues and affirmation that our holy quest was headed in the right direction. Several local men and women gave me odd glances at my intense upward stare and must have thought I was crazy. Then I heard my name, yet it was as if the voice came from a dream, until I felt a strong grip of a powerful hand on my arm.

"Lord Robert de Borron, are you okay?" the voice asked. My trance then vanished as I turned to see our new grand master, Gilbért de Érail.

"You have been standing here some time, for I was observing you from the blacksmith shop. Why are you so still? Have the sun's rays harmed you?"

"I am fine, *merci beaucoup*. We must speak in a secluded place," I stated. "Can you lead us to an isolated spot where no one can hear us? I must speak to you."

"*Oui,* I think I know a spot. Follow me."

We traveled to the outskirts of Huesca and sat down on a large stone block that appeared to be of ancient Roman design. A broken-down wall obscured us from the wandering eyes of the town plaza. Moreover, we sat under an oak tree with its remaining leaves to thwart the sun's rays.

"Grand Master Gilbért I saw something last night that appeared strange. Before retiring, I decided to stroll in the clear night air and refresh my lungs. My curiosity was piqued when I saw the *Mudéjar*-designed *église,* or as you call it a mosque. I wanted to study the unusual design and coloration, so I drew closer to the entrance. The stillness of the mosque was broken when I heard several horses whinnying and saw them tied to a post along a passageway next to the mosque.

"After the horses calmed down, I could hear voices from the interior of the mosque. There, through an ornate lattice grill, stood Commander Ramáirez. He conversed with a dark-skinned man who spoke in the local *Mudéjar* tongue to the commander. The odd features of the man were his clothes. He was dressed in white with a red-trimmed waistband, turban, red boots, and a large-curved knife, similar to Muhammad's ornate dagger. A black-hooded mantel obscured his head, which would make it difficult for me to recognize him, even if I saw him again. I wouldn't have mentioned this to you at all, yet before they concluded their conversation, a large bag of coins exchanged hands. The sack was so heavy Commander Ramáirez grunted as he handed it to the *Mudéjar*. It appeared to me a payment was being made for services rendered or forthcoming."

Grand Master Gilbért's face raced with paleness as if he had just died.

"This doesn't bode well, Lord de Borron. We may have a traitor in our midst." He pounded his fist against a tree. "I trusted Commander Ramáirez. Now, I am not so sure. Lord de Borron, you haven't written your letter to your wife and sent it by one of the commandery couriers, have you? I fear any information about our quest will be used against us."

"No, I did not." Then came a sigh of relief in Grand Master Gilbért's demeanor upon my negative reply. "There was a second thing I wanted to discuss with you. I met *Abbé* Miguel of San Pedro el Viejo. Do you know him, and can he be trusted?"

"*Abad* Miguel is one of the most trusted holy men in the *Royaume* of Aragón. He helped tutor the current *roi* of Aragón, Alfonso the Chaste, and me. He was like a real *père* to me before I became a Poor-Soldier of Christ. Don't worry,

Lord de Borron, I would stake my life and the lives of my fellow *chevaliers* on his holy judgment. I am glad you had the opportunity to meet him."

I felt a sense of instant relief, knowing there was somebody new in the town I could trust.

"It's a matter of fact that I am meeting him tonight to discuss who's traveling with us to Zaragozza. Would you like to accompany me after Compline?"

"*Oui,* I too promised to meet him tonight. I will ask him to deliver this written message to my *épouse*. He said he would have his natural *frère* to deliver it. *Abad* Miguel told me last night that his *frère* will be traveling to Cluny and would see to its delivery to Marie. I am now relieved knowing that I wasn't handing over my letter to a traitor."

As we sat there, the wind picked up speed and created small whirlwinds of dirt around the oak tree. I could tell Grand Master Gilbért was still worried about the unknown *Mudéjar* and Commander Ramáirez. He kept addressing what I had seen and continued to ask about every minute detail of that clandestine encounter, while shuffling his boots in the sandy soil.

"Lord de Borron, what else do you have to tell me before we leave?"

"I believe the monastery tympanum is both a clue and a signpost for us to follow and decipher. That was what I was fixating on when you approached me, thinking I was ill. Maybe there are clues in it, which *Abbé* Miguel can help us interpret tonight. The tympanum is telling us where to find the second set of *Sangraal* parchments."

"This is quite revealing information, Lord de Borron, but right now we must prepare to leave here soon. I fear the longer we stay here, the more of a threat that Cardinal Folquet de Marseille will become. Let's return to the commandery so our absence won't alarm anyone. Later tonight, we'll discuss with *Abad* Miguel what course of action to choose. Until then, I will be thinking of a proper excuse for our quick departure. Please alert me right away of anything unusual. Let's return so we won't be late for the office of Sext."

We then proceeded to the office of Sext after entering the commandery entrance. Afterward, I had a collation of cheese, bread, and wine in my cell before Nones. I used that time to update my travel parchments while hating the thought of riding once more and leaving the comfort of my cell. The cautious side of my nature told me that Grand Master Gilbért had our best interest in mind.

Before leaving for the office of Nones, I felt I needed to check my copy of the *Sangraal* parchments. I reached into my writing satchel, and, to my horror, it wasn't there! Sweat broke out on my palms and I started to swoon with fear. This forced me to upturn everything in my room with a frantic zeal. I caused several loud crashing sounds in my manic search. The question kept dancing through my mind, *What I was going to do?* My thoughts hammered against my brain until my hands started shaking, distracting me. I retraced my day's events and realized that the *Sangraal* parchments were there before departing for Terce and Saint Michael's mass. It must have been stolen after that, while I was returning from the plaza. How could I have been so careless? I fell on my knees and prayed for the *Sangraal's* recovery.

PART II

The Return

CHAPTER V

Anno Domini 37
City of Jerusalem
and Palestine

oseph's walls had so many scratch marks, piles of stone dust had accumulated at the four corners of the dungeon floor. It was hard to believe that he had been so faithful in keeping track of the days, months, and seasons. His Lord's miracle cup had sustained him all these months, not only in physical nourishment, but also in both intellect and spirit. His nephew's spoken words had saved his sanity, and his comments were right. "Man needs more than bread alone to survive."

Each day, Yoseph repeated his routine. He strained his memory for any missed words he might have spoken. Also, his mouse companion and he had an animated conversation with each other at mealtime. Yoseph would feed him from the stale breadcrumbs every two days. His mouse friend didn't seem to mind its hard, rock-like texture. If it was moldy, he would eat around the bad section until he was full. After each meal, Yoseph would repeat to him what he remembered in the presence of Yeshua. After Yoseph finished speaking, he would make a noisy squeaking sound until Yoseph started drinking the never-ending wine from the Holy Chalice. A fresh loaf of bread always appeared each morning. After his mouse friend ate his share, he would disappear until the next meal.

The routine with his mouse companion, writing his *Adonai's* holy words, and drinking and eating from his cup and paten was Yoseph's salvation each day. The rest of his time, he spent worried about his family. He prayed each day that they were well and alive. He wondered if Yosa was married, if his younger sister Enygeus had any children, or if Alein Yosephe was married. This longing to see them was the remaining incomplete part of his spiritual being. Not one day would pass without saying prayers for their safety and their reunion. Yoseph was always afraid of his thoughts concerning his family's welfare. These dark doubts crept and crawled out of the far corners of his mind when Yoseph's hope became eaten with despair in not seeing his family again.

Either his family had been harmed by the high priest, Yoseph ben Caiaphas, like himself or left *Yehudah* for places unknown. These same doubts always entered his mind just before he ate his *Adonai's* supper. After the wine and bread, his spirits and confidence would soar. The aftertaste was always hope. This was the driving force to endure each day.

He received his vermin-infested food around the time of sunset, but this evening he saw no food. *How odd.* Yet the guard appeared and told Yoseph to gather up his things, for he was to leave at once. At first, he thought he was dreaming until the guard grabbed his bony arm and pulled him to his feet.

"Yoseph, today is your lucky day. Caiaphas is no longer the head of the Sanhedrin and a new chief priest reigns. To show his forthcoming magnanimous rule, he and the Sanhedrin are releasing all political prisoners. You must hurry to leave, for you have until sundown to leave the city of *Yerushalayim.* If you are still here, you will be put back into prison."

Yoseph sensed, with every beat of his heart, joy racing through his entire body. He raised his hands to *El Shaddai* and thanked him for his release. Moreover, Yoseph gave thanks to Yeshua, his *Adonai* and Savior.

"Yoseph, I am leaving the door open, so when you are ready you can leave. However, don't tarry, I have to report to the Sanhedrin that you have left by my next watch."

"Thank you for your kindness," Yoseph stated,

not knowing the guard's name. "What's your name so I can remember you for your noble deed?"

"My name is Yoel, and I never thought you would survive these last four summers. It's a miracle that I am speaking to you this day."

"Yes, indeed it's a miracle you see before you, Yoel. Remember the name Yeshua the *Maishiach*, for his kingdom is now with us."

The Sanhedrin guard had a pinched face before he returned to his appointed rounds. Yoseph gathered his writing material, pen, inkwell, Holy Cup, paten, spear, cruets, and wrapped some of the objects in parchment paper before placing them in his large satchel. The sword he tucked into his tattered tunic cloth belt. The glass cruets he wrapped in some crumpled parchment paper and positioned them into the satchel. He used the remaining blank parchment paper to wrap around the cup and paten to keep each from *clanking* against the other before leaving.

The tall spear left him was a dilemma. This would attract considerable attention to him, which he didn't want. Yoseph reached to pick it up and the bottom half of the wooden shaft fell off from dry rot. This was quite fortunate on Yoseph's part, for he could now tuck it too in his tunic belt. He struggled to rise, for his back throbbed with a knife-like pain. His long confinement on the stone floor had wreaked havoc on his spine. Yet, his elation of now being a free man helped disguise the pain.

As he exited the doorway, he heard a familiar squeaking sound. Yoseph gazed down to see the tiny dark eyes of his furry little companion. His constant squeaking voice sounded as if he wanted to accompany him. Yoseph reached down and lightly grabbed his furry body and placed him in the front of his tunic belt.

Yoseph crept down the narrow stone corridor but was reluctant to stroll outside. After four summers of imprisonment, his dirty, smelly appearance would keep most people away from him in the streets of *Yerushalayim*. He knew a place at one end of the Temple Mount that he could hide until darkness came. It would be better if he traveled late at night, Yoseph thought. His beard had grown below his waist and his hair was over his shoulders. Yoseph knew the majority of the people would smell him before they saw him, and the thought of scaring little children distressed him. His clothing was nothing more than tattered rags.

He proceeded down the corridor until it turned a sharp direction north. Then he came before a large door that he knew led to an underground tunnel to the Temple Mount. He and Nicodemus had been into this end of the mount, and it led to the prison. He confided in Yoseph about a small underground room that he later showed him. Nicodemus stored some of his important papers that he had used after their council meetings.

From what Yoseph could remember, the room was dry, clean, and spacious.

He traveled some distance in the well-lit passageway until he came to a large wooden door with the star of Solomon carved on its surface. He knew now he was in the Temple Mount. He stepped inside the next corridor and there, in front of him, was the entrance door to Nicodemus's storage room. Yoseph's major problem was that he faced a locked door and didn't have a key.

He peered through the lock and saw what appeared to be a spare key on the other side of the lock. At once, it came to him on what he had to do. He tore off a large section of his threadbare cloak and edged it through the bottom crack in the door. It slid through, after which a majority of the cloth entered the other side of the door. He used his writing quill to stick through the keyhole and heard the key strike the covered stone floor with a muffled *clang*. Did the key land on the cloth or somewhere else on the floor? He pulled the cloth toward him, but it caught on something on the floor. The crack at the bottom of the door was wide enough for a key and cloth to come through. After several gentle tugs, the rag cloth eased out and there was the key. He thanked Nicodemus for leaving a spare key on the other side of the door. Yoseph proceeded to unlock it.

To his consternation, the lock froze halfway through the turning of the key. Right away he heard faint footsteps coming in his direction. A second turn of the lock with his full weight against the door caused it to edge some. Part of the door bottom hung on several paving stones. Yoseph tried to use his foot to kick it free, yet it wouldn't budge. The footsteps were coming closer, and a sense of panic overtook his body. The third attempt of striking it with his foot freed the door. He gathered up his cup and vials and entered the darkened room. This time, upon shutting it, the door cooperated with him. He could hear the steps coming down the passageway toward his darkened room. At once, he heard the large stone corridor door creep open, but to his chagrin, a squeaking sound started emanating from his tunic belt. His little friend wanted loose from his captivity.

Yoseph reached in his cloth belt and grabbed his furry body, which leaped out of his hands and scrambled to the dark interior confines of the room. Whoever was outside his door stopped and shook the door handle. Yoseph's heart pounded with fear, for he had forgotten to lock the door behind him. He put his full weight against the door to make it seem locked. The sound of jangling keys of what might have been a Temple guard gave the door an attempt to see if it would open. The next thing he heard were faint footsteps leaving and moving down the stone corridor.

Yoseph's immediate need was to fetch a torch from one of the holders in the passageway. After a small blessing of thanks, waiting a short time, he opened the door, and once again entered the passageway. After grabbing the torch, he returned to his new quarters. The torchlight revealed a dusty size library replete with many ancient scrolls, parchments, and several cobweb-covered writing tables. All of it not used in some time. He was fortunate there were several unlit torches mounted on each of the four walls. To his left were three grimy oil lamps on one of the writing tables. Yoseph reached for one, shook it for oil, and to his surprise, it was full.

He lit one of the torches mounted in the holders, then he retrieved one of the lamps he had shaken and lit it. *Yoseph*, he told himself, *this is your new home for now if you're careful.* He would use this seldom-used storage room to hide and then search for his friend Nicodemus and make inquiries about Yoseph's family. He surmised that Nicodemus hadn't used this room for many summers, and he feared that his colleague was dead.

The door was a major concern he needed to correct right away. Again, it was difficult to shut and lock. Then an idea came to him to use some of the olive oil from one of the lamps to lubricate the lock. He poured a small amount of oil into the lock mechanism and tested it. After several attempts, the lock turned with ease. He loosened one of the stones that was holding the door from closing and it swung forth. Now he was able to leave and return without any impediments. He suspected the guard would return at the same time each day and Yoseph would note it for future times. He wouldn't light any of the lamps or torches until knowing the daily routine time the guard made his rounds.

It wasn't quite dark outside, for he could still see the sun's narrow last, rosy-fingered rays. The western-facing slit window in the passageway was his sole source of natural light. Once he closed his door, he was in total darkness and at the mercy of his oil lamps and torches for light. However, he was used to this dim light after many seasons in prison.

Yoseph spied one solitary chair in the room, which he sat on right away. As he sat in this creaky wooden chair, a small cloud of dust motes issued forth while he contemplated his next move. He sat there and prayed for Nicodemus. He knew not of his fate after their trial before the *bet din.* His home would be his first destination tonight. Yoseph said a prayer of thanks to *El Shaddai* and for Nicodemus.

Every so often Yoseph would open his door and peek out to see if it was nightfall. Once it became dark, Yoseph hid all his holy gifts that he received from Yeshua and prepared to leave his newfound home. He waited for the Temple guard to make his late-night round before leaving. He extinguished the oil lamp to lessen the smell and waited for his arrival.

After a short time, he heard the guard's footsteps. All of a sudden it came to him he hadn't locked the door to the room again. He reached for the key on the table and placed it into the lock opening. The key turned right away, and the lock plunger secured the door. The *clanging* of the lock mechanism echoed in the room. Had the guard heard the lock turning? His palms started sweating and his throat tightened.

His footsteps were now by the door. He stopped and pushed his body against the door and paused.

CHAPTER VI

Yoseph could hear the guard's breathing as he grunted, pushing on the door; however, after several tries, he stopped, but wouldn't leave. The guard stood outside Yoseph's door as though he was trying to hear something. Yoseph held his breath on several occasions and didn't move. After what seemed an eternity, he left. Yoseph unlocked the door after giving the guard sufficient time to travel deeper into the Temple Mount passageways. Yoseph found a lantern in one of the storage boxes that he used to light his way.

He waited a while before entering the main corridor of the Temple, still fearing discovery. As he started to leave, his longtime furry friend started squeaking his displeasure, sounding as if he didn't want to remain. Yoseph reached down, grabbed him, and tucked his furry friend in his ragged tunic belt. He locked the door behind him and crept down the dark corridor to true freedom. As he drew near the exit; a sudden fresh breeze struck his face. At last Yoseph was back in the narrow streets of *Yerushalayim.*

His immediate destination was Nicodemus's house. It was close to the Temple, which meant he didn't have far to travel, but his weak body trudged toward the home. Yoseph's heart raced with anticipation as he saw a lamp lit in an upper room window. Nicodemus had been released before him, Yoseph thought as he reached the door. He gave a hardy knock on the door and waited for his friend to let him in. The door eased open, and a middle-age woman appeared with a man Yoseph didn't recognize.

"Is Nicodemus at home?" he asked. "I am a friend of his and haven't seen him in many seasons."

"There's no man by the name of Nicodemus living here," replied the woman in a curt manner. "Besides, we don't allow beggars near our home," said a man with glaring eyes standing behind his suspected wife.

"I am not a beggar, sir, and my name is Yoseph of Arimathea. This could be the wrong house of my friend Nicodemus, but I don't believe so. I recognize the carved-shaped fish on his door." Yoseph pointed at the top portion of the door and drew their attention to the fish design encompassing a sword.

"See, it's Nicodemus's seal design. You must know him. Please tell me where he is," Yoseph implored, hoping they were just afraid to say.

"Leave me, beggar, before I shout for a centurion on duty!" hollered the man as he stepped in front of his wife. With both of his hands, he shoved Yoseph out of the alcove into the street. The wooden door slammed shut and the latch bolt locked with a loud *clank*. Stunned, he lay there on his back against the cold cobblestones, staring at the carved fish and sword on the door.

From merchant to now a beggar, Yoseph surmised. This shouldn't be a surprise, he thought, after four summers in prison. Here he was lying in the street with tattered clothes, uncut hair, dirty face, and a smell that would drive camels away. On his arms and legs, he rose and proceeded to return home, thinking there might be somebody still there waiting for his return.

The passageways were dark and deserted. Yoseph became confused because of the changes in shop signs. His trip to reach home was quite a challenge traversing the narrow passageways of *Yerushalayim*. It was a maze of wrong turns and unfamiliar alleys. At last, he recognized King Herod's old palace and knew the way from there to his home. It was quite late when he approached his courtyard door. He spied his old *mezuzah* post and reached in to touch the prayer scroll, but it wasn't there.

To his right, over the door entrance was a sign. It said the high priest and the Sanhedrin had confiscated his home! The doorjamb had the red seal of the Sanhedrin with its insignia of the Ten Commandments tablets. He tried to force the door open, but it wouldn't budge. Then he remembered the iron gate on the other side of his stone wall. A quick trip around the back of his home met further disappointment. The gate was open, but there were several large wooden beams placed in a crisscross fashion, preventing him from entering.

He fell in front of the iron gate with an overwhelming sense of despair. Who could Yoseph seek out that might help him clean up? The fear of being in prison again mortified him. Then it occurred to him that he could return to the home of Eli, his old friend.

Yoseph's memory that it was some distance from his home, so he should start right away. However, there was an obligation he must perform. His hand reached into his tattered tunic belt and felt his warm furry prison companion. He knew he couldn't see to his needs; however, it was becoming quite bleak for Yoseph to care for himself. For a moment, he held him in his hands and stared into his dark glistening eyes before releasing him into his old courtyard. It was like saying goodbye to a human companion he wouldn't see again. Yoseph observed him scurrying toward the old cellar, and, for a moment, he thought he turned and stared back at Yoseph as if acknowledging his farewell.

The night was pitch dark and few people were on the streets and a dark moon blackened his image, but that presented another problem. It was so dark Yoseph stumbled at times. Then came the *clanging* sound of metal and the heavy thumping of sandals down one of the many passageways. In addition, in the distance, Yoseph could see the flickering of moving torches and uniform-shaped shadows on the buildings in front of him. His throat tightened so fast from fear, he thought he might faint. He felt the dampness starting to form in his palms, followed by the dreaded voice he didn't want to hear.

"Who goes there? You look like a thief, stop! I am Gaius Sertonius, the centurion on duty. Halt right now or I'll arrest you."

Panic seized Yoseph at once and he started running. The footsteps behind him grew closer as he raced down one passageway after another. There was some distance between them, but he was no match for well-trained Roman soldiers. Just as he thought his heart and lungs were about to burst, he spied a familiar building. It appeared to be his old business partner Eli's home and shop. He prayed that Eli and his sons still lived there.

The darkness left him in some doubt that it was his house. The centurion and soldiers were now closer; as he glanced back, he could see the torch shadow of a horsehair-plumed helmet. To Yoseph's relief, there were several camels tethered outside this building and one of Eli's sons was attending to them. He gazed in his direction and saw Yoseph running toward him and darted back inside, after which he returned with his brother. Just as Yoseph arrived winded, Eli also appeared.

"What is all the commotion about? I am trying to rest. Eliyah, who is this beggar?"

"Eli, don't you recognize me? It's me, Yoseph, your friend and former business partner," he implored with a wheezing voice. "A Roman centurion wants to arrest me and is just around the corner."

"You aren't Yoseph of Arimathea; he died in the *bet din* prison several summers ago. Why are you trying to pretend to be my late friend, beggarman?"

"Eli, I don't have time to identify myself. A centurion is chasing me; he suspects I am a thief. My brother-in-law's name is Hebron. Please hide me, I beg you."

At once, his old friend's brow raised, and his mouth gaped open from disbelief and fear. His oldest son ushered Yoseph into a small shop room and threw several large cloth bolts over him, thus concealing his whereabouts. Then he heard the centurion speaking to Eli outside and describing Yoseph as a thief. To Yoseph's chagrin, he said yes!

However, to his relief, Eli told the Roman officer that Yoseph had run down a side passageway toward the Temple Mount. If he hurried, he told the centurion, he would capture him. A great relief came over Yoseph upon hearing the rattle of the centurion's greaves and the thumping of his sandals running away. A short time later, Eli's footsteps approached his hiding spot.

"Whoever you are, you can come out now, the centurion is gone," Eli said, as he helped raise Yoseph from behind the red silk bolts of cloth, then gazed at him for some time. Eli appeared hardy and the past summers had been kind to him. There wasn't a gray hair on his head or any new wrinkles on his brow. His skin was quite taut, and his weight appeared normal. The dark bushy eyebrows showed no white in them. The clearness in his large eyes hadn't diminished and their piercing stare was as penetrating as ever.

"Eli, I know I don't appear the same, but, please, help me. I have no true home to rest this night. The Sanhedrin has confiscated my home and if I don't leave *Yerushalayim*, I will be thrown back into prison. The conditions of my pardon state I must leave *Yerushalayim* as soon as possible, otherwise, I am a doomed man."

"How do I know you aren't lying?" Eli asked.

"Ask me any question that you and Yoseph would know."

His hand reached up to his curly beard and pulled on it, searching for a difficult question to ask.

"Where was your nephew, the rabbi, born?"

Yoseph didn't hesitate to answer, but said, "A small village that means the House of Bread or Bethlehem! Our great King David was born in that village."

The quick response prompted Eli to ask another question.

"Who was the man that betrayed Yeshua and had him arrested?" Eli asked with a deep penetrating stare into Yoseph's eyes.

Yoseph's reply wasn't as quick as before, for it brought back painful memories. With a heavy heart, he replied, "Yudas Iscariot." Then his anger started to swell up inside him. "I curse the day that the dagger man and Caiaphas were born."

"Praise be to *El Shaddai*!" exclaimed Eli. "It's you, Yoseph of Arimathea, my old friend." He delicately touched Yoseph's shoulders with both of his hands as though he saw a ghost. A huge grin broke out on his sun-darkened face, and he embraced Yoseph for a long time. Both of his sons did the same.

"Yoseph, I can't believe you're still alive and not a wraith before me. It's a miracle that you are still here among the living. How did you survive over those many summers? Oh, it's rude of me to question you now. Eliyah, show Yoseph to your quarters so he can clean up and destroy his filthy rags."

Eliyah motioned for Yoseph to follow him, which he did with much enthusiasm.

"Yoseph, you and I are about the same size and build. Pick out anything you see and it's yours to keep. Also, there is soap, beard-trimming scissors, clean water, and towels. Please let me know if you need anything else. Yoseph, it's excellent to see you again. My *abba* has missed you these many past summers. He believes he is to blame for your captivity. Both my brother and I know this isn't so. He was brokenhearted when he heard rumors that you were dead. You have lifted his sadness tonight. Whenever you are presentable, come join us for a late-night celebration."

Eliyah left him to his ablutions, which he was elated that he had the opportunity to cut his beard, wash, and change his clothes. It had been four summers since he last cleaned himself. The hot bath water didn't do its job. Each time it was changed, it became a rusty muddy color. Not until the fourth bath, did he see a difference. He decided to trim his beard close like that of one of Eli's sons. He was no longer the same man that he once was. The successful merchant and member of the Sanhedrin didn't exist now. That man died in prison several days after his nephew died on that bloody cross four springs ago. He was now resurrecting himself for a new life.

The clothes he chose were plain with some purple color on the tunic belt. The shawl was a comfortable material of lightweight silk. To Yoseph's surprise, the robe had a small chalice design pattern woven into its fabric, which was invisible until the lamp shed its light a certain way. Oh, the joy of having sandals again. Eliyah's sandals fit fine on his feet.

Gazing around, he saw a silver-coated metal square reflecting light coming from one of the corners of Eliyah's room. He approached it with much apprehension, not knowing what he would see. He observed himself and saw a sunken and haggard face. His shoulder-length hair needed cutting and he had large crescent-shaped dark circles under each eye. The skin on his face was snow white from the lack of sunlight and seemed to hang from his arms and facial bones.

"Yoseph, how are you coming along?" he heard Eli's deep voice from an adjacent room.

"I am about done dressing," he replied. "Can one of your sons cut my hair?" He now experienced a helpless sensation of dependence on Eli's generous hospitality. "Your kindness is more than I deserve, Eli. I don't know how I can ever repay you."

"You stay there, Yoseph, and I will send my other son, Isaiah, to cut your hair. He has had plenty of experience cutting and grooming our camel herd. He should make quick work of it in no time. After he is finished, you must join us for some wine and celebration."

Isaiah came into the room with some large shears and a long comb. In what appeared an instant, there was a large pile of hair behind the back of Yoseph's chair.

"Master Yoseph, there is so much hair that we could make several large sitting pillows. Do you want me to save it?"

"No, my young man, burn it all with my old clothes. All of it reminds me of my imprisonment. Thank you for doing this for me. I wish I could pay you right now."

"Master Yoseph, don't worry. This is what *Adonai* has taught us to do for our fellowman in need. Now, come and join us for some much-needed refreshment."

He followed Isaiah into their large eating area with numerous large pillows stacked about in a semicircle shape in front of a sumptuous amount of food. There were large trays of dates, pomegranates, honey cakes, and a common bowl filled with stewed lamb. The steaming bowl gave off pungent smells of basil and tarragon. It was the first tasty food he had, other than the holy wine and bread.

As they sat down, Eli said a blessing for the wine, then the bread. By the time the blessings were finished, Yoseph's mouth was watering with hunger. He couldn't believe this event was happening after four summers of imprisonment. There was a big cup in front of him replete with wine that he wanted to toast to thank Eli and his sons. He raised it with a steady hand and started to speak from his heart.

"My dearest friends, I want to bless all of you

for helping me in my time of need. I am now a penniless old man. If I did have any money left, I would give it all to you. After my many summers in prison, I now see what wealth indeed is, it's a lasting friendship. I now raise my cup to honor the house of Eli and his sons. May *Adonai* always give all of you *shalom bayit* forever."

They then raised their cups and shouted, "*Shalom.*" Yoseph was quite anxious, as they started to eat, to inquire about his family. As a guest, he waited until the completion of the serving of the food before speaking with trepidation.

"Eli, I hope you have some pleasant news about my family."

There was a pause while he chewed his food. During this short time, Yoseph's heart raced with fear. Would the news be positive or otherwise?

CHAPTER VII

Yoseph, I haven't heard anything from your family in a couple of summers. The last news was that your family was afraid to return to *Yerushalayim*. All of your business and personal property was confiscated by the high priest, Caiaphas."

"Yes, I know about my home in *Yerushalayim*. Before I came here, I stopped by hoping I might see them. To my great disappointment, the Sanhedrin council had barricaded it shut. I tried to open every entrance and gate, but it was futile. Just for a moment, I broke down with despair and then thought of you. I was on my way here when one of the Roman guards on patrol spotted me. That was why I was running when you first saw me. If he had caught me, thinking I was a thief, I would have been returned to that cursed prison."

"Yoseph, this much I do know. If your family is

still alive, they may have left for Alexandria. They might have believed you had perished in prison and decided to leave *Yehudah* several summers ago. The last time I saw them was when I dropped them off near Arimathea. After your nephew's crucifixion, Eliyah told me you and Nicodemus were arrested. There were so many rumors after your nephew's burial. I didn't know what to believe. All I surmised from these terrible happenings that you and Nicodemus were unjustly imprisoned. A short time later, I approached Caiaphas and pleaded for your release. He told me that if I didn't leave his presence right away, he would try me as a zealot. Yoseph, I tried so hard to reason with that son-of-a-bitch, but it was useless."

"Why was Nicodemus's property sold and not mine? After my release, I passed by his home and saw someone else living there!"

"The first summer after your nephew's cruci-fixion, Caiaphas sold his property to pay off all his henchmen. Your property didn't sell, for all the prospective buyers thought *El Shaddai* had cursed it. It has lain vacant these four summers. It's now a thorn in Caiaphas's side and a reminder of his nefarious treachery. Praise to our *Adonai,* he is no longer the high priest, but his evil deeds continue. He saw to it that the emperor recalled Pontius Pilate to Rome and later the emperor exiled Pilate to a country called Helvetia. The new procurator, Marcellus, is even more oppressive than Pilate was. The evil Syrian prefect, Lucius Vitellius, controls him.

"Yoseph, I would be quite careful about your presence. Use your rumored death to your advantage. You are more than welcome to stay here tonight."

"I appreciate the offer, but you have risked the well-being of yourself and your sons for hiding me. Your hospitality and the gift of clean clothes have made me a new man. Besides, I have a small hidden room in the Temple Mount where I am hiding. Eli, I have seen and heard wonders that no man can comprehend. It may be hard for you to believe, but it was a blessing for me to be confined these four summers."

"Why do you say this, Yoseph? You could have died in that filthy prison."

"Yes, that could have happened, but didn't. My beloved nephew kept me alive. He appeared to me one day and gave me his Last Supper cup. This cup sustained me these many seasons along with a platter of bread. His Holy Cup was never empty of wine and the bread paten never stopped producing bread. During this time, I continued with my diary and wrote everything I knew about our *Maishiach*, Yeshua."

"Yoseph, your nephew was crucified by the Romans and died. Don't you remember, my friend? I was told you buried him in your new tomb. The Sanhedrin thought you stole his body three days later and you created the legend he rose from the dead. I know you are a truthful man, but, Yoseph, could those many hot summers in prison have tricked your mind?"

"No, Eli. I know what I saw in prison. Yeshua touched my hand when he gave me his cup from the *Pesach* celebration four springs ago. He was as real as I am sitting in front of you now."

Eli's son Eliyah spoke up and asked Yoseph a question about the last *Seder* he had with Yeshua.

"Master Yoseph, I heard from one of Yeshua's followers a short time after your nephew was executed. I believe his name was Thomas. He told me that there were several strange occurrences at the *Seder* dinner. The one that he told me was about the prophet Eliyah."

"Yes, I know. The cup for the prophet Eliyah mysteriously fell over and the door for his entrance closed with a sudden gust of wind. However, most there thought that Yohanan the Baptizer's spirit had entered the room, knocked the prophet Eliyah's cup over, and then his spirit left the room."

"Eliyah, what became of the rest of Yeshua's followers?"

"The majority of them fled the city of *Yerushalayim.* There was a rumor that they later returned and started having secret meetings at Yohanan Marcus's home. I am almost certain if they did, both the Roman authorities and the Sanhedrin spied upon them. Master Yoseph, I wouldn't travel there to see them if I were you."

"Thank you for the warning, Eliyah, but when I leave here, I will be traveling back to my secret room at the Temple Mount. In several days. I want to depart for Arimathea and seek out my family."

"Master Yoseph," Isaiah said. "I haven't told my brother or *abba* about what the disciple Thomas told me too. It was several days after Eliyah spoke to him."

They turned their heads in the direction of Isaiah. He had remained quiet through their entire conversation.

"Thomas Didymus, as he is called by Yeshua's disciples, said he saw your nephew at Yohanan Marcus's house almost nine sunsets after you buried him in your tomb. He didn't believe it was Yeshua at first. Not until he saw the scars from his healed wounds, did he believe it was him, but still, he had doubts. Yeshua then let Thomas touch the scars to see if he was made of flesh. Thomas at first thought it was a ghost. When he touched the scar on his side, Thomas yelled for all to hear, 'My *Adonai* and my *Eloheinu.*' Then Yeshua admonished him and said, 'Have you believed because you can see my flesh? Blessed are those among you that haven't seen but have come to believe.'"

"Isaiah, I can understand Thomas's doubts, for I felt them once. What my nephew and Savior has become I cannot say. He is beyond our understanding. All I know is that I believe in him, and he has changed my *kavanah* or spiritual direction.

Yeshua has given me a purpose to spread his knowledge and wisdom to others. Those who have no hope or thirst for something in their lives will now be my new charge."

"Eli or Isaiah, have you heard anyone speak about the Magdala woman? She was Yeshua's closest confidant."

Both Eli and Isaiah shook their heads in a negative manner, but to Yoseph's surprise, Eliyah answered.

"Master Yoseph, I heard from the market gossip that she stayed with Miriam, your niece, for a while. After several summers, she left *Yerushalayim.* The last rumor I heard was she sought out your daughter at Arimathea. I haven't had any further information since then."

"Thank you, Isaiah. I hope these rumors are true." Eli's family had given Yoseph a glimmer of hope that they were well.

"Eli, once again I don't know how to repay you."

"Yoseph, you need not repay me. Just remember us in your prayers. I know you will become a great teacher to Abraham's people. You'll become an instrument of *El Shaddai's* will. For now, I insist you stay with us tonight, and no argument about it. Let's retire and rest, for it's late."

That night Yoseph had a sound sleep in Eli's home. It was the first time in four summers he had slept on a real bed. Along toward morning, two things he hadn't experienced in a while awakened him: the sound of a cock crowing in the distance and the light of warm sunbeams touching his face. Yoseph's first thoughts were about his family and seeing them. Splendid anticipation came over his entire body as he finished his morning prayers.

"Yoseph," he heard his name called by Eli's deep booming voice. "Come join us to break the fast."

Yoseph proceeded down a long hallway to a bright open courtyard behind Eli's clothing shop. The morning sun blinded him for a moment, and he couldn't see Eli and his sons. Though his nose could smell the mouthwatering food, his eyes hadn't adjusted to the brightness of the sun.

"Eli, you must pardon me, my eyes are like those of a bat. All they have seen is darkness these four summers."

"Eliyah, help Master Yoseph to his cushion so he can eat," Eli ordered. "Yoseph, you sit next to me in the shade until your eyes adjust."

"I suppose that evil Caiaphas even plundered the Temple money for the prison torches, and I believe he would sell his daughter if someone would accept her." Eli smiled.

It felt wholesome to laugh as Yoseph sat down in the shade. Now he could distinguish the many dishes set before him. There were plates of dates piled high, stacks of honey cakes, apples, pomegranates, almonds, and a large ewer of pomegranate juice. As Yoseph's eyes adjusted to the sunlight, he spied two large patens of goat's cheese and eggs.

"So, Yoseph, what do you have planned today?" Eli inquired with a large wedge of goat cheese ready to enter his mouth. "I am wondering why you want to return to the hidden room in the Temple and not go at once to Arimathea. Why risk being caught?"

"Eli, my friend, I am returning to the Temple to organize my diary and review what I have written about my Savior's life. It should be completed in several days, and from there I will then travel to Arimathea."

"Please, be careful, Yoseph, when you proceed to the Temple. We wouldn't want you imprisoned again. Before you leave for Arimathea, come by and I will have my favorite camel ready for you. He was the one you left on, after attending the Last Supper with your nephew."

"Again, Eli, I thank you for your hospitality," Yoseph replied putting one last chunk of cheese in his mouth and washing it down with a cup of pomegranate juice. Everybody by now had completed their meals and Eli said the *birkat ha-mazon,* after which Yoseph stood up and gave each of Eli's sons an embrace. Eli handed him an ample supply of the food to last him several days and they too embraced. He put the sack of food over his shoulder and exited the courtyard by a small gate hidden by thornbushes.

He crept along numerous narrow passageways and kept close to the side streets. The people of *Yerushalayim* were beginning to stir as the sun rose over the tops of their homes. The fresh smell of baked bread wafted from the many bakeries as he passed the shops. He was almost at the Temple Mount when he saw Gamaliel from the Sanhedrin approaching him. He couldn't avoid him, there was no doorway or side street for Yoseph to hide. Their eyes met, and he greeted Yoseph with "*Shalom.*" He replied in kind and hurried past him. Gamaliel's footsteps stopped and Yoseph knew he had paused for a moment. He sensed his eyes focused on the back of Yoseph's head and a lump of apprehension formed in his throat. To his relief, his footsteps continued onward.

A short time later, Yoseph arrived at one of the many gates to the Temple. He was in a quandary over which to choose. In the darkness of last night, Yoseph didn't realize the many gates. Then he saw the location of the morning sun. The sole open window to the prison tunnel was an east-facing window. He then counted up from the Temple's two levels and surmised this was his room. There below the window was the Sanhedrin building entrance. He knew that he hadn't come out of that entrance last night. Farther down the lofty wall was an arch that braced a stairway to the Temple grounds. He then saw a small entrance underneath the large arch, which the sun's shadows had hidden. This must be the right entry, he told himself.

As he drew near to the entrance, the more he remembered. Indeed, this was the correct opening. Yoseph started running along the wall. By the time he entered the small passageway, Yoseph was breathing quite hard. It was still early in the morning and not many people saw him enter. His eyes adjusted fast to the darkness. Up ahead he saw a large door with the star of Solomon engraved on its wooden surface. The door opened without a sound, and he strolled a short distance to his room. He grabbed the torch next to the open window and reached in his tunic belt for the key.

The key worked without effort and the door closed with ease. The olive oil had done its job. The first things he wanted to check were the cruets, spear blade, sword, paten, his diary, the cup, and the written history of his Savior and Redeemer, all of it stashed in a chest hidden under a mountain of scrolls. To his great relief, everything was in order. He lit all the lamps, replaced the torch in the corridor, and then he sat down to finish his work. A thought came over him that he should make a copy of all his writing, just in case the authorities destroyed one. The other he would transport with him to Arimathea. If he couldn't return for some reason, he could always have it delivered by Eli. Besides, he would leave Eli directions on where he would be hiding in Arimathea.

He must have written way past sunset. One time he opened his door, gazed across the passageway, and saw the moon's beams coming through the slit-shaped Temple window. His stomach started growling, and hunger and thirst grabbed his attention. He stopped writing and drew near to the chest. Yoseph opened the lid and reached for the cup and paten. Both were still warm to his touch. He placed both on the table, hoping he would see both wine and bread appear. To his disappointment, nothing happened after staring into the cup and paten for a considerable length of time. Both gave off a glow of light, but neither wine nor bread appeared. *How odd*, he thought. Had he done something wrong? Was his time spent in prison the sole experience of the former miracles? Would the wine and bread ever appear again? His appetite and distress were now sharper.

He then remembered the food sack Eli had given him, reached for it, and consumed part of its contents. After finishing, he continued writing for the rest of the night. The sweet dates gave him plenty of energy and the pomegranate juice kept him alert. Every so often, he would glance at the paten and the cup to see if bread and wine would appear. Yet, nothing happened.

He had completed copying half of his Savior's life history when without warning he heard a noise. It must be the guard, he surmised. He blew out all the lights and remained still. The footsteps thumped louder and then there was a pause. At once, fear came over Yoseph, for the guard shook the latch and pounded on the door. Then a voice shouted.

"I know there is somebody in there. I can smell burnt oil."

Whoever he was tried to force the door. There were numerous hard thumping sounds as if he was lunging at the door with his body. Blessed be to *Adonai,* for the lock held. Then to Yoseph's further chagrin, he heard scraping from his sword blade, in an attempt to pry the door open.

CHAPTER VIII

After a short time, he gave up and shouted through the door again.

"I will be back tomorrow on my next watch. Right now, the high priest wants me elsewhere. Whoever is in there better be gone. Tomorrow I will have additional help and this door will come down! Also, I am notifying the high priest of your presence."

Yoseph remained quiet, yet he could hear his sweat dripping onto the table in front of him. The fear of returning to prison caused him to sweat further. To his relief, the guard's footsteps departed. He didn't relight the lamps until he heard the passageway door close. Then with ease, he opened his door and again used the passageway torch to light his lamps. His nervous state kept him wide awake, for he couldn't sleep. This was quite fortuitous, for his sleepless mind helped him complete his copy by dawn with no need for rest.

He ate some more food that Eli had provided him and sat there thinking about how he might hide his parchment copies and directions. His eyes focused on several loose stone blocks near the floor. A satisfactory portion of the mortar had fallen out of four of the stones. He reached to pull one loose. To his surprise, it slid right out. The other three did the same and now he had his hiding place. The hole in the wall was deep enough to place the small wooden chest into.

He grabbed the remaining *kodesh* written words from the chest that his Savior had spoken and then he placed these parchments in it. Afterward, he shoved the chest into the recess of the hole and positioned the stone blocks back in their original places. The broken grout, which lay on the floor, he used to secure the stones. His hands shook from fear that the chest of parchments might be discovered. He left one crack above the top stone to place his directions to the secret cave at Arimathea. Yoseph prayed that the right person would find his *kodesh* writings.

Gingerly, he replaced the remaining grout in front of the directions, concealing the roads and paths to the secret cave at Arimathea. He gathered up all the things that his *Maishiach* had given him and placed them in both his writing satchel and Eli's food sack. After finishing, he said another prayer, that if needed, Eli would find his nephew's holy words. By now, sleep had overtaken him, and it was time to rest before he departed. Yoseph sat down on the cool stone floor and fell fast asleep.

He awoke about the first watch of the evening rested, with no fitful dreams. It was now time he left *Yerushalayim*. All he had to do now was to return to Eli's home and retrieve the camel he promised him. He edged his door open to see that nobody was coming. He then locked it but left, taking the key with him.

Again, it was nightfall as he departed from the small underground Temple entrance. The sky was clear, and the moon gave him sufficient light to travel. Eli lived in the lower part of the city and wasn't too far from the Temple. Yoseph followed the viaduct to the southern part of the city and now approached Eli's house. Coming toward him were five bouncing flaming torches, with faceless hooded persons holding each. The dark band approached him at a rapid pace. To Yoseph's horror, leading them was Caiaphas! Then he heard him speak.

"Make way beggar, it's Yoseph Caiaphas, a Temple priest. Clear the passageway."

At once, a hot burst of hatred swelled inside Yoseph's heart. His warm-flushed face filled with anger and his hand reached for the sword in his cloth sack. He wanted to kill the "bastard" Caiaphas. Then as suddenly as his temper flared, it subsided. A strange sensation emanated from his hand as he held the bag with the cup and cruets. His fiery hot body and hatred stopped at once. It was as if a fast-moving thunderstorm had cooled his skin. His hand released its grip around the pommel and his fingers became numb. He became so relaxed that he thought he might pass out as Caiaphas passed within an arm's length of him. Yoseph didn't even make eye contact as he rushed by him. He was relieved that Caiaphas didn't recognize him. Anyway, he suspected in Caiaphas's mind, Yoseph had died several summers ago. The calm sensation stayed with Yoseph until he approached the front entrance to Eli's shop and house and then stopped. He knocked on the door and young Eliyah opened it for him to enter.

"Welcome back, Master Yoseph. Let me grab your belongings."

"No offense, Eliyah, but I rather keep them with me. I know I have imposed on your hospitality more than I can repay, but I need a place to stay. I believe the Temple guards have discovered my presence. One of the guards tried to break my door down, yet the lock held and prevented him from entering."

"Did I hear my great friend Yoseph of Arimathea enter my humble abode?" Eli asked coming out of one of his many shop rooms with a bolt of red silk.

"Yes, you're right, Eli, I have returned. One of the guards has discovered my secret Temple room. The guard tried to break the door down but to no avail. He is coming back tonight to finish the job. I thought it best I leave *Yerushalayim* before first light for Arimathea. Do you still have a camel for me to travel on tomorrow?"

"Yes, he is tethered at my gate behind the courtyard. You do know his wife will follow with you?"

"Eli, you don't have to loan her to me too! I suffer bad enough I can't pay you for your prize male camel."

"Don't worry, Yoseph, we will make this a loan between two friends. When you arrive at Arimathea, send them back by a courier. I will pay the expense. Now let us have some food, for I am famished from working all day."

"Eli, before we eat, have you heard anything about my family?"

"I will tell you what little I know when we start our repast."

They proceeded to the courtyard and a short time later Eliyah brought a large stone pot of lamb stew. Yoseph reclined on a large silk pillow and gazed at the hot steam from the stew circle above his head. The smell of vegetables and meat caused his mouth to water from anticipation.

"Eli, before we eat, I must tell you several things. First, I almost killed Caiaphas tonight.

On my way here, Caiaphas, accompanied by four other men, approached me in a narrow passageway. I recognized him, but he didn't recognize me. The element of surprise was in my favor. I had a sword I could have used. Also, I believe in his mind he thinks I am dead."

"What prevented you from killing him, my friend? We would all be better off if he was dead. Yoseph, you have more of a reason to kill him than any man in *Yehudah* does. Besides, he isn't the head of the Sanhedrin anymore. It would have been the perfect opportunity to rid us of that evil man."

"Eli, what stopped me was the miraculous cup of Yeshua, my Savior. It prevented my hot anger of revenge from using my sword. So many unexplainable things have happened to me that I still cannot comprehend them, yet my faith in this *Kodesh* Cup and Yeshua keeps me on his chosen path. I know I have been ordained with fire to tell his story to others and show the miracles of the holy items he gave me. Also, I have composed a written copy of my recent experiences with Yeshua. I hid it back in the Temple storage room behind a stone with loose mortar. If I need it, will you bring it to me?"

"Yes, Joseph, my friend."

Yoseph drew him a map to find it inside the Temple and then gave him the door key.

"I must say, Yoseph, I am starting to believe you and see your determination. This I know, my friend; it won't be long before you make a spiritual name for yourself. I am proud to have known you and I will miss your company. It's obvious your nephew has given you his 'light of truth.'"

There was a moment of silence before Eli continued. "Yoseph, I meant to tell you earlier about Hebron, but I forgot."

"He's not dead . . . is he?" A sudden lump formed in Yoseph's throat, and his heart started racing.

"No, no, Yoseph. That night after the crucifixion, a strange thing happened. I saw your big brother-in-law in one of the passageways close to the Temple gate. It was quite dark, and he didn't see me. The direction he was traveling wasn't toward your house. As I observed him, it appeared he was following somebody. I did notice his hand held a large dagger!"

"Did you meet him that night?" asked Eli.

"No, I proceeded home and fell asleep. That horrific day left me exhausted. I had given Hebron instructions not to return to *Yerushalayim*. I have no idea why he returned."

Then it struck Yoseph like a bolt of lightning. Hebron had come back to kill Yudas!

"Eli, what happened to the man called Yudas after the crucifixion?"

"The rumor I heard was he hung himself, but when he was found, his stomach appeared to be torn open. Whoever found him said his intestines were lying across his upper thighs. And there was one other odd thing that was told. The rope he used broke or was cut, for his body was found in a ravine along one of the cliffs near the tomb of Absalom."

"I pray, my friend, that Hebron wasn't a part of Yudas's nefarious demise," Yoseph said to Eli with a burning sensation in his throat.

"I don't believe so, Yoseph. Guilt was the instrument of this hanging. Caiaphas paid Yudas thirty pieces of silver to become a traitor to your nephew. Caiaphas will always be the author of what occurred four springs ago." Eli's words made Yoseph feel somewhat better, yet there was lingering doubt still in his mind.

"Eliyah, let's help Rabbi Yoseph with his belongings and assist him with his camel."

How odd to be called Rabbi Yoseph. All his adult life, he never thought of himself as a rabbi. The thought of teaching others about his Savior filled him with a sense of joy and happiness. Before leaving, Yoseph ate a hardy meal. The best in many summers.

They passed through the small gate, and there waiting for him were two of Eli's camels. He forced Boaz to his knees so Yoseph could climb on. Eliyah placed his belongings with Boaz, and on the other camel, called Ruth, he put a sack of food and some water. Before he mounted his camel, Isaiah came out of the courtyard to see him off. They hugged for a long while, after which Yoseph mounted his camel to depart. Tears of goodbye started streaming from his eyes. Right before he departed, Isaiah said a prayer for Yoseph's safety.

"Those people who traveled in darkness now have seen a great light; those who lived in a land of deep darkness—upon them, light has shone. Goodbye, Master Yoseph; don't forget us."

"I will never forget any of you. You will always be in my thoughts."

Yoseph's camel rose little by little from his knees. He guessed Boaz was like Yoseph, he didn't want to leave but knew he must. Struggling to rise from his knobby knees forced his camel to protest with a loud braying sound. After standing, Yoseph kicked him several times and he started to trot down the dark narrow passageway behind Eli's courtyard. After a short distance, Yoseph turned around and waved his final goodbye to three distant figures, made visible by the back-gate torches. There was both sadness and longing in Yoseph's heart. He knew he perhaps wouldn't see Eli and his family again. Still, his heart ached to see his own family.

Once he reached the *Yoppa* gate, he observed few travelers entering and exiting. The night sentry gave him a casual nod and motioned him on. He was through the gate and out on the *Yoppa* road in a heartbeat. Boaz's stride was strong and swift. He hadn't lost any of his speed from the four past springs. The moon was above the Tower of David as the road bore to his right. There was no need for torches tonight. The white moonbeams touched the road ahead, and it made Yoseph's navigating the big camel and his spouse easy.

As he passed the Hill of the Skull, a lump formed in his throat from the dreadful events of four springs ago. For a moment, he thought he saw three empty crosses, but it was dark shadows from some distant rocks. The night air was quite mild as the camels picked up speed on the flat open road. His heart ached to see Yosa, Alein Yosephe, Enygeus, and Hebron. He wondered how they had aged. Had any of his children married? Were they well? Then fear seized him. What if they weren't at Arimathea or alive?

PART III

The Cup and Symbol

CHAPTER IX

Anno Domini 1190
Early Winter
Huesca Commandery, Iberia

There was a quiet knock at my door that inter-rupted my desperate prayer. I rose from the side of my bed and proceeded to open the door, where I saw Grand Master Gilbért standing with a frown on his scarred forehead.

"Lord Robert, is there anything wrong? I heard loud noises coming from your room and thought you might be in trouble."

I glanced down to see his fist release its grip from a large dagger at his sword belt. For a short moment, he gazed over my shoulder to see the disarray of my cell room.

"You should also be more cautious in opening your door. What if I had been someone who wanted to harm you?"

"Yes, it was foolish of me to be so careless. Please, come in and shut the door, for I have a sorrowful confession to make. My mind is so upset that the fear of physical harm is of no importance to me. *Le Sangraal* copies have been stolen! Please, forgive my careless behavior. I have prayed for guidance and hope we will find them soon. As you can see, I have searched everywhere. We must find the *bâtard* culprit who did this at once!"

Without warning, Grand Master Gilbért's fist punched the closed door, and his face then displayed a fiery crimson color.

"Damn it, Lord Robert, you should have stayed in your room, but let's not panic. We must use stealth in how we accomplish the recovery of our copies. I haven't told you this, but there may be another plot against our quest. Yet, I know the archbishop of Toulouse, Cardinal Folquet is behind this new cabal. I have heard rumors in the past he has a man here in Huesca. I believe its Commander Ramáirez Sancho del Zaragozza." He said this in a hushed voice and then continued speaking while my mind tried to figure out this revelation.

"Never underestimate power and greed. Each comes in many disguises. They both can be rationalized at the expense of the poor and righteous. How a man or a woman handles power is a true measure of their character. Justice is the first casualty when power is misused. It's time we consult *Abad* Miguel and seek his counsel on what to do.

Let me help you straighten up before we leave."

It was late evening when we left through a back stairwell and exited a small sally port unobserved. We traveled behind the Templar commandery toward San Pedro el Viejo. The night air had a definite chill that showed our steamy breath. We were now in the month of November and the nights had a cold bite to our exposed flesh. A light from the colored glass of the church windows helped guide us. The candles inside gave off shimmering colors of yellow and red as we approached the ambulatory of San Pedro. There was a small, concealed entrance to a chapel, so we entered undetected. It was apparent that Grand Master Gilbért knew where he was.

The small arch-shaped wooden door creaked as we passed through. Its screeching sound echoed on the walls of the chapel, and I prayed nobody else had heard us. Inside the glowing chapel were several people praying as we proceeded from the chancel area. I couldn't distinguish their faces at first, but as they rose from praying, I could see that both were *moines.* Their distinct black robes contrasted with our white mantles and surplices as we approached them. The light from a large nine-candlestick holder revealed the first *moine's* face. It was *Abad* Miguel, the other *moine* I didn't know, yet he had similar facial features to *Abad* Miguel. Both men were the same build and their white-and-black-streaked beards matched.

"*Pax vobiscum*, Grand Master Gilbért de Érail and Lord Robert de Borron," *Abad* Miguel said with a large grin on his face. "I guess congratulations are in order too. There could be no better man deserving of being grand master of southern Gaul and Iberia than my former pupil."

They both embraced at once and *Abad* Miguel whispered something in Grand Master Gilbért's ear. From their physical closeness, I knew the two men had known each other for some time.

"Lord Robert, I just gave our new grand master his greeting when we would always meet. It's from Matthew, chapter ten, verses thirty-four through thirty-nine. As a young boy, he'd gain strength in what our Lord said and I knew one day he would be a Poor-Soldier of Christ. Oh ... I am so sorry not to introduce my *hermano*, Gabriel. He is the one who will be delivering your correspondence, Lord Robert de Borron."

"It will be an honor, Lord Robert, to deliver your letter to your épouse. My *hermano* and our pious *Abadt* Miguel said that Grand Master Gilbért de Érail wanted some correspondence delivered too."

"Yes, that's true *Hermano* Gabriel. Both of our letters are quite sensitive in nature, but I would like to discuss this in private."

There was a pinched expression on Grand Master Gilbért's face as the four of us entered the transept and proceeded along the clerestory. We then approached the entrance that I had gone through the previous night, which led out to the open cloister garth. The remaining enclosed cloisters led to a set of stairs that had one sputtering fading lit torch. At the top of the stairs, a long stone hallway ended in front of a large arch-shaped door. A wooden-carved cross, embedded into the full length of the door, awaited us as we approached and then entered. *Abad* Miguel's cell was quite spacious and had many scrolls and parchment scattered about his living area.

One end of his room had a large cupboard that reached the ceiling. The opened doors revealed full shelves with every size of book and tome. On the bottom of the cupboard, books spilled onto the floor. Next to the books, scattered about, was *Abad* Miguel's bed. Above his spartan bed was an ornately carved pewter crucifix. Yet, what caught my attention was a parchment paper with an unusual geometric design. It was lying on a wooden table in front of the sole open window in his cell. The room glowed with numerous candles and the candlelight seemed to be concentrated on the crucifix and the geometric design.

The grand master was first to speak as we sat on the four wooden chairs gathered by *Frère* Gabriel.

"It's quite pleasant to see you *Frère* Miguel, but I have urgent and dangerous business to discuss with you. I am glad you have already met

Lord de Borron. Both of us are on a secret quest. We require you and your *frère's* help to continue our quest. I need to send a message to our Holy *Père* in Rome. There is a warrant for my arrest by Cardinal Folquet. I cannot trust some of the men in my order to deliver my missive. There's a traitor among us. It's *Deus vult* that Lord de Borron and I complete God's Holy command."

"You are in search of the *Santo Cáliz*, am I correct? Or could it be a new holy gospel?" *Frère* Miguel said.

"*Oui*, you're quite intuitive as usual, *Abad* Miguel," Grand Master de Érail replied in a respectful manner of a student to his teacher.

"*Hermano* Gabriel keeps in close contact with the Cistercian *hermanos* at Clairvaux. There was word that you needed a scribe and a learned man to seek out an unknown *santo* book and the Cup of Christ. I would surmise Lord Robert de Borron is that scribe and learned man."

"*Si, Abad* Miguel, that's correct, and we have both gained in meeting each other. Lord de Borron has the divine gift to translate any ancient words written about our Savior, Jesus the Christ. He has made a copy of the first parchment scrolls that my order found in Jerusalem. The legate from the Curia in Rome demanded I turn the original holy parchments over to him. Lord Borron and I have had the sacred honor to touch the writings of our Holy Saint, Joseph of Arimathea. His sacred words, which Saint Joseph has revealed, may be used for nefarious purposes for those in power.

"He had left a hidden note at the Temple Mount instructing whoever he meant to find it to follow him. His note told me to travel to Arimathea and seek out a cave. Before I left the Levant, I found the cave where he stayed. A Saracen hermit resided in this cave and told me the Syrian Umayyad rulers conquered this part of Palestine and then conquered the rest of North Africa. It was this tribe that set up a sultanate over southern Iberia.

"My conjecture says the second set of parchments made its way to Toledo and is in some archives there. I believe Saint Joseph of Arimathea wrote his second set while he lived at his birthplace and there recorded the start of his ministry. I know how he hid the first set; it would then make sense he would do the same when he completed the second set. The old hermit there told me there were many empty clay ewers when he first arrived at the cave. Toward the back of the cave, I saw large pits with broken shards of pottery scattered about in the dirt, as if something of value was dug up."

"Gilbért, are you telling me that Saint Joseph of Arimathea was an apostle and wrote a never-before-found gospel?"

"*Oui,* and he's the first founder and leader of our church!"

"How can this be, my *hijo*? *Santo* Pedro founded our holy Roman church and *Santo* Jerome never spoke or wrote about Joseph of Arimathea doing any of this!"

Both *frères* fell to their knees and crossed themselves. They each said an undistinguishable prayer and then stood up with furrowed brows, waiting in silence for Grand Master Gilbért to continue his explanation.

"I will defer to Lord Borron for a more detailed explanation of what has been revealed to us. His holy gift of memory and translation has divulged much from what he has read."

"Lord Robert, tell both *frères* what Saint Joseph has revealed."

"I hope I will give our Saint Joseph the long-overdue respect that he deserves. The first manuscript he wrote told of his dealings with Pontius Pilate and how he obtained our Lord's body. However, more important, it tells of his close relationship as a great-uncle to Jesus. Jesus appointed him a furtive disciple of our Lord and gave him secret knowledge to start his ministry right after our Lord's crucifixion. A short time later, the high priest, Caiaphas, imprisoned Saint Joseph and there Jesus visited him.

"Jesus and his angels, Michael and Gabriel, gave Saint Joseph the holy spear, the sword of Saint John the Baptizer, vials from the cruci-fixion, the Holy Cup, and paten from the Last

Supper. The paten and *Sangraal* kept him alive by never emptying themselves of wine or bread. His lamps were always full of oil, so the flames never stopped burning. Saint Joseph wrote his first section with the unending parchments that the archangel Gabriel gave. Saint Joseph tells us that the Holy Spirit of fire visited him ten sunrises after our Lord visited him. He describes in detail how it felt and how the fire penetrated his body and soul.

"Don't you see, fellow *frères*, Saint Joseph was the first teaching 'fisher of men.' He is and was the first true fisher king, prince of apostles, and priest. He may have started the first Christian church!" I raised my voice with excitement. "His parchments revealed to me many details about his family, the disciples, friends, fears, and secret knowledge that our Lord and Savior had given him to start his ministry. This is one of the many reasons we came here to confide in you and your *frère*, Gabriel, about *le Sangraal* book."

Both men stared at each other and crossed themselves once again. *Abad* Miguel was the first to reply.

"Lord de Borron, if you had told me about this information by yourself, I wouldn't have believed you and said you were a blasphemer. However, my former student Gilbért wouldn't have picked you unless he knew of your integrity. It's still hard to believe there is a fifth gospel. What do you think, Gabriel?"

"I have heard rumors of the *Santo Cáliz* parchments for several years now. Our Cistercian *hermanos* have denied its existence for quite some time, but the rumors have persisted to this day. You said earlier in our conversation you seek the *Taza de Christo* too. If this is so, it's common knowledge the *Santo Cáliz* resides at San Juan de la Peña at the foot of the Pyrénées Sierras. Grand Master Gilbért knows that some of his men guard the *Santo Taza* that Saint Lawrence sent to us."

"*Hermano* Gabriel," I said. "There were numerous *Sangraal* cups that Saint Joseph of Arimathea saw. All the Marias, who were present at the crucifixion, possessed a holy cup or container. According to Saint Joseph, those cups became holy, for they gathered our Savior's blood. Saint Joseph used his *Sangraal* from the Last Supper to catch the blood that came forth from Longinus's spear puncture. Our Blessed Virgin Maria gave Saint Joseph her two vials she collected from her son's wounds. The cup you mentioned may have belonged to Saint Marie Magdalene. What's the cup made from?"

"It's made out of a blood-red glass, like a semi-precious stone," *Frère* Miguel described.

"Its description doesn't resemble what Saint Joseph recorded in his parchments. It's not the *Sangraal* of the Last Supper, for Saint Joseph said it was made from yellow bronze metal. In all probability, it belonged to Saint Mark. Saint

Joseph gives us detailed information on the whereabouts of the *Seder* dinner and described Saint Mark's home and the upper rooms. He says in his *Sangraal* parchments that our Lord, Jesus the Christ, gave him the *Sangraal* cup before he left to pray at Gethsemane. It's possible when we find the last remaining manuscript that Saint Joseph wrote, we'll find the Last Supper chalice.

"We came here tonight to elicit your help. My holy copy of the *Sangraal* manuscript, somebody stole from my commandery cell. In it were possible clues to help us find the location of the next manuscript. Grand Master Gilbért has a greedy traitor or traitors among his men. He suspects Commander Ramáirez of stealing my parchments. Also, I saw Commander Ramáirez last night conversing with a red-and-white dressed Moor."

"Where was this?" *Frère* Gabriel inquired.

"It was at the Muslim mosque."

"You mean the Mosque de Misleida," *Frère* Gabriel stated.

"*Oui*, and the commander was paying the stranger with a large sum of coins."

"I believe I know where your missing copies are. In the late afternoon sun, I saw Commander Ramáirez receive some parchments from a man with a dark cape, it was near the mosque. I followed him out of curiosity, and he led me to the old Roman gate, where he hid some parchments behind a loose stone block. I know where he put them. I will go and retrieve them now, which will be less suspicious as a native villager."

"Bless you, *Frère* Gabriel. I can never thank you enough. *Abbé* Miguel, Grand Master Gilbért would like a boon from you."

"*Hermano* Miguel, will you accompany us to Zaragozza and Toledo? I know we will need your exegesis on finding the next set of parchments. The three of us would make a powerful force in finding the next set of *Sangraal* parchments. Also, I am asking my chaplain at Zaragozza to travel with us to Toledo. There could be danger on this mission to find the *santo* parchments. What do you say, *mon* teacher and *ami*?"

"*Si*, and I am anxious to see *Rey* Alfonso. It will be like old times when you two boys would fight over my books on Odysseus and his epic adventure."

Both Grand Master Gilbért and *Abbé* Miguel gave each other a hardy embrace of agreement as a *père* to a *fils*, with both men expressing a toothy grin.

"*Abbé*," I spoke up. "I have been wondering about the wheel symbols over the entrances to the church and monastery. I believe they are signposts or markers trying to tell me about *le Sangraal*. Part of the wheel symbols are the Greek letters chi and rho. Can you explain the other pieces?"

"*Si*, it's called the Ichthus Wheel by our church. If you looked closely, it spells out the Greek letters ΙΧΘΥΣ with its spokes. This means fish in the

Greek language. Also, the letters are an anagram for 'Jesus the Christ, God's son and Savior.' The wheel represents many things. It symbolizes God's infinite universe and the presence of Christ moving over the face of the Earth with his ministry. The angels on each side holding the wheel are Saint Michael and Saint Gabriel. Some say Saint Gabriel goes by the name '*Taza* Bearer' instead of the messenger. You can also see the Greek letter tau, which forms a cross. I have been told this letter has a numerical value of three hundred."

"What about the snake coiled around the cross?" I asked, knowing the snake signified evil. "Does it mean evil?"

"No, quite the contrary. The snake is a Gnostic symbol that signifies wisdom that's used against evil. I know you will ask me why the holy wheel has eight spokes instead of Emperor Constantine's six-spoke labarum, yet don't forget, Constantine was the first emperor to organize the Christian church."

"*Oui, Abad* Miguel, but why are the other two spokes there?" Each question raised more questions in my mind.

"The eight sections or spokes tells us this is a baptismal cross too. Isn't the baptismal font eight-sided? How many days was it between Christ's entry into Jerusalem and his resurrection?"

"Eight," I replied with pride, knowing Saint Joseph had told me this in his writings. Now I could see why Grand Master Gilbért's intellect reflected the scholastic tutelage of *Frère* Miguel.

"The number eight placed on its side symbolizes infinity also," *Abad* Miguel continued in his explanation of the wheel's revelations. Then it struck me.

"Octave!" I said aloud, which earned me two bewildered stares.

"Grand Master Gilbért, don't you remember me telling you this was the word our Lord and Savior gave in secret to Saint Joseph of Arimathea. The word was octa. Also, Saint Marie Magdalene uttered it. This holy wheel's many symbols are a reaffirmation that we're on the right path to the second set of *Sangraal* parchments. They are giving us a roadmap of hints."

"Oh, there were several other things I failed to mention, Lord de Borron," *Frère* Miguel rubbed his piebald-colored beard before continuing. "The hub of one of the holy wheels has a lamb with a cross standard. This is the sign of Saint John the Baptizer. Some say his spirit was at the Last Supper. We know he baptized our Lord, Jesus the Christ, in the River Jordan and foretold of the Messiah coming."

"*Oui, Abbé* Miguel, Saint Joseph states in his book of a sacred or mysterious wind that overturns the cup of Elijah."

"What other truths or knowledge do you have about the wheel?" I asked.

"One last thing about the holy wheel, *Hermano* Gabriel has studied the Magus of the old Celts who once inhabited this peninsula. The wheel was the Tree of Life, which bore the Trinity. The Celtic priests claimed they could see the future as well as the past. The Celts were later killed or driven out of Iberia, and a few escaped to the land of Albion, which today we call the land of England."

The candles in *Abbé* Miguel's cell had burned to half their length and time seemed to flee with an uncanny pace. This left me with curiosity about the drawing on the table that was in front of me.

"*Abbé* Miguel, can you tell me about the drawing on the table?"

"It's strange you should ask. I just received it yesterday from the abbess at San Juan el Peña. One of the villagers gave her the drawing, who drew it after finding it etched on the wall of a cave. As you well know, our *Santo Cáliz* is housed in the *monasterio* at San Juan el Peña."

"*Oui*, but the drawing is telling us something more. I think it's another clue about the second *Sangraal* parchments. The ancient ones from the past are speaking to us. We are being guided by clues to find the second *Sangraal* manuscript and the cup of Christ."

Right away, I noticed the detailed geometric designs as *Abbé* Miguel handed it to me for perusal.

Whoever drew it was well-versed in mathematics, for all the parts were geometric in shape.

"I can see it's a cinquefoil design. There are five flower petals or circles enclosed in a roundel."

On closer examination, in each circle or petal was a fish design, thus creating five fish. The center had a five-pointed star with the single point pointing toward the top of the cinquefoil.

"What do you think this symbol represents, *Abbé* Miguel?" I hoped this new symbol might give us some additional information.

"Lord de Borron, there are several things I think it might reveal. As you can see, there are five fish. At the beginning of Christianity, this was a secret sign all Christians greeted one another with when they met. Half of the fish design would be drawn in the dirt by one party; the other would complete the fish drawing, thus acknowledging each other as Christians."

"*Oui,*" I replied. "Saint Joseph mentions this symbol in his *Sangraal* parchments. He first encountered it in a letter from Nicodemus. I didn't know it was a secret symbol among early Christian followers."

My mind raced with thoughts of what this mysterious cinquefoil was trying to say. Its enigma was reaching out to all three of us, harking for resolution.

Abbé Miguel continued with his observation of the cave drawing.

"The five petals or circles could mean the five wounds of Christ that were inflicted at his crucifixion. Don't forget, Lord de Borron, of the five loaves used to feed the five thousand and the first five books of the Old Testament or Pentateuch. Again, if you peruse one of the fish designs and complete its tail, you will see the figure eight or octave. Lying it on its side, you'll see the symbol for infinity. It's the same as the number eight that spoke to us in the Ichthus Wheel. It appears the numbers five and eight are leaving us *sub rosa* or with secrets yet foretold. The five-pointed star has left me in a quandary I cannot explain."

"*Abad* Miguel, can we take this drawing with us when we leave for Zaragozza?" the grand master inquired.

"*Si*, my *hijo*, and I will have *Hermano* Gabriel make some drawings of the Ichthus Wheel. He's a better artist than I am. Listen!" *Abbe* Miguel whispered. "*Hermano* Gabriel is returning from his search for the *Santo Cáliz* parchments."

CHAPTER X

All eyes focused on the open door as *Frère* Gabriel edged it closed. My heart leaped with joy as he started pulling out parchments from a large burlap bag used by the perpetrator. He placed each on the table next to the cinquefoil design. Right away, I noticed there was something wrong. He hadn't retrieved all the parchments; for a second group wasn't there. At once, my heart stopped beating and my stomach knotted. Posthaste, my hand grabbed the bag from *Frère* Gabriel, and I furiously searched its interior.

"Where are the rest of the parchments?" I demanded with warm blood coursing to my face. Right away, there were unexpected wide-eyed expressions of bewilderment at my loud displeasure. "*Frère* Gabriel, did you overlook any of the remaining parchments?" I asked with a tightened fist.

"*Ninguno*, Lord de Borron, this is all that I found behind the stones. I counted them before Commander Ramáirez placed the stone back in place. I reconfirmed their number on the way back to the *monasterio*. Nothing is missing. I am sorry, I know you are upset with me."

"*Non*, dear *frère*, let me be contrite for my sudden outburst of temper. I know you're not responsible for the missing parchments. It's my fault, but where could they be? The second set was bound with light cord, and this is what is missing."

"Lord de Borron, did you say that the caped *Mudéjar* stranger and Commander Ramáirez spent some time in the Mosque de Misleida?"

"*Oui, Frère* Gabriel, but what they exchanged was a large sack of coins. I didn't see any parchments. Why would the missing parchments be with the coins?"

"That's where your remaining parchments are located!" exclaimed *Frère* Gabriel. "The *Mudéjar* stranger kept them as security for his next payment. Now we must determine where that sack of coins is hidden. I say it's hidden somewhere concealed in the mosque and we must work fast. When Commander Ramáirez realizes his set is missing, he'll suspect we retrieved it."

"*Oui*, at once I will have Muhammad Nur Adin search the mosque!" Grand Gilbért whispered.

"Grand Master Gilbért, is he not a Saracen? Can we trust him?"

"*Pax, hermanos,* fear not, he is more than a true friend. I would place the safety of my life in his hands. He knows both the evil and the kindness of his people. Muhammad has an uncanny sense to see the cloaked evil in other men. *Bon frères,* you must trust my judgment with this man. I will leave right away and tell him what has happened. Wait for my return, Lord de Borron; continue discussing our plans for Zaragozza and Toledo with *Frère* Miguel and *Frère* Gabriel."

Grand Master de Érail jumped from his chair, opened the door, and slinked down the stone stairs. With faint thumps, I could hear his boots along the cloister paving stones.

"*Abbé* Miguel, we are to meet Grand Master Gilbért's chaplain and the *Roi* Alfonso when we arrive at Zaragozza. He said his name is Jeremiah Santiago de Compostela, a quite erudite member of his order. According to Grand Master Gilbért, he is the chaplain for the preceptory at Zaragozza. He further stated to me that he once had a Christian father and a Jewish mother. Are you familiar with this chaplain in Zaragozza?" I asked.

"*Si,* I know of this young man. The grand master is quite ecumenical with members of his order. He doesn't hold any prejudices or intolerance of anybody, even having such a young chaplain for his preceptory. The thing he hates is unrelenting evil. Did he mention any more about his relationship with his chaplain?"

"*Non*," I replied. "Is there more?"

"It's best that Grand Master Gilbért tell you himself."

How odd, I thought, *that the old abbé hadn't answered my question*. Up until now, he had responded to my inquiries right away. *Frère* Gabriel sat there for some time, not adding anything to my question. His furrowed brow indicated he was privy to some knowledge I didn't know. There was a long silence in our conversation until broken by soft footsteps coming from the garth of the cloister. These weren't the heavy footsteps of Grand Master Gilbért, but much lighter in sound. There was an almost cat-like silence in their movement.

CHAPTER XI

ll at once, the door banged open with the appearance of Muhammad Nur Adin. His dark eyes were darting from side to side as if he suspected someone might be following him. He stared at me and then touched his black turban in a greeting to all of us. *Frère* Gabriel appeared quite shaken by the sudden intrusion, for his eyes were bug-like in shape and his hands trembled. *Abbé* Miguel was the first to speak.

"*Pax vobiscum, hermano.* Lord de Borron, is this Muhammad Nur Adin I have heard about?"

"*Oui,* that's Muhammad."

Both *moines* stared at our sudden visitor, yet *Abbé* Miguel didn't seem shaken by the presence of Muhammad. He gazed at his appearance, as you would expect an excellent teacher might. We stood up and reciprocated the greeting bow, and then Muhammad said something I could understand.

"*Alaikum al salaam,* holy *frères*. Gilbért de Érail sent me here to give you this," he said in his heavy Saracen accent. His hand reached inside his cape and exposed a large sack, but also the steel scabbard of his large scimitar. *Frère* Gabriel spied the sword, and his eyes grew large with fear. Muhammad placed the sack in my hands and motioned for me to open it. My fingertips felt the bundle of parchments and my heart skipped a beat from joy. Now I knew I had the rest of *le Sangraal* parchments. When both *moines* saw the smile on my face, we crossed ourselves and said a prayer to our Lord and Savior.

The remaining codices of parchments appeared to be intact; still, I checked the numbered pages again. To my final relief, all pages were accounted for, and none were missing. Once again, all heads turned toward another sound of running footsteps. These were heavy steps of a man of considerable size. With our instincts, both Muhammad and I grabbed our sword pommels and unsheathed them. *Frère* Miguel motioned for us to lower our swords, then he bent and removed a wool rug, which revealed a hidden trapdoor. Just then, a familiar voice issued forth.

"*Pax, frères,* it's me, Gilbért, coming up the steps. Fear not, I am not being followed."

Then Grand Master Gilbért said something in the Saracen tongue that mentioned Muhammad Nur Adin's name. Muhammad replied with an affirmative sound just as Grand Master Gilbért reached the top of the steps and came wheezing through the open door. He emitted a deep gasping sound before he could catch his breath to speak.

"It appears as if Muhammad secured all the copies of the *Sangraal* parchments," Grand Master Gilbért said, as glanced down at the tied bundle.

"We must leave as soon as possible. Commander Ramáirez knows of the disappearance of the *Sangraal* codices. I was shielding Muhammad's back as he entered the mosque to search for their whereabouts, then I heard a voice I recognized. It was the voice of Ramáirez. From my hiding place, I couldn't see him, but I knew damn well it was him. He was speaking in the shadows. The dark image said nothing but motioned with his fist. When Ramáirez finished speaking to him, he made his familiar shuffling footsteps as he departed. The stranger then vanished.

"They are laying a trap for us when we leave tonight. Cardinal Folquet's *chevaliers* haven't attacked us at Huesca because they know I command all the Templar *chevaliers* here and would defeat them. The cardinal's men are cowards and will ambush us on the main road to Zaragozza. I believe that stranger gave the commander the writ for my arrest. I cannot return to the commandery; they are searching for all of us. I told Sergeants de Béziers and de Hoult to have our horses tethered behind the monastery."

"What about my writing satchel and the letter to my wife?" I interjected into the rapid conversation. At once, he reached down behind his sword belt and with a big grin handed me my possessions.

"Thank you very much, Grand Master Gilbért. I appreciate your valiant effort to retrieve my precious belongings."

"No more conversation, *frères*. We must leave now! *Abad* Miguel, are you ready to depart?"

"*Si*, my *hijo*."

"*Hermano* Gabriel, are you ready to deliver Lord de Borron's letter to Cluny and mine to our Holy *Padre*?"

"*Si*, my *hermano*."

"This leaves us with one problem. How can we leave without being seen?"

"I have a quick solution to that dilemma!" exclaimed *Abad* Miguel with a sly grin on his face.

"The Poor-Soldiers of Christ aren't the sole holy order that has secret passageways," *Abbé* Miguel kicked the rug he had replaced in front of his chair, which again exposed a large trapdoor underneath.

"There is a tunnel that travels some distance past the *monasterio* into a copse of trees. They won't see us, the brush is quite dense, and it will hide our departure. Let me fetch some lanterns to light our way. Lord Robert, would you please grab the drawing? *Hermano* Gabriel, you use some of this parchment to sketch the

Ichthus Wheel. I will be right back with our lanterns."

"Grand Master Gilbért, did you know about this tunnel to our horses?"

"*Oui*, but no more conversation."

The *abbé* exited from the front door of his cell and proceeded along a dark hallway. I folded the drawing and tucked it into my writing satchel along with the *Sangraal* copies. I felt great relief knowing I had them back in my possession once more. Grand Master Gilbért put a final red seal on the outside of his letter, and we handed *Frère* Gabriel our missives. He was still detailing the wheel when *Abbé* Miguel returned to the room with four lit lanterns. Grand Master Gilbért gave *Frère* Gabriel a farewell embrace.

Each lantern radiated a warm glow as Grand Master Gilbért proceeded first down the wooden steps. Muhammad followed right behind. I turned before traveling down the steps and saw both *frères* conversing and *Abbé* Miguel gave Gabriel some final instructions. Then *Frère* Gabriel recited a prayer.

"*Christo* be with all of you, *Christo* be within all of you, *Christo* be behind all of you, *Christo* before all of you, may *Christo* comfort and restore all of you, may *Christo* be above all of you and beneath all of you, may *Christo* be in your quiet time and times of danger, *Christo* in all your hearts and those that love you, *Christo* in all the mouths of friends and strangers that you meet. Amen."

The door closed in silence, and the lone sound heard was an occasional drip of water or the scurrying feet of mice. We stooped as we traversed the low overhead stone ceiling. After traveling a short distance, we came upon a large crypt. To my right was an ornately carved sarcophagus. I stopped just for a moment, raised my lantern for a better view, but was encouraged forward by *Abbé* Miguel.

"Who's buried there?" I inquired of the *abbé*.

"It's the *Rey Monje* Ramiro II de Aragón. He was the current *rey*, Alfonso the Chaste's *abuelo*."

How strange this land was, a *roi* who was a *moine* and grandfather to a *roi*. We continued some distance down the dank tunnel until we approached a set of stone steps. They proceeded upward at a steep incline, leaving us gasping for breath.

"*Hermanos*, please help me push this heavy stone slab away so we can exit," *Abbé* Miguel said. "My bones aren't as strong as fifty summers ago."

Grand Master Gilbért and I helped the *abbé* lift the slab covering our exit. We scrambled out of the square hole into a damp foggy night. I was quite disorientated as I stood there trying to visualize where we had arrived. A thick fog prevented me from seeing our horses. I whispered into Grand Master Gilbért's ear asking the whereabouts of Sergeants de Hoult and de Béziers.

Just then, Muhammad mimicked the hooting sound of an owl. Grand Master Gilbért put one finger in front of his lips to signal all to be quiet. There was a short pause before Muhammad made another hooting sound. Then came a faint reply. It started soft and then grew louder. Muhammad changed the variations of his sound to test the response. Each signal mimicked the same response.

Then I saw ghost-like men and horses ambling through the dense fog. Out of instinct, I drew my sword from its scabbard. A red cross appeared on a dark green tunic, and I knew it was Sergeant Jacque de Hoult. Trailing him with the horses, to my relief was Sergeant Guy de Béziers. We mounted our horses and with stillness left the fog-shrouded copse. Grand Master Gilbért had *Abad* Miguel ride with him for lack of a horse. We traveled about a quarter of a league and then heard running water.

"*Frères*, we'll stop here to plan our route to Zaragozza," Grand Master Gilbért whispered. "This is the Rio Isuela and Muhammad will water the horses. I suggest we travel a different road and not the normal road to Zaragozza, even if it's longer. The cardinal's men will be guarding that road. I'll have Muhammad transport the packhorses with a feint toward Monzón. There we have a large *château* and a commandery. That means we'll travel on foot for several leagues before Muhammad returns. I know this is risky, but Muhammad has fooled these men before with his diversions. We'll travel back into the Sierra de Guara and there wait for Muhammad. I know of a canyon hidden from the trail. It's well-protected from the cold and the rain and located at the western end of the canyons and the mountain range. In addition, there's a ford on the Rio Gállego we can cross, and this will put us on the Ebro plains, while still making decent time from there to Zaragozza."

How odd, I thought. I was just complaining of too much riding on horseback and now I would find out how strong my legs were.

As we reached the river's edge, the fog had not dissipated. Muhammad was first to ford the river with the horses. To my surprise, the river water touched the hocks of our horses, making the crossing uneventful. As Muhammad reached the far side of the bank, he leaped on his horse, Buraq, and spurred her onward. Then he and all our packhorses galloped into the night fog. The rest of us reached the far bank just as the sunrise made a vain attempt to penetrate the fog. The cold river water had left us wet from our thighs down to our feet. Right away, we started climbing toward the top of the riverbank unobserved, then several of us slipped and fell backward toward the river.

Some distance from Huesca in the streaked dawn, we decided to make a fire to dry our clothes. I helped Sergeant de Hoult gather some dry fire-wood. Afterward, he applied the starter flint, and the wood caught fire at once. It burned with a clean warm flame, and in no time, we were dry and on our way. In the distance, as the morning sun rose above us, I observed snow-capped *montagnes* and fir tree-lined canyons some distance to my right that drew nearer as the day ensued. The fog had burned off as the sun approached its noonday position.

"Let's stop here and rest for now," Grand Master Gilbért said as he pointed at a large outcrop of boulders.

"We won't be seen by anybody for some distance. Sergeant de Hoult, you secure the first watch at the crest of that large boulder. I will travel back down the trail and oversee our rear. Lord de Borron and Sergeant de Béziers, both of you scout ahead about a league. Survey what you see and then meet us back here about the time of Compline. *Abad* Miguel, I will give you the food sack so you can prepare our evening meal. Everybody must obtain enough water before you leave for your post. We'll let the horses rest here and travel on foot."

Sergeant de Béziers drew a long draft from the water skin and handed the container to me. The water was warm to the taste and clean of any debris. We both strolled west while hugging the base of the canyon walls for some distance. The trail was rocky at first but leveled out after a short distance. Overhead, there were a few stringy-appearing clouds and the sun now started warming my white tunic and coif of chain mail, yet the rays were still pleasant on this late autumn day.

We stopped to rest on a large boulder after about a half-league distance. Behind the large stone came a noisy squeaking sound. I gazed down to see a nest of chipmunks scurrying about from our intrusion. They would each stand on their hind legs, sniff the air, stop for a moment, and then bark their complaints at us. This continued for some time, holding Sergeant de Béziers and me in a trance as we observed their repetitive posturing.

Until now, I hadn't had the opportunity to ask Sergeant de Béziers about the healing of his wounds.

"Sergeant Guy, how are your wounds healing?" I inquired to start up a conversation with him.

"*Très bien, merci beaucoup,* Lord de Borron. My old self has returned. I always did heal fast. The many years I was in the Levant, injuries were a part of life living in the Crusader states. All of us learned many things from the Muslim doctors. Several worked in our hospital at our fortress called La Roche-Guillaume in the principality of Antioch."

"Tell me why you entered the holy order of the Poor-Soldiers of Christ. I know you are a seasoned veteran and fought many years in the Outremer, but where did you join?"

"I grew up in the small town of Béziers, one of six *frères* and five *soeurs. Mon père* was a fisherman and merchant. He traveled the entire Mediterranean

Sea during his lifetime. Every so often, I would sail with him on his trips and assist him. It was hard to survive as one of eleven children, and I knew at a young age I had to leave to lessen the food burden that my *frères* and *soeurs* faced. Traveling and adventure appealed to me, and my sailing experience came in handy. Sailing jobs came easy, and I sent a large sum of money home each month until my *frères* and *soeurs* were grown.

"Then one day while I was home on leave, a Templar *chevalier* visited our village. He said he was on the way to the Holy Land and was recruiting men to protect Christians and their pilgrimages to the Holy Sepulchre. He knew I had sailing experience and wanted my skills to help transport pilgrims to the Levant. The Templar *chevalier* said the food was *bon*, and there would be plenty of meat and wine. I told him I didn't know how to use a broadsword. He replied he would teach me to be a skillful fighter.

"At my *mère's* urging, I decided to join. The night before we left, she had a dream that our Lord spoke to her about me. Our Savior, Jesus the Christ said that I would seek his *santo* words that would lead to the Cup of Truth. Also, she said there would be many trials and tribulations before my odyssey would end. I knew then my life's adventure was God ordained. Anyway, how can you refuse Grand Master Gilbért de Érail's request? You yourself know that all too well."

"*Oui*, you are right, *mon ami*. It's apparent that our Lord and Savior, Jesus the Christ, has ordained us both on this holy quest."

Our conversation ended at once with the sound of a screaming eagle that leaped from its disturbed perch, not by our conversation. As it flew upward, I spied a large dust cloud in the distance. The pitch-black cloud covered the western horizon as far as I could see and was moving at an enormous speed. In front of it were about twelve small funnel-shaped whirling clouds of dirt and debris. Each funnel measured the height of three or four men and the dirt funnels bounced back and forth with each other traveling in no set direction. It appeared each whirling finger was sucking up anything in front of its erratic path. I hadn't seen anything like this in my sheltered days in Burgundy. This strange phenomenon grabbed me in a fascinating trance and my fear came forth when Sergeant de Béziers yelled, "Dust devils, head for the shelter of those rocks!"

We both ran as fast as we could to a crop of large boulders and slid in between them. I feared for my compatriots some distance away and the holy worded parchments. There wasn't much room to maneuver my body and crouch down for protection. The roaring sound of the storm made communication impossible. Then came the high-pitched sound of each dust devil. The closer each funnel came caused pain to my ears, and it felt as if minute daggers were entering my head.

Then they struck with their full fury and pressure. Rocks, tree limbs, bark, and clods of grass pelted me, causing body stings from the debris. The worst sensation of all was my body lifting into the devil maelstrom.

I pushed myself farther down into the narrow part of the rock while praying I would be wedged too tight for the tug of war going on with my body. To my relief, it worked, and the dust devil funnels passed, after which I said a quick prayer of thanks. However, the dust storm itself hadn't arrived. The loud rumbling sound raced toward us, which sounded as if it was a stampede of horses. The dust was so thick that daylight turned to darkness and then I started choking. I pulled my tunic around my face and felt as a turtle entering its shell for safety. The gritty taste of the black dirt penetrated my nose and mouth, while I wondered how long I could endure this storm.

After what seemed an eternity, daylight resumed as I glanced up with grit-filled eyes. The roaring sound hadn't stopped, but the air was clearer, and I was able to breathe in a normal way. My entire body had a sticky black substance covering it. I appeared as if I had been stuck in a chimney flue. Then I heard a faint muffled voice. It grew louder as the roar of the storm subsided.

"Lord de Borron, are you alive? Can you hear me? It's Sergeant de Béziers. Please tell me you're all right."

"*Oui*, I think I am fine. What about yourself?"

"Other than small cuts and bruises, I am fine."

"Lord de Borron, let's wait a little longer before we come out from behind the safety of these rocks."

"*Oui, mon ami*, I agree." Sergeant de Béziers wouldn't hear any disagreement from me on his caution. I sat there hunkered down, thinking how this peninsula was such a land of many contrasts. If the second set of *Sangraal* parchments existed, Grand Master Gilbért was right that there would be many dangerous trials ahead.

Without warning, a hand grabbed my shoulder and startled me. I glanced up to see Sergeant Guy's black-stained face and white toothy grin.

"Hope I didn't frighten you, Lord de Borron. I think it's now safe. We must continue scouting ahead."

We climbed down from the boulders and stepped back onto the path. The sky was now clear, and visibility ahead was excellent as we traveled the remaining length of our scouting distance undisturbed. There was an occasional whistling sound from eagles overhead, but other than that, it was uneventful. We then turned around and retraced our footsteps back to our rendezvous point. By now, the sun was setting behind us, and I knew our camp wasn't far. Out of nowhere, Sergeant de Hoult appeared from behind a boulder to greet us. Again, our reactive instincts made us grab our swords.

"*Pax, frères*," announced the sergeant as he crossed in front of our path. I don't think he recognized us at first, because of our sooty appearance. Then he started laughing aloud.

"It appears both of you fell into a tar pit and had a hard time climbing out. At first glance, I thought you were the cardinal's *chevaliers* dressed in black. I just now recognized *Frère* Guy's hooked nose. Both of you two bedraggled-looking black swans are still waddling on your feet. Let me find you some water and cloths to clean up."

It appeared our fellow *frères* were some distance away and had missed the storm. Sergeant de Hoult appeared clean from any debris. My conscious mind never thought how silly we both appeared. I still lingered with fear in what we had just seen. Sergeant de Hoult left at once to obtain the rags and the water, while still shaking his head and laughing all the way to our campsite. It became quite humorous, after sitting down by the campfire, for even I gave out a belly laugh at my expense. The laughing started all over again when Grand Master Gilbért said we shouldn't clean ourselves. He thought we would be almost invisible at night. The hilarity continued and it gave us some relief from the present threat of the cardinal's men.

That night we sat around a small campfire hidden from the main trail. We consumed some dried venison and berries, which left my mouth thirsty for some *vin*. After we partook of the wineskin with large gulps, I stared at the large boulders surrounding us. There was a light frost forming on the parched grass. This sight moved me closer to the campfire. All around us, the ground started glistening from the moon's reflection off the small ice crystals. I was the first to fall asleep, for my watch would be next.

The next thing I remember was Grand Master de Érail telling me it was my time for sentry duty. "Lord de Borron, everything seems fine on the trail from whence we came but be alert. Wake me if you see anything unusual."

The moon had risen to its high point in the sky as I climbed the tall boulders to my lookout point. Upon reaching the top, a cold wind stung my cheeks as I settled in for my watch. The full moon lit the trail, mountaintop, and boulders for some leagues. I sat there thinking about my home, wife, and children. These thoughts prompted me to pray, asking my Lord and Savior to protect them from harm. Then a glint of light caught my eyes. The moonlight had struck something with its beams. My eyes strained to focus better, yet it seemed as if the glint or metal object was moving at a fast pace. I scrabbled down the boulders and shook Grand Master Gilbért to awaken him.

"Something is coming our way and traveling quite fast. Come and see! It might be Muhammad, yet we need to arm ourselves."

Grand Master Gilbért hadn't removed his sword belt and sprung to his feet ready to fight. We both ran to my sentry point and climbed back up to the crest of the boulders.

"See there, below that last peak. Something is moving fast."

"*Oui,* I now see it. We must return and warn the others. It appears as if there are six or seven riders. We can hide in the boulders until we can determine who it is. Let's leave now!"

I followed Grand Master Gilbért back down the boulders and ran toward the campsite. We aroused the camp with stealth and informed the two sergeants and *Abad* Miguel of our unknown visitors. We tossed the campfire with dirt and gathered up our belongings to hide. Grand Master Gilbért left for a high spot in the boulders and the rest of us were scattered throughout the boulders. I lay listening for any sound, and then I felt a vibration coming from the ground.

Hoofbeats were now heard coming up the trail. The steady thumping turned into rumbling sounds. Then the noise stopped. Did the riders dismount? I eased my sword and dagger from their scabbards, yet I heard not a sound other than the wheezing of several horses. Then came a faint chirping sound and I searched around to see if I had disturbed a nest of chipmunks. That sound was followed by a distant reply and the voice of Muhammad Nur Adin.

"*Salaam alaikum, Mujahid* Gilbért."

"*Alaikum al salaam, Mujahid* Muhammad," replied the grand master to my relief. We came from our hiding places and gave a respectful bow with smiles of happiness. "Muhammad has completed his deception," the grand master said to *Abad* Miguel and me.

"Lord de Borron and *Abad* Miguel, Muhammad has lured Cardinal Folquet's men in traveling to Monzón. Our plan has worked for now. Let us break camp while we have a full moon and travel to our next destination. The hidden canyon should be about eight leagues. We should arrive there this time tomorrow. The next day we will ford the Rio Gállego. The horses are tired so we must trot at a slow pace to help conserve their remaining strength. Now jump on your horses!" he shouted.

I grabbed my writing supplies, the *Sangraal* parchments, and placed them in my waterproof leather case. Earlier, my attention was to write in my journal and reread Saint Joseph's words for new clues, but it didn't happen. My horse was happy to see me, for she licked my face with her large rough tongue. I put one foot in my stirrup, climbed on, and then we trotted off to our canyon destination. Still, an uneasy sensation grabbed at my stomach, so I kept looking over my shoulder at the moonlit trail behind me.

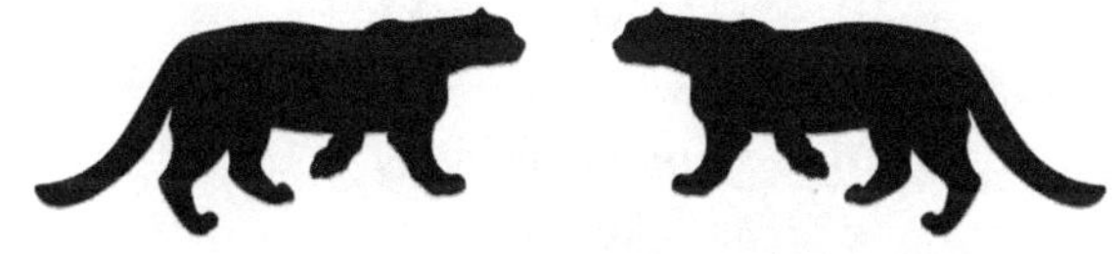

PART IV

The Leopards

CHAPTER XII

Anno Domini 37
Yehudah

The *Yehudah* night sky darkened as fast as a sudden-appearing kestrel in flight. Glancing up, Yoseph saw a milky haze of endless stars in the heavens and a windy chill penetrated his robes. The desert night was upon him and he must stop and rest after his escape from *Yerushalayim*.

The camels wanted to continue, but his body succumbed to today's travels and his sore tailbone told him otherwise. Their physical energy far exceeded Yoseph's. After much *braying,* they both yielded to his demand to stop and kneel. It was a well-sheltered spot for his first night's camp. The oasis was in a small depression between two rocky sand dunes. A small spring gurgled near an out-cropping of rocks to form a small pond. Yoseph placed his blankets close to the spring and readied himself for some much-needed rest. It wasn't long before Yoseph's fire ignited, and he hunkered next to a grove of date trees with his blanket.

He sat there staring into the fire thinking about what he would find in Arimathea. His eyelids began to flutter as he continued to gaze into the flames of the fire, causing his head to every so often drop and rebound with a sudden jerk. Yoseph thought it best to lay his head down on a small mound of sand and sleep. He wrapped his blanket tightly around his head, gathering the warmth of the fire as the bubbling spring lulled him to sleep.

Two piercing screams caused him to bolt upright. The unearthly sounds triggered the hair on the back of his neck to tingle from fear. Through the darkness of the night, he saw two large leopards circling the outskirts of the oasis. Their eyes glowed like bright coals of fire. The camels started braying and jumped up while kicking their hind legs. Yoseph couldn't tell who was making the louder sound—the braying of the two camels or the screams of the two large spotted cats.

The cats' orange-red eyes kept Yoseph's atten-tion as they circled the oasis. However, each time they completed one circle; the leopards came closer to the fire. Their fiery-eyed stares froze him with fear. Neither his hands nor his feet wanted to move. Each came closer and closer until he could smell their breath, which reeked of rotten human flesh. He knew this putrid smell from his many travels. Neither cat stalked his camels, just him. He tried to grab his leather pouch that had the spear of Longinus and the Holy Cup of his *Maishiach*, but Yoseph's arms moved so sluggishly, and he doubted that he could grab the bag in time for protection.

Each leopard now faced him with crouching muscles ready to pounce. He prayed to Yeshua to be with him in his time of trial. Right away both of his hands moved, and he reached for his bag. Yoseph grabbed the spear and thrust it at the first cat as it sprang in midair to pounce on him. At the same time, the Holy Cup rolled out of the sack right in the path of the second cat as it sprang. At once, both cats vanished. Yoseph couldn't believe his eyes. *What just happened here?* The night air had brought two demons to kill him, but his faith in Yeshua and his Holy Cup and lance had protected him. It was another of Yeshua's many miracles and further upheld Yoseph's faith in him.

The rest of the night, he stayed awake. It wasn't the fear of more demonic creatures, but a great gladness that he would be preaching the good news of Yeshua, his Savior.

The sun began to peek over the horizon with jagged morning colors of pinks and oranges. The moon was still full as he loaded up Boaz for his departure, estimating he would reach Arimathea late tonight. There would be five leagues to travel before reaching his old home place.

The weather stayed pleasant until his little caravan reached Tel Tzora, and then storm clouds appeared on the distant horizon. A wind picked up in speed and forced him to place his shawl over his face. The road ahead had vanished with the forthcoming rain. The downpour was so great that the strong winds forced the rain sideways, making visibility impossible from traveling any farther.

Yoseph stopped his camels at an outcropping of large rocks for shelter. Boaz and Ruth were quite recalcitrant in kneeling, making it even more difficult to seek safety. Each pulled with all their might to remain standing. He then used his long stick to coax them to lay down. It worked just as the full force of the storm struck. He thought they would have some protection from the storm, but the rocks weren't sufficient in height to protect them. The driving rain stung like small pebbles thrown against his eyes and his mouth. The camels' bodies gave Yoseph some shelter from the roaring storm, yet it seemed the wind would suck him up at any time. As he tried to wedge himself between both camels, the satchel with the holy relics of his *Maishiach* started drifting away.

He lunged at the satchel with all the strength of his right hand and wrapped the reins from

Boaz around his left hand and arm. Terror seized Yoseph as he felt his body pulled upward and raised from the ground. He continued to rise above the ground until Boaz jerked his powerful neck in the opposite direction. Yoseph then fell back to the ground as the storm lessened in intensity. As he glanced up, there were large pieces of debris swirling in the sky as the storm moved on its frightening path. His eyes followed the storm as Yoseph's mind thought that without Boaz's great strength that could be him in the storm's debris. Eli's dear trusty camel had saved his life.

Aloud he prayed a prayer of thanksgiving, "*El Shaddai*, blessed be. You have protected me, a wretched old man, twice from death." As Yoseph rose to search around, to his surprise, the sun came out from behind dark clouds. His emotions had run from total fear to an exhilaration of relief in just a short period.

Both camels started to rise as they saw him stand, ready to continue their expedition. Yoseph gathered up his satchel, forced Boaz back down, and vaulted on him to proceed on with his journey. The road headed due north out of the valley of Sorek and his next destination was the oasis of Tel Gezer. It was a small village from the time of King Solomon and noted for its stone agricultural calendar.

The rest of the day was clear, and there was a warm sea breeze penetrating inland out of the west. He reached Tel Gezer about dusk, rested his camels, and let them drink their fill. Yoseph noticed there were few villagers about as he listened to the drinking slurps from Boaz and Ruth. The stone watering troughs were in the center of town, which should have been busy with the village folk. Sitting against the stone trough, Yoseph sat there thinking of his family until the sun started to set. As he started to stand, a sharp pain shot through his lower back. The many years in prison had weakened it and any prolonged sitting made it hard for him to stand up.

The sun was gone, and night had fallen on Tel Gezer. The ink-colored sky was clear, and the stars and the moon were shimmering with light. The rays of each star seemed to double their size in appearance. As Yoseph peered around, there were several oil lamps lit, yet no sign of people moving on the small pathways. In the earlier part of the afternoon, the village appeared shoddily built. However now, he felt a strange sensation as if somebody unseen was observing him.

Then several small designs caught his eye in the moonlight. He saw etched on the outside surface of the stone watering troughs figures of fish. There must have been twelve in number, all the same size, and pointing in the direction of the road leading to Arimathea. All at once, he had the urge to pick up a sharp stone and etch an additional fish above the twelve, but he didn't. He stared at the symbols, thinking of Nicodemus's fish-designed ring. Was this a beneficial sign? He hoped so and mounted back on Boaz to finish his trip. The remaining road to Arimathea was without trouble.

It was quite late when he reached a small ridge on the outskirts of Arimathea. He peered down on the darkened village, thinking how peaceful it seemed. The moon reflected off the roofs of the taller homes to give him some light to see his destination. Yoseph's mind told him he should wait until dawn when everybody would be awake. Then it struck him. It was silly to think anyone would now recognize Yoseph of Arimathea. Here was an old man with no beard, with considerable weight loss, appearing as a beggar.

He decided to stop and rest for the night, next to a small copse of date palms. It was well-sheltered by a grove of small hawthorn trees. There was a small indentation in the earth close to the thorn trees that would make a suitable campsite and sleep for the remaining night. He secured both camels to a large date palm and proceeded to make a cloth pallet as a bed. His back still ached with an intense pain as he struggled to recline on the blanket. Yoseph hoped this pain wouldn't be a harbinger of how the rest of his night might be. To his surprise, once he reclined, the pain subsided. The last thing he remembered, before falling asleep, was the fear that his family might not reside in Arimathea.

The next morning, several crowing cocks in the distance rousted him from his rocky bed. The sunrise was clear of clouds as he tried to raise himself from his outdoor crib. The first thing he felt was the sharp jabbing pain in his lower back. His rest hadn't cured his earlier discomfort but exacerbated it. The pain forced him to hunch over as he attempted to untie his camels. There was no way he could mount Boaz for the ride into Arimathea. His main physical concern was being able to travel. Near where the camels stood, was a sturdy wooden limb that had broken off from a white hawthorn tree. With faltering motion, he reached down and grabbed the long straight limb. It became a helpful staff to straighten himself and to journey the rest of the way to his destination.

The cave in which he prayed his family resided was on the north side of Arimathea. It wasn't far from the main road to *Yoppa*. A small path descended from the ridge he was standing on, which traveled straight into the main square of Arimathea. His painful back forced his feet to shuffle the remaining distance to his old home village. It seemed forever to reach the central market square. Each step was laborious to make, and the pain hadn't abated. With each step, his emotions were in turmoil. Inside him were sensations of apprehension, anxiety, anticipation, and fear. The back pain started to ease as he entered the village.

After reaching the marketplace, several townsfolk greeted Yoseph, which he somewhat recognized from his early manhood.

"*Shalom,* stranger, what brings you to our humble village?"

"*Shalom aleichem,* friend. I am a humble traveler on my way to visit some relatives. I am just stopping here to water my camels before I leave."

"You said you are visiting relatives. Could it be someone I know? Oh, please, excuse me if I have been too bold in my inquiry."

"No, my friend, not at all. Would you happen to know of a family who lives on the outskirts of Arimathea? A large man with a close-cropped beard would accompany them. Also, there could be a smaller man with two or three women."

"No, I am afraid I haven't seen them, for I am quite familiar with the people here in Arimathea. Maybe they lived here for a short time and then left. I have been a lifelong resident of this town and have known many people my sixty-two summers."

Yoseph recognized this man. His name was Yosiah, and he was about ten summers older than him. Yoseph kept thinking Yosiah had died of old age and remembered his *abba* was Simeon the prophet. His hair and beard had turned snow-white since he last saw him. His severe bent back kept him from focusing his large brown eyes on Yoseph's. They were still clear and flashed back and forth trying to identify him. Over many years,

Yoseph and Hebron had had numerous business transactions with the man.

"Have you traveled far, stranger?" he asked while gazing on Yoseph's plain clothes.

"No, just from *Yerushalayim.*"

"I see you too were caught in the rainstorm we had yesterday," Yoseph stated seeing dried mud stains on Yosiah's clothes.

"Yes, the storm pelted me about the third watch yesterday while bringing a load of olive oil back from *Yerushalayim.* Blessed be to *El Shaddai,* I wasn't swept away with the rain and wind. The heavy clay ewers weighted my camels down and saved my life."

"It seems I have met you before, stranger," Yosiah said, while shuffling closer to see Yoseph's face. "Could it be years ago?"

Yoseph knew what he would say next. He would ask Yoseph's name. What would Yoseph tell him? Even if he told him the truth, he wouldn't believe him! Most people in *Yehudah* thought Yoseph died in Caiaphas's hellhole. Yet, Yoseph feared his lateness in leaving *Yehudah* would become common knowledge, and he didn't want to go back to prison. It would be better if he changed the subject and leave as soon as possible. This old olive oil merchant would soon figure out something by his many questions.

"I don't think so. It has been quite a while since I have visited Arimathea. Please, don't think me rude, but I must leave now. It has been a pleasure speaking with you."

"Stranger, if you need any help in finding your relatives, my name is Yosiah, and I live in that house with the clay ewers scattered about."

Yoseph acknowledged his offer, pulled his camels away from the watering trough, and proceeded to leave. With each step, his back felt better, yet his stomach stayed tighten from the nagging fear that his family wouldn't be at the cave.

A short time later, his birthplace was behind him, and his two camels were on the smooth road to *Yoppa*. If his memory hadn't failed, it would be about half a league to the cave. He still didn't want to attempt riding for fear of his back pain returning. Instead, he strolled alongside his lumbering beasts, holding his new hawthorn staff. This made traveling easy as he crested the top of the road and spied a low ridge of hills and knew he was close to the cave. Yoseph's pace quickened, and so did his heart as his camels started making a *clopping* sound as they trotted next to him.

The cave entrance was well-hidden from the road. Its opening faced the side of a sharp-pointed hill, away from the road that traveled down into a gully and stream. His heart now hammered with anticipation. Then, without any thought, he started running and he let loose of the camel reins and held his staff as he came upon the dark cave entrance. There wasn't a person anywhere as he surveyed the premises in front of the cave. After a short period of searching for signs of habitation, he started shouting names.

"Hebron, Yosa, Enygeus, Alein, Nicodemus, is there anybody here?" Yoseph repeated their names several times but received stillness. The bottom of his stomach started to tighten with despair. The bile began to rise in his throat, and he threw up near a large flat rock. Afterward, a swoon came over him and he thought it best to sit on a large flat rock. Both of his hands were clasping his face, which flooded with tears of disappointment and dread. His family had promised four summers ago not to leave the cave until they were all together. The air around him was as still as a tomb.

He sat there in trance, not knowing what to do next, and then he felt a cool breeze emanating from the cave followed by a cold dagger blade against his throat. Was this the day of his demise? Would a robber kill Yoseph for his precious sacred objects? He surmised what his fate might be as he clutched his satchel bag. For a short moment, the warmth of the bag distracted him from his would-be murderer, still, Yoseph prayed, hoping to grab his holy sword or spear. Then his unseen attacker spoke.

CHAPTER XIII

Who are you, stranger, to intrude into my home? Have you been sent to kill us?"

Right away, Yoseph recognized the voice, though he couldn't see his face.

"It's me, your brother-in-law, Yoseph." The sharp-edged dagger eased some from his neck, but not enough to relieve Yoseph from harm's way.

"Turn around so I can see you and also keep your hands at your sides."

Yoseph's head eased to face Hebron. He had changed little in four springs. His dark olive-colored eyes were still alert and penetrating. However, his beard was bushier and streaked with white hair. Hebron's muscular build hadn't deteriorated, and both arms were tense with many rippling muscles. His prominent jaw jutted out for action, yet he still didn't recognize him.

"Hebron, my dear blessed brother, don't you recognize me?"

"You are still a threat and a stranger to me and my family. Yoseph of Arimathea is dead. He died in prison four springs ago, put there by that evil bastard Caiaphas. Have you been sent by Caiaphas or the family of that other evil monster, Yudas?"

"No!" Yoseph shouted "Please, my praiseworthy brother, hear me now. I have shaved my beard, cut my hair short, and lost weight since I left prison. As you can see, my hair is snow white. I know I don't seem like the same man you once remembered."

"You are trying to deceive me, whoever you are. It's a cruel joke you are playing on me. I won't listen to any more of your tricks. You shame the name of my beloved brother-in-law. Yoseph was a kind and generous man and died trying to give our nephew a proper burial. Yet I will give you one chance to prove yourself. Just our immediate family knows about this gift. Four springs ago our family received an ornate silver box. Who gave us this gift and who delivered it?"

At once, Yoseph knew he had to convince Hebron who he was, and fast. His dagger hand shook, and his jaw muscles further tensed.

"Hebron, listen with care to what I am about to tell you. The gift came from King Arviragus of the Celtic Isle. The small casket displayed a cup design on its lid and Alein Yosephe, my son, gave it to us. Also, one night, that same four springs ago, you saved my life in front of Nicodemus's house. You cut Yudas on his arm with your dagger. In addition, Nicodemus wore a ring on his finger that had a fish and a sword as a signet design. Is this correct?"

"Yes . . ."

"I have the cup of the last *Seder* that Yeshua gave me before he was crucified."

Yoseph reached for the cup in his satchel, and then Hebron pressed his dagger closer to his throat. When the bronze chalice came out of his bag, the sun struck it, blinding Hebron. The radiance was more than just the sun's reflection. Hebron touched the glowing rim, yanked his hand away, which forced him to drop the dagger and fall to his knees. He then cried out,

"*Barukh ata Adonai Eloheinu Melekh ha'olam ha-tov v'hameytiv,*" and then started crying and sobbing with intensity as he continued to repeat the blessing.

Yoseph reached down with one arm and pulled him up so they could embrace. Tears of joy rolled down his face as he kissed him on his cheeks. For a long moment, they embraced before he placed the Holy Cup back into his writing satchel. The "Cup of Truth" had melted away Hebron's doubts.

"My eyes still deceive me, Yoseph, that you're back among the living, yet my heart knows that it's you in front of me. Let us sit here on this rock and discuss what has happened in the last four springs. Oh! How thoughtless of me, Yoseph. Let me fetch you some water to drink. I am sorry I haven't any wine for you."

"Hebron that's fine, but are the rest of our family here?" Yoseph braced himself for bad news.

"Yes, some are working some distance behind this large hill, and some are hiding until I tell them to come out."

Yoseph said a silent prayer of thanks to *El Shaddai* and felt as if Sisyphus's boulder had lifted off his shoulders. The cool water from Hebron's large wooden bowl tasted cold and sweet. After drinking his fill, Yoseph commenced telling of his terrible events with Caiaphas. Also, the loneliness of the jail, about the resurrected body of Christ, and how his holy gifts had sustained him those four summers in prison. After he had finished, the appearance on Hebron's forehead wrinkled with disbelief. He must have thought Yoseph had lost his mind after he'd finished.

"So, our nephew is the *Maishiach* foretold by the prophets Zechariah and Isaiah. The magdalener has visited us several times since the crucifixion. She claimed the same and saw Yeshua several times after his burial in your sepulcher. Miriam told me she left for the tomb the next day with Yeshua's mother, and upon arriving saw it was unsealed and the body was gone. The lone thing left was the shroud that you and Nicodemus had wrapped him with. She further told a strange story that she saw a man at the back of the tomb. Miriam said he told her not to search for Yeshua there, for he had conquered death. Without warning, he vanished in front of the women.

"Our niece, Miriam, folded up the shroud, after which she left with her sister. Miriam of Magdala stayed behind and prayed. She knew that grave robbers had stolen her rabboni and she hoped by praying they would bring his body back. She told me that after some time she gave up and left the sepulcher. Miriam strolled out into your garden and thought she saw a man who was a gardener. At first, she didn't recognize him, but when he began to speak to her, she knew at once it was Yeshua. Miriam couldn't believe he was alive.

"Yoseph, I now know how she felt, which I doubted her too when she told me her story. I contributed her tales to her emotional state and the love of her teacher. Yoseph, she was the first person to see him resurrected.

"Yeshua told her to run to Yohanan Marcus's house and speak to the others. She then ran to tell the hiding disciples of the incredulous news. None of them believed her because she was a woman, yet both Shimon and Yohanan bar Zebedee raced back praying he was there. When they arrived, he had vanished. Now Miriam felt quite foolish in the eyes of the men, for they all thought she was lying.

"Several days later there were reports that Yeshua was sighted on the road to Emmaus. There were other sightings; however, proof arrived about ten days later. All the disciples met at Yohanan Marcus's house for an evening meal. They barred the doors after all were present, for fear the authorities might find them. Yohanan Marcus noticed a bright *kabod* in the corner of his room and a voice spoke from the light and said, 'Peace be with you, my brothers and sisters.' It was Yeshua who miraculously appeared in their midst. Then he spoke again and said, 'I bring you *chesed*.'

"They all gathered around and marveled at his healed wounds. He continued speaking to those who had doubted him and said, 'Blessed are those who have not seen and yet have come to believe.' A short time later, he appeared again at the home of Yohanan Marcus. The disciple Thomas was there and thought Yeshua was a ghost. He had much doubt in his mind that it was Yeshua and had to touch Yeshua's scars. Yeshua admonished Thomas along with the rest of the disciples for a lack of faith. He further told them to return to Galilee and proclaim the superb news about his resurrection.

"Yeshua outlined what they would do in his name, 'The one who believes and is baptized will be saved; but the one who does not believe will be condemned. And these signs will accompany those who believe: by using my name you will cast out demons; you will be able to speak in any language; you will pick up snakes in your hands and not be harmed, and if you drink any poison, it won't hurt you.'

"The last two things Miriam of Magdala told me before she left was further hard to believe. She said Yeshua told his disciples they would be able to heal the sick and raise the dead in his name. He and the forthcoming *ruah*, or a wind of fire, would change them all. The holy fire would rest on their heads and this flame would anoint them.

"Yoseph, he said he would come again to stamp out all evil, and then his throne would rest upon a New *Yerushalayim*. He didn't want us to search for this New Kingdom, for it wouldn't come by searching the skies. It won't be said, 'Behold here! Or behold there! Rather my Father's kingdom is spread out upon the earth and people don't see it.'

"At last, Miriam told me after forty days of being seen by the faithful, he left them from our garden on Mount Olive. Listen with care, Yoseph, to what I am about to say. Miriam said a hand-shaped image appeared, which was that of *El Shaddai* and lifted him up from the ground and pulled him through the clouds. He told his followers as he left, this was how he would return. There were radiant-appearing men, who accompanied Yeshua into the clouds, and they repeated his same words. They told the witnesses to preach to the world about what had just transpired.

"Yoseph, please help me make sense of all this. My heart aches for an explanation."

"Hebron, we will have plenty of time to discuss these matters. I want to see the rest of my family so I can touch them."

"Yes, and our bedraggled group has grown."

At once, Yoseph fell on his knees, reached his arms toward the heavens, and shouted a blessing, *"Barukh ata Adonai Eloheinu Melekh ha'olam ha-tov v'hameytiv."*

Tears rolled down his cheeks again as he wept for joy, followed by another sigh of relief. All his fears and anguish melted from his body like spring snows in the mountains.

"I want to see my precious family." Yoseph searched for them with his tear-filled eyes.

"Yoseph, the women are near the stream washing clothes. Alein Yosephe has just departed for *Yoppa* to obtain some supplies. The Baptizer's son is hiding in the cave as I've instructed him. Miriam of Magdala is due to arrive with Thomas Didymus tomorrow."

"Hebron, show me the way to the stream."

"Yes, Yoseph, follow me around the face of the cave. It's but a short distance from here."

He followed his brother-in-law over some large rocks that formed a small valley that led to the stream. Up ahead, he saw three women instead of the expected two. There was a sweet song coming from them as they washed the clothes on the rocks near the streambanks. Oh, happy the sound. Yosa was the first to turn and see their approach.

First, she put her hand on her forehead to block the sun. She stood up, straining to see who this stranger was.

Yoseph shouted her name, "Yosa! Yosa! It's your *abba*!"

Then she started screaming, "*Abba! Abba!* You are alive!" She ran toward him with a quickness of an African cheetah. Yosa embraced him with a force that knocked them both down on the rocks. She was crying and kissing Yoseph at the same time. Then he felt another person grab him with an embrace. When he turned, he saw Enygeus, who shouted, "My brother! My brother, Yoseph, you are alive!"

"Yes, my sister, I am back among the living," he said, while continuing to embrace all his loved ones.

"Let me gaze upon both of you. I must say there are still no prettier women in *Yehudah* than Enygeus and Yosa."

"Oh, *abba*, you are just saying that because you haven't seen us in so long."

Their eyes still had that youthful glistening appearance that the aged and downtrodden lack. Enygeus had some narrow streaks of gray hair, and her clothing was tattered from wear. Yosa favored her *amma* even more. She now had a mature appearance of a woman of twenty summers. Her hair was long and braided. Both of their hands were red and rough from doing manual labor. Their feet were dusty from living outdoors, and the sandals they wore were almost missing their leather soles. The outdoor sun had weathered their fine pale skin to a dark brown glow.

A woman was standing behind them with a young boy child. She wasn't familiar to Yoseph but reminded him of Miriam of Magdala. The little boy started calling to Enygeus and pulled on the hand of the unknown woman. He whispered, "*Amma, amma.*"

"Yoseph," Enygeus said, "this is my son Enoch who was born to Hebron and me shortly after you were imprisoned." There formed a dimpled smile on his sister's face as she told him her happy news.

The young boy broke loose from the woman holding his hand, ran toward Enygeus, and clung to her lower legs. Yoseph reached down to grab him and put him in his arms, but he started crying. His little hands and arms flailed against Yoseph's face as he struggled to reach his mother.

"Enoch has the strength of his father," Yoseph smiled as he handed him back to his sister.

Yosa turned toward the unknown woman and introduced her. "*Abba*, this is Martha from Bethany. She is Miriam of Magdala's sister. Martha has been kind enough to stay with us while Miriam preaches the great news of Yeshua. Martha was indispensable in helping Enygeus deliver young Enoch. Her brother Lazarus is in *Yerushalayim* with Miriam. I pray that both will be here tomorrow, and I know Miriam will be happy to see you. I am afraid our faith wasn't as strong as hers, for we felt you were dead. She knew all along that Yeshua would protect you. Miriam was so right, *abba*. I am ashamed."

"Don't blame yourself, my child, I am here now and that's all that matters. I have many marvelous things to tell all of you. Let's return to the cave. I am famished for some food."

They began their saunter to the cave. "We don't have a lot for you to eat, *abba*. We're waiting on Alein to come back from *Yoppa*. He promised that there would be some food at the synagogue for us."

"Why is he traveling there? Can't he buy food in Arimathea?"

"*Abba*, we have no money! Alein was hoping the priests in the synagogue would give us something to eat."

Hebron, Enygeus, and Yosa all bowed their heads in shame, making Yoseph experience an awkward moment.

"What about the money we hid in the cave? Also, where is the money we packed with us before leaving *Yerushalayim*?"

Before Yoseph could say another word, his hawthorn staff struck him in his head. The blow stunned him but just for a moment, and he tried to recover his senses. Then he remembered he'd laid it near the cave entrance. Yoseph glanced down to see a scared, wide-eyed child of about six summers in age. The wildness in his face unnerved him as if he was staring into the eyes of a wild beast. Both Hebron and Yosa grabbed hold of the young child and tried to comfort his fear.

"Zechariah, stop this at once. This is Uncle Yoseph," Yosa said, as she rubbed her hands through his dark curly hair. Hebron wrenched the staff from his hands and gave him a glare of displeasure. By this time, the young boy was breathing hard from excitement, yet the wild-eyed appearance stayed on his face.

"Whose child is this?" Yoseph asked, still unnerved by the boy's stare.

"Don't you recognize him, Yoseph?" his sister asked. "He is the Baptizer's son."

"He fears strangers ever since Yosa started taking care of him. I think he thought you had come to abduct him from us or maybe harm Hebron. Zechariah will calm down soon. Give Yosa another embrace, so he can see you won't harm us."

Yoseph gave Yosa a soft hug so the child could see he meant no harm.

"Hebron, did you teach that boy how to use a staff like that?" Yoseph asked with his head still aching from the boy's hardy blow. "His quickness and stealth are to be commended."

Hebron grew a large grin before he began to speak. "I have trained him well, Yoseph, but he is a natural when it comes to wielding a wooden sword or staff." They sat down on the rocks near the cave entrance.

"Hebron, what happened to the money we brought with us when we left *Yerushalayim*?" Yoseph asked, wondering how well they had survived these past four springs.

"Yoseph, it's gone. We paid most of it to the mediators that first spring in trying to acquire your release. The rest was hidden in the cave and used for protection money in Arimathea, which has kept mouths shut from speaking of our where-abouts. There are rumors that we're spied on and now our protection money is no more. I believe the possible watchers are not from Caiaphas, the Sanhedrin, or the Romans."

"Who is it, then?" Yoseph inquired with angst.

"I don't know, Yoseph. This is why you received an unwelcome reception by Zechariah and me. We have practiced vigilance in the last four springs. So far, I don't believe anybody knows where we are, except Eli and his sons and Miriam of Magdala."

"So how much food do you have left?" Yoseph asked, changing to a less-sensitive subject.

"We have about one day's supply left. After that, I am hoping Alein will come back from *Yoppa* with satisfactory news. Miriam of Magdala helps us when she can. We're anxious for her visits, but they've been less frequent, for the authorities observe her every day. The Sanhedrin stoned several of Yeshua's new followers to death. There's a new member who sits in the Judgment Hall, called Saul of Tarsus. He hunts down Yeshua's followers in an evil manner and then has them executed or imprisoned. This Saul hates anybody associated with Yeshua."

"What has happened to my friend, Nicodemus? I pray he is still alive."

"Nothing has been heard from him, I am sorry to say, Yoseph. He thought you died in prison. You can ask of his whereabouts when Miriam arrives about the third watch tomorrow. I wish I knew more, Yoseph, but it is too dangerous for us to ask many questions. Maybe she will bring some splendid news that he's still alive.

"Now, tell us about your troubled times in prison, Yoseph. We want to hear about what miracles happened that kept you alive by our *Adonai's* grace."

"Hebron, would you bring me some more water? Then I will begin my narrative."

The water was cool and tasted clean as Yoseph began to tell of the crucifixion, the tomb, his arrest, and his prison confinement. All the faces in front of him were awestruck with great amazement. The sole exception was young Enoch, who was playing with a stick on Enygeus's lap. When he told them the specific details about the crucifixion, everyone cried. He stopped at once to let them regain their composure.

He told his family to hold any questions for him until he had finished. Then Yoseph continued about Yeshua and the two *malachs*, Michael and Gabriel, who brought the *kodesh* items to him in prison. Above all, the cup and the miracles it performed in keeping him alive. Yosa and Enygeus started crying again, and he stopped there to have Hebron hand him a cup of water to sip and then he passed it to the others.

He showed them the holy lance and the holy sword, which had decapitated Yohanan the Baptizer. Young Zechariah stared at the long sword with his beastly intense eyes fixated on the rusty blade that had killed his *abba*. His lower lip curled with anger and his red flushed head held its color until tears rolled down both cheeks. Yoseph thought it best to put the sword back into his satchel. Once more, Hebron wanted to see the Holy Cup of their *Maishiach*, even though it had burned him when Yoseph first arrived at the cave.

"Hebron, great reverence has been bestowed to this cup of salvation. We shouldn't treat it with indifference or as an object of fascination. As my time goes forth with you, its purpose will amaze you. The many mysteries that will emanate from this cup will become quite clear to all of you. In addition, the glass vials that Miriam gave me at the Holy Sepulchre have the same mystery and reverence. Remember, my family, what our *Maishiach* Yeshua said at the last *Seder* when we gathered with him. Please try to lift your foggy memories of these past seasons and search your minds and souls for his words. Then contemplate these words. You'll learn to speak the 'way' soon. Right now, we are like rough stones in need of cutting, shaping, and polishing to form a solid foundation for the New *Yerushalayim*. Here we will tell the world what Yeshua said to his disciples.

"Now I am tired and must rest. Yosa, wake me by the fourth watch before the sun sets."

"*Abba*, let me show you where you can sleep undisturbed. Follow me to the back of the cave. It's quiet there and the children won't bother you."

CHAPTER XIV

Yoseph grabbed his satchel of precious objects and followed his daughter into the cool cave that reminded him of the one at Gethsemane. It was narrow and damp and ended with a large hewn chamber. There were privacy curtains hung for each of the cave dwellers. Small wooden stick toys were lying about the damp floor. Glancing up toward the ceiling of the cave was a narrow shaft of light. It appeared to be a smoke hole, for the roof of the cave was a sooty black. Small wooden food utensils were arranged around the firepit from a previous sparse meal.

"*Abba*, please use my sleeping pallet. I must leave to finish washing our clothes and think about what you have just said. I knew all along that my cousin was a great man, teacher, and healer. Now I know it's true. I will wake you right before the end of the fourth watch as you wish."

Yoseph's eyes remained fixed on his daughter as she ambled down the narrow passageway to the cave entrance. She hadn't changed in her kind demeanor and was always responsive to his wishes. Yet, he sensed a new maturity in his daughter, which wasn't present before his imprisonment. Then he noticed young Zechariah waiting for her at the cave opening. He was still apprehensive of Yoseph's presence and didn't want to follow her into the cave. Once she reached the Baptizer's son, he gave her a great embrace and she then knelt, put both hands on his small face, and kissed him on his forehead. She must have said something to him, for Yoseph detected a small smile on his face as they both left.

The bed was quite tempting and right away he reclined on the soft cloths stuffed with palm leaves. There was even a small pillow to rest his head, and he said another prayer giving thanks to *El Shaddai* for reuniting his family and knowing they were all alive. The remaining angst in Yoseph's heart was still there for his friend Nicodemus. He hoped and prayed he was still of this earth.

Sleep came fast, and his slumber slipped into a dream about the disciple Philip. He was speaking to him in a place Yoseph wasn't familiar with. There were dense woods all around them and the trees weren't the types that were prevalent in *Yehudah*. It was icy cold and to his amazement, a snow-whipped wind buffeted his back. Philip was speaking to him, but he couldn't hear what he was saying. His mouth moved, yet no words came out. All at once, there were words; however, the voice was that of his daughter.

"*Abba*, it's almost the end of the fourth watch. Come and eat some lentils. See, *abba*, young Zechariah wants to apologize for striking you with your staff."

The young boy came forward from behind Yosa and gave Yoseph a long embrace, after which they both gazed at each other and smiled. Yoseph stooped down and gave him another hug of reassurance. They strolled out into the waning sunlight where he smelled cooked lentils stewing in a small steaming pot. Out of the cave, Yoseph carried his precious satchel over his shoulder to show his family their *Maishiach's* bounty. Everyone sat down on the dusty ground while Enygeus dipped a small portion of the steaming food into a wooden bowl for each person.

"I am sorry, Yoseph," Enygeus said, "we haven't any bread or wine. This is the last remaining portion of our food supplies. I hope Alein Yosephe procures some food tomorrow. Please, forgive me, my brother. It hasn't been easy living here these past four springs."

Yoseph tried to assume full blame for the hungry state of his family. "You need not apologize, dear sister. I am the author of your misfortune. Besides, after the meal is over, I will show you the glory *Adonai* fulfilled in his new covenant with us, those four springs ago. I hope all of you have had time to contemplate what he said the night of his Last Supper."

A tear started trickling down Enygeus's sun-bronzed cheek. As Yoseph stared at his small bowl of lentils, he soon knew he would give them hope with his *Adonai's* cup. He placed his bowl of lentils in front of little Enoch and Zechariah, after which both young boys devoured them in the blinking of an eye. He reached into the satchel's large confines and pulled out the cup and the paten. Everyone stopped eating and focused on his every movement. With care, he placed the cup in front of him and in the same fashion, the paten.

"What I am about to do will show that our *Maishiach* is present with us now. Again, remember him and the words he spoke that night four springs ago."

Yoseph raised his hands toward the late afternoon sky and said the *Shema*. "*Sh'ma O Yisrael Adonai Eloheinu Adonai Echod. Barukh Shem k'vod walkout l'olam va-ed. V-ahavta et Adonai b-chol l'vaucha u-v-chol naf'sh'cha u-v-cho m'odecha.*"

The air around them became still and the birds stopped chirping. The silence was so great they could hear each other breathing. Yoseph stopped the *Shema* and they glanced at each other anticipating what Yoseph would say next.

"Remember what our teacher said that night of his betrayal. 'Where two or three are gathered in the remembrance of me, I will be there with you.' Remember what else he said, 'Love your fellow neighbor as you love yourself. There is no greater love than to lay down one's life for one's fellow man or woman. Always seek the trustworthy in humankind.' These were the new commandments he gave to all of you."

Yoseph knew at that moment the *Maishiach* was standing next to him, for happiness and joy came over him that he couldn't describe. The blessing for the bread and the wine rolled off his lips with no thought or effort.

"*Barukh atah Adonai, Eloheinu melekh na-olam, ha-motzi le chem min ha-aretz.*"

He raised the paten overhead and when he lowered the plate, it was stacked with bread! He then placed it on a large flat rock in front of him. At the same time, he reached for the bronze cup and said a blessing for the wine.

"*Barukh atah Adonai, Eloheinu melekh ha-olam, borei p'riy ha-gafen.*"

He raised the *Kodesh* Cup toward the pink-streaked blue sky and once again he lowered the cup replete with wine! It too lay next to the *kodesh* plate. Then a great *kabod* of yellow light emanated from both *kodesh* items, followed by a faint whisper that said, "This is my body which is given to you. Do this in remembrance of me."

Then before their eyes, the bread was broken into pieces so they could eat it! The whispers grew louder, and it spoke again, "This cup that is poured out for you is the *brit chadashah* in my blood that forgives the sins of the world. I Am the Ladder whereby you reach the Kingdom of Heaven. Climb with wisdom upon its ten rungs and say my words each time you have my supper. For my body is now your new temple. Yoseph, you are now my shepherd who will lead the scattered flock of *Yisrael.* When the Gentiles seek out what you say, you will speak of my quenching words that will slake their thirst. Proceed to that thirst with the wine of the *brit chadashah* and raise my cup for all to see and drink. It's the cup of righteousness and truth to forever remember me. I am the way, truth, and light of the world. *Shalom aleichem,* Yoseph, and your family."

There followed a prolonged silence after his whispering words had stopped. Yoseph glanced down to see his entire family and Martha on their knees, heads bowed, tears of wonder streaming down their cheeks and even the son of the Baptizer was praying. The sole person not knowing what had just happened was little Enoch. His little nephew was playing with a small stick and heard the others praying. "We bend our knees, bow, and acknowledge our thanks to the King who reigns over all kings, the *kodesh* one, who is blessed."

Yoseph stood there in silence and observed them finish their prayers. All eyes then focused on Yoseph, searching for answers. Hebron was the first to speak.

"Yoseph, I don't know what just happened here and my mind says this cannot be possible. Was this the voice of Yeshua we heard?"

Everybody drew closer to hear his response. Yoseph's mouth had become dry from the sudden elation, causing him to hesitate before he answered.

"Yes, and these were the *kodesh* words of Yeshua, our *Maishiach*, and they were more than a didactic lesson. Our *Maishiach* is telling us of a new 'spiritual way' we will live and teach. For the rest of our lives, we will have a new *kavanah*, or direction for preaching his worthy news. As the voice of our *Maishiach* said, 'You will speak of my quenching words, which will slake their thirst.' We will seek out both the Gentiles and our lost people and tell them the superb news of Yeshua. The supper we have just received here, you will recite and serve to all who thirst and hunger for love, truth, and salvation. All gathered here with me tonight are my new *mathetes*. You will follow what I do here at this *kodesh* feast and teach others after I am no more of this world."

He reached for the cup, then a piece of bread, stood, dipped it in the wine, and ate it. Then Yoseph raised it over his head and exclaimed, "The cup of salvation and the body of Christ!" He lowered the cup back down to his lips and then swallowed a large draught of wine. His entire body then shook with joy as he motioned each person present to come forward.

"Each of you do the same as I have done in remembrance of our *Maishiach*."

To Yoseph's amazement, the first to step forward was Zechariah. His small fingers reached for his piece of the bread from the paten Yoseph was holding, dipped it in the wine, ate it, after which he sipped a small drink of the wine. Zechariah's intense eyes met Yoseph's and again Yoseph blessed the cup and the paten with the words, "The cup of salvation and the body of Christ," causing a great smile with tears of joy streaming down Zechariah's face. Hebron, Enygeus, Yosa, and Martha followed him. All sat back down with the same expressions of joy on their faces.

"My dear brother, I too agree with Hebron. The miracles that have transpired here are hard for my mind to understand," Enygeus stated.

"My dear sister, it's not for us to understand at first, but to believe in what our *Maishiach* has given us. If you believe, faith is the sole understanding you need. You as a pupil and later as a teacher of the way will show and teach others the new law our nephew has given us." He turned to his daughter, "How are you, Yosa, at this moment? Is it an impression of fullness from hunger and a sense of great joy?"

"Yes, *abba*. I haven't felt this way since that night of the *Seder* dinner with my cousin . . . I mean our *Maishiach*. That sense of joy and happiness had left me until now. These past four springs have been nothing but sorrow and hunger. We didn't know that our *Maishiach* had bestowed the mercy of *El Shaddai* and these teachings on you." The others shook their heads in agreement.

"Don't ignore the sensation you now have. Its renewal will come each day when we have our evening supper. The first lesson I'll teach you, which I learned from experience these past summers, is that material things bind you to things of this earth. The true power you'll receive from *El Shaddai* is doing without. Give what you can to the point it won't endanger your spirit or physical body. If he asks of you to give more, don't be dismayed. Our *Adonai* will provide as you have just seen.

"Protect the *Kodesh* Cup, paten, vials, spear, and sword. This is our armor we will use against the powers of darkness. Remember the *logos* of our Savior; it will be your battle cry to gather the Gentiles and the lost sheep of *Yisrael*. Let us now say grace."

Yoseph stood to lead their small group. In unison they started, "May the name of *Adonai* be blessed from this time forth and forevermore. With the permission of all present, let us bless him, *El Shaddai*, whose food we have eaten. Blessed be he, *El Shaddai*, whose food we have eaten and in whom goodness we live. Blessed be he, and blessed be his name, Omein."

They stood there in the presence of the *Kodesh* Cup and plate. The *kabod* of its light still radiated the joy of hope into their hearts. The yellow light little by little dissipated, and the cup and the plate were once again empty. Darkness had fallen and the chill of night had come. They stared up toward the starry heavens, and the night sky was aglow with dancing lights that swirled back and forth. Yoseph knew that *Eloheinu* was pleased with their honoring of his son.

Hebron had started a fire and the crackling of the burning wood drew Yoseph's attention back to earth. Martha was standing across from him, and the firelight danced in her eyes. She favored her sister Miriam but was more nervous in her demeanor. She sat there in silence gazing into the flame, but her hands had a restless manner about them.

"Martha." She stopped helping Enygeus clean young Enoch from his nightly meal and gazed in Yoseph's direction. "How's your sister?" Yoseph asked. "How is she doing in *Yerushalayim?*"

"Rabbi, she has been in hiding at the homes of Yohanan Marcus and Shimon the zealot. She has been teaching Yeshua's special wisdom to all who will listen. Miriam's love of learning and *chokmah* exceeded the everyday chores of life. She has spoken of your kindness often and often thought you still survived in prison. I know there will be a great longing in her heart to see you. She has become a leader among Yeshua's followers, though she and the man they call Cephus don't agree."

Yoseph always thought Miriam would assume a leadership role in his nephew's ministry. He too longed to see her.

"Your sister is a smart and persuasive woman. I know our *Maishiach* knew what each of our destinies were and challenged us to fulfill them. Cephus, the rock, also challenged him to be his new leader."

"My sister Miriam spoke little to us about the crucifixion. I think it's hard for her to remember that horrid day. Both Lazarus and I were in Bethany when it happened. After Yeshua was crucified, Miriam and I thought to escape with the Baptizer's son and hide him here with Hebron."

"Was there some danger for him in *Yerushalayim*?" Yoseph inquired with a slight nervousness forming in his stomach.

"Yes. Herod Antipas and his whore of a wife were searching for him. Somehow, they knew he was still in *Yerushalayim* and hiding with Yeshua's disciples. Miriam will tell you more when she arrives tomorrow. I know there will be great joy in her heart to see you."

Yoseph saw fleshy bags under her eyes and realized the woman exhibited exhaustion. He didn't want her to answer any more of his questions.

"Martha, we can continue this conversation tomorrow. You need to rest. We need to strengthen ourselves for the coming days."

"Bless you, Rabbi. I will leave now."

Martha strolled from the campfire and trundled toward the cave entrance and entered its darkness. It was apparent she was weak from hunger, and Yoseph surmised the rest of his family suffered from hunger too. He mostly worried for the young boys. Yet, he knew this would change henceforth. His fingers felt the warm outline of the *Kodesh* Cup inside the large satchel on his lap. He ran his hand down the sword blade and it gave him further faith to overcome whatever dangers they might face. The spear tip protruded from the satchel and caught a glint of firelight on its metal. He gazed at the reflection of the fire dancing across the spear tip.

"Yoseph." A voice drew him from the spear tip to find Hebron standing before him.

"I need you to stand guard for me tonight. Yoseph, I know they have spied on us, yet they haven't made themselves visible. After four springs of living here, I thought I would have detected them. They leave food remnants and campfire charcoal in the numerous caves surrounding this area. Both Alein and I have searched in vain for their whereabouts. This has necessitated that we do guard duty day and night. Young Zechariah has helped me some, while Alein has been gone, yet I fear he isn't as wise as you and me."

"Hebron, tonight I volunteer to replace you on sentry duty. Our *Adonai's* wine and bread have refreshed me, and no fear or tiredness will come to me. Show me my post."

He followed Hebron some distance from their humble camp and Yoseph started climbing a set of rocks that led to a steep path. After hiking some distance, they reached the summit of a small mountain. Even in the darkness, he could see in all directions. A thin crescent moon gave them some light, but it was the stars that provided a brilliant glow.

"Yoseph, sit here on this rock and rest your legs, and I will relieve you at dawn. If you see anything at all, come and tell me. No matter how insignificant it may seem. I will see you at dawn."

A blustery wind picked up just as Hebron started to depart. "Wait, Hebron. I have some questions to ask."

Hebron turned toward Yoseph.

"What happened that last night four springs ago? What did Yeshua say to you right before we left Yohanan Marcus's house? And why did Eli see you later that night after the crucifixion?"

Hebron stared into Yoseph's eyes, and then sat down to tell his story.

PART V

The Romany

CHAPTER XV

Anno Domini 1190
Northern Iberia

We crossed the Rio Gállego at dawn and headed a due west direction. The sunrise was warm on my back and helped relieve the ache from the cold weather. My horse's nostrils exhaled two steamy streams of breath as we proceeded out of the canyons. The downhill trail was smooth and well-worn by previous travelers. This gave me some consternation knowing that we could be recognized by anybody we might meet. The trail ended and spilled out onto a large open plain. One could see in all directions with the few exceptions of hillocks. The wind was strong as we headed our horses into the westerly gusts, making conversation impossible because of the buffet-ing sounds.

Grand Master de Érail motioned for Muhammad and Jacque de Hoult to ride out and scout our flanks. I scrutinized both men until they appeared ant-size on the right and left of me, then disappeared. We had ridden about three leagues when Sergeant de Hoult returned with some

news. He didn't seem concerned as his horse came alongside me and then spoke to his grand master.

"Your excellency, I spotted a Romany caravan about two leagues in front of us. I counted eight wagons of about forty men and women. Their leader wanted me to conduct a mass for them, as he thought I was a chaplain. They appear harm-less, yet I sense they could be helpful to us. I told their leader we had a priest traveling with us, but I needed your permission to meet them."

"Accompany Sergeant de Béziers and tell them we will meet this evening before Compline. Oh, one other thing, give their leader this holy medal." Grand Master Gilbért reached into his saddlebag and pulled out a small silver medallion on a chain.

Jacque de Hoult grasped the holy medal that Grand Master de Érail handed him, gave it a cursory glance, after which he tucked it into his surcoat belt. He spurred his horse along with

Sergeant de Béziers and galloped off in the direction from whence he came. My curiosity nagged me. Through the howling wind, I asked Grand Master de Érail about what had just happened.

"Grand Master Gilbért, what was that medal you gave Sergeant de Hoult?"

"It's the *santo* medal of the Romany patron saint, Saint Sarah. She protects them from harm. It's made of pure silver and the *santo* medal is powerful in their eyes. Just the silver metal itself is supposed to ward off the 'evil eye.'"

"Do you believe this about Saint Sarah?" I inquired with skepticism of our leader.

"Faith may have many disguises when it's used against evil. Who am I to say that it's wrong? Lord de Borron, remember what our Lord said to his disciples. 'For whoever is not against you is for you.' We have many friends who know true evil. They are a great defense on our quest for the *Sangraal* parchments. Sergeant de Hoult said the Romany people were camped in the canyon rocks. That is our next destination. I think you will be quite intrigued by these people when we meet them."

We spurred our horses as both sergeants raced ahead to tell the Romany people we were coming, yet our pace drew to a slow trot with *Abad* Miguel and Grand Master Gilbért riding double. After some distance, his horse started to limp, causing the poor *abad* and our leader to alternate turns riding with Muhammad and me. *Abad* Miguel started to complain about a muscle cramp in his leg, prompting us to stop and rest next to a small stream. My horse, without urging, ambled over to the stream and started drinking her fill. As I dismounted, my eyes caught the sight of three foxes stopping to stare at us. They too were drinking from the stream until we startled them.

"Observe, *Hermano* Miguel, we have visitors!" I said to gain his attention. He turned to gaze upon the horizon and replied, "The *zorro* family has come to hear my mass tomorrow morning." A large grin broke across his bearded face as he placed his feet in the stream.

"How far to the Romany camp, *Frère* Gilbért?" inquired the *abad* as he continued rubbing his aching leg.

"Maybe a league. We should reach it before sundown. Do you see those canyon rocks in the distance? Search for the one that's shaped like a human face."

As Grand Master Gilbért pointed in that direction, my eyes followed the stream past where the foxes drank. This led toward the jagged-shaped canyon rocks. We mounted our horses and *Abad* Miguel rode with me. Muhammad rode up ahead some distance, scouting on each side of the stream. Alongside me, Grand Master Gilbért led with his lame horse.

After some time, I saw in the distance a horseman galloping in our direction. The sun was sinking on the horizon with its final rays obscuring my vision. But I knew it was Muhammad from his high-pitched Saracen voice as he shouted his greeting. His vocal tone didn't convey any alarm, but firm confidence in spotting our camp destination. The few words I understood told me we had nothing to fear. The canyon walls began to swallow us as we approached a narrow passageway. Dark shadows from the evening sun put a chill on me as my horse traveled deeper into the canyon interior.

Around the next turn of canyon walls, a smoky smell penetrated my nostril. The scent of burnt wood and roasting meat caused my mouth to water. Then I spied a drifting blue haze growing in intensity as we came to a large opening. This revealed an open field that stretched for some distance in front of us, with the canyon walls concealing its presence even to the sharp-eyed observer.

My eyes caught the last rays of the sun glowing on the flamboyantly designed wagons that I hadn't seen until now. Each had large solid wooden wheels connected to square-shaped living compartments. Over each of the compartments were round rigid tents stretched to cover them. The colors of each varied from wagon to wagon. Some had blue, green, and red-striped canopy coverings. Others were yellow, black, and orange.

Yet, what caught my eye as we approached

closer, were the ornate carvings on their wheels and carriages. Each had symbolic designs that were unfamiliar to me. However, for some unknown reason, I reached into my surcoat and clasped my hamsa protective medal. Its hand-shaped design gave me some reassurance we were among *amis*. I remember Commander de Polignac's message to return it after our quest was completed. The visit at *Château* Carcassonne seemed more than a year ago to me.

Sergeant de Hoult was the first to greet us as he jumped up from a huge fire that was roasting a large animal.

"Lord de Borron, why are you late?"

"As you can see, we are riding double because Grand Master Gilbért's horse has pulled up lame. We traveled on foot part of the way here. Is that a deer I smell roasting on the spit?"

"*Oui*, my lord, and it's about finished. Come and let me introduce you to the *roi* of this Romany band. The *roi* and his family band are quite honored that we want to sup with them. He told me his food is the least he can offer us to repay our holy gift."

A young boy with tar pitch-colored eyes ran up to my horse as I dismounted. He said something in an unrecognizable language and motioned for me to give him my horse. Sergeant de Hoult told me to hand him my reins and then the boy ran off toward a green pasture, which held other horses.

In front of me were about fifty sets of eyes that had the same dark color as the young boy. The orange flames of the fire reflected from their eyes as the crowd gathered around the four of us.

Their large number concerned me, but several displayed large grins on dark faces. Their skin, hair, and facial features favored Muhammad, but were different. The shapes of their faces were longer than Muhammad's round face. Their hair was straighter and longer. Skin tones were darker, and the men were all clean-shaven except for mustaches. The women wore long red, blue, and green-dyed skirts with small open vests over lacy ornate blouses. Their black hair was long but single braided. Some of the older women had their snow-white hair covered with loose-fitting red scarves. Each woman and young girl wore wool knitted shawls covering their bare shoulders. The majority were barefoot with large gold or brass ankle bracelets that made a quiet *clinking* sound as they approached. On closer observation, the women and young girls had the same twisted golden bracelets on their wrists too.

Each man wore black baggy-fitting pants, dark-brown leather boots, and a loose-fitting white shirt. Tucked into their large-buckled belts were large-pointed daggers. Every boot had a smaller dagger sticking out of the rim. The men's heads were covered with red-dyed *biggens* that were left untied. Every man and woman had some type of cross or holy medal around his or her neck. A tall man approached Sergeant de Hoult and me.

"Let me introduce you to Andreas. He is the leader and *rey* of the Romany in this part of Iberia. *Rey* Andreas, this is Lord Robert de Borron, a leader of his family in Northern Burgundy. Next to him is my grand master, Gilbért de Érail, and the other *caballero* is Muhammad Nur Adin from the Levant. We have fought for the protection of *Jesu Christo's* grave and home. The Saracen was once a prince in his homeland. We call him *amigo* as he has helped save our lives on many an occasion. I think you know *Abad* Miguel."

"*Si*, he has been kind to us in the past. When no one would let us water our horses and camp on their land, *Hermano* Miguel received us into his *abadia*. Which one of you gave me this precious holy metal of *Santo Sarah-la-kali*?" Andreas's dark penetrating eyes searched each one of us for a reply.

"I am the one," replied the grand master, with a grin on his face. The *roi* grabbed his hand and kissed it, while I spied a small tattoo of a chalice on his inside wrist. Could this man have any clues to help us on our quest? He then motioned for us to join him near his wagon. We followed and then sat cross-legged on the soft frosted grass. Andreas had *Frère* Miguel sit to his left and Grand Master Gilbért sit to his right. His animated expressions showed he was quite pleased with our leader, and he kept holding the holy medal in his hands and every so often kissed it while praising Grand Master Gilbért de Érail's name.

"Andreas, I received the silver medal of *Santo Sarah-la-kali* from the *abbé* at the church of *Saintes-Maries-de-la-Mer*. It was sained there with holy water from the church. I never quite knew what the connection was between your people and this dark-skinned *santo* woman. I've heard the people of Iberia discuss the *Gitanos* and their *santo reina*, but my *amigos* and I would like to hear more."

Before *Rey* Andreas started speaking, he motioned for two women to come forward. One appeared about Andreas's age, the other younger.

"This is my noble *esposa* and *hija*. My *esposa's* name is Esmerelda and my *hija* goes by Adriana. I will have them bring us some *vino*."

Rey Andreas was somewhat hard to understand, but our native languages were similar enough that we were able to make ourselves understood. The *Gitanos*, called by my compatriots, had an unusual dialect. It wasn't the sound of the *Mudéjars* or the Iberians. The Romany accents had a slow rhythmic sound with each word that trailed off in a soft tone. One had to listen well to each sentence to understand them.

Both women returned with two large *vin* skins painted with a strange design on each. It was a large five-petaled flower in the shape of a cinque-foil. In the center of each flower was a five-pointed star. After closer observation, I was surprised to see it was identical to the drawing design found at the San Juan el Peña cave. The geometric shapes mirrored the one given to *Abad* Miguel by the abbess. Had the *Gitanos* known about this symbol before the recent discovery by *Abad* Miguel? It appeared clues were forthcoming to us, not by serendipity, but preordained encounters. I swallowed my draft of wine and gazed transfixed on the colorful designs.

"Lord de Borron, are you keeping the *vin* skin or sharing it?" Grand Master Gilbért asked. He hadn't noticed the design but had plunged himself into conversation with *Rey* Andreas.

"I am sorry for being rude, my thoughts were elsewhere. Here. Partake, your excellency, and don't let me interrupt your discussion." After their conversation was over, I felt the need to speak. "Please, *Rey* Andreas, tell us more about your people. I have a curiosity that I would like satisfied."

Andreas gulped down a long draft from the wineskin, then began to speak.

"I am a *rey* of two tribes; one is called the *Beticos*, and the other is the *Herari*. Some of my ancestors came to this peninsula with a tribe of people called the Visigoths. We were fighting with the Visigoth's *rey*, Reccared, when he conquered Córdoba. The rest of us were slaves for the *Umayyad* caliphate of Damascus. Some of us fought with the caliph as he conquered North Africa; others were blacksmiths to his many horses. His great armada set sail to conquer the Iberian Peninsula and that is when we bought our freedom.

"Part of my kingdom is still on the Andalusian plain. The *Herari* tribe became a pawn between the *Mudéjars* and the Mozarabs. We moved north into the Pyrénées Sierras to escape persecution. We stayed in that region for two centuries until now. Over the years, a few of my tribe have come from the east. There are many more of us in slavery across the sea. It will be many lifetimes before my people are free to join us. The wars for the tomb of *Christo* and Jerusalem have kept the rest of my people from coming here."

The women handed us wooden plates of hot juicy venison. Andreas continued speaking after biting off a large chunk of meat that Esmerelda had given him.

"Part of the year my tribe, the *Herari*, spends the summer months and early fall in the Pyrénées. There we travel from village to village and do blacksmith work for the locals. It pays well and keeps us fed. When the snows creep down the sierras in late fall, we move south."

Andreas had strayed some from his history and ancestry, which I needed to know more about.

"Andreas, can you tell me where your ancient

ancestors once lived? You said there were many more of your kind beyond the Levant."

"*Si*, we were once mighty warriors who spoke an ancient tongue called *Hindi*. The land of our origin was a region called Punjab. There we lived along an enormous river called the Ganges."

"Tell me about this design on your *vin* skin. Do you know what it represents?" I asked, pressing Andreas for additional pertinent information.

"I don't know. Some say the design is the symbol for a man or sailor who traveled with our *Santo* Sarah. My family told me the man was a *Judio* who came across the great sea and brought her to Gaul."

"Have you seen this design anywhere else?" I asked as my anticipation grew greater.

"*Si*, these are signposts marked in the Pyrénées Sierras where we spend our summers. Some of them have *trishuls* or the trinities etched next to these symbols. All of my tribesmen think they have magical importance." At once, Andreas made the sign of the cross and continued with his story.

"My *esposa* Esmerelda can tell you more about the meaning of these symbols. She is a *drabardi*, one who can see into the past as well as the future. After our feast, I will have my *hijo*, Shandar, escort you into our wagon. Esmerelda is excellent at helping *gadjes* with their unanswered questions. Enough of this discussion, let's be entertained, my *amigos*."

Two Romany men appeared from behind a wagon. One carried a stick that had fire coming from its tip. The other was juggling four leather balls in his hands. Both circled the campfire, which still had the half-eaten deer carcass roasting on the spit. The man with the fire stick raised the flaming tip to his lips and, to our amazement, swallowed it. The second man continued juggling his leather balls but added a large dagger to his collection, which caught the glint of the firelight as it flew over his head.

The Romany crowd began to chant their names. One name sounded like "Tomas," while the remaining others shouted "Boldo!" The one called Boldo grabbed additional daggers from his belt and boot with each completed pass of the campfire. Before long, he had replaced the four leather balls with five daggers that he now juggled. The chant grew louder without interruption, Boldo threw each dagger, one at a time, at a red five-pointed star carved on one of their wagons.

Again, to our amazement, all five daggers stuck into the precise tips of the star. The crowd roared with approval at this unbelievable feat. Now our attention centered on the other man holding five fiery lit sticks, their flames made a flapping sound like that of a cape in a strong wind. He held my eyes to the flaming patterns against the night sky. He appeared juggling them in a certain sequence. Then it came to me: the patterns against the night sky were cinquefoils!

On his next pass around the campfire, he stood still right before me and stared into my eyes. The direction of his gaze was obvious, and his jet-black eyes glistened in the flames of his small torches. He wasn't concentrating on his flaming sticks as he juggled them but staring at my face. I felt I was in a trance and couldn't move. All at once, he dropped all five flaming sticks causing me to come out of my trance. As I stared at the ground where they fell, I was in awe of the pattern they formed.

It was a burning pentagram. The ancient geometric sign originated from the time of *Roi* Solomon and later represented the five wounds of Jesus the Christ. At once, I observed Grand Master Gilbért's reaction too. His opened mouth of awe spoke for itself. He glanced in my direction with his searching eyes, wanting to know what this meant and how the Romany accomplished this feat. The number five once again repeated its direction and hinted we were traveling to our next holy destination. The crowd didn't cheer this time but remained silent, yet I could see a multitude of dark eyes focused in my direction. They weren't speaking to me with words, but their liquid-black eyes were telling me to heed this clue and continue on my quest.

"Lord de Borron and Grand Master de Érail, I hope you have enjoyed our entertainment so far, for we aren't finished," *Roi* Andreas stated.

"Your *alteza* has given me not just excellent entertainment but sharp insight into what direction we should travel," I replied first to *Rey* Andreas. Gilbért Érail echoed my words and asked the Romany *roi* to continue the fine amusement.

A young barefooted woman of about sixteen summers came forward and stood near the center of the camp circle. In each hand, she held two wooden shell-shaped objects. The young woman wore a red velvet skirt and several ankle bracelets that were tinkling on each leg. Her bare shoulders held a mint green-colored shawl. The young woman's upper body had an ornate lace-trimmed blouse. Around her waist was a large black belt with an even larger silver buckle. Moreover, my eyes noticed an odd-looking, silver-colored, upside-down crescent moon that she wore around her neck. The silver beads that held the crescent were small pomegranate-shaped objects. The silver medal around her neck caught the light from the campfire and began to sparkle. She had another necklace with a plain crucifix that hung low between her breasts.

"Lord de Borron and Grand Master Gilbért, this is my other *hija*, Ashena, and the young man who is now joining her is my *hijo*, Petrus. One day he will be *rey* of all my tribesmen. Petrus is my oldest and wisest *hijo*. They are the best dancers in all of Iberia."

The *rey's* or *roi's hijo* was taller than his *père*. He stood three to four hand lengths taller than the rest of his tribesmen. Standing side by side, next to his *soeur*, he appeared as a giant. He wore a loose-fitting shirt that was open at his chest. and he had a large red *biggen* that covered most of his thick curly black hair. Both knee-high boots had a silver hilt dagger protruding from them. Around his neck was the medal that Grand Master Gilbért had given his *père*.

"Now, my *amigos*, listen to the music and see my children dance," the *roi* said, pointing at three men with musical instruments. One held a flute, another a small drum, and the third strummed a lute-shaped instrument. At once, our ears heard a sound coming from the raised hands of Ashena. Each hand started making a slow rhythmic clicking sound as her *hermano* circled her. His hands were on his hips and ever so nimbly he would stomp his feet to the music. A small cloud of dust formed under their feet as the tempo of the music grew louder.

"My *amigos*, join in with the rhythm and start clapping," the Romany *roi* said with a gleam in his dark eyes. "It's our custom, be happy tonight, for tomorrow may bring us sorrow."

As the *roi* motioned for us to clap, the rest of the *Herari* joined with shouts of approval. Both dancers grew faster in their steps, and Ashena's hand seemed blurred as her musical instruments hummed like a field of crickets. Petrus's ever-faster stomping feet raised enough dust to create a haze over our campfire. Ashena threw off her shawl and revealed beads of sweat trickling down her bare neck. She circled her *hermano* several times with her skirt whirling in the night air.

Their dancing and the music continued playing until the full moon was high in the night sky and then stopped when Ashena fell to the ground in exhaustion. This was followed by a roar of approval and clapping from the entire tribe. *Roi* Andreas stood up near the center of the large campfire and began to speak.

"My dear guests and *amigos*, I hope you have enjoyed yourselves tonight. Our honored guests have traveled many miles to visit our tribe and present us with the medal of *Santo Sarah-la-kali*. This medal was sained with *santo* water from her shrine. Thus, we now have a great sign of friendship between our people and the *santo* warriors. Let us acquire some rest, and tomorrow *Abad* Miguel will say mass for us."

The crowd of *Gitanos* started dispersing, strolling back to their wagons. Grand Master Gilbért, *Abad* Miguel, both sergeants, and Muhammad stood speaking to *Roi* Andreas about our horses and the cardinal's *chevaliers*. While listening to their conversation, I felt a presence behind me. Upon turning around, I saw the *Gitano reina*, Esmerelda.

"*Barón Roberto*, please follow me to our wagon." The *Gitano reina* strolled in front of me with her many silver bracelets making a rhythmic tinkling sound. She was small in stature yet strolled with the confidence of someone with authority. Esmerelda's clothes displayed several bright red and green colors, and her knitted shawl surrounded her face.

As I approached her wagon, the largest of the *Herari* tribe, I saw more unusual carved designs on the sides of *Rey* Andreas's wagon. Two of them caught my eye as we started to step into the interior. One was the same open hand-designed necklace that Commander Armound de Polignac gave me at the Carcassonne commandery. They were identical, except one was wooden and mine was pure silver. The other symbol was an upside-down, silver-painted crescent moon with beads. It too was identical to the silver necklace Ashena wore around her neck.

The interior of the *rey* and *reina's* wagon lay strewn with numerous objects. Suspended overhead were various dried herbs that smelled so pungent my eyes started burning. In one corner were two conical-shaped metal lanterns that gave the inside of the wagon an eerie glow. Each lantern had punched holes that emitted tiny shafts of light, which focused on Esmerelda's face. Next to the lanterns was a parchment with the same symbol that was on the *vin* skins. There was a large silver cross fixed to the wooden side of the wagon that overlooked a bed. At the foot of the bed was an altar, in the shape of a small square stone with a small crowned, black-faced doll placed in the center. On closer observation, I saw dried rosebuds arranged in a geometric pattern around it. In front of the image, a red glass votive flickered with light.

"*Barón Roberto*, I see you are drawn to our *Santo Sarah-la-kali*. She is a signpost for you. Her holy image has led you to me. You seek the five hallows that she saw over eleven hundred summers ago. The second *santo* parchments are within your grasp. Once all three sets are found, the other four hallows you will see."

"How do you know about these things?" I asked as we sat down on small wooden stools.

"I have been given a special gift by *Santo* Maria, the magdalener. She appeared to my *madre* when I was born and said I would see the future and know the past of others. You have seen our *Santo* Maria several times within the last two full moons, *si*?"

"*Oui* or *si*! That is correct, but I am still filled with doubt about your auguring abilities. Can you tell me the names of my children?" Her dark gaze focused on my eyes, and I saw her face inside my head. Esmerelda's lips murmured and said, "Brian and Henri. Is this not so?"

"*Si!*" I stated, sensing my gaping mouth.

"You're carrying an amulet that a warrior *caballero* gave you. It's called a hamsa, and it will protect you from the evil eye of others who want to kill you. Your second set of *santo* parchments will be difficult to find. Remember what *Santo Maria* told the man who buried our savior."

"And what were those words that were told Saint Joseph of Arimathea?" I asked. The more I spoke to this *drabardi* woman, as the Romany people referred to a seer, my doubts at once faded.

"The words were *penta* and *octa*. As Saint Joseph heard these words, so too will you face the same challenge. Search for your next parchments under the sign of the *octa*, above will be the *penta*. His words have lain hidden and forgotten for many centuries. I see the pages in my mind's eye, but their location is misty. That's for you and your companions to find. My destiny draws me elsewhere. Your future holds numerous new revelations you'll see and write about. You will complete your quest and be amazed beyond human belief. Others will try to destroy what you have written. Another eight hundred and fifteen summers will lapse before one like you will come to tell your completed story. He too will have many trials in authoring your story. Yet the truth of the *Santo Cáliz* will never die."

A contorted expression came over Esmerelda's face and her eyes closed tightly. She had predicted another would come after me in *Anno Domini* 2006. I wondered who he might be and the astonishments he might see.

"I see much torture for the men of the red cross and the distant future holds the flames of false retribution. A fair-faced *rey* and a weak *santo padre* will be the author of their demise. The final leader of the red-crossed men will die with a burning curse on his lips, but like the *Santo* Lazarus, the red-crossed men will rise again from the ashes of their destruction."

She awoke from her deep trance-like state with an exhausted sigh and her dark gaze met my eyes once more.

"*Barón Roberto*, my visions of the future are done. It's quite late and I need my sleep. Tomorrow you will leave us and head south on your quest. My people will help protect you from the evil men who track you."

We both stood up from the cramped quarters of the wagon and started to step out into the cold night air. I didn't know whether to thank her or just say nothing. Upon leaving, I observed a silver, five-pointed star pinned to the top cover of the wagon. It was a solid silver star designed as the one on the *vin* skin, her wagon, and the drawing we brought with us from Huesca.

"*Reina* Esmerelda, does this star have any special significance by itself?"

"*Si*, it's a solid pentagram and was the symbol

of an ancient *rey* of the *Judios*. It's also the shape of an amulet to protect you from harm. As you can see, it has five points. Many meanings lay hidden in this star symbol. Remember it well, my *amigo*."

CHAPTER XVI

I left the *reina's* wagon similar to a *vin* cup overflowing with too much *vin*. She had revealed so much information; and my thoughts and many conclusions were spilling over onto my body. The cold night air grabbed me away from my thoughts and drew my body to the warm campfire. The rest of my *frères* had gone to sleep near the fire. I found a spot next to a large chunk of burning wood, knowing it would last the night. While lying there, I saw the moisture from my exhaled breath be snatched by the fire. For some time, I gazed on the disappearing motion of the moist air, while ruminating on what Esmeralda had revealed to me, until I fell fast asleep.

"Lord de Borron, it's time to leave," a distant voice sounded in my ears, which was Grand Master Gilbért calling me to wake up. "We have many leagues to ride before reaching Zaragozza and time now must be spent changing our horse-shoes. The Romany men are putting new shoes on them as I speak. Muhammad and Sergeant de Hoult left before daybreak to scout ahead and behind. The Romany women have packed us enough food to last until we arrive at Zaragozza. *Abad* Miguel will be saying mass quite soon, as he promised *Rey* Andreas. I want you to find your horse and lead it to Boldo for new shoes."

All the horses, both the Romany animals and ours, danced in a corral at the far end of the box canyon. I proceeded to exit the camp and strolled toward the area where four young boys were overseeing all the horses. One young boy ran toward me shouting, "*caballo, si, caballo, si.*" He stopped in front of me and stared down at my sword. His eyes widened with both awe and fear as I eased it from the scabbard and handed it to him. With grunting sounds from his throat, his small arms fought to raise the sword from the ground. The crescent-shaped smile on his face was a wonder to see, along with his jet-black eyes growing as large as dark walnuts. After several failed attempts to raise it, he handed it back to me, after which he trailed behind me as I searched for my horse. The plentiful big Andalusian horses of the Romany people made it difficult to spy my mount, but she saw me before I saw her.

At once, my Arabian horse galloped up to the rope fence and reared up on her hind legs to greet me. She then whinnied with a sharp tone telling me of her hunger. There were several rope harnesses tied to the corral fence. I untied one, and then placed it in her mouth, around her ears, and then under her neck. The young boy untied the corral and I led her in the direction of Boldo and his portable blacksmith shop. His hammer *pinged* each time he struck the anvil and horseshoe. The *clanking* noise reverberated off the tall canyon walls with a rhythmic sound that was telling me something. The sound was speaking a word or phrase. I stopped for a moment to listen closer. The word sounded similar to "solo-man."

It made no sense to me, and I proceeded to where Boldo stood over his anvil. The acrid smell of hot burning coals grabbed my nostrils at once as another man pumped the bellows, while Boldo formed the cherry-red glowing horseshoes. His arm muscles were the size of round wooden bowls and large sinew lines bugled from each forearm. Boldo's bare shoulders glistened with sweat, and their large ball-shaped muscles flung out more sweat with each quick blow of his iron hammer. What impressed me was his quickness. The old shoes of each horse came off with a quick *thud* and each new one was attached at the same speed. I don't believe our horses realized they were wearing new shoes, for not a sound of displeasure came from any of them.

My horse was the last shod. She stood motionless

as Boldo grabbed each fetlock and replaced the shoes. He proceeded to the rear and then reached for each cannon bone and finished the shoeing. His quickness was incredible. He was both a master with knives and shoeing of horses.

"*Muchas gracias*, Boldo, for taking care of my horse with such great speed; she didn't raise her voice or complain when you grabbed her back legs."

"*Barón Roberto*, it's not just my experienced skills, but the Moor traveling with you has trained them well. All your *caballos* gaze at his every move. You're blessed to have a *caballero* who knows his horses."

We saddled all our horses, packed them to ride, but before leaving, *Abad* Miguel finished a crude outdoor altar to say mass. A stream of people came out of their wagons and stood in rows behind the priest. Boldo shed his apron, washed his hands, and followed me to a back row of his people. There was no censer for *Abad* Miguel; instead, Esmerelda gave him some herbs that gave off a sweet smell as they burned. He waved them throughout the crowd and over the table that had two large candles. On the table was a large bowl and a silver plate covering its contents.

All around the altar were *fitchée* crosses stuck into the ground that our Grand Master had placed. A large loaf of crusty bread was next to the bowl and candles. With reverence, *Abad* Miguel sliced it into many small pieces. He then gave a short homily about the great hospitality of the Romany people and a newfound relationship with *la Hermandad de Christo*. After he finished, he distributed the Holy Eucharist as the quiet crowd moved in a single file to the altar. Grand Master Gilbért assisted his longtime mentor with Holy Communion, and I saw *Rey* Andreas kiss his *Santo* Sarah medal before he ate his bread and swallowed his *vin*.

The next thing I knew we were mounted and ready to leave our band of new friends. Grand Master Gilbért began saying his farewells.

"*Rey* Andreas, *Reina* Esmerelda, Boldo, and the rest of my *amigos*, it has been a great pleasure to be in your presence. *Pax vobiscum* and *adios*."

Grand Master Gilbért spurred his horse causing it to rear with a whinny, and we followed him, waving *adieu*. I glanced back at the cheering crowd and their many colorful wagons leaving me with a sense of sadness. A forlorn sensation came over me, and I knew I wouldn't see these same people again.

We rode all day and stopped once to water our horses. The swiftness of the leagues flew by due to our horses' long rest and new shoes. In addition, *Abad* Miguel had his own mount, which *Rey* Andreas gave him as a gift.

Toward evening, we stopped at a small stream to make camp. It was isolated between two large canyon walls and gave us enough concealment to build a fire. A hoary frost had formed on the low-lying rocks and dead grass in front of the canyon entrance, forcing Grand Master Gilbért, Muhammad, *Abad* Miguel, and both sergeants to pull their hoods over their heads as we sat down next to the fire. We were exhausted and searching for relief, as we scooted closer to the crackling flames. I surmised it was close to Saint Andrew's feast day and the latter part of November. Since we weren't in the *montagnes* anymore, the days still had a little warmth, but the nights were colder.

"How far have we come today?" I asked Grand Master Gilbért. His beard appeared whiter in the light of our roaring campfire.

"About six leagues; it will be another two leagues before we come to a small village called Ejea. It faces the Rio Arba. From there we will travel southwest along the Rio Arba until we reach the mighty Rio Ebro. There's a ferry boatman there whom I know well. He'll float us to the other side of the Rio Ebro, and from that side of the river, it's another ten leagues to Zaragozza. There's an excellent road that runs due east into *Rey* Alfonso's capital. Once on this road, the cardinal's men and his Moor lackeys won't be a threat. My men patrol this road every day to protect the pilgrims on their way to the seaport city of Tortosa."

"What about before we cross the Rio Ebro?" I inquired, still worried about our rear.

"Before we left *Rey* Andreas's camp, I spoke to him about helping us with the cardinal's *chevaliers*. He said he would have Boldo and his men scout behind us. The Romany people are experts in concealment and sabotage. They'll do enough trickery to stop or slow down the cardinal's men."

"I hope this won't put *Rey* Andreas's people in harm's way," I replied, as I stared at the smoke rising into the star-filled night.

"No, they're cautious people born out of necessity. I would like to change the subject and speak to you about our quest and finding the next *Sangraal* parchments. I know the difficulties we faced, leaving little time for discussion. Besides, the time we have spent racing on horseback since leaving Montpellier. Do you believe the clues we have discovered will help lead us to a specific place in Toledo?"

"*Oui*, once we arrive in Zaragozza and with the aid of your chaplain and *Abad* Miguel, its whereabouts will become clearer. Both my heart and mind tell me we are growing closer, but I fear Cardinal de Folquet's men will intercept us first. Why can't you and your *chevaliers* at Zaragozza hunt them down and kill all of them?" I asked.

"It's not quite that simple. My men have either fought in the Levant against the army of Saladin or the Moors of Iberia. Some of them have even fought both armies. We could, with little effort, rub them off the surface of the earth, but politics deem otherwise. *Rey* Alfonso the Chaste needs my men to protect

Iberia and Aragón from his rivals and the Moors. There has been an accord struck with *Rey* Alfonso and our *Santo Père* in Rome. A portion of whatever lands and possessions we conquer in Iberia, a portion is given to Rome. We soldiers of God will receive a small portion to fund the Crusades in the holy land and a greater portion is contributed to *Rey* Alfonso. I am responsible for executing this agreement.

"Cardinal Folquet and his dead *bâtard* seneschal, de Tournay, knew of this accord. The cardinal desires to steal this money too as well as the *Sangraal* parchments. He's a feared and powerful man in the Curia. I must discredit the cardinal and let him hang in his own noose of guilt. When the time is right, I will know when to act." He shook his head. "We have a long trip ahead of us tomorrow; let's sleep."

"One other thing before you retire, Grand Master. *Abad* Miguel said you should tell me about *Abbé* Jeremiah, your chaplain at Zaragozza. What should I know about him before I meet your priest?"

Without any reason, I glanced over to see *Abad* Miguel's reclined form, yet his eyes were still wide open. He hadn't fallen asleep, and he must have overheard my question, for the reflection of our campfire danced in his large dark pupils.

A long period of silence ensued before Grand Master Gilbért replied to my question. His large fingers kept rubbing his beard and he kept staring into the fire as if remembering something or someone many years ago.

"I . . . should have mentioned to you a while back about my relationship to Chaplain Jeremiah. Please forgive me that I wasn't forthcoming with you. He's my *fils* by a *Juive* woman. His *mère* was from a wealthy merchant family who lived in Santiago de Compostela. They were quite successful in selling wine and supplies to all the pilgrims who traveled to the holy shrine. She was the child of Benjamin and Esther. Right before I joined the order, *Abad* Miguel sent me there. He wanted me to see the shrine and obtain sained holy medals for the poor. He knew that members of his church couldn't afford to travel there. Benjamin's shop was close to the église, and I arrived in town during the heat of the day. It was the first place I stopped to rest, and I still remember to this day the cool breeze that came through his shop. As I gazed at the back entrance of the shop, there stood a lithe silky black-haired young woman."

Grand Master Gilbért paused in his conversation, and I saw his eyes moisten and again transfix on the flames, followed by a long uneasy silence before he continued.

"Her name was Deborah and was about twenty summers in age. She was holding a large clay ewer of water and she asked if I would like some to drink. Her hands were small and showed no sign of hard labor. The prominent features of her appearance were her eyes. They had a dark liquid intensity yet displayed a searching intelligence. Her lips were full and wide and moved in a soft-spoken manner. She knew I wasn't from her region, because of my northern accent. We conversed until the sun was sinking behind the church and cast dark shadows into the shop. I told her I had pressing business and must leave, which we both agreed to meet later that night.

"I stayed on at Santiago de Compostela for a fortnight until *Abad* Miguel sent a letter to the *abad* there requesting I come home. I believe I could have stayed there with her for the rest of my life, but God willed otherwise. When time allowed, I would travel to visit her. It was during one of my visits she told me she was with child, after which we shed many tears. Her *père* found out about us and forbid me from seeing her again. However, I would send Deborah missives with what little money I earned from helping *Abad* Miguel and told her how much I loved her. The last letter I received said we had a *fils*, and she was naming him Jeremiah. After three months of not receiving any letters, I became worried. I obtained permission from *Abad* Miguel and traveled to Santiago de Compostela. Her parents refused to let me in their shop or answer any questions about where she and my *fils* might be."

There was another long pause before Grand Master Gilbért began to speak again. He asked for the *vin* skin next to me. I saw him swallow several large gulps before he continued. As he started speaking, his eyes filled, and a tear rolled down his cheeks.

"I saw the *abad* there and made some inquiries. He told me I should travel to a place a short distance from town. He gave me some directions, blessed me, and said no more. The location was off the main road close to a grove of oak trees. Somewhere in the trees, I remember hearing an owl hoot. To my horror, it was a cemetery; I forced my legs to move as I approached numerous grave slab coverings. It wasn't a Christian cemetery, but a *Juive* cemetery. At the far end of the graveyard, I saw a new dug grave. Right away, my eyes focused on this location. I gazed down on the new stone slab with its scattering of small rocks. My trembling hand brushed them out of the way and to my horror found Deborah's name.

"It said in the *Juive* language, 'Deborah daughter of Benjamin and Esther.' Both *Abad* Miguel and Deborah had taught me enough Hebrew to read the inscription. She had died a month before I had come back to see her. My heart sank with unbearable grief. I don't know how long I stood at the gravesite. It was almost dark before I fell to the ground with exhaustion. The next thing I remember was my horse nuzzling me to wake up. My horse's hunger had compelled her to arouse me from my deep trance. I reached out for her halter, grabbed one of the straps, and pulled myself up on wobbling legs.

"The sun began to rise with a strange orange crescent shape above the eastern horizon. The air was cold, and I knew I had to leave. Before I left, I put additional rocks on the stone slab, said several prayers, and left."

"What happened to your *fils*?" I said, interrupting Grand Master Gilbért without thinking how I sounded, yet he showed no offense but continued. He stated all this information in a low voice for *Abad* Miguel and me to hear.

"I returned to the old *abad* and told him what I had found. He told me everything. Deborah had died from some disease of childbirth. Her parents wanted my *fils* schooled in their Sephardic faith when he came of age and hid him with a rabbi. However, before the old *abad* died, he wrote me a letter stating that Deborah's parents had died from the plague, and he knew the rabbi who was raising Jeremiah and where he lived. His final words were that the rabbi was old like him and feared that the *garçon* would go to an orphanage. By this time, I had become a *chevalier* in the Poor-Soldiers of Christ. Jeremiah must have been six or seven summers old when the old rabbi died. The new *abad* wrote that I should come to Santiago de Compostela and obtain my *fils*.

"After seeing him we traveled to the Sorbonne in Paris for his religious studies. He excelled in all his studies and earned his college letters at the early age of thirteen. I knew he would be intelligent because he had his *mère's* eyes and quick intellect. As I rose through the ranks as a soldier of Christ, *Abad* Miguel saw to his further scholastic training as a priest. After I came back from the Levant, I saw to his martial training. He's now a chaplain of the Temple and has both the mind of a warrior and that of a scholar. My love for him I cannot explain with words. I can't express myself in words or the written language as you do. All I know is God has *sained* me with a gift of my *fils*.

"Very few people are aware of our relationship, and I know I can trust you with my secret. It's best that I keep it this way. My men at the priory at Zaragozza are unaware their chaplain is my *fils* and born of a *Juive mère*. Lord de Borron, please don't write of this in your journal until I am no more of this earth."

"I won't betray your trust in me, Grand Master Gilbért. I know God has smiled on what you have accomplished with your *fils*."

CHAPTER XVII

The next morning, we broke camp and passed the outskirts of Ejea about the time of Sext. From there we headed southwest along the Rio Arba. About Nones, we stopped to pray and afterward eat near a riverbank that hid us from the road. Here we placed our *fitchée* crosses in the ground and Grand Master Gilbért read from Psalms fifty-six and fifty-seven. They were both quite appropriate passages. Trust in God while being pursued by evil forces and seeking God's wings of refuge from a destroying storm.

I think the Psalms gave us additional spiritual encouragement to continue our journey to Zaragozza. We finished Nones with thirty-three *Pater Nosters* and Glory Bes. After the divine office, I grabbed my horse and led her to the Rio Ebro to drink. She paid no attention to me as I checked her gaskins and fetlocks. Then I checked her shiny new shoes and saw they were all holding tight. Boldo had done an excellent job.

"Lord Robert, come join us for some food," shouted Grand Master Gilbért. The sergeants echoed his request.

"What do we have to eat?"

"It's not a *rey's* banquet, but it's something *Abad* Miguel brought with him when we left the *monasterio*."

My curiosity and hunger pains were insatiable, so I left my horse and proceeded to investigate. To my surprise, *Abad* Miguel gave me a large slice of cherry pie. Right away, my mouth started watering before I could put it up to my lips. The sweet-tart flavor was delicious, and the crust was soft and buttery to my mouth. The large pie disappeared within a blink of the eye and not a crumb leftover.

"*Abad* Miguel, your order eats as well as the Soldiers of Christ," I stated as I swallowed the last piece.

"Lord Robert, the kind *senoritas* from Huesca bring these pies by our *monasterio*. They think my fellow *hermanos* are always on a fast and fear for our health. I don't have the heart to turn them down. When we break the fast tomorrow, I have another pie we can eat. It's a spiced apple pie. This should last us until we reach Zaragozza, besides, we still have the Romany's venison they packed for us."

We didn't drink any *vin*, holding it for tonight. Instead, we washed our pie down with cool water from the Rio Arba and then proceeded to our horses and left.

It was past Compline before we again stopped for the night. The night air had turned cold, and our breath emitted a jagged stream of moisture. I kept my mantle closed with my hands and hoped a fire would be started soon. To my dismay, the grand master said we were stopping for a short time to rest and soon as there was enough moonlight, we would leave. I tried to find some shelter from the icy wind that blew from the north. Several bushes were growing next to some large rocks that seemed dense enough to stop the wind. I crawled in between them and sat there drinking from one of the remaining *vin* skins after which a freezing rain started falling obscuring the rising moon. It appeared this night would be one of the worst for us to travel since we left the snowy peaks of the Pyrénées Mountains.

"*Frères*, it's time to leave and meet the ferry boatman," the grand master commanded as the rain turned to sleet.

Sergeant Jacque lit two pitch torches and gave one to Sergeant Guy. They mounted their horses and led the way. I searched around for Muhammad, but he had disappeared. Muhammad must have exercised his great ability of stealth and disappeared unseen by me.

"Where is Muhammad?" I called to my companions who were leading the way.

"He has gone ahead to see if everything is okay

with the boatman," replied Sergeant de Hoult. "He will return and let us know if the way is clear of the cardinal's men. Listen for his signal; it will be that of a screech owl."

With the speed of bee stings, the sleet pelted my face and started making a dull *plinking* sound on everything it struck. I was afraid we wouldn't hear Muhammad's signal or see him through the icy curtain of rain. The sleet stuck to everything that it fell and formed a glazy film on bridles, chain mail, saddles, and mantles. The pathway became slippery, and travel slowed to a turtle's pace. After about two leagues of riding, we heard Muhammad's signal. A frozen-covered ghost appeared before the sergeants' torches. The fiery light made his stillness appear as a carved glistening statue. He stood there motionless on Buraq before he spoke, "*Salaam alaikum,*" eliciting a reply from Grand Master Gilbért of "*Alaikum al salaam.*"

"*Sadiq*, the way is clear to the boatman," said Muhammad, as he motioned us to follow him. We traveled about one additional league until we came upon a frosty haze of yellow lights in the distance. There on a large hill was the small village of Tauste. According to *Abad* Miguel, the ferry boatman was just a short distance down in the valley.

We descended the trail with caution, yet several of our horses slipped on the downward path. This forced us to travel off the path, causing our horses to whinny with fear. At once, Muhammad spoke to them, which gave the horses some confidence, after which they were calm. My ears told me we were approaching a riverbank, for the sound of a mighty *rio* roared above the *plinking* noise of the sleet.

At last, the riverbank flattened out to a long sandy and ice-encrusted beach. There I spied several faint stationary torches emanating from a long dark-shaped object jutting from the beach. The crunching sound of our horses' hooves continued down the beach until I heard the faint words, "*Bienvenu, amigos.*" I now recognized the dark object as our barge.

PART VI

Dagger

CHAPTER XVIII

Anno Domini 37
Hidden Cave and
Lookout Point Near Arimathea

Joseph, it's hard for me to speak of that night four springs ago," Hebron said. After which, his head fell dejected on his chest before continuing. "The next night was even worse for me. I couldn't let you be alone to confront Caiaphas and the Sanhedrin. Besides, afterward Yudas stayed in *Yerushalayim*, still loose planning his next nefarious activities. Remember Yoseph, Yeshua spoke to me in private that night after his Last Supper in one of Yohanan Marcus's upper rooms. He spoke about future events, not just those days after his crucifixion, but many events into the future, my future. He said I wouldn't kill Judas, yet he knew evil surged in my heart forcing me to seek revenge for my nephew's death. The search for him was a primary concern along with my hatred. Later, it burned even hotter when I heard how our nephew died.

"The next night I tracked him along the cliffs near the tomb of Absalom, where I spied a rope in his hand as he ascended the cliffs. After a short distance, Yudas stopped in front of a dead olive tree and threw his rope over the largest tree limb and then put a noose around his neck. That's when I confronted him. I had stolen a *Gladius* sword from a sleeping legionnaire and pointed it at him and hollered his name. He saw me as he stepped near the precipice. Yudas told me that my sword was unnecessary, and he was sorry for what he had done.

"Without warning, he tied off the loose end of his rope and jumped off the cliff. Even in the dark of that night, his face turned bright red, and the whites of his eyes seemed to bulge out of their sockets. He swung there just a short time until a strong wind blew his body back and forth, then the limb snapped. Yudas fell some distance down into the ravine and struck several large sharp rocks below. I crept to the edge, glanced down, and saw his bloody entrails lying on his chest. My emotions were all confused, yet I didn't know if his fate had cheated me of my revenge or his suicide was a blessing for me. Then the words that Yeshua spoke to me came whispering in my ears. 'My *Abba* told me that vengeance is his alone.'"

"I am relieved you didn't kill him, Hebron.

There's no darkness of guilt residing in your heart. Yeshua has shown you the way to our *Adonai Eloheinu.* What else did Yeshua tell you?" I felt both relief and curiosity as Hebron started to answer my question.

"He spoke to me about where we would travel and what part I would play in the New *Yerushalayim.* Yeshua said I would be a fisher of men and help build the new Temple of Solomon. To my surprise, he said I would have a son called Enoch. Also, he said that my young son Enoch would help build this temple too. Enoch would one day be a fisher king and Zechariah would become a warrior king. Both Alein Yosephe and I would start a line of soldiers to guard the cup of Yeshua and his *kodesh* remembrances. None of this made any sense to me when he spoke that last night. Several things he said have come true. You have brought all the *kodesh* items he told me you would have. Yeshua said you would be the first fisher king and show us the way. Oh, one last thing I remember. Do you recall when he was a young boy of thirteen summers and you sailed with him to the Isle of the Celt?"

"Yes, why do you ask?"

"He said we would build a new tabernacle there, and it would one day become as great as King Solomon's temple."

"How could this be possible? We don't have any boats, money, or crew!" Yoseph exclaimed, still pondering what Hebron had revealed.

"I don't know, Yoseph. Maybe he will give us a sign or provide for us. He has already given us wine and bread."

"If what you say is correct, Hebron, please forgive me for my doubt. I am still guilty of thinking in the material world. You are right. In due time, all will be revealed to us."

"Yoseph, I haven't spoken to anyone else of these things I have said here tonight. As you can see, part of what I have told you makes me ashamed. It's time I leave and acquire some rest. I will see you in the morning."

Hebron started back down the mountain path and slipped into the dark shadows of the rocks. He was a virtuous man, and Yoseph was proud to be his brother-in-law. He sat there gazing at the stars and gathered his robe for warmth that Eli had given him. One star seemed much brighter than the rest. It was the star the Romans called Venus and the Greeks called Aphrodite. The cold air, what Hebron revealed, and the hard ground helped keep him awake for his guard duty. The coming sunrise was colorful with streaks of purple, yellow, orange, and sea blue in the morning light. It enthralled Yoseph for some time as he said his *Shakharit* morning prayer.

From the east, on the plain in front of him, came a small dust cloud. It didn't appear to be a dust devil, for the shape of this dust cloud was long, narrow, and close to the ground. Could it be Roman soldiers or Temple guards? After a short while, he could see images forming at the head of the cloud. It appeared eight individuals were coming in his direction. Yoseph hurried toward the rocky path, which dropped down the side of the hillock. The ever-increasing daylight made it easier to step down at a rapid pace. Once Yoseph stumbled and bloodied his knee on a jagged rock just before reaching the flat ground. Yet, his fear for their safety made him ignore the pain. As he saw Hebron trying to start a fire, Yoseph shouted his alarm.

"Hebron, I spotted what I think are soldiers, headed off the road in our direction. Maybe less than a third of a league from us. They could be Roman legionnaires or Temple guards. It's difficult to tell. The sun and distance kept me from distinguishing between the two. We must hide right now!" Yoseph demanded as both Yosa and Enygeus rushed out of the cave upon hearing his shouts to hide.

"Yoseph, what did you see?" his sister asked with wide-eyed panic on her face.

"Eight riders are approaching from the east," Yoseph replied, not knowing where to hide.

"Hebron, where is the best place to hide when strangers approach? Is it the cave?"

"Yes and no, Yoseph. There is a hidden exit to our cave. It's for our protection and helps us escape on a rear path. Yoseph, you, Martha, Zechariah, and Yosa hurry to the back-cave entrance. Yosa will show you the way. The rest of us will remove any traces of our camp here and inside the cave. There is a large boulder inside that hides a tunnel to the rear of the cave. I will lift it so Enygeus and little Enoch can squeeze through. They will meet you after we hide our belongings. Now leave while we still have time."

Right away, the four of them ran toward the riverbank. It twisted some distance behind the cave yet traveled in an easterly direction around the small mountain and then flowed north. Right at that change of direction was a set of large bushes near a talus.

"*Abba*, help me spread apart these thick bushes," Yosa said in a gasping voice. "It's under these bushes that the rear of the cave is located. Be careful; there is a steep decline leading down into the cave. We will have to lie on our backs to enter, after a short distance we'll be able to stand."

As soon as Yoseph parted the dense bushes for the others to enter, a cool blast of air struck his sweaty face. It felt soothing at first until the thorny branches tore at his arms as he slid down behind the others. For a short time, his eyes had to adjust to the darkness. When his vision returned, he saw his arms were dripping with blood. Then Yoseph heard a shuffling sound from the tunnel behind them.

"Yoseph, Yosa, Martha, and Zechariah is that who I see in the shadows?" His sister whispered as she covered little Enoch's mouth.

"Yes, my sister, and where is Hebron?" Fear at once seized Yoseph when he didn't see his brother-in-law.

"He has climbed halfway up the mountain to a hidden lookout point. From there he can see anybody departing off the main road and heading toward our camp. Don't fear, my brother, there's a path down the side of the mountain that ends a short distance from here. We have been doing this for four summers now and hide just when they travel off the main road."

He hated to see his family living with fear, but they all seemed well-prepared. It was apparent Alein Yosephe and Hebron had planned this drill in military fashion.

"Yoseph, if you hear the cooing of a dove, you will know that everything is safe. If the sound is of an owl, we must be still as the owl's prey, for danger is quite close at hand," Enygeus said.

Without warning, Enoch started crying. At once Martha snatched him and hurried back into the tunnel while humming a quiet song to stop his crying. The sole sounds he heard were their shallow breathing and the whimper of baby Enoch. The wait was unbearable until soft crunching footsteps approached. Then in the distance, Yoseph heard several indistinguishable sounds, but neither mimicked an owl nor a dove. They were human voices and many of them. *Oh, Yoseph,* he thought, *you have arrived so far with the cup of Yeshua. Pray this won't be the end.*

The voices grew closer, and his mind realized they knew where they were. Even in the cool cave, sweat broke out on Yoseph's forehead. As he reached for his satchel, he then touched their Savior's *Kodesh* Cup, fear at once vanished from his body. That's when he heard a voice that he hadn't heard in four summers.

"Yoseph, my friend, it's me, Nicodemus. Are you down there?"

He couldn't believe his ears and turned to Yosa and Enygeus for confirmation. They both broke out in smiles and tears rolled down their cheeks. They stood in the dank cave and started jumping up and down with happiness.

"Yes, my dear friend, it's me, Yoseph!" After which he shouted "yes" many times until little Enoch once again started crying.

"Yoseph, there are several people who are with me that would like to see you. Meet us at the front of the cave. We can then greet you in proper fashion."

Yoseph gave a positive reply and hurried through the dark caverns toward a faint torch-light. When they reached there, Yosa asked them to help her push the large boulder out of the way. Once completed, there was another round speck of light off in the distance. This was the entrance to the front of the cave. Yoseph's legs ran with excited anticipation to meet his old friend and his companions.

Upon reaching the front entrance, his eyes blinked several times trying to focus on the images before him. The bright morning sun made his eyes see eight purple-blotched forms. He put his hand up to his forehead for shade and, to his surprise, there stood Miriam of Magdala, Yohanan the writer, Thomas, Philip, Nicodemus, Shimon the Zealot, Philip's longtime friend Nathanael, and an unknown man embraced both by Martha and Miriam of Magdala. All the faces were staring at him with various expressions of disbelief, wonder, and tears of happiness on their faces.

"Now I know how the crowd felt when they saw me come out of my tomb those many summers ago." The unknown man said with a tear rolling down his cheek, which started everyone crying. Then each of Yoseph's friends gave him a hardy embrace and spoke into his ears, welcoming him back.

"Yoseph, let me introduce you to the man who just spoke." Nicodemus pointed at the stranger in their midst. "His name is Lazarus and is the one our *Maishiach* brought back from the dead. Do you remember the dream I spoke to you about four springs ago? Now you see him in person. Both of you were once dead and now you are among the living.

"Oh, it's so great to see you alive, Yoseph. I had many sleepless nights in prison wondering if you were alive. I tried to bribe the guards to tell me if you were alive or not, but under the penalty of death, they could not say. I surmised that Caiaphas had condemned you to a slow death. Yoseph, I am so sorry I gave up on you. My faith was weak. Please forgive me, my old friend."

"Nicodemus, you don't need my forgiveness. I too had doubts, but let's discuss how you escaped and why you no longer live at your home."

"I escaped about the time of *Yom Kippur* after we were put in prison. A new guard was careless in locking the door. When nightfall came, I made my escape. There were tunnels under the Temple Mount that I knew and nobody else was aware of. This helped conceal my escape. I started for my home when I saw that Caiaphas and his lackeys had confiscated it. There were locks everywhere and the windows were nailed shut. Later, I heard the greedy bastard sold my property to a man and his wife and he then kept the money. Being a fugitive forced me to seek shelter elsewhere. Then the figure of a dolphin popped into my mind. Remember, Yoseph, the bronze doorknocker on Yohanan Marcus's door was in the shape of a dolphin when we traveled to Yeshua's Last Supper."

"Yes, my friend."

"Right away I proceeded to his home, looking for the porpoise-shaped doorknocker, which at last helped me locate his house in the darkness of the night. I threw some small pebbles near his sleeping quarters where a light from an oil lamp illuminated one of the windows. I then heard the thumping of bare feet on the stone tiles. Yohanan Marcus, with a faint voice, asked me to identify myself. Even through the thick wooden door, I was able to hear him. After I had identified myself, the door eased opened, and I saw three shadowy figures. Right away, I recognized Yohanan Marcus, for he was holding his oil lamp close to his face. The other two had swords in their hands.

"When each of the two dark shadows spoke my name, I recognized the biggest one first. He was the Galilean fishing merchant called the Rock. The other smaller man was Philip. Yohanan Marcus encouraged me to come in and we embraced. As I entered the dark courtyard, I heard a wooden clunking sound coming from the door I had just entered. When I turned, Yohanan Marcus was placing a large square-cut wooden timber into two angle irons, one on each side of his door. It was apparent something was wrong.

"Yoseph, all of Yeshua's followers were in Yohanan Marcus's house. The entire upper floors lay covered with pallets of sleeping people. I felt some security that night at Yohanan Marcus's home, yet his wooden barred door worried me. The next day everyone was asking me if I heard from you or if I knew whether you were alive. My ignorance of any news didn't lift their spirits. We prayed for you every day that I stayed there. I told Yeshua's disciples that I had some money hidden and would use it to make some inquiries. The rest of the disciples, who weren't at the crucifixion, poured out their thanks to both of us, for helping to bury our Savior.

"They all knew what you had sacrificed, in both material and emotional loss. Even after the great *ruah* wind came, they used you as a *kodesh* example of someone willing to give total love at the risk of your life and that of your family. They knew you had defied the powers of both Rome and Yoseph ben Caiaphas. Theirs was an earthly power, but you, Yoseph, held the sword of *El Shaddai*."

"Nicodemus, I am so honored in what you said, my friend, but I am not ready to become an apostle of Yeshua's teaching. I have much to learn."

"My inquiries didn't turn up anything new, many people I spoke with were in fear of their lives and said nothing. This caused a problem for me and our band of new teachers. My possible whereabouts became profitable information to others, for Caiaphas always paid for information with gold talents. We thought it best if we should split up and travel in different directions."

"Who was the informant, Nicodemus?" Yoseph asked, worried they would have another dagger man in their midst.

"I don't know, Yoseph. Caiaphas's threats sealed many lips. All my usual information sources left *Yerushalayim* or disappeared. Many of us thought you were dead because of their silence. From *Yerushalayim*, I traveled to Bethany to stay with Lazarus. A few of our new teachers are staying in various houses in *Yerushalayim*, hidden from the clutches of Caiaphas. Yet there is a new fear that has risen. We're being shadowed by someone other than the new procurator's men or Caiaphas's spies."

"Could it be one of Herod's men?" I was thinking of that night four springs ago, when Hebron chased after one of Herod's lackeys spying on them.

"Yoseph, I can't say for sure it's one of his men. Hebron, Miriam of Magdala, have you felt the same shadowy person lurking near you?"

Both nodded in agreement with Nicodemus.

"Just yesterday," Yoseph said, "Hebron mentioned this presence to me. I was standing guard for this unknown person or persons from my hidden perch." He looked at each person gathered. "My friends, let's not lose sight with worry and fear. It's prudent to be cautious, but we have a new covenant to fulfill. Tonight, you will see the glory of our *Maishiach* and Savior. Yeshua left me with a new suit of armor that no mortal army can penetrate, and we now carry a new banner and sign to teach his *kodesh* words."

"What do you mean, Yoseph?" Philip asked.

"Philip, our *Maishiach* has given me a mission, remembrance symbols, and a ceremony for the forgiveness of our sins."

Miriam of Magdala stared at Yoseph's face and he felt her gaze searching in his mind. She hadn't aged the past four summers that he was in prison. Miriam's skin was a smooth light-almond color and there were no wrinkles evident around her large eyes. Her hair still held its red-streaked tint, without a trace of gray or white. The brass arm and ankle bracelets were still there, but not the fine robes she once wore. Her robe, tunic dress, and sandals showed fraying from repetitive use. Even though, with old clothes, she still appeared regal in bearing as she sat facing him. A slight smile formed on her face as if she knew great events were forthcoming.

"My friends and fellow teachers, tell me of further news from *Yerushalayim*," Yoseph searched their faces for pleasant news. Nicodemus was the first to speak.

"Yoseph, it isn't great news. My remaining sources say a man, who was a pupil of mine, is persecuting all followers of Yeshua. His name is Saul, and he has become a powerful member of the Sanhedrin. After he left my training, he became a pupil of Gamaliel. You remember him, Yoseph, he was a fellow member of the Sanhedrin."

"Yes, I saw him one night before I left *Yerushalayim* for Arimathea. Please continue."

"Young Saul's power grew soon after he completed his studies. He sought out all believers of our *Maishiach* and when they would speak at the

Temple, he incited the people to stone them to death. What I heard was many followers died under his persecution. One of the first was a man by the name of Stephanos. He was one of our first leaders and helped convert many people to the way.

"Is this not so, Philip?" Nicodemus directed his question to Philip sitting next to him.

"Yes, it's true. Stephanos used his house to feed the poor widows and orphans. The rest of his time, he would speak on the Temple grounds telling of our *Adonai*. Saul saw him as a threat to his rising power and started malicious rumors about Stephanos. One day, about two summers ago, he came to speak at the Temple. By now, the rumors of his blasphemy had increased to a sufficient level, causing the people to drag him from the Temple Mount. After surrounded by his accusers, he was stoned to death. I heard from others his dying words were, '*Abba*, forgive them of their sins.' He then died our first martyr. Many more followers of the way died after Stephanos. Yoseph, they won't kill all of us, for the words of our *Adonai* have formed roots too deep to dig out."

"Where is this Saul now? Could he be the one following you, my friends?" Yoseph searched the small crowd for somebody to speak.

Yohanan bar Zebedee, the writer, replied. "Master Yoseph, I spoke to Shimon bar Yona three nights ago. He and Ya'akov, our *Maishiach's* brother, told me Saul had gone to Damascus to persecute more followers of the way. There are rumors that something happened to him on the road to Damascus."

"And what would these rumors be, my young writer friend?" Yoseph asked, wanting to dispel the paranoia.

"He saw a great light, heard voices, and then the light disappeared. This was just a rumor I heard in the bazaars."

"Maybe he's a prisoner and held for ransom. It's obvious he has many enemies."

Yoseph remained silent for a moment.

"More important tell me about my niece, Miriam. Has she been well these past four summers?"

Yoseph thought of the misery she saw at the cross, his imprisonment, and her wondering what became of him. She had nobody to care for her, but young Yohanan now sitting in front of him. He still had the wrinkle-free young face of a boy, yet now a dark beard covered his cheeks.

"She's fine, however, we move quite often and stay in many houses of our followers. They all want to know about Yeshua's past and what he taught. She has asked about you many times and prayed she would see you once more. Miriam still speaks about what risks you encountered for her son. She will be thrilled to know you're still alive, Master Yoseph."

"Yohanan, please don't call me 'master' any-more. I am a master of nothing and now a servant of our *Adonai*. We are teachers for our *Maishiach*. None of us possesses material wealth or position and I am just a fisher of men and women, who has been adjured by *Adonai* to start a new kind of synagogue with hallowed gifts to convert and lead others."

Yohanan cast his eyes downward.

"I hope you won't be offended of what I just said, it wasn't meant to chide you, Yohanan. Forgive me if it did."

"No, Yoseph, it didn't offend me. My per-sonal emotions have toughened these past four summers. Though Shimon bar Yona and Ya'akov bickered all the time about who will be the leader of the way, this strained my patience. They won't teach to just anybody other than the descendants of the patriarch, Ya'akov!" Yohanan's face flushed with emotion. "I know if Yeshua were alive right now, he would be saddened and disappointed with them!"

Yohanan's voice rose with an intensity, causing all of them to focus on his rising anger. He paced back-and-forth until the blood drained from his face and then spoke once more.

"Yoseph, I am glad you are alive and hope you can help us teach the *kodesh* words our Savior has taught us. I haven't spent much time writing Yeshua's final words he expressed to us. Four summers have gone by with moving, teaching, trying to evade the high priest, and confronting the fears of new followers. How has your writing been? Were you able to do any writing in prison or after you were released?"

"Yes, indeed, it helped me keep my sanity while I languished in that filthy prison of Caiaphas's. That was one of the many miracles I received in prison. My lamplight, writing parchments, ink, and quills never ceased. Also, I have to thank Nicodemus for helping me after I was released." Yoseph glanced over and saw a furrowed brow on his old friend's face.

"But, Yoseph, I thought you were dead. How could I have helped you?" Nicodemus asked.

"Do you remember your scroll room you kept at the Temple Mount?"

"Yes, of course, I do."

"I hid in there, after my release, having nowhere to call home. If I didn't leave *Yerushalayim* right away, they would rearrest me. It was a temporary base for me while I contacted Eli and his sons. May *El Shaddai* bless his family and descendants for all eternity. I finished my writing there and hid the parchments behind some loose ashlar stones. I am revealing this to all of you, for my name has been stricken from all records and I am banished forever from *Yerushalayim*. You're my witnesses to where these *kodesh* words are hidden."

"What do you want us to do with the *kodesh* words and life of our *Maishiach*?" Nicodemus asked.

"Nothing!" Yoseph retorted to all sitting there. "A time will come when believers and nonbelievers will see and read my parchments. However, that time of revelation hasn't come to me. The *kodesh* book is secure and fear not, my friends, the few who know of its whereabouts are Eli and his sons and now all you. Besides, I made a copy, which I brought with me. I intend to do a second *kodesh* story, telling about leaving *Yerushalayim* and the start of my ministry."

"Yoseph, I would like to help you with telling the *logos* of our *Maishiach*," Philip stated. "I can do the blessing of the *kodesh* waters and tell the faithful how it came about. Zechariah can assist me, just as his *abba* showed me many springs ago. Now we have something to give, in telling of the way. I see all of us as a powerful body of teachers. Do you agree, Miriam?" Philip deferred to Miriam for approval.

"First," Miriam responded, "I would like to say my heart is filled with joy sitting here with all of you, which causes my mind to hearken back to that time five springs ago. We traveled to many towns and villages with our *Adonai* and Savior, where he spoke to thousands of people. I know the days ahead will be even greater. Philip, I think it's an excellent idea that Yeshua would approve. What do you say, Yohanan? Can we count on you with our *kodesh* mission?"

"Yes, Miriam. I too sense this new zeal. We have spoken of Yeshua's remembrance and preached his teachings, but this will be an organized effort centered on Yeshua's last meal with us."

Yoseph's sister, Enygeus, began to protest. "But Yohanan, Yosa, and I have no experience in preaching. Besides, we are women. Who will listen to us?"

"Our *Adonai* will show us the way. Have you spoken to other women, and haven't they listened to you? Yeshua will give you the authority over men, women, and children when you speak his words. Tell the stories you know about our *Adonai*.

"The people of Abraham and the Gentiles' thirst for new hope and salvation. Once you start speaking about his life, you will be amazed at how the people will react. All of us here have experienced these holy events. Am I right, my weary travelers?"

Everyone nodded in agreement with Yohanan.

"Enygeus, does this help you with your doubt?" Yohanan's eyes searched the faces of the women there. Yoseph's sister nodded her head in confirmation, a smile on her face.

"It was wrong for me to doubt, please forgive me. Now, it's late and I must find something for us to eat. Pardon me, while I leave to prepare the food."

"No, sister, please sit still," implored Yoseph. "We'll partake of the feast Yeshua has given us."

"Let's do as Philip has suggested. But first we must each be cleansed by the Spirit before we drink from the cup of our *Adonai*. This is our new beginning for us to celebrate Yeshua's remembrance and tell what he taught us. Now, let's wash ourselves in the kind of water that the Baptizer gave Yeshua. Follow me down to the riverbank."

Philip, along with the rest of those present followed Yoseph to a small path that circled an outcropping of rocks. The sun was low on the horizon as their band of Yeshua's followers ambled down to the riverbank. Philip dropped his robe and tunic on the ground and entered the water first. Young Zechariah joined him, taking his place in the running water next to Philip. When Philip raised his arms overhead, Zechariah followed his lead. Then Philip began to speak.

"We have traveled with the lamb of *Eloheinu,* who removes the sins of the world. We are one voice crying out in the wilderness; make straight the way of our *Adonai.* We come here baptizing with water for all to see the *kodesh* dove of *El Shaddai.* My beloved friend, Yohanan the writer, spoke to me five springs ago of this event. He now stands here as a witness to this *kodesh* ceremony. Yohanan, please join me in the *kodesh* embrace of these waters."

Yohanan removed his robe and tunic, then joined Philip and Zechariah midstream. He stood there with his naked back exposed to the late evening sun. The remaining followers of Yeshua soon stood by the riverbank, allowing Philip and Zechariah to pour water over them. A gentle wind came from the side of the mountain and blew upon their faces as though it was an affirmation of their actions.

When it was Yoseph's turn for the *kodesh* ceremony blessing, the spirit of his *Adonai* filled him with gladness. The sun's late rays caught the water as it flowed over his head and down his body. As the water sparkled and shimmered on his skin, he felt a profound sense of calm and joy. Philip and Yohanan were speaking to Yoseph, but not all his senses reacted as he allowed the calm to sluice through his body. The sound of the gushing waters disappeared when an unexpected howling wind blew forth and replaced it.

He observed Hebron as the water cleansed him, seeing tears roll down his face as Philip and Yohanan blessed him.

"He who came to remove the sins of the world, blessed be he forever and bless this new teacher. Let him spread *Adonai's* words like the waters spread over the face of the earth. Glory be to his reign."

This was the same blessing conferred on the others, with Miriam of Magdala being the last one baptized. With her head bowed, she moved out of the river and the wind blew even stronger. Then a loud ear-piercing blast of wind came from the direction of the mountaintop that seemed to say: "*You have done well, my children. My son is quite pleased. Now leave and start a new house in which I can dwell.*"

CHAPTER XIX

At once, they fell, prostrate with trembling arms and legs of fear upon the muddy riverbank. The mountaintop glowed with streaks of fire and smoke that issued forth from its summit, which was accompanied by a hot blast of air. Their gaping mouths expressed both fear and wonderment. It appeared *El Shaddai* had overseen the actions of their humble band and given his approval. The streaks of fire lingered for a moment before it disappeared as though nothing miraculous had occurred.

Yoseph shook with disbelief, but now their teaching endeavors were blessed by *El Shaddai* as the others lay silent but also shaking with incredulity. They were now more than just a nomadic band of strangers.

"My friend, Yoseph, what has happened here?"

Nicodemus asked. "Have my eyes deceived me?"

Miriam of Magdala spoke second. "Yes, Yoseph, tell me what I just heard and saw is true!"

"It must be, Miriam, since I too experienced it. The tongue of *El Shaddai* just gave his approval." Miriam wiped at the mud on her face as Yoseph continued. "We have been given a heavy burden to carry, yet we will bring terrific news to all those who thirst for our Savior's knowledge."

Miriam moved toward him, grabbed his hand, and began to laugh. The mud from the riverbank had covered each of them in reddish-tinged brown color. He surveyed himself and then the others around him, and afterward, he joined in the laughter. They were now blessed to teach the words of their *Maishiach* but appeared as a ragtag group of outcasts standing there holding hands with mud covering them from head to toe.

"Come, join me, and let's discuss what just happened," Yoseph announced. The men were still lying on the muddy river with their legs in the water.

"Yoseph, I am afraid to open . . . my eyes," Philip said. "What if the fire and smoke returns? We may be struck down."

Yoseph saw gaped mouths of fear and awe from the rest of their small band of followers.

"No, my friend, you must not have heard what the fiery wind said. Come and listen to Miriam and me."

All three trudged up the riverbank, still fearful. Philip with caution, gazed at the last rays of the evening sun.

"Yoseph, what was that? I am afraid and confused about what I just experienced. Can you explain?"

"It was the *Shekhinah*," Miriam stated, indignant that Philip had directed his question to Yoseph, a male, instead of her. "It was the presence and words of *El Shaddai* giving his approval to our endeavor. Philip, you let your fear overcome you and didn't listen to the fiery wind. Fear not what is unpleasant to your ears. His *kodesh* tongue blessed you on evoking his son's name. Now let's wash the mud from our skin," Miriam admonished Philip.

Yoseph knew that Miriam lacked credibility with the previous twelve disciples, and they didn't believe her or what any woman said. In addition, they were jealous of her closeness with Yeshua. At one time, Miriam was a woman of business and independence, and he admired that. Now they were different with new lives to live.

Their group found a dry place on the riverbank. Enygeus grabbed her cotton cloth shawl and used it to wipe the mud from their faces, arms, and legs. Afterward, they returned to their campsite and put on clean robes. Philip continued discussing the miraculous event with Hebron and Enygeus.

"I now consider I am chosen and confident to preach to the people of Moshe and the Gentiles.

Like you, Miriam, I won't be intimidated by men and now will gain their respect with the testimony that *El Shaddai* his given us," Enygeus stated. "What about you, Martha?" Enygeus asked.

"I too agree, and I will have my sister to remind me to testify in what I have just seen and heard. Yeshua's words and truths will be powerful working tools for the masses to join us. Lazarus, my brother, what do you think about what we just saw?"

"Yeshua brought me back from death, and with all my heart, mind, and soul, this is a major sign to continue our *Maishiach's* memory."

The sun slid behind the mountain and gray shadows started to create hidden spots in the rocks. Faint stars started appearing. Hebron placed lit pitch torches around the campsite and the cave opening. It was now time to celebrate the supper of their *Maishiach*.

"I would like Yohanan, Miriam, Martha, Yosa, and Zechariah to assist me for the supper of our *Adonai*," Yoseph said. "Moreover, I would like the rest of my fellow rabbis to be seated at our humble table outside the cave. I'm sure *El Shaddai* won't object if our table is made of soil."

Right away, the small group of members assembled.

"Now!" Yoseph exclaimed. "I ask you to listen with both ears. I hope each of you will follow my instructions with reverence for our *Adonai's* last night on earth among us. Yohanan, grab the brass oil lamp and make us sons and daughters of the light. For this night, brothers and sisters, you will lead the way. Any other place or night, we will help each in this procession.

"Miriam, please hold the *Kodesh* Cup and vials close to your heart. However, don't stare into the cup. Martha, hold the paten that held the Passover bread from which Yeshua partook. Yosa, I am giving you this spear. Carry it with reverence, for it's the spear that pierced the heart of our beloved Yeshua. Zechariah, I am giving you the sword that struck your *abba*, to honor his remembrance. None of Yeshua's followers should ever use this sword to harm others.

"I will follow carrying the *kodesh* words that I have written about our *Maishiach*. With care, place all these hallow gifts on the flat rocks that are elevated in front of the unlit firepit. Then find a spot to partake of the wondrous events that will ensue. I will do the rest from there."

Yoseph removed the brass lamp from his satchel and gave it to Yohanan, who was startled when the lamp lit itself. Next was the cup and the vials. Miriam's long fingers reached out to grab these glowing objects as they came out of the leather satchel. Martha approached Yoseph, and he gave her the shimmering silver paten. With reluctance, Yosa moved forward as Yoseph handed her the broken wooden staff of the spear of Longinus. Last to come forward was young Zechariah.

"Young man, honor this sword. Your *abba* died for the righteous ideals that all men and women should uphold. When you are of age, guard it well."

Yoseph's hand reached into the satchel for the last time and retrieved the copies of the *kodesh* parchments. His fingertips moved across the crinkled sheets of parchment and the pages were warm to touch from the cup and the vials that had been resting on them.

"Let's now travel out into the darkness of night, my fellow teachers, and partake of the feast of our *Adonai*," Yoseph proclaimed as Yohanan led the way in front of them.

Halfway out of the cave, Yoseph heard gasping breaths. Zechariah turned the sword blade from side to side, staring at the words appearing on both sides of the blade. In front of him, Yosa was crying, and Miriam had her free hand over her eyes from the intense light of the cup. It was a slow solemn procession as they moved out of the cave entrance. Their squinting eyes made it difficult to focus on the glaring rays of light emanating from the center of the *Kodesh* Cup. Each beam of light reached up into the starry skies. Everyone, who first stared, now covered their faces as the light's brightness turned a brilliant white color. Still, they marched around in a procession to place the *kodesh* objects on the stones.

As Yoseph peered at the spear, red drops of blood ran down its tip and then disappeared before reaching the ground. The miracles of *Adonai* were ever-flowing and never-ceasing as Yoseph stood in his place at the center of their group and placed the parchments behind the glowing cup and vials.

When he was able to focus his eyes, he could see the etched fish pattern on the chalice's rim. He reached out, grasped the hot bowl of the cup, and lifted it overhead. The night became quiet as a tomb. Then a whisper of wind issued forth from the west. While they gazed at the cup, its rays changed to a fiery red.

"*Sh'ma O Yisrael Adonai Eloheinu Adonai Echod. Barukh Shem k'vod malkhute l'olam va-ed. V-ahauta et Adonai b-chol l'vavcha u-v-chol haf'sh'cha v-v-chol m'odecha.*" Yoseph shortened the *Shema* once more and repeated what their *Maishiach* told them at the Last Supper.

"All remember what our rabbi said that night of his betrayal: 'Where two or three are gathered in the remembrance of Me, I will be there in your presence.' My friends and fellow teachers, remember what else he said the night before his crucifixion: 'Love your neighbors as you love yourselves. There is no greater love than to lay down one's life for one's fellowman or woman. Always search for the goodness in humankind and love *El Shaddai* with all your heart and being.'"

Yoseph heard murmurs of agreement all around him as he spoke their Savior's holy words. Once again, there was a cool presence touching

Yoseph's face and abundant joy overcame him as he felt his presence. Voices surrounding Yoseph cried, "Yeshua is with us!" Sensing Yeshua's consent, he placed the cup on the flat rock in front of him. Raising the paten overhead, he spoke the blessing for the bread.

"*Barukh atah Adonai, Eloheinu Melekh ha-otam, ha-motzi lechem min ha-arctz.*"

When he lowered the paten, it was stacked with bread for each of them to partake. Lowering it to the flat rock next to the cup, the sounds of amazement greeted the unexpected gift. Even little Enoch gave out a tiny response of "Ah," as his baby eyes glistened in the glowing rays. The cup beckoned Yoseph to clutch it. Yoseph's fingertips touched each fish design pattern on the rim as he held the bowl of the cup and raised it upward. He gazed into the starry sky and saw the rays spreading across the firmaments. His confidence surged as he continued speaking the words taught them by their *Adonai*.

"*Barukh atah Adonai, Eloheinu Melekh ha-olam, borel p'ny ha-gafen.*"

As he lowered the cup, they saw it fill with ruby red wine, and once again their souls became nourished. As Yoseph placed the cup on the rock, the wind whispered in their ears. Yeshua's voice said, "This is my body that is given to you. Do this in remembrance of me." As the sound increased, they heard, "This cup that is poured for you is the *brit chadashah* in my blood that forgives the sins of the world. I AM the ladder whereby you reach the Kingdom of Heaven. Tread with caution upon its ten rungs. Say these *kodesh* words each time you have my supper. My body is now your new temple. Listen to Yoseph, for he is the fisher king for the souls of men and women. It does not matter in my *abba's* kingdom whether you are sons and daughters of Abraham or Gentiles. Yoseph is now the architect of the New *Yerushalayim*. Assist him as he teaches others as I have taught you. *Shalom aleichem.*"

"My master, please don't leave us," cried out Yohanan.

"Yeshua, my rabboni, please stay with us tonight," lamented Miriam.

"I won't doubt you anymore, Master. My faith doesn't require my eyes to see!" shouted Thomas Didymus.

"This is Philip, Master; tell us where we must travel to preach."

Lazarus said nothing but appeared stunned and then bowed his head in reverence.

"My fellow teachers, he won't come back tonight," Yoseph stated to the little band of apostles. Many expressions were passing across their faces—bewilderment, sadness, happiness, longing, and amazement.

Miriam held back her tears but began to speak with a choked voice. "Yoseph ... what does ... this all mean?" Her eyes searched for an answer. "Can

I speak to my rabboni again tomorrow?"

"Yoseph, whom does this cup serve? Why is Yeshua speaking to us at this special supper?" Philip asked.

"My friends and fellow teachers, he is reminding us of each time we sup that he sacrificed his body and blood for our sins. We now serve him and all humankind. Miriam, I can't say he will speak to us each time we have supper, but he will always be in our presence. We must be servants first before we can teach his *kodesh* words. By this vessel, we are sifted and if worthy we are elected to teach his *kodesh* words, for the cup doesn't allow any sinners in its presence."

Yoseph glanced to his right and saw Thomas's large eyes gazing at the still-white *kabod* surrounding the *kodesh* chalice. He was in deep thought, but then his head turned up and he began to speak.

"Yoseph, now I know what Yeshua meant when he said, 'Let not him who seeks cease until he finds, and when he finds he shall be astonished.' Today I have been astonished more than ten lifetimes of existence. We agree that *Adonai*, Yeshua, has given us instructions to teach the ceremony for the forgiveness of sins."

Yoseph saw total agreement on their faces and heard a low murmur of "yes" coming from their mouths.

"Let me continue with our *Adonai* remembrance supper, my friends. He has instructed me in the parts that we must perform. You will now see and know all that will be revealed."

Yoseph lifted the cup from the flat rock and stood, sniffing the sweet smell of roses that hung over the whole camp as he held the cup to his chest. Each of his friends also remarked at the smell that penetrated their nostrils.

"Miriam, would you please stand and hold the paten and follow me?"

"Yes, Yoseph, it would be an honor to serve and remember my rabboni."

She stood close to him holding the paten stacked with many slices of bread. To his surprise, two wondrous events occurred. The *Kodesh* Cup's *kabod* grew with a lightening-colored whiteness that surrounded the entire chalice. And then, as he started to serve supper to his fellow teachers, he heard a quiet flapping sound. Over the top of his head flew a glowing white dove. It hovered just above the cup and made a gentle cooing sound to let all know of its presence. All eyes were transfixed on the dove's appearance. Then without warning, it soared back into the darkness of the night sky and disappeared.

Yoseph and Miriam were the first to partake of Yeshua's feast. Her fingertips held him a slice of bread to eat. Its buttery taste was slight but left a memorable honey flavor on his tongue. He grabbed the cup of wine in his hands, raised it, and then swallowed its smooth liquid, which slid down his throat. After finishing his cup, he reciprocated with Miriam, after which she favored him with a tender smile. They then served the *kodesh* supper to the others with a more renewed sense of reverence.

"The cup of salvation, the body of the *Maishiach*," Yoseph said to Philip, who stepped forth first. He tore off a large thin piece of the crusty flatbread and then ate it. Yoseph then gave him the radiant chalice, from which he sipped a drink of the ruby-colored liquid. He said a prayer that Yeshua had taught him: "Our *Abba*, who is in heaven, hallowed be his name . . ."

Yoseph realized that Yeshua had reminded him of these *kodesh* words the night of his betrayal. After the Last Supper, he hadn't listened to what prayer he said in Yoseph's ear. Miriam ambled to each member of their band and placed the paten on his or her lap for them to partake of the bread. Even young Zechariah was included in the *kodesh* ceremony. Yoseph reasoned he was mature enough because he'd experienced more things in his short lifetime than many older men had experienced. He felt assured he knew the significance and honor of this *kodesh* ceremony bestowed upon him.

The *Kodesh* Cup as usual never ran out of its shimmering liquid. The bread always replenished itself until each member had eaten and drunk of *Adonai's* goodness. Thereafter, they recited Yeshua's prayer, which he had taught them, into the night air.

It was a wondrous sight to see and hear as Yosa's face mimicked the others in reverence of being included in the feast. He and Miriam placed the *kodesh* paten and cup on the flat rocks, after which Yoseph moved to the center of the camp and said the *birkat ha-mazon*. The old blessing for their unlimited food was a special ceremony for all their members. Would their old blessing change henceforth? How would their old religion evolve?

"May the name of *Adonai* be blessed from this time forth and forevermore," they said in unison. Then Yoseph said, "With the permission to all present, let's bless him, *Eloheinu*, whose food we have eaten." Then again in unison, "Blessed be he, *Eloheinu*, whose food we have eaten and in whose decency we live." At last, he ended grace with, "Blessed be he, *Eloheinu*, whose food we have eaten and in whose goodness we live. Blessed be he and blessed be his name."

Yoseph knew there would be many questions after he recited the *Hashkiveinu*. It was late as Yoseph placed with care all the *kodesh* symbols back into his large satchel. The chalice had a slight glow around its rim, but the liquid had vanished. The same with the paten. Its silver surface was devoid of any bread. He couldn't see even a remaining crumb on the plate. The spear tip was clean of any blood drops, and the sword didn't reveal its words any longer.

The lone thing still glowing was the oil lamp sitting by itself on the flat rock near Yohanan. Hebron grabbed some dried palm branches and cedar logs and started a fire. When the flames were sufficient to see, the lamp flame disappeared from the tip opening. Yohanan waited for it to cool, and he handed Yoseph the lamp to put away.

Yohanan glanced up at Yoseph. "Yoseph, does this lamp represent the light that always shines in the darkness, and Yeshua is that true light, which has conquered darkness for all those who believe?" He asked the question as if he knew the answer but was seeking affirmation.

"Yes, my young man, you're correct. Each of these *kodesh* objects are to demonstrate that Yeshua was the sacrificial lamb who will remove the sins of the world. It's our calling to teach of these miracles of his life. As Thomas Didymus has learned, to believe what you have seen here tonight, first you must believe beforehand. To sense from the heart and the mind's eye can conquer all adversity. Loving wisdom is born out of both knowledge and experience. In the days ahead, we'll use both."

Standing close to the crackling campfire, young Zechariah asked him a question. "Master Yoseph, what did the words say that appeared on the *kodesh* sword?"

"Zechariah, the words said, 'Beware to he who uses this sword in evil, for he would be torn asunder and so will this blade.'"

"What were those many polished stones on its hilt?" Zechariah asked, as his inquisitive eyes searched for answers.

"My son, it represents the twelve tribes of Ya'akov. Each stone is a specific tribe. Herod Antipas, who murdered your *abba,* thought he was king of the remaining tribes of Ya'akov. You and I now know who's the true King and *Maishiach* that rules over the earth."

Zechariah's glowing eyes widened as he searched for the meaning of what he had said. Then Yoseph remembered what Yeshua had said to him about the Baptizer's son. That he would one day start a long line of kings in the Celtic Isle.

At this moment, how could this be? Yoseph was penniless and the Isle of Britannia seemed as far away as the moon from Arimathea. This perplexed him for a short while, yet he laughed at himself for such thoughts. Yeshua always provided a way for the fulfillment of his prophecy, and he shouldn't worry.

Next, Lazarus asked him a question about their new ceremony. "Yoseph, may I participate tomorrow evening at the next *kodesh* supper?"

"Yes, you may, and each night we will change the one in charge of the processional. All will serve the hallows of the cup of our *Maishiach.* Each of us will be servants for the people who believe in Yeshua and his words. That's who we will serve until we are no more of this earth."

Yoseph paused, then said, "But now, Yohanan, tell me more about my niece. Is she well? Who is caring for her?"

"Yoseph, she is staying with her sister at Emmaus.

Her health is well, yet I wonder about her happiness. So much tragedy has befallen her in the last four springs. She doesn't seem sad, but contemplative. However, when she speaks your name, we see a smile on her face. She and Miriam of Magdala have spoken often of seeing you again. I think her faith believed you were still alive, and this helped her cope with Yeshua's horrible death. She foresaw Yeshua's resurrection, but not knowing at what cost. The next time Miriam of Magdala and I travel to Emmaus, we will tell her the valuable news that you are alive. After which we'll bring her to visit you at your cave. It will be by the next full moon."

"Yes, that would be excellent. We'll have many things to discuss."

It was late, and the rest of their little band of new teachers was abandoning him for sleep. Yoseph strolled out onto the vast desert plain before him, then stopped and gazed at the stars. His body and mind were still in the grasp of the *Kodesh* Cup of Yeshua. A cool breeze whipped across the plain, making a low buffeting sound. His eyes stared into the ink-black night sky while thinking where Yeshua's cup and teachings would carry them. What places and destinations would they travel?

"Brother," at once his sister's voice pulled him from his wandering thoughts.

"Yoseph, I see you couldn't sleep either. It's hard for me to contemplate what you have said and what I've seen in the past two evenings. I hope with time I will understand." She looked out over the plains, then back to him. "Where do you think we'll travel to speak our *Adonai's* words?"

"I wish I could tell you, but right now there are many before us who long for his words. It's valuable that some of us have written what Yeshua said and what we know of his life. The world ahead will be our edifice to grow in teaching these written words spoken by our *Maishiach*." He saw the concern in Enygeus's eyes as a crooked smile formed around her mouth. "Yoseph, let's try to gain some sleep, for Alein Yosephe will arrive early tomorrow."

They strolled back to the torchlit entrance while clasping each other's arms. As they entered, there was a slight whistling sound from family and friends fast asleep. Yoseph lay down on a feather-filled pallet and fell fast asleep, reassured knowing his brother-in-law was on sentry duty.

The next morning Yoseph awoke, not from the new light of day, but rather by the morning smell of burning wood from their campfire. A smoky blue haze drifted into the cave entrance as they started their morning ablutions. Upon leaving the entrance of the cave, he saw Hebron adding more dry palm branches with flames issuing forth with *popping* and *cracking* sounds.

"Excellent morning, Yoseph. I trust you slept well."

"Yes, indeed, knowing all my friends were

with me," Yoseph said while realizing he sounded like an *amma* hen *clucking* in glee about her baby chicks. The lone exception was one stray chick, his son. He traveled some distance from the cave entrance and found a large rock that would hide him as he sought to relieve himself. As he finished, he spied a small dust cloud from a lone rider.

To see a better view, Yoseph climbed to a higher advantage point on the side of the mountain. There, in the distance, was a man riding a donkey. He wore a cloth protecting his face from dust, which also obscured it. Was it Alein Yosephe or somebody else? From his advantage point, he couldn't tell, but he scurried down the rocks and announced their unknown visitor.

"Yoseph, did you see the face of the rider?" Miriam of Magdala asked. "Could it be your son?"

"I don't know, his face was covered with a cloth to protect the stranger from dust."

The rest of the women became agitated from his alarm and little Enoch started crying and clinging to Yoseph's sister. To his surprise, young Zechariah rushed into the cave and came out with three rusty swords. They were the same swords they carried with them on that fateful night they had their Last Supper with his nephew.

"Yoseph, I don't think we have anything to fear, it's probably Alein Yosephe; besides there are eight men here against one unknown rider," Hebron said. Yet, he grabbed one of the rusty swords and ran out to meet the rider, still the cautious Hebron. Yoseph too joined him, followed by Zechariah, while the rest of the men raced behind the Baptizer's son.

"*Abba*, you are alive. Praise be to *El Shaddai*, I feared you were dead. Please tell me you are not a ghost." Alein Yosephe raced toward Yoseph while uncovering his face.

"No, I am not a ghost and praise be to *El Shaddai* too it's you, Alein Yosephe. I thought you were a stranger and sent here to do us harm. We weren't expecting you until the fourth watch in the afternoon." At once, Yoseph's eyes filled with tears of joy that caused him to see Alein Yosephe in a watery blur. They hugged each other as their bodies shook with happiness.

It was after their embrace that Yoseph was able to focus on his son's features and could see Alein had lost a considerable amount of weight. His face was drawn, and his beard was long and uncut, along with streaks of white hair, as were his eyebrows. He was thirty-seven summers in age but appeared much older. Yet, Alein's high-cheeked smile and enthusiasm reminded Yoseph of his wife during her short lifetime.

"*Abba*, we thought you were dead, yet Miriam of Magdala and my cousin Miriam were both certain that Yeshua had protected you. *Abba*, you have shaved your beard and it makes you appear younger, while it appears I've grown your beard.

Now let's return to the camp and sit down so you can tell me all about what happened while you were imprisoned," Alein said with a toothy grin.

They both strolled to the camp with their arms around each other's shoulders. Hebron, Yosa, and Enygeus rushed to embrace Alein, grateful for his safe return. Both sat on two flat rocks while each gave a summary of what had happened over the last four summers. They spoke until the next watch of the day, sharing a meager midday meal.

"So, *abba*, we are now teachers of Yeshua's way. Is this true?"

"Yes, it is, my son."

Yoseph saw a wrinkled brow of concern on Alein's face. His son had grown up as a merchant in his childhood and would follow Yoseph each business day that he would leave home. He never became bored counting merchandise or totaling figures. People liked him because of his gregarious personality. Yet, Alein Yosephe seriously practiced his business dealings with vigor but had a fine sense of humor when speaking to other merchants and clients.

"*Abba*, I am anxious to be baptized by Philip and Zechariah. Can it be done today?"

"No, not today," Yoseph replied. "I will speak to them about doing it tomorrow. Now let's reacquaint ourselves and then enjoy the goodness of the *Kodesh* Cup."

"What's this *Kodesh* Cup you speak about?" his son asked.

"It holds the wine, which is the blood of Yeshua, and the bread we serve is his body."

"*Abba*, please explain, for I am confused."

"We now honor the blood and body of our great teacher and *Maishiach*. It's now drunk and eaten for our everlasting salvation. *El Shaddai* transforms it to wine and bread so we can absorb his divine truth into our bodies. The sacred ceremony is the bridge whereby each of us becomes one with his spirit. *El Shaddai*, the Son of Man, and the *kodesh ruah* are all in one with his presence at the *kodesh* supper. My son, when you drink from Yeshua's sacred cup, you will become like him and hidden things won't be a secret to you. He shall give you what no eye has seen, what no ear has heard, what no hand has touched, and what has never occurred to the human mind.

"You'll be the teacher to the ones who seek. They will not stop seeking until they find they will become troubled. They'll then be astonished and will rule over all things with their goodness. Just in the last several days, our little band has experienced *kodesh* voices, signs, and miracles because of their baptisms and the hallowed supper. These will prepare you to teach Yeshua's way."

His son sat there pondering what Yoseph had just said while rubbing his overgrown beard.

"*Abba*, it appears I have a new *brit chadashah* with my *kodesh* cousin. It seems I am no longer a merchant of olive oil or wine, but a merchant of *kodesh* words and a seller of the wine and bread created by Yeshua."

"That's a wonderful way to interpret it, my son. As one door closes, another opens for a person's destiny to travel through. Now, Alein, tell me about your trip to *Yoppa*. Did the rabbi give you any food?"

"No, he just gave me an ass to sell or to use, whichever is more important. The wheat crop in Egypt was sparse this past year, and the Roman army confiscated the rest."

"What about the boats we purchased for our escape four springs ago, did you sell them?"

"Yes, *abba*, I did, and it was all used for protection money to keep our whereabouts unknown. The remaining amount was used to help obtain your release from prison right after that bastard Caiaphas confiscated all our property, silver, and gold."

"Alein, we must forget the past and not bear any grudges or act on revenge."

"But, *abba*, he destroyed our family. We have no food. Think about young Enoch and Zechariah, for they need food to grow. Also, the protection money has run out and soon everybody will know where we live."

"I know it's hard not to seek revenge, yet you'll see tonight the new army that will protect and sustain us in its bosom. Our family won't be destroyed, and none of the children will be denied food."

The evening sun slid behind the mountains creating a red-hued sky. Close to the end of the evening's first watch, Yoseph gathered the ones for the cup procession, and they again marched from the cave opening. The ceremony continued the same as the previous night. Alein Yosephe ate his bread, then drank his wine from the sacred *Seder* chalice. The whispering voice of his cousin returned, now their *Maishiach*. The rays of light from the cup and Yeshua's voice caused his widened eyes to fill with tears. He swallowed a long draft from the never-ending liquid and at once fell to his knees asking mercy for his past sins.

The voice of Yeshua told him to rise and preach to the Gentiles and tell of this ceremony. Alein gave an affirmative reply and Yoseph could see that Alein's thirst and hunger had vanished this night. The rest of their band of teachers partook of their holy supper, which strengthened all who ate and drank from the *Kodesh* Cup and paten. At once, each person displayed a pink glow on his or her face as the ceremony ended. Each sat down with high-cheeked smiles of wonder as they discussed with themselves what they would say to the Gentiles.

"Should we convert the Gentiles to the faith of our forefathers and ask all males to be circumcised?" Philip asked. "Is this what our *Maishiach* would have wanted?" This caused a murmur of discussion as they considered Philip's query.

Miriam of Magdala gazed through the camp-fire and then asked Yoseph, "What do you think about Yeshua's directive?"

"Did not our *Maishiach* and *Adonai* preach to the Gentiles when he was of this earth? Philip, you once spoke of a Gentile woman at Sychar who lived in Samaria. Our *Adonai* came to Ya'akov's well and asked for a drink of water. He told the woman, 'Believe in me, the hour is coming when you will worship the *Abba* neither on your mountaintop nor in the Temple of *Yerushalayim*,' did he not? You told me many Samaritans became believers that day."

"Yes, that's true, Yoseph."

"Miriam, you told me about a time in the region of Tyre when our *Adonai* traveled to a Gentile's house where a Syrophoenician woman stayed. She had a child possessed by an evil spirit and our *Maishiach* cleansed this child of the demon because she believed in him. Also, don't forget what the prophet Isaiah wrote, 'For my house shall be called a house of prayer for all peoples.'

"All of you can give many testimonies that our *Adonai* preached and visited the Gentiles. They all believed in him, and he asked nothing from them in return. Have not the scribes, Pharisees, and lawyers burdened us with enough rules? Haven't they restricted us in what food we can eat, how far we can travel, and when we can help the sick?

Didn't my nephew speak of the *brit chadashah* and how we should treat all our neighbors? For these questions, you know the answers, my fellow teachers. It will be a new dawn for all humans who will hear our words. Now let us retire and then tomorrow further our discussion."

"*Abba*, may I speak to you alone?" Alein Yosephe asked, before rising from the campfire.

"Yes, let's climb up the side of the mountain. It's my turn for the night watch."

After a rocky climb, they both sat down at the summit to catch their breath.

"*Abba*, I am thrilled you're alive. Today has been the happiest day of my life. The two empty holes in my heart you have now filled. You are alive and the *Kodesh* Cup has slaked my spiritual thirst. Yet I am alarmed about two things. The first is the baptism of being born again tomorrow and, second, the fear of discovery after I left *Yoppa*. I know in months past we've been spied on, yet I sense an even great danger than before."

"My son, fear can be useful or a bad thing. The fear of *El Shaddai's* judgment is the beginning of wisdom. You being reborn in the *kodesh* waters is spiritual wisdom that *El Shaddai* bestows on you. Rest with ease that tomorrow *El Shaddai* will place his *chesed* upon you. Fear can eat at your insides, just as maggots eat upon dead flesh. You'll find safety in the chalice from fear and see that it will lead us along Yeshua's predestined path.

Now, Alein, rest, while I look out for intruders, for tomorrow will be a busy day."

"*Abba*, I am so glad we honored our pledge from four summers ago and we didn't leave here until we were all reunited."

Alein Yosephe left with a smile on his face after their discussion and Yoseph sat there alone listening to the gusting wind. All along knowing one day when he was no more of this world, Alein would be giving his son or daughter the same advice. *It's strange*, he thought, *about knowledge and experience. It's like a muddy river that flows many miles until it becomes the clear waters of wisdom.*

The night was uneventful until the middle of the fourth watch. Yoseph then spied a dark shadow moving toward the entrance to their cave. From his viewpoint, a part of the mountain obscured the entrance. Yoseph moved around the side of a large outcropping of rocks and saw Alein's donkey in front of the cave entrance. He didn't think any more about it until dawn arrived. That's when he heard a blood-curdling scream come from his sister.

At once, he raced down the mountain to hear his name called out by the lone thunderous voice of Hebron. Once he arrived at the base of the mountain, the whole camp was aroused. Hebron was holding his sword and young Zechariah was holding a large wooden club. Yoseph's sister was holding little Enoch and still screaming. Martha and Miriam were trying to quiet his sister and console her, but it was to no avail. Her wailing stung Yoseph's ears until Hebron had to shake Enygeus to bring her to her senses.

Miriam grabbed the baby from her arms, afraid that Enygeus might lose control of herself and harm him. At that instance, Enygeus lunged at Miriam until Hebron's powerful grip stopped her. The small blanket that covered little Enoch had fresh splattered blood covering it, which gave Yoseph a sick knotted sensation in his stomach as he considered what they might see.

"Yoseph, Yoseph, please tell me he isn't dead," his sister continued to wail throughout their camp. Hebron couldn't move, for fear had frozen him into a marble-like statue as Yoseph reached to remove the bloody blanket from his little nephew. Yoseph said a frantic prayer to Yeshua to protect this baby from harm and asked for the intercession of the cup and vials, plate, lance, manuscripts, and sword to shield them. With trembling hands, he reached to pull back the bloody blanket from Enoch, the son his sister had long waited. Afraid of what he might see, a tightness formed in his throat as his fingers grasped the crimson-stained covers.

CHAPTER XX

ith ease, he unwrapped the bloody blanket from young Enoch as Miriam held him for Yoseph to examine. Yoseph's heart raced beyond comprehension. Then he saw the child's small belly heave up and then down as great relief came over him like a sudden gust of wind.

"He is alive!" Yoseph shouted, while still examining him for puncture wounds. "Glory be to *El Shaddai*!" He continued to check his small body, which looked fine. Yoseph wondered where the blood had emanated from on the blanket. Enygeus had fainted from both grief and relief and was lying at his feet. Martha tipped her water jar, reached in with her cupped palm, and then sprinkled some water on Enygeus's face. Out of the corner of Yoseph's right eye, he saw Alein Yosephe running toward him holding a bloody single piece of parchment and dagger.

"*Abba*, my donkey's throat has been cut . . . here's the dagger that cut his throat and a warning message. Someone must have come late at night when we were asleep and crept along the ground, that bastard lizard!"

Yoseph glanced off in the distance and saw the poor creature lying in a puddle of blood. The blood gave off a putrid sweet smell from Enoch's blanket and the dagger, causing bile to rise from his stomach.

"What does the parchment say, Alein?" Yoseph demanded.

"*Abba*, let me read it to all present, if that's all right."

"Yes, please do."

"The warning is quite explicit in what will happen."

Yoseph of Arimathea, you and your fellow apostles will be under my dagger until you're all dead. Not even young children or your friends can escape the blade of my knife. This is your sole warning and there will be no more. I will pick the time and place to kill all of you at once or one at a time. Search for me in the shadows of the moonlight, the darkest part of the night, in your times of doubt, and no matter where you flee, I will be there. Seek me not, for I reside in the abyss of Sheol. My name is Barabbas and remember it well.

The threatening note ended.

"Yoseph, let's track this bastard at once and give him his due!" hollered a flush-faced Hebron. "This demon came close to killing my son. No innocent baby should be under this kind of threat."

"I agree with Uncle Hebron, *Abba*. Let's chase after this fiend. We'll dispatch him in less than a full watch. We can ride your camels and overtake him."

"My friends," Nicodemus said as he interrupted their emotional conversation. "Let's keep cooler heads and ask ourselves why this evil person wants to kill us."

"There must be some motive for this and I don't believe Caiaphas is the author of this deranged person. Do any of you know who this Barabbas might be?" Yoseph asked.

Nicodemus replied, "Now I believe I know of this man. I saw him the first time when we were before the Roman prefect. He was on trial for suspected murder. The crowd and Caiaphas wanted him to be released. They continued to shout his name and said to let him go. The mob and the Sanhedrin threatened Pilate. The Sanhedrin said they would go to the Roman emperor and ask for Pilate's recall if he didn't execute Yeshua. Nobody knows where he is from; however, the rumors say he has murdered eight people for no apparent reason. We are dealing with an evil monster who kills for the pleasure of killing. He's as cunning as a cat in stalking its prey and like a cat playing with the mouse before he kills it." He glanced at Miriam.

"Did Yeshua ever speak of Barabbas?"

"No, Nicodemus, but Yudas always spoke about a killing insurrection and not much else. If the evil one possesses this man, he needs no motive to kill us. However, I do now remember him speaking to Yeshua about a relative he was afraid of. We have much to fear, for if he is a close relative of Yudas, he'll focus his wrath toward all of us who were close to Yudas. Yoseph, his demented mind may think you and Hebron are the instigators of Yudas's demise. This has made a random murderer into a nonhuman. I fear him, yet I know that Yeshua and the *kodesh* cup is with us to protect family, friends, and others who will believe in Yeshua."

The insight of Miriam and Nicodemus calmed them some, and his sister had regained her senses to hear what both had said. Miriam pulled the bloody blanket off Enoch and handed him to Enygeus to hold. He awoke with a smile on his face when he saw his *amma*. Martha reached into her sewing bag and retrieved another blanket on which she had just finished embroidering the symbols for the twelve tribes of Ya'akov. Yoseph noticed the center of the blanket had a gold-colored figure of the lion of *Yehudah*. After giving the blanket to Enygeus, Martha traveled to the stream, accompanied by Alein Yosephe, and washed the blood out of the old blanket.

"It's apparent, Hebron," said Yoseph, "that Barabbas was spying on you for some time. Didn't you say you saw near here small campfires in front of the surrounding caves and countryside?"

"Yes, Yoseph, but I thought they were spies of either the Tetrarch Herod Antipas or the High Priest Caiaphas. It never occurred to me that this monster may have been from the house of Yudas, the dagger man. I am responsible for bringing this monster to our camp. I beg all of you not to say anything to Enygeus about me witnessing his hanging. She doesn't know about that fateful day four springs ago when I followed Yudas. She still thinks I traveled back to *Yerushalayim* to search for you, Yoseph. It now appears I made two big mistakes that night. Please don't put my shame on her at this dreadful moment."

Yoseph nodded in agreement.

"Master Hebron," Nicodemus said, "you are a *tzaddik,* and *El Shaddai* has a way of guiding our lives with his omnipresent hand. Your intentions that night were without concern for yourself, but for the safety of Yoseph and other members of your family. *El Shaddai* had other plans for you than confronting Yudas and trying to help Yoseph. Yudas's fate had the seal of the evil one. Yoseph and I were to be the ones to help bury our *Maishiach*. *El Shaddai* knew our fate before we did and guided us in the right direction.

"Hebron, you could have been arrested or worse, killed. Who would be there for Enygeus and be the proud father of a handsome son? You're the strong rope that binds your family and now this band of teachers. Don't be hard on yourself, our *Abba* and his son have given us divine *chokmah*. Use this *chokmah* to nourish your *kavanah*. The past we cannot change. None of us here holds any animosity toward you. You have become one of *El Shaddai's* witnesses on earth of our *Maishiach's* teachings."

Nicodemus gave Hebron a big embrace, followed by Yoseph. He thought what his friend Nicodemus said helped increase Hebron's spirits, for a slight smile formed at the corner of his mouth. Enygeus returned from the stream with Alein, and Yoseph motioned for them to join the group in a blessing of thanksgiving. They joined hands and young Yohanan the writer prayed for their excellent news.

"*Barukh ata Adonai Eloheinu Melekh ha'alam ha-tov v'hameytiv.*"

There was a long moment of silence after young Yohanan spoke. Yoseph believed they knew in their hearts that *Eloheinu* had protected young Enoch from harm by Barabbas, or whomever it was, and his hand was pouring out his righteousness for the followers of his son.

Hebron, Alein Yosephe, and Yohanan helped bury the carcass of the donkey, leaving nothing visible of the poor animal's demise. Yoseph knew what his sister had seen couldn't be erased as fast in her mind as the recent burial. Her trauma prompted him to speak to her in private.

"Enygeus, please follow me, we need to speak."

With some hesitation, she handed little Enoch to Miriam and gave him a reassuring kiss on his forehead.

"Let's travel down this path toward the stream; it will be quiet, and we can speak in private."

She followed closely as they ambled down the dusty path to the stream. They continued beside it until the stream emptied into the river, where they had performed the baptisms. She said not a word until she grabbed his hands, stopped, and stared into his eyes.

"Yoseph, I am afraid. Let's leave this place. How can Hebron and I raise more children knowing they could be under the dagger of a sick, demonic . . . man?"

Her shifting, widened eyes sought answers from Yoseph that he wasn't sure he could give her. He hoped to vanquish her fears, yet Yoseph knew the threat from this diabolical killer could devour his sister's mind. He knew this fiend was toying with all of them, before he would murder their band. He knew this Barabbas would murder them in their sleep. Killing one of them on a random night until they were all gone from this world. All true cowards worked this way.

"Enygeus, let me pray on what we shall do. I know Yeshua will give us a solution to keep this evil miscreant at bay. You must have faith in *Adonai* and our *Maishiach,* for good and evil have been with us since Adam and Eve. Yeshua has given us a battle standard against evil. Doubt and fear have always been the tools of the dark forces of life. Never doubt Yeshua's words or presence. Little Enoch and Zechariah are destined to accomplish great things in the name of our *Maishiach.* Fear not, my sister, our nephew will be with us for all eternity."

They continued traveling along the riverbank until the late spring season sun was high above the mountains. As they approached a small pool of water ahead, both noticed some wild ducks swimming about emitting a nervous quacking sound.

"Yoseph, you have helped comfort me this terrible morning. A sister couldn't ask for a finer brother. I too will pray tonight for protection and understanding, but I see myself as a helpless insect in this mighty universe of *Eloheinu.* I know we must seek his mercy and protection, yet he speaks to us in ways we cannot understand as humans."

"You're right, sister, but now we have his son we can speak to."

"That's true, my brother, and I can relate to him as my great nephew and much more."

A small, crooked smile broke out on his sister's round face and they both embraced each other for some time. Yoseph held her by her shoulders, protecting her from any harm, as they headed back to their camp. Upon reaching the cave entrance, Miriam came out holding Enoch in the embroidered blanket her sister had made. Enygeus ran over to her and held out her arms for him. Miriam slipped his little body into his mother's arms. She hugged him, causing him to protest that he wanted down. As Yoseph turned around, there was Zechariah with his staff.

"Uncle Yoseph, are we chasing after that man who tried to hurt Enoch?"

"No, not today, for there has been enough emotional upheaval for us this morning. Besides, we need a plan, and I would like you to be part of that plan." Yoseph thought it best to use this young boy's enthusiasm for the best of their family's advantage. "I want you to guard the camels and the trail to the river. Have Philip go with you and lead the camels to drink and make sure nobody steals them. Use my staff, if you must, to beat off any intruders. This will give me time to plan and pray what we must do. You have an important job, Zechariah, now hurry and water the camels."

Zechariah's puffed-up chest let Yoseph know he was proud as he raced off toward the camels. Yoseph knew Hebron had trained him well to defend himself. The boy moved quicker than most men and his demonstrated power equaled theirs too. Besides, Yoseph still had the lump on his head from several days ago from the strength of this young boy. The single thing Zechariah feared was that of abandonment by his new family and Yoseph knew that wouldn't happen.

He sat down next to Yohanan and Yohanan Marcus to converse about their future mission and the terrible incident this morning.

"Fellow teachers and *kodesh* brothers, what are your opinions on what happened this morning?" Marcus glanced up after drawing a fish symbol in the dirt.

"Yoseph, I think this horrible event was meant to be, with *El Shaddai* in his omnipotent wisdom telling us to leave this place. I keep hearing in my head what the Prophet Isaiah said, 'For my house shall be called a house of prayer for all people.' We are to leave this desolate place and speak the *logos* of our *Maishiach*."

"Yohanan the writer, what do you say?"

"Yoseph, I don't know where we should travel first, but if we are to teach the way, the further from *Yerushalayim*, the better our chances to obtain new followers. However, I have the responsibility of looking after Miriam, Yeshua's *amma*, and cannot go far. I know Philip will go wherever his *Maishiach* asks him. Miriam of Magdala speaks wisdom. She knew the heart of Yeshua and felt his thoughts before they were told to us."

Philip was with Zechariah, helping him lead the camels to the river. Miriam heard her name spoken and inquired if her presence was needed. Yohanan Marcus jumped up and hurried to seek out Philip. A short time later, they gathered around one another, including Miriam and Martha's brother, Lazarus.

"Yoseph, I say we leave here as soon as possible!" Philip replied. "Our whereabouts have been compromised and it won't be long before Caiaphas finds us too. The next village is Lydda. Is this not so, Yoseph? Also, *Yoppa* isn't far from there, true?"

"Yes, you're correct on both accounts; however, Philip, who will travel with us?"

There was a moment of silence as each person standing gazed at one another for agreement or disapproval. Miriam was the first to give an affirmative response.

"Rabbi Yoseph, I believe my sister Martha and my brother Lazarus will journey with you, and so will Philip." All three nodded in agreement and then Lazarus spoke.

"Philip can confirm what I am about to say is correct. Two men, who have denied Yeshua's ministry to the Gentiles and his authority of a universal synagogue, are leading our *Yerushalayim* brothers and sisters. Cephus, you know as Shimon, and Ya'akov are now the leaders and so-called apostles of our

Maishiach. I have nothing against them for they risk their lives in the presence of Caiaphas and his minions, the Tetrarch Herod Antipas, and a new upstart of the Sanhedrin. I think both Nicodemus and Yoseph know about whom I am speaking."

"Is it the man called Saul from Tarsus?" Yoseph replied, gazing at Nicodemus for confirmation.

"Yes, Yoseph, and I feel some responsibility for my former pupil's actions. Yoseph, don't you remember the young man who came to your house with a message from me to proceed to your supper at Gethsemane? He's the one who had brother Stefanos stoned to death. I pray that he will find a new *kavanah* in his life and not succumb to power and fame.

"Cephus and Ya'akov don't want to teach to the Gentiles," Lazarus continued. "They consider them unclean. My sister Miriam can tell you that Cephus can be stiff-necked about his views. She has tried to speak to Cephus on numerous occasions, but he wouldn't listen to any woman."

"My brother speaks the truth," Miriam said. "Our *Adonai* has come to me in dreams and spoken of the Prophet Isaiah on several occasions. In my dreams, he spoke to me also, saying, 'My house shall be called a house of prayer of all people,' just like Yohanan Marcus said. After I told Cephus of my dream, he gave me a glance that told me he thought it was another one of my demonic illusions. Yoseph, you and I know the heart of Yeshua. I say we pray tonight and sleep on our discussion."

"I agree with what Miriam said about her numerous fitful dreams," Philip interjected. "I too have had the same dreams and another where Yeshua has spoken to me about the Prophet Yeremiah. He would tell me what *El Shaddai* said to Yeremiah: 'I will make a new covenant with the houses of *Yisrael* and *Yehudah* . . . I will put my law in their minds and write it on their hearts, instead of on tablets of stone.' He's telling us to journey to all people and not stay in this remote hideaway. The presence of this evil man named Barabbas was meant more than to threaten us; it's a sign to begin our teaching soon. I say we leave tomorrow after Alein Yosephe is baptized."

"Philip, my friend," Yoseph said, "let me do as Miriam has suggested. I will pray tonight after we have our *kodesh* supper. I know Alein, Enygeus, and Yosa will teach wherever our *Adonai* tells me we must travel. The question we must ask ourselves, my brothers and sisters, is this: Are you willing to leave your homes and never return?" Once again, each person sat there staring at one another wondering how to reply.

The rest of the day was uneventful as they continued with their chores. Hebron and Alein were more vigilant and circumspect, searching for any trace of their new devilish tormentor. They agreed to post double sentries at the cave entrance at night and not post a guard on the mountaintop. In addition, this evening, two guards would oversee the camels. Hebron then surveyed the mountain close to their cave, while Alein mounted one of Eli's camels, then left to survey around the desert plains. Later, he returned and reported a century of Roman soldiers marching on the road to *Yoppa*. That night they had their *Kodesh* Cup supper and again Alein Yosephe was amazed at the procession and the meal. Toward the end of the supper, once again they heard the whispering voice of their *Adonai*.

"Yoseph, it's time for your leave-taking and the start of your ministry to all people of the west. You have done well in joining my chosen army of spiritual soldiers. Be not afraid, my teachers, for the blood of my cup and the bread of my body, will protect you as long as you believe in me."

Yoseph didn't have to pray alone for his answer, they were all witnesses to their *Kiddush Ha-Shem*. There was no doubt in anyone's face or heart what they needed to do. After hearing those whispery words, the band of teachers ambled to the cave they called home and prepared to leave their ancestral homeland to unknown western lands. Yoseph spent the rest of the night writing in his parchment journal about what had transpired since he left *Yerushalayim*. It was almost dawn before he had brought it up to date.

PART VII

The Charon and Zaragozza

CHAPTER XXI

Anno Domini 1190
November
Northern Iberia

he sleet came down harder as we approached the eerie fog-shrouded barge. On the stern stood a tall man waving a lantern to direct us to the wooden boards of the gangplank. I imagined the stranger was Charon, the ancient Greek ferryman to the underworld of Hades.

Muhammad spoke to him in his native language, and he replied in kind. At first, the horses were reluctant to climb onto the wooden planking and into the shallow belly of the barge. Several refused to board until Muhammad, our own Orpheus, charmed them with his whispering words to move forward.

The *clopping* sounds of their horses' hooves hitting the wooden hull bottom made it sound as though the ancient three-headed monster, Cerberus, was preventing us from reaching the far shore. We gathered up several long icy-glazed wooden poles and placed them in the pitch-black water of the Rio Ebro. Muhammad approached the ferryman, who by now had carried his lantern to the bow of the barge. There Muhammad placed a small sack of coins in his right hand to pay for our crossing. Every so often, the ferryman would whisper something to Muhammad, who, in turn, spoke to Grand Master de Érail, and he would direct us where to position the poles into the river. We were fortunate the river current wasn't too swift, for our labors gained quick passage to the opposite bank.

We docked at a sturdy slip, which made it easy for our horses to disembark. In front of us was an icy narrow route from the slip's edge up to the side of the bank. The ferryman climbed this path until he reached the top of the bank and stood there shining his lantern down for us to see. We mounted our horses and spurred them up the trail until we arrived at the flat plateau of the embankment.

Muhammad said, "*Salaam alaikum*," to the *Mudéjar* boatman, who replied, "*Alaikum al salaam*," and then gestured goodbye with his lantern.

Dawn was some time away and visibility in the icy storm and fog made traveling slow, if not dangerous. We rode at a slow trot until daylight arrived. The fog was still thick, but the ice storm had stopped. Grand Master de Érail said it would be about another eight leagues before we would reach Zaragozza. The slow pace at which we moved could mean it would be the next day before we arrived at the palace-fortress and greet *Rey* Alfonso II.

There was a defined esplanade along the river that helped us see the ice-covered road ahead. Right before the divine office of Sext, the fog burned off, allowing the sun to light up the clear azure sky. We stopped to say our *Pater Nosters*, Glory Bes, and Muhamfound a clear spot on the ground to do his *salats*. The ice started melting from the sun's rays as we shared some apple cinnamon-spiced cobbler from *Padre* Miguel's leather bag in breaking our fast. The ground I sat on was half-frozen and muddy, yet this didn't deter my appetite for the sweet cinnamon-crusted dough.

As I sat there, I wondered what day it was. Were my *épouse* and children missing me? Had my letters made their journey to my épouse and *soeur*? Sadness overtook me, causing a great longing for my home and my épouse. I knew it was close to Saint Andrew's feast day and also Advent, yet I felt too many days had vanished on our quest. It had been two months since I last saw my *épouse*. Doubt began to creep into my mind. Would we ever see the second set of Saint Joseph of Arimathea's writings?

At once, my attention refocused from my gloominess to an unexpected shout from Muhammad to Grand Master de Érail. His high-pitched warning voice focused my sight on a high bluff on the opposite shore of the Rio Ebro. There I saw a brief glint of light from metallic helmets, which caused us to mount our horses and then race down the frozen esplanade toward Zaragozza. Our torrid pace continued for about two leagues until we felt safe enough to slow down to a military canter.

"Grand Master Gilbért, who do you think they were?" I asked, fearful of his reply.

"There's little doubt the cardinal's *chevaliers* have found us. They don't want us to reach the *rey's* fortress at Zaragozza. The cardinal's men will be waiting for us at the next ford of the river. I'll send Muhammad ahead to scout for a probable spot to expect an ambush. In the meantime, prepare yourself for battle. If God wills it, we may die today, then so be it, but let's not die without the approval of Saint Michael's judgment. Seize no prisoners and don't retreat. Lord Robert and *Padre* Miguel, you must escape if the battle doesn't seem favorable. Swear to me and God you will both do as I say."

"*Oui*, Grand Master Gilbért, I will do as you wish," I replied to his not-so-sanguine assessment of our forthcoming battle.

"Stay on this icy road that follows alongside

the Rio Ebro into Zaragozza. The fortress is close to the river bluff. Both of you should ride at once to Marshal Poncho Díaz de Vivar and tell him what happened. *Padre* Miguel, you will testify along with Lord Robert and give complete details of our quest. After that, seek out Jeremiah Santiago de Compostela, our chaplain. He has a vast knowledge of Hebrew and Arabic history. Young Jeremiah will assist you in any way with the clues to the whereabouts of the second set of manuscripts."

"Gilbért," *Abad* Miguel said, "I am a man of God and won't abandon a sainted child of his in times of danger. I cannot swear before God to do as you say. God wants me here to help protect us from the evil forces who want to destroy you and Lord Robert. He knows how important this quest is in honoring his *hijo* and his *hijo's Santo Taza.*"

It was apparent that the *Abad* Miguel would stay with his former student to the end, if necessary. Grand Master Gilbért shook his head with disappointment but knew *Abad* Miguel's stubbornness would win in the end.

We rode another league-and-a-half until we saw Muhammad racing in our direction on Buraq; she had icy streams of breath coming from each nostril as Muhammad reined her in alongside Grand Master Gilbért. The two men spoke in Arabic for a short while until Grand Master Gilbért turned to me.

"Fifty *chevaliers* are waiting in ambush at the next ford in the river. They're scattered among the trees and hills covering both sides of the road. No one can penetrate their trap. Beyond them ride thirty more *chevaliers* heading in our direction. Muhammad suspects there are even more *chevaliers* behind the thirty, for he saw a large murder of crows fleeing in our direction."

Knowing now where we stood with our enemies, we crossed ourselves and then drew our swords from their scabbards. The metallic hiss from our blades sounded loudly enough for the people in Zaragozza to hear us.

"Lord Robert, I want you and Sergeant Guy to ride straight southwest along the Rio Jalón to our fortress at Calatayud. It is a shorter distance than Zaragozza, maybe a league-and-a-half from here. If God wills it, we'll meet there. Now leave at once!" he shouted.

He swung the flat blade of his sword and swatted the hindquarters of my steed. She reared with surprise and raced off with a swift gallop followed by Sergeant de Béziers. We raced ahead some two leagues before we rested our horses with a slow-gaited trot. So far, none of the cardinal's *chevaliers* had spied us. This was odd because there should at least be some scouts behind us. We traveled another half-league and entered a small gully surrounded by steep sides. To my horror, blocking our exit from the ravine, were the cardinal's men.

There were at least eight of them and our lone way out was a hasty retreat from where we came.

As we prepared to turn and escape, the *chevaliers* shouted in unison, "*Rendre! Rendre!*" They charged forth when they saw we were retreating and drew their swords. Both Guy and I spurred our horses, and just then I remembered what Muhammad had said to make our horses fly across the icy ground. "*Allahu akbar!*" I repeated these words three times and then I was thrilled with wonder as our magnificent steeds outpaced the horses of our pursuers.

Soon we were out of their sight, yet we knew they weren't far behind. Sergeant Guy motioned for me to stop; however, my indefatigable horse was hard to rein in. Guy grabbed hold of my reins and forced her to stop with his horse.

"We must return to the ford and the ferry boatman. Our upmost chance to evade capture is to cross back over the river and follow the short road to the fortress at Calatayud. They knew we would travel the shorter road to arrive at the Zaragozza palace as soon as possible. Let's hope we can reach the ford before the cardinal's men. Now let's pray we can arrive there and cross the river in time."

We both crossed ourselves and said Psalm twenty-three while racing back toward the boat slip and the ferry boatman. Up ahead, along the horizon, was a thin finger of black smoke rising from the direction of the ford. As we drew closer, we could see orange flames reaching above the riverbank. Once arriving and glancing down, we saw the charred twisted skeleton of the ferry boatman lying next to the burning slip. Somewhat submerged in the icy water were the smothered remains of the ferry. We were now trapped between the river, in the pincer trap of Cardinal Folquet's men. It appeared we were doomed.

"Lord Robert, I must ride to aid my excellency, Grand Master Gilbért. You do God's work and follow your heart to Calatayud and protect the holy documents. If you don't follow me, I won't think less of you. I once heard tell the English Plantagenet *roi* say, 'Adversity sheds light upon the virtues of humankind. Brave men conquer nobly or die gloriously.'"

With Sergeant de Béziers' final words, my honor as a *chevalier* wouldn't abide by his command. I trusted in God and his son's will to deliver us from evil. We galloped in the direction of our ill-fated *frères.* I kept glancing over my shoulder, expecting to find the cardinal's *chevaliers* behind us at any time. As we raced closer toward our original jumping-off spot, I began to hear faint trumpet sounds.

The morning sky was blue as a robin's egg and visibility was clear in the direction of Zaragozza. Up ahead, I could see with horrid clarity, fifty *chevaliers* with the cardinal's standard flapping in the wind surrounding my companions. I knew the warrior-*moines* of Christ wouldn't allow themselves to be captured, for they always fought until death. We raised our swords, spurred our horses, and shouted Psalm 115, as we raced down the road to God's greater glory.

CHAPTER XXII

I heard the trumpet blasts coming closer as Sergeant Guy raced ahead shouting, "*Non nobis, Domine, non nobis, sed nomini tuo da gloriam.*" Then I heard what I thought was his echo as he finished shouting. To my surprise, I saw a tall stiff piebald flag in the air, accompanied by at least fifty Templar *chevaliers* and sergeants. They were racing from the direction of Zaragozza.

The sun's rays caught their fifty raised blades, and the glint for an instant blinded me. I turned in my saddle when my ears caught the shrill blast of a second trumpet, not more than twenty or thirty horse lengths behind me. To my great relief, the road behind me had another fifty Templar *chevaliers* and sergeants.

They were blasting with their trumpets to signal their fellow warriors of Christ to rally behind their battle standard, the *beauséant*. When the cardinal's *chevaliers* saw their approach, they scattered like cockroaches discovered in the dark by a well-lit candle. Some of them tried to escape down the bank of the ford, but our men cut them to pieces from behind. Others tried to escape in a flanking direction from the river, yet some surrendered. A few foolish souls stayed and tried to fight, but it was futile. The wall of red-crossed shields engulfed them like some red and white ravenous dragon that was devouring all the prey in its path.

The noise was overwhelming, with screams of pain, dying horses, cursing, the snake-sounding hiss of arrows, and the ever-present *clank* of metal striking metal. It was all over in just a short time. Grand Master Gilbért had entered the bloody melee accompanied by Muhammad, who raised his circling flashing scimitars over his head. Both Sergeants Guy and Jacque were chasing five of the cardinal's men down the side of the riverbank. Two of the men fell off their horses into the river and drowned. The other three tried to fight while crossing the swift river. The tenacious fighting of my fellow Templars killed all three of the men. The whitewater current pulled the bloody bodies of all three and sucked them into the depths of the muddy brown water. *Abbé* Miguel and I separated from the main battle. We ended up in a ravine not visible from the main conflict.

Behind me, *Abbé* Miguel prayed in his saddle repeating several Psalms with his eyes closed. I had stopped my horse to observe and saw two of the cardinal's *chevaliers* heading in my direction. One had a sword raised to strike, the other had a rope in his free hand. They wanted to either capture or kill me and my blood was up to their challenge. I spurred my horse hard in her flanks and drew my sword to meet their oncoming rush. The *chevalier* with the sword tried to maneuver me so that his fellow *chevalier* could throw a rope over my body. Their desire at this moment wasn't to kill me; yet once captured, they would torture me for information. Afterward, my life was finished. However, how did they know who I was?

The *bâtard* Marcel de Tournay was the singular one capable of identifying me and rallying his men, but he was now dead in the *montagne* avalanche a fortnight or better ago. Praise God he was now in hell. I appeared no different from any other mounted Soldier of Christ on this killing plain. Had he had time to describe me to all the cardinal's men?

As I lunged at one *chevalier* with my sword, the other threw his rope around me. Right away, I tried to throw it off, but the line tightened. Then he jerked me off my horse. With God's blessing, I kept my sword as my body struck the wet, cold ground. After which I sliced the rope line free. Both *chevaliers* dismounted and approached me to fight. To my dismay, the same *chevalier* had another rope. This time he reached for my horse and the *Sangraal* parchments, while the one with a sword came after me. Their efforts were to separate us, furthering my dilemma in what to do next. I decided to advance toward the *chevalier* with the rope and protect the *Sangraal* parchments. He too drew his sword and a fight ensued.

To even the odds, I drew out my long mercy dagger, which didn't frighten them, for they both grinned, exposing their rotten teeth. As I lunged with my dagger and struck with my sword, I spun my body around to strike the *chevalier* with the rope. My blow struck his left shoulder causing him to drop the rope. His broadsword struck down on my dagger and broke it into several pieces. My back was now against my horse and to my surprise, she reared and struck the other *chevalier* with her hooves. At once, he fell to the ground with a large dent in his helm.

A quick sword thrust into the *chevalier* with the rope forced spurting blood from his mouth to strike my face. After this, I pushed him away hearing his gurgling sounds and placed one foot in my stirrup to leave. This is when the second *chevalier* awoke and then lunged at me with a large dagger. At once the dagger penetrated my hauberk but stopped when the hissing sound of crossbow quarrels made loud thumps penetrating his back. Right away, his grip gave way, yet I still felt the sharp tip of his dagger enter the flesh of my right shoulder. I fell backward on top of the dead *chevalier* and passed out.

"Lord Robert, are you all right?" a familiar voice asked. Grand Master Gilbért shook me to consciousness. "I see you're still among the living. It seems Muhammad has saved you once more. You have lost some blood, yet the dagger didn't reach any vital organs. God has protected you in his arms with the help of one of his Saracen children."

I turned my head to one side and spied Muhammad with a large toothy grin forming on his face.

"Pilgrim, you have the protection of *Allah*," he said while bending to treat my dagger wound. He and Grand Master Gilbért placed me back on my horse and we started our last half league to Zaragozza.

"Lord Robert, we were quite blessed by God that my men from our priory were protecting this road. In the past, I have instructed them to use four different squadrons of *chevaliers* and sergeants to patrol along the Rio Ebro."

Just as Grand Master Gilbért said his last words, a large group of about thirty *chevaliers* appeared on the far shore opposite our riverbank. I could see the cross of Toulouse and the *fleur-de-lis* battle standard of more of the cardinal's men. Racing in front of them was a helmeted *chevalier* holding two severed heads. To my horror, it was the Romany heads of Boldo and Ashena. He flung both heads into the muddy Rio Ebro and shouted out.

"My foolish Soldiers of Christ, see what you have caused. There are many more heads besides these, and you sons-of-bitches have caused their deaths. Whoever tries to protect you will receive a similar fate. Oh, by the way, don't expect your precious *Roi* Alfonso to protect you. Cardinal Folquet has spies everywhere. *Oui*, one other thing, I had the Romany *princesse* dance for me in my personal tent before I killed her."

"*Mon Dieu*," the words at once rolled off my lips, which caused my heart to sink into my stomach. "Here is another evil man as diabolical as de Tourney," I told Grand Master Gilbért. Out of the mass of Templar *chevaliers* appeared a young man who rode up to Grand Master Gilbért on a large white Andalusian horse.

"*Su excelencia*, shall my men pursue these *bastardos*?"

"*Non*, Marshal Poncho, that's what that *diable* son-of-a-bitch wants us to do. He knows we outnumber him three to one. Some of the cardinal's men have fought in the Levant and have learned the battle tactics of the Saracens. His men will wait in ambush with their crossbows and try to cut us down one at a time if we cross this treacherous ford. Tell your men, Marshal Poncho, to close ranks and not charge any of his men. They will continue to bait us on with their crossbow attacks until we reach Zaragozza. My men and I need time to rest and figure out how we can chop the head from that snake, Cardinal Folquet.

There was an incredulous mouth-opening face of disappointment on the young marshal's face as he ordered his men to line up in formation. It was a superb sight to see one hundred red-crossed white surcoats and their white cloth-draped horses followed by the dark uniforms of the sergeants. In the center of the ranks was the *gonfanier* holding the battle flag of the Soldiers of Christ. The stiff piebald flag blazed with a blood red pattée cross in its center as our captured prisoners were cowering among the marshal's men.

We had traveled just a short distance, when on the opposite bank behind a copse of trees came the hissing sound of crossbow arrows. Just as Grand Master Gilbért had said, they were using the stealthy battle tactics of the Saracens. The quarrels fell short with their first volley. The marshal broke ranks spurred his horse, and raced toward his grand master. I noticed the sword in his hand was long and had an Eastern geometric design on the hilt. He reined in his horse in front of Grand Master Gilbért with a scowl on his forehead.

"*Su excelencia*, what do you want my men to do in thwarting the next batch of quarrels? They will soon be in range to hurt our men and horses."

"Do you still have several sergeants who are Englishmen with longbows?"

"*Sí,* I have *seis hermanos.*"

"Accompany them with the *seis* other sergeants and *seis* pouches of arrows and form in front of the line of trees on the far bank. Give the order to the rest of the men to flank shields. Make sure the longbowmen can fire without obstruction from our shields. The cardinal's men will have to come out from behind the trees to fire next. Now ride at once, don't delay."

"*Sí, su excelencia,*" the marshal replied. Once again, Poncho spurred his horse and left, shouting orders to his men. The quick movement of a hundred men and a hundred shields turned as fast as a well-oiled lock. There was one continuous metallic thud as the red-crossed, teardrop-shaped shield formed an impenetrable fortress that no arrow could pierce. Even each horse's head and flank had protection.

Then came the quarrels toward us fast and furious from the now visible men. It sounded as if hail was pelting the shields. The center of the Templar men edged open and twelve sergeants, six of whom had English longbows, appeared. They arched their bows in the air and released six arrows as fast as a heartbeat. Their assistants were feeding arrows to them so fast the sky above us appeared as if hundreds of birds were swooping down to land.

Across the Rio Ebro, the arrows came down on the unprotected crossbowmen. The accuracy of these English sergeants was unbelievable, which caused the arrows' metal tips to strike the helmets or chest of each crossbowman. Within several breaths, all was silent and twenty to thirty of the cardinal's men lay dead. A great cheer broke out among the Templar *chevaliers* and sergeants, praising their new Grand Master of Iberia. "*Viva poss nuestro excelencia, viva poss nuestro orden, viva poss nuestro excelencia!*"

Without warning, there was a trumpet blast from the marshal's retinue and all the men became silent as we continued marching toward Zaragozza. The morning air had turned cold, and the sky became clear as the late fall sun reached its high point of the day. There was much sorrow in my heart for the loss of our Romany friends. I knew Boldo and the Romany *roi* put up a decent fight in our defense, yet at a great cost. They were no match to men without heart or honor. How many more friends would sacrifice their lives in our quest for the *Sangraal?* A deep dejection came over my demeanor and our grand master at once saw that I was troubled.

"Lord Robert, you have a doleful expression on your face, even after this victory. Might I inquire what is troubling you?"

"It seems that anybody I meet and befriend dies at the hands of that devil de Tournay and the evil dogs of the cardinal. Doubt has entered my mind, Grand Master Gilbért, and I fear soon it will seize hold of me and not release its grip. We don't have a tangible clue that this second set of parchments even exists. The Saracens may have destroyed it hundreds of years ago when they left the Levant for North Africa. My intellect says I am searching for ants in the dark. God hasn't answered my prayers in recent times, nor has our Saint Marie Magdalene visited me. I am wondering, are we searching in the right direction?"

There was a moment of silence by Grand Master Gilbért before he replied to my thoughts. The sole sound I heard was the steady clopping of more than one hundred horses' hooves trudging along as he ruminated on what I confessed.

Then he spoke. "Evil is all around us, *mon ami*. Some of us ignore it, others join it, and some of us oppose it. Our Lord and Savior knew this and so did his disciples. He asked them all, 'Will you drink from the same cup that I am about to drink from?' Truth is a merciless taskmaster both to the righteous and the men of evil. With the lone sword of truth can we conquer pure evil. *Le Sangraal* is our sword of truth and taskmaster. Evil men want to kill this truth. Yet remember your divine gift is far greater than the *Tizona* sword that young Poncho carries. Are you willing to drink from the same cup as our Lord and Savior, Jesus the Christ, *mon ami*? That's a question you must answer. Truth and freedom always come at a great sacrifice."

He smiled. "Enough of my didactic preaching, for now, let me increase your spirits. We've had a dearth of beneficial news and humor. My new commander, Hugo de Joffre, and Chaplain Jeremiah will give you some cheer. Commander Hugo has the cheeriness that would make the dead smile. Both he and my—I mean my chaplain—will see to giving you some new confidence when you listen to what they have to say."

His words were encouraging, but my body and mind were numb, for I had ridden, fought, and wrote for almost two months. I had seen death, smelled it, and caused it. The next set of parchments seemed like a rising mist from the Rio Ebro. Something I knew was there but couldn't grasp my hands around. I felt quite defeated at that moment, not caring if I reached Zaragozza today or ever.

Then up ahead of the *chevaliers*, I heard shouts of "Grand Master de Érail, Grand Master de Érail," and I saw two riders approaching from Zaragozza. One appeared to be about twenty-five years old and the other maybe forty years in age. The oldest one wore the standard coif of chain mail and the white mantle of a *chevalier*. The other wore a forest green mantle with a red pattée cross over his chest. He appeared to be a chaplain. The closer he came, I could see he was wearing a small round brimless hat. It was obvious to me it was Grand Master Gilbért's son. His eyes were darker, and his facial features were finer, yet he was his son. His build was muscular, and he rode long-legged in his saddle.

"*Su excelencia*, Zaragozza is just a short ride away. Marshal Poncho sent a rider to our priory and informed us of your troubled arrival," the young priest said with a familiar dimpled grin on his face.

"Great to see you again, Commander Joffre and *Padre* Jeremiah. God has been with us on our journey. Yet, to my dismay, I lost my faithful squire . . . *Chevalier* Hughes de Montbard. He died trying to protect one of my sergeants from the quarrels of a crossbow."

There was a brief silence as we crossed ourselves and said a quiet prayer. The stillness of his memory continued until Grand Master Gilbért apologized for not introducing me to his commander and his chaplain.

"Both of you know *Abad* Miguel."

"*Si, pax vobiscum*," replied the young chaplain and the commander.

"And also to both of you, my *hermanos*," replied *Abad* Miguel with his white beard bouncing up and down on his chin with a jovial smile.

"I am sorry I haven't introduced both of you to *Baron Roberto*, *Señor* de Borron y Northern Burgundy. He is accompanying us as a gifted chronicler and troubadour. *Señor Roberto* is wearing our mantle and surcoat to travel incognito on our holy quest. It's imperative that his identity, our purpose, and our destination to Toledo stay hidden. I want both of you to swear before God, our Lord and Savior, not to reveal anything that we discuss here or in the future. Can I have your oath of secrecy here now before God and his kingdom?"

"*Sí*," was their response as both men swore together their loyalty to God, Jesus the Christ, and Grand Master Gilbért. Each man had a vexed expression on his face, not quite knowing what they had just sworn to. This reminded me of myself many weeks ago back at the priory fortress at Montpellier. It was the typical method employed by Grand Master Gilbért, giving out a smattering of information when needed. You had to earn his trust not just keeping quiet, but also proving your worth. I suspected he knew a spy was in our midst, but he wasn't ready to divulge to me until he had enough proof.

It was late in the day when I observed what seemed similar to a giant square peg, off in the distance. It was trapezoid in shape, with several ascending levels of windows. The roof tiles were red clay that stood out against the now clear blue sky. As we approached closer, I saw a mighty fortress of some unknown design.

"Grand Master Gilbért, what's that square-roofed tower to our east? It's not a keep. There's no wall around it."

"It's la Zuda tower, the old Moorish governor's

palace. There's an even more impressive palace and fortification that you'll soon see. It's Aljafería, where *Rey* Alfonso II and *Reina* Sancha reside. I believe you haven't seen any other palace similar to this one. It's quite unusual in its design and living quarters."

We followed the Rio Ebro until we reached what appeared to be an old Roman wall, with sections of the stone blocks missing that revealed remodeled buildings under construction. All our *chevaliers* and sergeants entered through a Roman-arched gate and followed Grand Master Gilbért past the Zuda tower. A lone man exited from the tower dressed in a black mantle and sur-coat. He had a white-splayed cross that covered the majority of his chest and his remaining body bore chain mail from head to foot. He carried a long double-edged broadsword.

"*Su excelencia*, Gilbért de Érail," shouted the warrior-*moine*. "Congratulations on your pro-motion to Grand Master of Aragón, Catalonia, Provence, and Roussillon, and I know you'll soon be grand master of your entire order. You're a brave and fair man!"

"God has willed it so, Commander Ramáirez; however, thank you for both compliments. I see you have a new hospital in la Zuda tower."

"*Si*, my fellow *hijo* of Christ."

We trotted on and didn't stop to further speak to this military *moine*. *How odd*, I thought, *for*

Grand Master Gilbért not to converse with a warrior-moine of the hospital. His demeanor wasn't such that he would pass an opportunity to listen and gather information. My curiosity wanted to know more, and I had to ask why he didn't further acknowledge him.

CHAPTER XXIII

"Who was that *moine*, and what order does he represent?" I asked with a hush as I rode up next to Grand Master Gilbért.

"He is Ramáirez Rodrigo de Tarragona, commander of the Holy Order des Hospitalliers de St. John de Jerusalem. He's responsible for treating the sick and lame in *Rey* Alfonso's kingdoms. Sometimes they fight alongside our order against the Moors in Iberia and the Saracens in the Levant. They're a rival order and often there's animosity between us. Our relationship right now isn't on the best of terms."

Grand Master Gilbért said nothing more until we approached a bizarre-looking church. It appeared part *Mudéjar* in architecture with an added Christian Romanesque façade. The windows showed the *Mudéjar* influence of checkered *Jacques* stonework.

"That's the Cathedral of San Salvador that King Alfonso the Battler captured. The cathedral replaced an old mosque constructed by a friend of the first Muslim leader Muhammad in the eighth century of our Lord and Savior. King Alfonso the Chaste and his royal retinue pray here on high holy days."

A short distance later we were heading on an opposite road as Grand Master Gilbért led us in a southwestern direction. That is when I saw what he meant about a forthcoming impressive sight. Up ahead was a large fortress with twelve tall round towers and one massive square tower. The whole *château* structure stood on a high foundation that formed its base. The merlons weren't similar to any in my country. They appeared massive, but the tops were intricate decorated arches in stone. The outer walls of the *château* were horseshoe-shaped in design, which appeared to strengthen the battlements.

This didn't appear to be a palace, yet a *château* built for siege warfare. One large square tower seemed older than the rest of the structure and showed its age with many indentations of missing bricks from years of battles. We approached a long dirt ramp that led to a wooden drawbridge guarded by two barbican towers. Here stood the small entranceway to the interior.

Grand Master Gilbért's sergeants, Muhammad, the *château* commander, and the prisoners preceded us inside the fortress. We had to dismount to enter through the entrance opening. After Marshal Poncho Díaz de Vivar's arrival, we dismounted in a small reception yard. Just Grand Master Gilbért, *Padre* Jeremiah, *Abad* Miguel, Muhammad, and I were present. The rest of the *chevaliers* and our sergeants attended to the horses and the prisoners.

"You have quite a following of powerful and dangerous men wanting to kill you," stated the young marshal with his left hand tapping at the large-hilted sword at his side. "Grand Master Gilbért de Érail, you are either carrying important parchments or protecting an important person. It could be both, yet I know you are now in the crossbow sights of those remaining men we didn't capture."

"I will discuss this further with you when we have a convent meeting of all officers. For now, I would like to wash up, eat some food, then sleep, and I speak the same for my companions," Grand Master Gilbért said in a martial fashion to his young subordinate.

"*Su excelencia*, it will be done at once. The *rey's* seneschal has been expecting you and your men. In the meantime, enjoy a warm fire just inside this door. I will send one of *Rey* Alfonso's servants to show you to your quarters."

Young Marshal Poncho Díaz bowed his head in respect and left at once. I scrutinized an unusual heraldic crest carved into the wooden arch of the door we were entering.

"What does this heraldic crest mean?" I inquired of both *Abad* Miguel and Grand Master Gilbért.

"It represents the Kingdom of Aragón, *mon ami*. Notice the quarters divided on the shield. That oak tree represents the Celtic Tree of Life. The cross on top shows how the faith of Christianity converted this once Celtic land. The second part of the quarter shows a silver *fitchée* cross representing *Santo* George in heaven coming down to intercede in the battle to conquer Huesca. The four heads or kings were the Moorish governors of ancient Aragón who were defeated by the Christian armies. The gold and reddish-orange stripes in the last quarter symbolize the conquest of Aragón, Catalonia, and Barcelona. Let's proceed into the chapel of San Martin and warm ourselves."

We started to enter, except for Muhammad, who waited outside for further instruction. Grand Master Gilbért directed him to proceed to a small palace mosque, which was on the eastern side section of the northern palace wing. This palace was something to behold, a palace with both a mosque and a Christian chapel on the same ground. This city and the *rey* showed a tolerance I wasn't used to seeing in Northern Burgundy. The *Mudéjar* architecture was everywhere. The stucco and stone carvings were delicate leaf and tendril designs.

Columns of brown or red marble supported the interior arcade arches, revealing lacy geometric patterns at the bottom of each arch. The top of each column held a designed Corinthian capital of unknown plant architecture.

As I stepped inside the dimly lit chapel, my eyes focused on another contrast. The small chapel was part Romanesque in design and heavy with the *Mudéjar* influence of geometric patterns. There were triangles, squares, half-crescent arches, and the ever-entwined repeating arches. We strolled forward, dipped our hands in the holy water stoop, and gave thanks for surviving the journey from Montpellier. After giving thanks to our Savior, I prayed for Hughes de Montbard, asking for our Lord, Jesus the Christ, to hold him in his arms for all eternity. I also prayed for my *épouse*, Marie, and my two *fils*, hoping our Savior's hands protected them. As I glanced up at the chancel, my eyes caught the sight of a glimmering flash of light. It moved backward at first toward the apse of the small chapel, where a golden nimbus began to form along with the whispering sound of a woman's voice.

"Robert, so far you have done well . . . listen and tread with care this forthcoming Advent season."

I gazed around at my fellow companions, who were still praying and observed their fingers counting their *Pater Noster* beads. They seemed oblivious to the voice I had just heard. A light started forming into the shape of a woman. Was it Saint Marie de Magdala appearing in this small chapel? Again, I glanced around and saw *Abad* Miguel gazing straight through her. He didn't seem to see anything, yet she glided right in front of him.

"Robert, there will be a son from one of the tribes of Jacob who will help guide your way to your next destination. Study with him each day to seek out the clues to the next parchments written by Joseph of Arimathea. You're drawing nearer to the words of our Master and Savior, Jesus the Christ.

"I have come here to tell you two important things. First, young Hughes de Montbard is in the house of the *Père* Almighty. All true martyrs who propagate the faith of his son reap the rewards of divine grace. Also, your family is safe at the *Château* Montbéliard, and all is well with the children, yet your *épouse*, Marie, so misses you. She cries every night before retiring and prays often for your safe return.

"The second thing I have to say is beware of temptation, Robert. Temptation doesn't just affect your mortal soul, but those around you. Observe whom you meet, for there are many forlorn and troubled souls in our midst." She gazed at me with a fixed stare. "It's now time that I must leave, however, don't depend on my visions to help complete your quest. It's not mine to give; for the *Père* Almighty knows the outcome of your future travels. You were preordained from birth to seek out these holy parchments and the Cup of Salvation."

Within an eye's blink, she disappeared, leaving me with the droning sounds of my fellow companion's prayers. Still kneeling, I didn't know what to think about the warning. It was cryptic and left me perplexed with many thoughts racing through my head. A short time later, my companions had finished their prayers, crossed themselves, and stood up to leave.

"Lord Robert, you seem distraught. Is there something wrong?" Grand Master Gilbért asked.

"*Oui*, I had another vision of our Saint Marie de Magdala. She told me in my vision that my *épouse* misses me with a saddened heart and that I should beware of temptation. She also spoke to me that an ancestral son from one of the Jewish tribes of Jacob would help us in our quest. Is she referring to your *fils* . . . oh, please, pardon and forgive me for my loose tongue?" Right away, I searched the dim chapel to see if anybody had heard me. The remaining person was *Abad* Miguel.

"No harm is done, Lord Robert, and you're forgiven. Yes, you're correct in your assumption. Chaplain Jeremiah will speak to you about our quest after the convent tonight. In the interim, let's proceed out into the courtyard and meet one of *Rey* Alfonso's servants, who will show us to our living quarters so we can clean up."

We moved out of the chapel and met a well-dressed servant in a red velvet, fur-trimmed robe. He motioned for us to follow him toward another ornate columned arcade, which led to a small flight of steps. The spacious stone hallway glowed with sunlight from large interior windows covered with a strange material. It appeared as clear sheets of ice placed in the window openings. I stopped for a moment and touched the clear material. It was cool to the touch, but not icy cold, like a frozen pond. Grand Master Gilbért saw me pondering what it was, smiled, and commenced to respond to the curious expression on my face.

"Lord Robert, the founders of this palace knew the art of creating large sheets of this material to keep out the cold wind. In the beginning, they called it *klass*. The Moors brought this invention from North Africa. It's the same material, but smaller pieces, we use in our churches, except we add color to the *klass* to tell biblical stories."

"*Oui*, and expensive for most *châteaus* in Northern Burgundy," I replied

"Come. we must follow *Rey* Alfonso's servant to our living quarters and clean up. This evening should be busy; let's make ourselves presentable for *Rey* Alfonso, *Reina* Sancha, and their courtiers."

We continued down the long corridor until the three of us approached three large wooden doors carved with crosses in the style of the Saint George cross. Below each cross was the Aragón heraldic seal similar to the one on the chapel door. The servant showed each of us our rooms and waited in the corridor to see if we were pleased.

"*Su excelencia*, is everything satisfactory?"

"*Si, muchas gracias*, but before you leave tell my commander, Hugo Joffre, to bring us some new tunics, surcoats, and mantles to wear. Oh, one other request, see to it that my Saracen *amigo* is roomed close to us tonight. He was once a *principe* in his homeland and I value his close counsel."

"*Si, su excelencia*, I'll undertake it at once."

After a slight bow to Grand Master Gilbért, the servant disappeared with the quickness of one of Muhammad's Arabian horses. I turned to view the interior of my new quarters and was amazed. To my right was a large stone-carved fireplace with lion's heads on each side holding up a large mantle. A crackling fire lit up the room and caused my cheeks to tingle hot from the blue-orange flames. To my far left was a large wooden canopied bed.

The bed was fit for an important dignitary, a lavish gold-threaded comforter covered it. On my right was a large wooden buffet that held a washing bowl, cloths, towels, and sweet-smelling soap. Next to the soap was an urn full of water. Several dark-colored oak chairs stood near the fireplace. Each chair had a red silk velvet cushion affixed to the seat. On the square-shaped ceiling, moldings were stone stucco designs. The design pattern was the same delicate geometric shapes as found in the courtyard arches. This was so dissimilar from any keep I had seen in my native land. The nobles in my homeland of Burgundy wouldn't believe my recollection.

The walls were tight-fitting ashlar stones, with two of them covered with *Mudéjar*-designed rugs displaying vines, geometric blocks, and various flowers. I strolled over to my bed and sat down on its edge to rest. The surface was as soft as the fur of a kitten. The temptation was great to sleep, yet I told myself to clean up first.

At once, my coif of chain mail came off, which allowed me to wash my face and beard. Lying on the buffet, I found a comb, brushes, and a silver-plated hand mirror. I was hesitant to gaze into the mirror for fear of what I might see. Then a slight chuckle came over me and I told myself that I was alive and nothing else mattered and to hell with my appearance. The image in the mirror wasn't as frightening as my mind's eye thought. There were some new white hairs at my temple and my beard was speckled with white-tinged hair against a dark-bearded background. I removed the dirt covering my face and neck with the lavender-smelling soap. The comb and brush tugged at the tangles from my hair. Without warning, a strong thumping on my chamber door startled me.

"Lord Robert, it is Gilbért, and I have some clean clothes for you."

I ambled over to the door, reached for a large iron ring, and pulled on the door.

"I see you have started your ablutions, and this is perfect timing on my part. Here are your fresh clothes. I think you will find everything you need, but if not, the floor servant is in this corridor to your right. How do you like your accommodations? I am certain it's far better than the rocky terrain of the Pyrénées *montages*."

"*Oui,* and the bed is par excellent. I am sure my body will catch up on many missed nights of sleep."

Grand Master Gilbért hesitated for a moment in the doorway and asked, "May I speak to you in private?" He edged close the door behind him and approached the warm fireplace before he spoke. "I fear two things . . ."

CHAPTER XXIV

I believe our quest for the second *Sangraal* book has become even more complicated and dangerous. Commander Hugo Joffre has told me that there's a rumor of a spy in our midst. He also said that the holy order of Saint John knows of our quest. Furthermore, Hugo revealed to me they know of your divine gift of being able to read and translate ancient words. I fear for your life, *mon ami,* and will speak to the *rey* tonight to strengthen this part of the *château* with his guards. Right now, it's circumstantial gossip whether Cardinal Folquet has influenced the Hospitalliers to stop us. Joffre doesn't have any definite proof, yet I am more disturbed with the rumor of a spy among us. It's hard for me to believe I have been betrayed. I pray it's just hearsay. Yet, our movements and locations have been checked by the cardinal's men."

"Who would do this? Why wouldn't the spy just steal the information we've already received or kill us in our sleep?" I asked my companion. I felt my face hot from angry disappointment, yet this man had known my companions far longer than me. I knew at that moment he was under a great strain of frustration and that we now faced another setback. His disenchantment contorted Gilbért's face as if a different man stood before me.

"I cannot answer your questions, other than they want you alive to translate future documents and the rest of us to lead them to the location of the parchments. No mercy will be given to this traitor once he has been identified."

"How can we complete our Lord's quest, while knowing that our every move is conveyed to Folquet and his men and now to the Hospitalliers? Also, how factual do you believe this spy information to be?"

"To answer your second question first, let us think about the past six weeks. I have the three best scouts and trackers in all Christendom. My men have tricked, lost, confused, and evaded the great army of Saladin in the Levant for many years. This doesn't make any sense that the cardinal's *chevaliers* have checked each of our movements.

"I know the Hospitalliers have some excellent scouts; however, they have no Saracens helping with their tracking. Another thing, I haven't been honest with you in my correspondence with *Abad* Miguel. He has known all along of our quest. This is before you met him a fortnight ago. You and I have seen the visions and heard the words of Saint Marie Magdalene. Now we must often meet in secret to plan our strategy. We'll give the rest of our group false information while laying down a trap to snare our traitor and the cardinal. After Vespers each evening, we'll meet in the small mosque here at Aljafería. There we can plan and share information in completing our quest. Speak to no one about this meeting or the time we'll meet. There are other alliances with *Rey* Alfonso and the *Santo Père* in Rome, so don't speak of our quest to his nobles, courtiers, or any member of the Royal court.

"For now, finish cleaning up and dress, for we have a convent to attend and thereafter be presented at court."

Grand Master Gilbért left, leaving me in a state of disbelief, while numb to the thought that any three of my close companions could be a traitor. I grabbed the urn, poured out another bowl of clean water, and splashed it on my face. This helped alleviate my mind from the unsettling news I had just heard. The clean clothes made me appear as a new man and gave me back some of my old enthusiasm. I left my room, proceeded into the corridor, and met both sergeants preparing to leave for the convent meeting. I didn't want to stare at both men, but suspicion circled inside my mind. We acknowledged each other and joked about how different we appeared after cleaning ourselves.

"Lord Robert, you appear resembling the person we first encountered at Montpellier, except your wrinkled brow seems frozen with thought. Is something troubling you or is that dagger wound still bothering you?" Sergeant de Hoult inquired with a searching expression in his large blue eyes.

"*Non*, other than I need some rest."

Sergeant Guy smiled but didn't say anything as we retraced our steps back to the chapel, revealing a long line of *chevaliers* and sergeants waiting to enter. They were all lining up according to their rank and length of service as Soldiers of Christ.

I didn't know where to position myself until Grand Master Gilbért pointed in the direction where I should proceed. It was an impressive sight of red-crossed white tunic *chevaliers* and red-crossed dark-green tunic sergeants. One young sergeant held a banner with the heraldic crest of the Kingdom of Aragón. Another banner was the half white and black *beauséant* carried by the *gonfanier*. Behind all the banners and flags was *Padre* Jeremiah carrying a banner with the head of a man, an ox, an eagle, and a lion divided into four quadrants. All at once, there was a unison shout of "*Non nobis Domine non nobis.*" The shout then erupted into a chant as the Soldiers of Christ proceeded into the chapel. The whole bailey area echoed with their voices. The holy men of Christ spilled out of the chapel entrance like an overflowing chalice of *vin*. Each had his designated place to stand as the procession completed its entrance.

I stood near the right side of the chancel as Grand Master Gilbért seated himself in a stone chair near the altar. His commander was to his right, his marshal to his left. *Padre* Jeremiah and *Abad* Miguel had seats to the far right, closest to the altar. Grand Master Gilbért nodded, and the men seated themselves. He turned to his marshal and asked, "Is the chapel secure and our horses ready to defend the cross of our Lord?"

The marshal answered, "*Si, su excelencia.*" This allowed the grand master to convene the convent.

"What matters shall we discuss, holy men of the Center of Earth?" asked Grand Master Gilbért of his men.

"*Su excelencia*, what shall we do with our prisoners?" shouted the men.

"*Padre* Jeremiah, what counsel do you advise us in this matter?" asked Grand Master Gilbért.

"I say we ask the *Santo Père* in Rome why these men were attacking his defenders. We are all disciples of Christ. Should Christians attack Christians? Our *hermanos* in Christ have sinned. Let the *Santo Père* decide their fate. He's the ultimate agent of our Lord and Savior. Let their perdition be determined by him."

"That's true, *Padre* Jeremiah," Commander Hugo Joffre stood and spoke, "yet how do we know the *Santo Père* won't be persuaded by influential members of the Curia who don't believe in our cause? Furthermore, we know the dangerous influence Cardinal Folquet has with the Curia. We have reason and evidence enough to execute all of them."

At once, the bulging chapel erupted with shouted voices of "*Si.*" They repeated it several times until Grand Master Gilbért stood up. Right away, the entire nave of warrior-*moines* became quiet.

"My fellow *frères, oui,* these men deserve punishment for killing fellow Christians, yet it's also their leaders who deserve punishment for their evil deeds. Under the threat of death, our prisoners went to do battle. People close to our *Santo Père* want me killed."

Once again, a unified voice spoke out shouting the words, "*Ninguno.*"

"It's these leaders we must seek out, discredit, and have proof of their guilt," continued the grand master. "I have written a letter to our *Santo Père*, with the approval of the grand master of our entire order, naming and implicating these leaders and traitors. Their avarice dogma and evil intentions, soon all Christian kingdoms will know. *Hermanos,* you know what I tried to accomplish in the Levant and not all of it done by a sword. I attempted a lasting peace with our Saracen neighbors. The hilt of our swords won't sustain Jerusalem. There must be treaties and alliances made for Jerusalem and the Kingdom of God. It's this reason I have been pursued along with my close friends."

At that moment, Grand Master Gilbért stared straight into my eyes. As I sat there in my cold stone chair, I saw the multitude of stares focus on me. Their gazes made me uneasy until Grand Master Gilbért spoke Cardinal Folquet's name followed by boos and hisses coming from all the warrior-*moines*. He then continued.

"In my letter to the *Santo Père*, I have proof that Cardinal Folquet wants a claim to all of Occitania for himself, including what our beloved *Rey* Alfonso the Chaste claims: Provence. Do you want the cardinal on the doorstep to the Kingdom of Aragón? Do you Soldiers of Christ want the corrupt archbishop of Toulouse to invade your homeland?"

Once more, there arose a thunderous roar of "*Ninguno,*" and every warrior was on his feet with swords raised. This demonstration continued until *Padre* Jeremiah arose and stood beside his grand master.

"Fellow *hermanos,*" shouted *Padre* Jeremiah, "let's seek God's counsel in this matter. Let us pray."

I said a silent prayer for *Frère* Gabriel to deliver our letters. Grant Master Gilbért's evidence was a key part to our further search for Saint Joseph de Arimathea's parchments. This proof would end Cardinal Folquet's power and greed. My letter to my *épouse* would ease her fears for my safety. I missed her so much and longed for home.

The *padre* began officiating the mass, while I sat there not knowing what to think. I was a part of the focus of Grand Master Gilbért's speech, while not knowing until now about undisclosed information sent to the *Santo Père*. I now realized the serious desire of the cardinal to grab lands and invade the Kingdom of Aragón. None of this made any sense. I thought the cardinal and his men were just after me and the parchments of the *Sangraal*. I knew Grand Master Gilbért couldn't divulge information on our quest to all his men. However, was this speech a ploy to throw off the unknown traitor in our midst?

The mass lasted until the holy office of Vespers, which when completed we then moved out of the chapel with the rest of the men. I sensed the men's eyes staring at the back of my body while following me. My uneasiness at last left when I reached my chambers and opened the door and entered. To my surprise, Grand Master Gilbért was leaning against the fireplace mantle waiting for my return. His eyes stared at the flames of the crackling fire and his face stayed frozen with contemplation. His head turned in my direction and he spoke.

"Lord Robert, I must apologize for using you in front of my men. I couldn't tell you what my letter said until now. It wasn't just an appeal to prevent my arrest, but to protect the lands in Occitania. Cardinal Folquet wants to use any of the found *Sangraal* parchments to manipulate the *Santo Père* in Rome. The cardinal now knows the apostolic succession from Saint Peter isn't true and our proof shows earlier that our Saint Joseph of Arimathea formalized the first Christian church, celebrated the first mass, preached to the Gentiles, and *Juive* converts. The Holy *Père* in Rome doesn't belong to the true line of apostolic succession."

"But . . . I don't understand about wanting the lands in Occitania and Aragón," I responded, still confused about the cardinal's machinations.

"Don't you see what is motivating him, *mon ami*? It's his greed, power, and the use of extortion. He will tell what evidence he has found to the *Santo Père*, forcing him to agree to a crusade against the lands of the Cathars and their allied nobility. He will use the parchments as a pry bar to force the Curia and the *Santo Père* to his will, giving their approval to this oncoming slaughter. Cardinal Folquet cares nothing for these sacred parchments; it's just a means to justify his grasp for greed, land, and power. The more of Saint Joseph's parchments he can steal, the stronger his control. His subterfuge has reached all way into the Levant and kept me from the grand mastership of our entire order. To this day, my sources say he is trying to confiscate the lands of both Christians and Saracens in Palestine. When I was commander there in Jerusalem, I tried to maintain peace between Saracens and Christians. He is the devil's tool to see that Muslims and Christians won't live together in harmony."

"What can we do to stop this evil man?" I replied, now seeing his full treachery.

"I have evidence showing he has abused his office both spiritually and to the secular members of his Toulouse archdiocese. He has stolen money from the poor and nobles to outfit many *chevaliers* to do his bidding. He has used the church's tithes to bribe two members of the Curia. Some of his personal servants have come to our order and complained of two mistresses he keeps in several of his *châteaux*. He has several *bâtard fils* who the Curia and the *Santo Père* don't know exist. *Hermano* Gabriel has these never-before revealed facts in a letter he's presenting to Pope Innocent the Third. He should be delivering my letter any day now. To further protect our safety and the holy quest we seek, I had a second letter sent to the grand master of our entire order. This should be enough evidence to discredit Cardinal Folquet and bring him to trial before the *Rota Roma*.

"I am not saying that our *Sangraal* quest isn't important. It's urgent that you translate and copy alé parchments that we find. As I told you back at my commandery at Montpellier, you're the appointed one who will reveal their secrets when the time is right. Lord Robert, your heart will tell you that proper time. I hope you have forgiven me, *mon ami*. I was afraid of confiding in you for fear of your capture and torture. I see now that my fears were groundless. You have suffered and displayed the utmost strength and fearlessness. I know now I can trust you, no matter what befalls you."

"*Oui, mon ami*, you have become like an older *frère*, mentor, and confessor to me," I said, seeing a slight smile of relief come over his face.

"Lord Robert, let's prepare to leave and present ourselves at the court of *Roi* Alfonso. You will be quite pleased with the huge banquet he will have thereafter."

I finished arranging my clothes, chain mail, brushed my now shoulder-length hair, and then proceeded with Grand Master Gilbért to my door to leave. There waiting in the passageway was *Abad* Miguel and Chaplain Jeremiah.

"Is this the new lord of Burgundy that my eyes befall upon here tonight?" asked *Abad* Miguel with a face of wonder and a slight grin coming through his wavy white beard. "You aren't the same man who came with me from Huesca, are you?"

"*Si*, it's just the simple wonder of clean clothes and the miracle of soap and water. This would be what my Marie would see, back at our *château* in Borron. However, my *fils* Brian and Henri might not recognize me with long hair and a beard."

"Those clear blue eyes betray your Norman lineage. We can tell you're a man from the North Country, even if we didn't know your name. Dirt wouldn't obscure that fact."

Abad Miguel was right, though I hadn't thought about how I appeared to my companions. Most had dark hair and dark eyes. This was most true of *Padre* Jeremiah. His dark black curly hair, swarthy skin, and pronounced Semitic nose was a marked contrast to my fair complexion and chestnut-colored hair.

As we approached, small crowds of fancy-dressed nobles were milling about next to several ornate *Mudéjar*-carved pillars. To my astonishment, all their heads turned at once as we approached. They knew Templar *chevaliers* didn't appear often at court, and the courtiers stared with concern. Yet, their total consternation seemed not directed toward us, but the sudden appearance of Muhammad Nur Adin dressed in his finest multicolored silks and a jeweled scimitar at his waist. His habit of coming out of nowhere still startled me after these many weeks.

As the five of us waited, in front of the courtier line, I could hear a constant murmur of voices asking who we were. Their whispers stopped when we heard the heavy thumping footsteps of the palace guard, followed by the lord high chamberlain. The palace guards were dressed in the usual military type hauberk and coif. Their dark blue tabards had the royal crest of Aragón emblazoned on each guard's chest.

The chamberlain wore a velvet surcoat the color of rich dark wine. Under it were the tips of black-brushed suede boots. Instead of wearing a hauberk under his surcoat, there was a high collar of light blue gambeson. He held a long thick wooden pole topped with a red and blue-jeweled medallion showing his office of authority. On his head was a black arming cap. Around his neck and shoulders, he wore a royal court neck chain with red and blue stones affixed on each of his silver badges. At his side was a small silver-hilt dagger attached to a wide black leather belt. The scabbard matched the leather of the belt except for its silver-plated tip.

The chamberlain barked out, "*Atención!*" followed by the word, "*Seguir mí,*" which moved us forward up a small flight of steps that spiraled through one of the round turrets. After reaching the landing, the hallway became an ornate gold-colored passageway that led to the palace throne room. Upon entering this large chamber, my eyes squinted from the brilliance of hundreds of blazing candles held in holders of solid gold. The walls appeared to be made from solid gold too and the ceiling the same. Also, the carved recessed gold squares of the ceiling intensified the candlelight, leaving me for a moment blinded.

Above, on all four sides of the rectangle throne room, were small gallery openings. These came down from the ceiling and were just tall enough for one person to peer out and observe the procession of courtiers. I estimated fifty such openings, with every one occupied with a person gazing out at our procession. The room filled at once with barons and nobles as we approached the elevated thrones. The presence of scaffolding and unattended tools indicated that the palace room was under renovation. On a raised dais were four vacant plain dark oak throne chairs, whose backs were in the shape of a triangle. They were in stark contrast to their opulent surroundings.

The chamberlain positioned himself next to a small mushroom-shaped door opening where the palace guards raised their herald trumpets and blew out a shrill sound before he commenced to speak. Grand Master Gilbért and I, along with rest of our band, drew closer to the dais to hear and to be seen.

CHAPTER XXV

tención! By the grace of *Dios*, *Don* Alfonso the Second, *rey de* Aragón, *condé de* Barcelona, Catalonia, Provence, Cerdanya, y Roussillon."

In proceeded the *Rey* de Aragón, holding a cross-topped golden orb in one hand and a golden scepter in the other. He appeared to be in his mid-thirties and was wearing a green velvet robe trimmed in ermine. On his head was an ornate crown with encrusted jewels of rubies and emeralds alternating on each gold cross. Under his velvet robe was a long-sleeved tunic made of the finest red silk. Around his waist, he wore a gold-threaded silk sash, with a solid gold scabbard enclosing a large dagger. A full dark-reddish beard and mustache covered his face and his brown eyes sagged with weariness from his responsibilities of ruling a vast empire. Following him was his *reina*.

The chamberlain again barked, "*Atención!* By the grace of *Dios, Doña* Sancha, *reina* de Aragón, *condesa* de Barcelona, Catalonia, Provence, Cerdanya, y Roussillon." She appeared to be about the same age as *Rey* Alfonso the Second, though her eyes were jet black, flashing back and forth with energy as she surveyed her subjects. She was a diminutive woman with snow-white skin, lacking the olive-colored complexion of her husband. The *reina's* face was oval-shaped; her head was covered with a green and gold velvet head roll, topped with a gold leaf-shaped tiara encrusted with diamonds. A white gauze veil hung under the head roll. Small black ringlets of hair protruded from her forehead. She was better than plain in her facial features, yet what caught my eye was the entrance of a woman whose beauty was from heaven.

When the chamberlain announced her presence, one thing that distracted me was the loud rapping of his long staff of office, as he spoke. "By the grace of *Dios, Doña* Helena, *princesa* de Aragón, *marquésa de* Barcelona, *castile y* Provence. The widow of the late *Don* Pedro Bernardo Ramón, *principe de* Aragón, *marqués de* Barcelona, Provence, martyr of the battle *de Hattin, y hermano* to our beloved *Rey* Alfonso the Second."

Helena was taller than the *reina*, with a slender face and high cheekbones. The *marquésa's* neck was long and graceful. Her skin was a healthy pink color with no blemishes. She had full moist lips that flowed down to a fine pointed chin. However, the greatest striking feature of her beauty was her eyes. They were blue gray, topped with two exquisitely formed auburn-colored eyebrows. Her nose was small and straight, above which was a full forehead. Her head held a black velvet hood encompassed with a halo-shaped crown made of gold and pearls. A small black veil extended down the back of her hood, which revealed some of her auburn hair. She wore a gold and ruby necklace that ended in a gold filigree cross; a large tear-shaped pearl lay between her breasts.

The princess's dress had a square gold-trimmed bodice made of blood scarlet-colored velvet. Each draped sleeve exposed the inside material made of gold and scarlet diamond patterned silk. Both of her long arms were encircled with gold bracelets and fingers with rings of garnet cabochons. There was a large gold broach pinned just below the gold trim of her bodice. Yet, quite prominent was her dress, which had a chain belt of gold draped around her waist. The center of the chain had a sizable oval buckle containing a large sapphire in the center. The rest of the girdle belt had alternating square and oval-shaped medallions of smaller sapphire and ruby stones. Extending from the gold belt was a long single gold chain, which dangled down across a gold and scarlet-colored brocade skirt that ended with a rectangular solid gold box. The unusual box was about the size of a man's hand.

I didn't even notice the bishop as he entered the throne room, for my stare had transfixed on this angelic-faced woman. I looked to see if my stare was obvious, but the rest of the courtiers and guests were focused on their *rey*. When all four were seated on their thrones, that is when we bowed in respect; then did I relinquish my stare. After the courtiers had seated themselves, once more my eyes transfixed on Helena's stunning face. As I stood close to her, I feared she would hear the rapid beating of my heart. I couldn't remove my eyes from her, and the more I stared, the warmer my face became. *Princesa* Helena was quite regal appearing while sitting on her large throne chair. Her bearing was ethereal. Once, I caught a glimpse of her staring at me, but our eyes met just for a few heartbeats.

There was a moist sadness in her eyes, as though they were staring into the past. Again, she glanced in my direction as the chamberlain started announcing members of the court of *Rey* Alfonso the Second. This time she didn't stop staring at me, but her eyes told me she didn't know who I was. Another trumpet blast from the palace guard allowed the chamberlain to announce the various visitors and courtiers from the Kingdom of Aragón. It was obvious that the *rey* and *reina* were familiar with their nobles, speaking the name of each noble as they gave homage to their liege lord.

When our time came, Grand Master Gilbért came forward, holding his long silver staff of office, and bowed before the *rey*. The sudden rising of the *rey* surprised the assemblage as he embraced the grand master and said, "*Bienvenido, amigo.*" *Doña* Sancha and Helena smiled their approval as *Rey* Alfonso continued to embrace and shake the hand of Grand Master Gilbért. Then I remember what *Abad* Miguel said about teaching these two men as boys.

The sole person who wasn't pleased to see Grand Master Gilbért was the bishop. Most Roman church bishops didn't approve of the Poor-Soldiers of Christ and their special favor the *Santo Père* gave them. His scowl of displeasure changed with the announcement of *Abad* Miguel and his *abadia* at Huesca.

Next to appear before the *rey* was Muhammad Nur Adin. All eyes fixated on the Saracen lord from the Levant as he bowed before *Rey* Alfonso, using his hand to touch his black silk turban to show homage. I hadn't heard Muhammad's full title of nobility until the chamberlain barked it out. "*Principe* Muhammad Nur Adin, emir de Jazzin," he announced to the court of *Rey* Alfonso.

"Lord *Roberto*, *Barón* de Borron *y* Northern Burgundy, writer of letters, poet *y trouvère* de Northern Burgundy *y* Normandy. Hail most esteemed of storytellers."

The entire room clapped their approval of my presence, which shocked me. These were total strangers to me, yet they all smiled with approval of me being at court. As I gawked toward the elevated platform of throne chairs, *Marquésa* Helena clapped harder than anyone else, displaying a large grin. Second in intensity was *Reina* Sancha. The *rey* was smiling from ear to ear; however, the bishop was staring with a stoic face. After my unexpected introduction, I stood there wondering how the *rey* knew that I was a *trouvère*. My baffled thoughts were right away distracted, when the chamberlain declared, "Lords and ladies, your *rey* desires your presence in the banquet hall for a royal feast."

The trumpets blew again and the *rey, reina,* and *marquésa* rose and moved out the side door of the golden room and disappeared. The chamberlain motioned for us to follow him. We traveled down a stone-columned corridor that led to a large mushroom-shaped entrance. Inside the entrance was a large hall, with many long wooden tables arranged in a systematic pattern. The banquet hall wasn't as bright as the palace throne room, yet many large lit candles gave it a warm enjoyment of the forthcoming festivities. The bright flickering candles reflected off the silver-plated salvers, which were arranged on fine dark-blue damask silk tablecloths that covered each table. At the right end of the banquet hall, on an elevated stone platform, were *Rey* Alfonso, *Reina* Sancha, and *Marquésa* Helena, all seated at a long table with four empty chairs. The chamberlain whispered something into Grand Master Gilbért's ear and then he turned to speak to each of us.

"We have been requested to sit at the *rey's* table as his guests of honor. Let's follow the chamberlain and he will seat us according to the *rey's* wishes."

I was both nervous and surprised to have the privilege to sit between the *reina* and the *marquésa*, while Grand Master Gilbért grabbed his chair next to *Rey* Alfonso, followed by Muhammad and *Abad* Miguel. This left the bishop to the far left of the *rey*.

I sat there in silence, not knowing what to say or how to say it. The Iberian language wasn't familiar to me. My eyes just stared at the large silver saltcellar positioned in front of the *rey,* which resembled a toy boat. At once, I sensed both charming women gazing at my face, waiting for me to speak, while a faint fragrance of vanilla perfume teased my sense of smell. I was stunned when the *reina* addressed me in my native tongue.

"*Bienvenu, Seigneur* Robert de Borron to our Kingdom de Aragón. I hope you will enjoy our festive banquet tonight and I am thrilled you are entertaining us with your *trouvère* talents." *Reina* Sancho had a pleasant smile on her round face.

"*Merci beaucoup*, your highness. It's an honor to be at court and dine at the *rey's* table. As far as my *trouvère* talents, that may be debatable."

"You're too modest, *Seigneur* Robert," the *marquésa* said. "It's not every day we have a baron come from Northern Burgundy to visit our court. Besides, your writing reputation has preceded you."

I turned my head to acknowledge and stared into those blue-gray eyes I first noticed about *Marquésa* Helena. She gave me a slight smile and waited for my reply. Instead, *Reina* Sancha spoke again.

"*Seigneur* Robert, my husband, the *roi*, is a troubadour too and keeps up on the current poets, writers, and *trouvères*. You may not know this, but *Roi* Alfonso is a cousin to Richard I, *le Coeur de* Lion, who is a *trouvère* as well. Your poems and reputation have come to us from Normandy by way of Aquitaine."

"*Oui, Seigneur* Robert, and also your fighting prowess," said Helena. "Bless my husband's martyred soul; if he were here today, it would be an honor for *Principe* Pedro to meet you and once again see Grand Master Gilbért." She looked concerned. "How is the dagger wound you suffered at the hands of one of Folquet's *chevaliers*?"

Again, I was amazed that *Marquésa* Helena and *Reina* Sancha knew so much about me. The *marquésa* had me enthralled in her enchanted gaze as she inquired more of my life.

"The dagger wound wasn't too deep, and I am mending quite well. *Merci beaucoup* for your concerns, your highness."

"I am sure you are wondering how I know that Cardinal Folquet has you in his crossbow sights. Grand Master Gilbért and my late husband were close friends in the Levant, so it's my job to keep track of all my husband's devoted friends. For weeks, there have been rumors of a great writer and fighter following Grand Master Gilbért dressed as a Soldier of Christ. The thing I don't know is why you and Gilbért are here. My sources say it has something to do with an old book. Is this true?"

I hesitated to reply at that moment, trying to think of something to say that wouldn't divulge our true purpose. All of a sudden, the chamberlain entered and hammered his staff to the stone floor, his distraction help save me from responding. "*Señors, señoras, caballeros, y* clergy, supper is now served."

From two side doors, servants scurried in with large silver salvers of boar's heads, peacocks, finches, cranes, eels, quail, different colored cheeses, and large brass flagons of ale and *vin*. The *rey's* table had its *vin* poured first into large silver chalices. I glanced toward the *rey's* chalice, which glowed with pure gold. After a short time, all the food appeared on each table, and then the bishop rose to say the blessing.

He admonished everyone to eat all their food and if any was left over, they were to give it to the poor. After which, *Rey* Alfonso rose and proposed a toast to his lifelong friend Grand Master Gilbért, to his tutor *Abad* Miguel, and both *Principe* Nur Adin and me for coming such a great distance. The entire court stood with cups raised and gave out a loud voiced "*salute!*" followed by quiet gulping of their drinks.

I then knew I must come up with an answer to satisfy the *marquésa's* curiosity as we began our repast.

"I will answer your question with several questions, if I may, your highness?"

She nodded her head to continue.

"Aren't *Rey* Alfonso, Grand Master Gilbért, and *Abad* Miguel lifelong friends? *Abad* Miguel has wanted to reacquaint himself with his former pupils and reminisce. He has spoken of this for at least a fortnight. Was not the *rey* responsible for helping in the promotion for the grand master? Grand Master Gilbért wants to give his thanks for the *rey's* influence. As for as an old book, I accumulate a lot of my writing material from old books. However, Grand Master de Érail may have a better answer to your question. I am just along on research business. You should address your inquiries to him."

"That I will, *Seigneur* Robert de Borron, for our court life is filled with intrigue, some of it is harmless, while other new visitors threaten our kingdom. All strangers are my business. I hope I haven't offended you for saying that or you think of me as some knave. All in our royal family are cautious. Besides, you already know the machinations of Cardinal Folquet. He wants to confiscate all the lands of the Cathars, their noble sympathizers, and neighboring kingdoms. Any evidence of us being heretical, no matter how small, could have us burned at the stake. He's an evil man, just ask the *Comte* de Toulouse. His Cathar sympathies have landed him in the Cardinal's spiderweb. *Roi* Alfonso is a strong leader and has considerable influence with the *Santo Père* too as well as a close friendship with your entire order's grand master. This is a strong fortress to defeat the cardinal, yet we shouldn't underestimate our enemies."

Our first course arrived, which consisted of herb-spiced quail that I washed down with one of their excellent Iberian red *vins*. Then arrived a diced vegetable broth, filled with carrots, parsley, cabbage, onions, and sage. This course was followed by salvers of tangy aged cheese. Accompanying the meal were numerous flagons of ale, poured by young squires.

"*Seigneur* Robert, I see that you are enjoying our feast. Do you know what tomorrow will be?" asked the *marquésa*.

"*Non*, I do not."

"It's the first day of Advent. You can see your arrival was the right day. Fasting will start tomorrow, and we won't see these meats again until the Christ Mass."

She was right. I had lost track of time, and the days had become meaningless to me. It was as if time had disappeared within a blink of an eye, yet I felt I had been catapulted from the present into the past as I sat there speaking to the Greek goddess Aphrodite of mythology.

"*Seigneur* Robert, I am still not convinced as to why you're wearing the mantle and surcoat of the men of the Center of Earth. Is there some reason you want to be celibate and give up your lands? This seems strange for a *trouvère*."

Once again, this noblewoman had forced me to explain why I was traveling with the warriors of Christ. *What should I tell her?*

CHAPTER XXVI

Grand Master Gilbért thought we could travel much faster with me wearing the clothes of a Soldier of Christ. As you said earlier, my writing reputation precedes me throughout Occitania and the Kingdom of Aragón. As you well know, most kingdoms don't stop or question men of the Temple." I raised a slice of cheese to my mouth and saw *Marquésa* Helena staring at my face while sipping her cup of dark-colored ale.

The next course of our meal came with the swiftness of an arrow. I hadn't finished my first piece of cheese when a baked peacock and boar's head lay before us on our table. I hadn't seen this much food since I left my *château* at Borron, and even then, we didn't have such a variety of viands.

"Tell me, *Seigneur* Robert, what is it like to live

in Northern Burgundy? Do you have snow most of the winter?"

"*Oui*, the ground stays blanketed with an icy covering of snow for several months." I think I'd satisfied some of her prying questions. For now, she appeared interested in my homeland.

"How do the noblewomen dress in Burgundy? Please don't spare any details."

She seemed spellbound as I provided her with a man's description of women's clothing and fripperies. I couldn't keep from staring at her delicate swanlike neck as we discussed fashions until the next course of eel and fish arrived, thus interrupting our conversation. We both partook of the fish instead of the eel while joking and laughing about the fear of snakes.

"So, *Seigneur* Robert, please continue about the women of Burgundy. What colors do they prefer?"

It was difficult to concentrate on the questions she posed as I continued enthralled under her spell of loveliness. My answers must have satisfied her as she moved on to another fashion topic. However, if anyone asked about our conversation, I couldn't have given them an accurate response.

"What style of shoes do they wear?" she asked. I had to force myself not to stare into her eyes, as she seemed to read my thoughts, which I prayed she couldn't do. I was so attracted to this noblewoman of such a high degree my entire being ached to hold her. She too stared into my eyes, which made me even more unnerving. A sudden guilt came over me and my *épouse's* face came into my mind's eye, causing my palms to sweat.

"My ladies in waiting will be pleased to hear about the fashions of Burgundy. I hope I am not boring you with this conversation on fashion and styles. I do have one more question to ask you, but I must admit it's of a quite delicate nature. The courtiers say I am a bold woman, so I will ask you about ladies' undergarments. I assume you are knowledgeable in these matters since you have written about courtly love in some of your poems." Regarding her question, she then qualified it, "You don't have to answer this last question if you would prefer not."

With a warm-faced smile, I gave her a silly answer. "Your highness, since we men have always been surprised by your feminine wiles, I will leave it at that." She laughed, and then I laughed too as we drank another mouthful of ale.

"I see you are a diplomat as well as a poet, *Seigneur* Robert. Please tell me more about your writings and poetry."

"My benefactor, *Comte* Gautiér de Montbéliard, has helped me sell my poems and writings to numerous duchies and counties. His influence with the many courts of northern and southern Gaul has made it a propitious time in my writing career. I owe a great debt to the *comte*. He saw God's gift in me to be a writer. Before I left my home, I was working on a story about Percival, a *chevalier* of *Roi* Arthur's roundtable."

She started to respond, but I interrupted. "But enough about me, tell me something about you, your highness." Just for a moment, she distracted me by her right-hand tapping on the silver cup that held her ale. Her fingers were long and soft in texture with each nail oval-shaped, and her right ring finger held a large gold ring with garnet stones circling it. She still wore her wedding band on her left ring finger.

"Do you have any children, your highness?"

I observed her hands tighten around the ale cup, followed by a short silence before she replied.

"I had a *fils* named Diego who died at birth. Diego lived one day, just enough time for me to hold him in my arms." At once, small tears rolled down her cheeks and she said nothing more.

"I am so sorry to bring back tragic memories; please, forgive me."

"*Non*, please don't apologize. It's something that is part of life. I am still young and may yet marry again."

I thought it best to change the course of our conversation to a more neutral subject. Yet I didn't think it was the appropriate time to mention I was married. Helena seemed quite alone and wanted somebody to listen to her sentient past. Her demeanor and voice appeared cathartic as her spoken words flowed from her beautiful lips.

The next course of our meal arrived, and the young squires brought the last *entrement* that consisted of fanciful foods called *solteties*. To my surprise, they were honey cakes shaped in the form of a chalice. Each salver had a large cake chalice covered with gold-colored icing. At its base were white pearls surrounded by pomegranates and an orange round fruit ringed with nuts and grapes. As each silver salver arrived in front of the courtiers, more squires followed with brass flagons of wine. I sat there wondering if there was some significance in the unusual-shaped cakes.

After they finished serving, something came over me to count the number of cakes. Again, to my amazement, there were a total of fifty-eight, the same two numbers, penta and octa that our Savior whispered to Saint Joseph of Arimathea after the Last Supper. Was it a divine clue or hap-penstance? However, my heart told me that it was God's will and not chance. All my vexed thoughts vanished by the soft voice of the *marquésa* asking me another question.

"*Seigneur* Robert, is there something wrong? You appear as if you are somewhere else. I hope I am not boring you with my presence."

"*Non*, please forgive me again for being rude. A recent thought caught my attention. Where was I? Oh, how did you obtain your title? I am curious to know."

"It was a title bestowed on me after my last brother died. He was a *march seigneur,* between his march, the *Royaume de* Castile, and the Moors. My *frère* was *Roi* Alfonso the Eighth de Castile. *Reina* Sancha is my *soeur.*"

"So, you are telling me that *soeurs* married *frères!*"

"*Oui,* that is correct. My oldest *frère,* the *roi* wanted to strengthen the hold on Iberia from the Moors. He pledged my *soeur* and me to marry both *Roi* Alfonso the Chaste and his *frère,* Prince Pedro, my beloved husband. I agreed to do this if I could keep my late twin *frère's* march and it wouldn't be a part of my dowry. His memory was important to me."

"Well, I must say you have quite a business head on those beautiful shoulders, but what did the late Prince Pedro say to this matter before you were betrothed?"

"*Merci beaucoup* for the comment, *Seigneur* Robert, it's not often I hear someone say something pleasant about me. Numerous subjects think I am still in mourning for my husband, which I am. My older *frère* and I insisted on this arrangement and *Roi* Alfonso the Chaste didn't object. I think back on it now and see that material things shouldn't be the memories in our hearts. It's the memory of loved ones in our mind and heart that God wants us to remember. Don't you agree, *Seigneur* Robert?"

"*Oui,* the matters of nobility and wealth are worthless unless we use it with God's design for the widows, the orphans, the poor, and the lame."

By now, the chalice cake slices were served to each of us sitting at the table of honor. Alongside the cake were pomegranates and several strange round-shaped bright orange fruits unfamiliar to me.

"Your highness, what shall I do with this orange-colored fruit? How must I eat it, without embarrassing myself?"

"They are called oranges and are grown by the Moors along the Mediterranean Sea near a southern coastal town called Valencia. Use your knife to start peeling it. Observe."

Her delicate fingers clasped the table knife from her salver, and with refinement she started removing the rind from the fruit. After peeling it, she broke the pale-orange-colored interior into sections and removed the seeds from within. Smiling, she held a section of the orange to her full lips, then without a sound sucked the juice from it and ate the flesh. Helena then used the finger bowl in front of her to wash the sticky juice from her fingertips and dried them on a napkin.

It was a sensuous sight as I gazed at her eating each piece of the orange. My heart pounded faster with each section she put to her lips. With my distracted eyes, I started to peel my fruit wrong, then sensed her warm fingertips grasp my orange and peel it for me. After peeling the fruit, she handed me the fleshy sections, put her fingertips on mine for a moment, and released the fruit to me.

"See how it's done. Now hurry and eat it so you can enjoy the sweet taste. The pulp will release its sweet taste by sucking and chewing on each section." Her provocative words had me squirming in my seat, which left me in a trance with her demonstration.

"Each morning I have one of my servants prepare me a cup of its orange juice after I awake. Before you leave us, I will give you some oranges for your journey."

"I appreciate the gift, your highness, and I know that it will be consumed with vigor." After finishing my orange, I neglected the pomegranate and started eating my section of the chalice cake. It had a light buttery taste and the icing melted in my mouth, leaving a sweet-tart sensation on my tongue. I finished my piece and resumed my conversation with *Marquésa* Helena.

"What are your courtly responsibilities in the Aragón *Royaume?*"

"See those flagons of *vin* that are being served? My estate produces enough of our splendid Iberian wine to export to England. *Roi* Alfonso has worked out a business arrangement with his cousin, Richard I, *le Coeur de* Lion, to ship all my excess *vin* to *Roi* Richard's subjects. I share part of my profit with the *roi*; the rest goes to my *château* at Maluenda. Tell me what you think of my *vin.*" Just then, one of the squires poured a large portion of the dark garnet-colored liquid into our goblets. I raised my chalice and gave a toast.

"To a remarkable noblewoman, who *Roi* Alfonso is fortunate to have in his court," I declared. There was the traditional metal clinking sound as our two cups met, after which a smile broke out on her exquisite face, exposing two rows of perfect white teeth. With grace, she put the cup up to her moist lips, as did I, each of us swallowing the divine liquid. Indeed, she did produce a celestial tasting wine. Its rose-smelling bouquet lingered in my nose long after I finished the first cup. The aftertaste was that of sweet cherries, grapes, and the strange orange fruit I had just eaten.

"What do you think of my *vin*, *Seigneur* Robert?"

"It is the best wine I've consumed. I would appreciate another cup."

At once, her long silk brocade-covered arm raised, and a squire appeared to pour a second cup. Our conversation continued with *Marquésa* Helena asking about my writing and songs.

"Can you tell me about your latest *cantos*?"

"I haven't written any recent songs of *amour*, just a *chanson de geste*."

"What are they about, if I may inquire?"

"By all means, your highness. They are about the prophet Merlin and the goodly *Chevalier* Percival."

"How intriguing that one of your *chansons* is about *le Sangraal*. I have always enjoyed the epic adventure of Percival and his quest for the Cup of Christ. Tell me, where did you acquire your material?"

"My *père* passed down the stories of Percival to me. Also, my *mère's* family lived near the coast of Brittany and heard many tales of druids and their menhir stones. As a young child, this excited my imagination and started me writing these tales into romantic stories."

"I hope you would sing one of your chapters for our courtiers. All here know your native language and your performance would top off our supper meal."

"But the *roi* is planning to have his jester entertain his courtiers. In most courts, the *roi* has him last," I argued, raising a protest, and not wanting to be the center of attention. "Besides, I didn't bring any instruments with me."

"That shouldn't be a problem; the court jester is accompanied by musicians. They are the best men in the *royaume*. I will have one of the musicians loan you his lute. The others will accompany you on their hurdy-gurdy, recorder, and harp."

"Did I hear *Seigneur* Robert say he will be our *trouvère* entertainment tonight?" *Reina* Sancha asked.

"*Oui,* it's true, *Reina* Sancha, *Seigneur* Robert is too modest to say, yet I can see it in his face he wants to show us his skills." *Marquésa* Helena had a beguiling smile on her face. Helena's round-shaped eyes had me at her command. I couldn't refuse either one of these regal women. The *reina* turned to her husband, and he motioned for the chamberlain to come forward. The *rey* whispered in the man's ear and he left at once to announce my up-and-coming performance. After three whacks of his staff of office, the man spoke.

"*Atención*, courtiers, our gracious *Rey* Alfonso is providing for you tonight the noted and illustrious *trouvère* from Northern Burgundy, *Seigneur* Robert de Borron. He will be performing the *chanson de geste* about the *caballero* Percival."

As I arose from my seat and then moved to the center of the banquet hall, the entire court broke out in applause. After the applause ended, one of the musicians placed a large white pine and chestnut framed lute into my hands. I glanced toward the *rey's* table of honor and saw the *marquésa* urging me on with her long slender fingers. Turning to face the many fancy-dressed courtiers, I saw their eyes widen with surprise to see a dressed Templar troubadour. Their gaping mouths at once prompted me to begin my *chanson de geste*.

"There was once a most chivalrous and godly *chevalier* by the name of Percival, who left his home of his grieving *mère*. He traveled to the great court of the wise *Roi* Arthur; there he met many brave *chevaliers*. Thus, he starts the quest for his great adventure. One day at the time of

Pentecost, all the *chevaliers* met at the round table of the departed Uther Pendragon. Around the table were thirteen seats. Before sitting down, *Roi* Arthur declared a great tournament to determine the bravest *chevalier* in his *royaume*. After considerable jousting and sword fighting, the *roi* declared Percival the greatest fighting *chevalier* in all his *royaume*.

"Arthur's mighty lands stretched from the Picts in the north, the Hibernians across the sea in the west, to the Bretons across the sea in the east, and the Isles of Lyonesse in the south. All of Arthur's *chevaliers* wanted Percival to sit at the thirteenth seat of the Round Table and be their leader. *Roi* Arthur agreed, and the young *chevalier* seated himself in the chair, though the great prophet Merlin warned it belonged to the most righteous *chevalier* in the land. Once seated, Percival saw his seat tremble and shake and the floor in front of him opened.

"Unbeknownst to Percival, his grandfather was the fisher king foretold by Merlin. Thus, young Percival didn't fall into the abyss of hell. His lone sin was ignorance. *Roi* Arthur would suffer a great deal for his decision. The Cup of Christ appeared before the Round Table and the Holy Spirit declared that the greatest sained *chevalier* in Christendom would come to redeem *Roi* Arthur's broken *royaume*.

"Percival was to seek out the fisher *roi* and must

ask, 'What is the *Sangraal* and who does it serve?' Once the questions are answered, the fisher *roi's* wounds will be healed and *Roi* Arthur's *royaume* would once again see his Round Table complete. For seven years, Percival continues his quest, fighting evil *chevaliers*, pursued by fair damsel temptresses, and the greatest foe of all, ignorance.

"The prophet Merlin knew of each trial before young Percival experienced it. He followed his progress. After seven years, he appeared to Percival and told him his quest would end in one year and God had tested his faith. After a year he came to the *château* of the fisher *roi* and met his grandfather, Bron, who then asked, 'What was the purpose of the *Sangraal?*' To which he replied, 'It serves in the name of truth and God's love.' He heard other mysteries of the *Sangraal*, which told him those who confess all their sins before God could stand in the presence of the Cup of Christ. Bron whispered the sacred words that our Savior told Saint Joseph of Arimathea the night he visited him in prison. The one worthy knows these words.

"After three days his grandfather Bron gave him the Cup of Christ and the other hallows. Bron then died and was lifted into the arms of our Lord, Jesus the Christ. Percival was the new fisher *roi*, guardian of the *Sangraal*, and the other hallows used at the time of our Savior's life. *Roi* Arthur's *royaume* was once again strong, his *chevaliers* and the Round Table were now complete. The stone seat, Siege Perilous, was no longer broken, and the lands were no longer barren.

"What is the *Sangraal*'s *raison de être*, and whom does it serve? To you noble *seigneurs*, *comtes*, princesses, and *Roi* Alfonso the Chaste, I pose these questions."

CHAPTER XXVII

Silence reigned over the entire banquet hall and the occupants were perplexed. Whispers broke out and one young noble shouted, "Truth!"

However, I retorted, "Whom does it serve?"

Again, silence held sway. I gazed around the room as no one rose to speak until *Marquésa* Helena stood.

"*Seigneur* Robert, *le Sangraal* serves those who are sinless, seek the *Santo Verdad*, and love one another." Helena spoke with an answer that echoed throughout the entire hall. "It's the ladder to our salvation. The other hallows are our reminder of *el Rey de Reys* and his death for the remission of our sins. Each hallow leads us closer to the Kingdom of Heaven and God's *santo* grace."

Glancing at the bishop, he nodded his agreement and both he and *Abad* Miguel crossed themselves, showing their approval. *Roi* Alfonso then gave his approval to *Marquésa* Helena by crossing himself, followed by all in the banquet hall. *Abad* Miguel rose and began to speak.

"The fisher *rey* was to be healed with the *Santo Verdad* of Christ; thus, the cup is service to Christ. Percival was Christ's agent on earth to find the *Santo Verdad* and use it to stamp out ignorance."

Again, the *roi* crossed himself and the entire court of Alfonso the Second followed suit.

"What of the sacred words, my fellow courtiers?" I asked. "What words did our Savior say to Saint Joseph of Arimathea and later pass on to the fisher *roi* and Percival? Can you tell me what these words were?"

I knew there wasn't anyone in the hall who could answer that question. If there was an answer to that question, the next set of parchments, if they still existed, would reveal it. I was ready to finish the story of Percival and *Roi* Arthur, but before I had a chance to pick up my lute, young Jeremiah Santiago de Compostela stood and addressed me.

"*Seigneur* Robert de Borron, many hidden words and their meanings are as a rule right before our eyes. Our *Seigneur* and Savior spoke in parables and metaphors to his disciples. He was testing his followers to see if they were listening with both their hearts and their minds."

"*Oui*, that's true what you say, *Padre* Jeremiah, yet we still must interpret their meanings to find what we seek."

The young chaplain displayed superior wisdom, and I suspected he knew what we were searching for with our trip to Zaragozza. Did he know about Saint Joseph de Arimathea's parchments? He made me uneasy among the crowd of banquet revelers. Glancing at their many faces, I saw a glazed-eyed stare resulting from my inquiry. I shouldn't have proposed that question, the injury was all mine. How would I extricate myself from this major error on my part? Before I could think another thought, Grand Master Gilbért gave a subtle nod to Chaplain Jeremiah, and he sat down. He rose, proposed a toast to me, and my great story of Percival, and begged me to finish the *chanson de geste* about Percival and his *roi*, Arthur.

I continued strumming my melodious sounding lute to the tempo of Arthur's many successful battles in Gaul against the Roman legions. "*Roi* Arthur would have conquered Rome and declared himself emperor, were it not for his nefarious traitor nephew, Mordred, who held Arthur's wife, Guinevere, as a hostage. A great battle commenced at Camlann; Mordred died, and *Roi* Arthur sailed to the sacred Isle of Avalon to recuperate from his grievous wounds. There he rests until the people of the Celtic lands need his bravery once again to fight the evil foes of darkness. As far as the fisher *roi*, Percival is still guarding *le Sangraal* and its hallows, while waiting for the new fisher *roi* to answer the questions of what the *Sangraal* is and whom it serves. Thus, ends the *chanson de geste* of Percival, *le Sangraal,* and the goodly *roi,* Arthur."

The entire banquet hall stood and gave me a standing ovation. It appeared I had accomplished two things this night. My poetic and musical abilities had ingratiated the court of *Roi* Alfonso the Second and diverted the attention away from the question of the sacred words told to Saint Joseph and what was conveyed to the fisher *roi,* Bron. After a considerable amount of applause, I returned to my seat at the *roi's* table.

"*Seigneur* Robert," Marquésa Helena addressed me. "You have lived up to your reputation as a great *trouvère.* I most enjoyed the story of Percival and his quest for *le Sangraal.*" She stared into my eyes with a sincerity I hadn't seen since the day I left my wife to visit my sister. It was obvious to me it wasn't a diplomatic compliment.

"It's a shame that you already have a benefactor, *Seigneur* Robert," *Reina* Sancha said. "Is there any way that my husband can persuade you from your commitment?"

"*Merci beaucoup*, your *altesse*, but I don't think my brother-in-law, the *Comte* Gautiér de Montbéliard would approve, as well as my *épouse, Dame* Marie de Borron."

Both noblewomen's eyes widened at my reply; moreover, *Marquésa* Helena's lips turned down.

"We didn't know you were married and the *Comte* Gautiér was your brother-in-law," *Marquésa* Helena said. Even with a crinkled forehead, she was still gorgeous. Her face still radiated a statue-like quality, reminiscent of Aphrodite with well-proportioned carved lines.

"*Oui*, we are surprised," said *Reina* Sancha, "for your dear brother-in-law is one of the best swordsmen in four *royaumes*. Is your sword as sharp and penetrating as *Comte* Gautiér's?" she inquired with a beguiling grim.

"I don't know if that question is true, however, on several occasions, I forced him to yield to my sword. We fought out of boredom and nothing else. If I had been a *chevalier* of the Sultan Saladin, I think he would have treated me otherwise. Besides, I can testify that Grand Master Gilbért is the best swordsman in Christendom and the Levant. There's no greater determined fighter anywhere."

"You are too kind; all the Soldiers of Christ fear no man and martyr themselves to God. They swing with zeal the sword of Saint Michael's judgment."

Reina Sancha then turned to whisper something into the *roi's* right ear.

"*Seigneur* Robert, please tell me about your *épouse* and your home." Marquésa Helena queried, "Do you have any children?"

"*Oui*, I do have children, Henri and Brian. Both boys like to fight with their small wooden swords and shields. They use our servants as their enemy and that causes my *épouse* some consternation. I miss seeing them so much, for two months have passed since I last saw them." Right away, their small smiling faces appeared in my mind's eye and a moment of sadness came over me. I prayed to myself that *Frère* Gabriel had delivered my letter to my *épouse*, Marie.

"Does one of your boys favor you and the other favor your *épouse*?" the marquésa continued.

"How did you know that?"

"When you said you had boys, an image of two young boys appeared in my mind. One has light hair and blue eyes, like you; the other has dark hair and eyes, which I suspect are like your *épouse*. Once in a while, the ability of 'sight' comes over me like a thin veil. It's not always perfect, yet it gives me the capability to see things in the future and know about what people think. Right now, the images of your young *fils* are clear in my mind's eye. However, your *épouse's* face is misty shrouded. Describe your *épouse* to me and tell me about her personality."

"She's tall like you. Marie's hair is darker and so are her eyes, yet her prominent features are her beauty and demeanor. It's much like yours, exuding an air of confidence that many women lack. Rich or poor, many lack the self-confidence I see in both you and my *épouse*. She dresses quite well, which is often complimented at the court of my brother-in-law."

"*Merci, Seigneur* Robert for the tribute. May I call you Robert?"

"*Oui*, that's fine."

"Also, you may call me Helena. Then it's agreed, we will dispense with the formalities for now. Tell me more about your Marie. What makes you think we are similar in disposition?"

"She also oversees our vineyards at *Château* Borron. This gives me time to write and compose my *chansons*. Marie loves being in the fields and vineyards, riding on horseback, conversing with the peasants. She wants the families of our crofters provided for, that's why we give them a small payment from the sold *vin*. This instills a sense of pride and security in their households. Do you do the same, your highness . . . pardon me, Helena?"

"*Oui*, I even have a hospital on my estate that is visited by the *chevaliers* of St. John. This ensures that my workers are in decent physical health to maintain the demands of *vin* production."

"That is an excellent idea for me to share with Marie."

This noble femme is independent in her thinking, innovative, and benevolent, I thought, *along with all her beauty.* However, I still sensed a void in her life, which reflected in her gray eyes.

"If the weather is clear tomorrow, Robert, would you accompany me to my *château* and see my vineyards?"

"*Oui*, that is an excellent idea, but I must see if Grand Master Gilbért has anything planned."

"And don't worry about safety. *Rey* Alfonso's

chevaliers will accompany us on the road to the *château*. You can have one of the palace guards send me a note later tonight if you desire to accompany me. I will be leaving at first light, right after Prime.

The courtly entertainment continued with jugglers, fire-eaters, and several annoying court jesters who mocked the Poor-Soldiers of Christ to the glee of the bishop. Grand Master Gilbért accepted the verbal barbs of his order losing the holy city of Jerusalem in stride. However, the jester didn't know Grand Master Gilbért and his men weren't even in the Levant at that terrible time. The expression on his face was one of ambivalence, reflecting his thick skin to their words.

The jester then turned on the bishop and the holy church in Rome. He made the bishop shift in his seat with tales of several *épouses* in his cathedral and compared him to the caliphates and their harems. He then pantomimed the bishop counting his tithes and the wonder of the many coins. At once the bishop jumped up from his seat, moved toward the banquet hall exit, while expressing indignation, causing the entire hall to erupt with laughter. The senior court jester then pranced around the hall waving, with his ribbon staff raised over his head with a large grin.

The courtiers continued laughing until they heard angry shouts coming from the palace guards. All heads turned toward the hall entrance and saw the *seigneur* chamberlain approach the *roi* and then whisper something in his ear. To my unbelief, *Marquésa* Helena leaned next to my ear and whispered, "Marcel de Tournay." A spine-tingling horror of doom coursed through my body as he appeared with ten *chevaliers* wearing Cardinal Folquet's *fleur-de-lis* and the cross of Toulouse embroidered on their mantles.

It can't be, I told myself. *He must be a ghost. He died with his men in the Pyrénées montage avalanche.* I realized at that moment that *Frère* Gabriel had failed to deliver the evidence to the *Santo Père*. Cardinal Folquet's cur dog was still alive and functioning under the cardinal's power. My heart further raced with anxiety, also knowing my missive didn't arrive at Château de Montbéliard.

"Your royal highness, I have a writ for the arrest of the grand master of Iberia, Provence, Montpellier, and his men. The archbishop of Toulouse, Cardinal Folquet, has signed it as the supreme leader of the Roman Curia and demands at once that you turn over to me, the cardinal's seneschal, all who are part of this group at your court. This includes the *abbé* of Huesca, Miguel, or Michael. Failure to obey with this Curia writ will mean that your *royaume* will be under interdict in holding mass, baptisms, confessions, marriages, and last rites."

"Who are you to threaten me and my *royaume*, you are nothing but a *bastardo* and lackey!" *Roi*

Alfonso's face turned crimson red with anger. Next came the metallic hissing of *roi's* guards and courtiers drawing their swords. Then the women shrieked and scrambled to move out of the way. Grand Master Gilbért and Muhammad leaped across the banquet table with swords drawn ready to kill Marcel. In rushed more palace guards, surrounding de Tournay and his *chevaliers* to protect their *roi.*

"I didn't mean to offend your highness. I am just a humble messenger doing the work of the église by delivering this order."

"Humble isn't one of the words I have heard to describe you, *Monsieur* de Tournay. You can return the cardinal's writ and tell him to stick it up his ass. My ambassador will call on him within a fortnight. Now get the hell out of my presence or you will be fed to the rats in my palace *oubliette.*"

"Sire, please don't find fault in me, for I have come a long way to bring église justice from Rome. Pardon my boldness, *adios* to you, and your court." De Tournay backed away from *Roi* Alfonso and crept back into the stone corridor with his *chevaliers* and disappeared.

Grand Master Gilbért, Muhammad, and I with raised swords ran toward Marcel and his *chevaliers,* however, the palace guards prevented us, upon the *roi's* orders. Grand Master Gilbért's widened eyes gawked at his royal *ami* with bewilderment.

"*Mon bon amis* Gilbért, Lord Robert de Borron, and *Principe* Muhammad, that *bastardo* wants a confrontation with all of you. Without a doubt, the news of a fight at court wouldn't bode well with the Holy *padre*. Let's adjourn this banquet and follow me to my private quarters. *Seigneur* Robert de Borron, put your sword back into its scabbard and both you and *Abad* Miguel follow me."

CHAPTER XXVIII

My heart pounded with anger that the *bâtard* devil Marcel had evaded justice. As we left the hall, the courtiers sounded like a nest of angry buzzing bees that just had their hive disturbed. The four of us followed the *roi* and his guards down a stone passageway. We passed several iron-made torch holders that lit a smaller passageway that ended in front of a blank stone wall. He dismissed his guards and waited until they were out of sight before he spoke.

"My nobles will think we are conversing in my private quarters and not realize that I have a secret chamber. Not even the *reina* knows of this place."

He crept back to the last iron torch holder and pulled it forward from the wall, which caused the entire stone wall to pivot enough for us to slide through one side. *Roi* Alfonso was the last to enter as the large wall returned to its original position. We faced another narrow corridor that had numerous lit torches perched along both walls. This corridor led to another blank wall. *Roi* Alfonso glanced back with a bearded grin. He placed his large right-hand ring into one inconspicuous notch in the stone and pressed his weight against the wall. There was a slight pause, followed by a rumble of the wall, which caused the sharp grinding sound from the bottom stones. The hair on the back of my neck raised as the wall pivoted on its unseen axis.

Facing us was a quite ornate chamber. A narrow slit of a window was the lone visible opening. At the top of the arrow loophole glowed the evening star. In a corner stood an iron brace of candles providing internal light and, to my surprise, I saw the room contained a large bed. This secret room gave *Roi* Alfonso a secluded chamber from prying eyes. We weren't alone upon entering, which forced me to grab the hilt of my sword as I spied a small dark-haired man in part concealed by a curtain. The *roi* didn't show surprise or fear at the appearance of this stranger.

"Let me introduce you to my sergeant of arms and head of royal security. His name is *Don* Rodrigo de Balaguer. Gilbért, you remember the skinny little *muchacho* who used to follow us around when *Padre* Miguel finished our lessons?"

"*Si*," replied Grand Master Gilbért with both he and the *rey* glancing toward *Abad* Miguel for agreement.

"*Si*, I remember the little scalawag." *Abad* Miguel laughed. "He was always sneaking food out of the refectory as my fellow *monjes* sat down to eat. I see you are now sneaking around for the *rey* in an official capacity. Is this not so?"

Both the *rey* and Rodrigo forced a grin, not knowing if the blessed *abad* was criticizing or being sarcastic. At once, *Abad* Miguel and the grand master embraced the small man, showing him their affection. Rodrigo was clean-shaven, except for a thick mustache and chin whiskers. His clothes were dark black with calf-length suede boots. Around his waist was a small silver hilt dagger.

"Who's this man you are with, Grand Master Gilbért? I know your Muslim scout, but I don't remember him nor recognize him."

"This is *Don Roberto, Barón* de Borron from Northern Burgundy. He is traveling with us on our way to Toledo."

Rodrigo's large forearm and hand reached out to shake my hand, clenching it in a powerful grip.

"*Don* Rodrigo, where did you acquire that strong grip? Was it fighting against Saracens in the Levant?" I asked.

"Quite the contrary; it was in the service of fighting the Moors in Iberia. My *rey* has been generous in letting me be in the forefront of all the major battles."

"*Si*, and now he's in my private employment; few people know he is working for me as a spy.

He knew you men would arrive today and prepared this wine for us. As *rey de* Aragón, I now must wear a different kind of chain mail that keeps accusations and nefarious plots away from me. In the old days, my great uncle and namesake, along with my grandfather, Ramiro the Second, would have beheaded their adversaries to the last man. These days, it pays to use a different tactic. *Mon bon amis*, therefore, I have asked you to come here after encountering that snake de Tournay. Please, sit down while Rodrigo pours us some of *Marquésa* Helena's excellent wine."

Rey Alfonso pointed at a large carved table. It was five sided with detailed carved designs of grapes, leaves, and vines. Sitting on top of the table was a pure silver vase with large silver cups sitting on a gallery tray. *Don* Rodrigo poured wine into each cup with care, then lifted the silver tray and brought it to each one of us.

"*Seigneur* Robert," *Roi* Alfonso spoke in my native tongue with ease. "Do you like the taste of our Iberian *vins*?"

"*Oui*, it's quite different from the native *vins* of Burgundy. It's not as dry but has a fruitier taste. The color is deeper as well. Does it have a greater strength?"

"*Oui*, so be careful of the amount you drink, because we have important business to discuss." Muhammad refrained from drinking the *vin* due to his religious laws.

"I have several posts that *Don* Rodrigo gave me yesterday. Tell Grand Master Gilbért where you have traveled."

"Grand Master Gilbért and *Padre* Miguel, my travels were to Rome," said *Don* Rodrigo. "It was to see the Holy *Padre*. My *rey* wanted you to have a promotion. As *Roi* Alfonso's secret envoy, this was done with relative ease."

"I haven't thanked you, *mon* old *ami*," Grand Master Gilbért said as he bowed his head in appreciation.

"Well, it was long overdue, Gilbért. However, I don't think you will thank me for being a bearer of bad news. My mentor and *amigo*, *Padre* Miguel, this post is for you too." The *roi* handed one note to Gilbért and the other to *Abbé* Miguel. I could see the red wax seal on each post was embedded with an image of two *chevaliers* riding a single horse. Both men read in silence and then Grand Master Gilbért and the *abbé* raised their heads.

The first thing I noticed was their faces had drained of color. *Abad* Miguel dropped the post from his hands. At once, he crossed himself and cried out, "*Madre de Dios*, my *hermano* Gabriel was murdered. It was right before he entered Rome on the Via Francigena. I have felt for a fortnight he was in trouble, for my heart has ached since we departed Huesca. I remember when we were young *muchachos*, we always knew when the other was in pain, for our hearts would ache. I can't believe he is gone. My body seems as if I am missing a large chunk of flesh and soul in his passing. He was such a worthy assistant at our *monasterio*. Everybody at Huesca loved him, in particular the young *muchachos*. How will I tell them he's now dead?"

We sat there in a state of disbelief. I pondered, in silence to myself, who had divulged his destination. Our small band knew who was culpable of doing this evil act. As we continued in our moment of silence, I could taste in the air the smell of revenge rising in that secret chamber of *Roi* Alfonso.

"Let us pray for his soul to find an everlasting peace, rest, and honor through our Lord, Jesus the *Christo*. Please pray with me," *Abad* Miguel said with a dolorous tone in his voice. "Let us not find cavil in these men who killed him, for the devil has made his home in their souls."

The prayer began with a doleful droning sound that echoed throughout the hidden chamber. My heart ached for the *bon père supérieur* as tears rolled down my cheeks. I asked God why an innocent holy man had to die by the hands of an evil power. He wasn't a threat to anyone, just a messenger to the Holy *Père* in Rome. How would the ramifications of his death affect our quest? Moreover, the pending arrest of Grand Master Gilbért, the indications of a spy among us, and the poor emotional state of *Père Supérieur*

Miguel. None of this boded well for finding the next *Sangraal* parchments.

"Who gave you the letters?" I inquired of *Don* Rodrigo, breaking the silence of our sorrow.

"I stopped at a commandery near Poggibonsi for rest on my way back from Rome. The local commander said his men were speaking about an Iberian *monje* who died on their watch. They patrolled that part of the Via Francigena and the commander, like his men, felt responsible for his death. He was more reticent to speak to me of the details when I confided in him my mission to the Holy *Padre*. The documents from the Holy *Padre* on Gilbért de Érail's elevation prompted him to give more specifics of the murder.

"The local villagers who found his body said there were no letters or documents on his body. They said he had thirteen stab wounds, yet he didn't die right away. In the dust, at the side of the road, his bloody hand marked it with a word and two symbols. The word was Huesca and as you can see in the letter, the commander drew the symbol of a *fleur-de-lis,* but the second symbol was a mysterious circle with a five-pointed star in the middle surrounded by what seemed like five fish and a cinquefoil flower. The commander made some inquiries and found out who the *monje* was and where his *monasterio* was located. I know the dying *monje* was telling us that Cardinal Folquet was responsible for his death, yet it didn't appear that way.

"After several days of rest, I thanked the commander for his hospitality and prepared to leave. Right before my departure, the commander told me where the evil act occurred, which was on my route home. I decided to investigate for myself. After one league, I found the spot. There alongside the road was a large dark stain of dried blood in the dirt. There were no symbols or words in the dust or dirt, which may have blown away. Yet, some distance from the road were footprints still visible in the soft mud. I bent down to examine them and noticed these weren't the footprints of the local people. The shape of the shoeprint was the style of our Moorish neighbors.

"Just then, the creaking sound of wagon wheels coming down the Roman road broke my thoughts. Up ahead was a farmer and two young boys sitting in a wagon. They stopped when they saw me approach. I could see the fear in their eyes while thinking that I was a *bandido*. I reassured them I wasn't a robber and gave each a small silver peso. They explained to me that each day they traveled to the local market in town to sell some of their grain. The older man said he and his sons do this each day around the time the sun is overhead.

"I asked if they knew about the *padre's* death. They responded with silence. The oldest boy appeared to know something, but after glancing at his *padre*, he continued his silence. I slipped three silver coins into their hands and again asked the same question. This time the oldest boy said the strangest thing. He told me that there were four brown-hooded *monjes* following *Padre* Gabriel. The boy believed the *padre* didn't know they were following him. The last thing he saw was the four *monjes* speed up their pace and greet the black-robed *monje* on his journey.

"The road I am told is much traveled by the clergy. It's quick, easy to travel, and has several monasteries along the way to Rome. The older boy said they didn't encounter anyone else that day. I was more confused after speaking to him and observing the Moorish-shaped footprints. It appeared these were the last people to see the martyred *monje*."

Don Rodrigo ended his story.

"There's something here that doesn't seem like the cardinal or de Tournay's modus operandi," I added. "Yet, I believe somehow his bloody hands were involved, for it still smells of the cardinal and his minion."

"I agree," *Roi* Alfonso concurred along with his spymaster and nodded in agreement to me. "These weren't common highway robbers. There was a definite motive. What do you say Gilbért?"

"I am sorry to say that I agree with your assessment. Earlier, I told my commandery here at Zaragozza, about the damnable evidence collected against Cardinal Folquet. Until this time, nobody outside *Padre* Miguel and *Padre* Gabriel knew of this evidence. The leak had to originate with one of my people from Montpellier. I haven't seen any suspicions in the men near me. They've all been loyal for many years. I know we can't underestimate the cardinal and de Tournay; however, it's hard for me to believe I have a traitor in my midst. These men helped rescue me out of some dangerous battles in the Levant."

"Has anything changed in their personal lives? I am thinking about their immediate families, such as Guy de Béziers told me about his *mère* and *père*. Could they be held hostage by the cardinal?" I asked. This thought caused my mind to race with other possible nefarious webs to extort disloyalty. My dolorous mind kept returning to poor innocent *Padre* Gabriel's horrible death. Why would another order of *moines* kill him? None of this made any sense, yet my half-closed tired eyes told me to put off hearing any additional information until later, and then organize it in my daily journal. Mornings always seemed to make things clearer, and the written word could show clues. Right now, my emotions had drained me of reason.

"*Don* Rodrigo, where is the *bâtard* de Tournay now hiding? Do you know the location of his camp?" My tired inquiry grabbed the attention of Grand Master Gilbért.

"My sources say he is at Tauste along the Rio Arba. His men, what's left of them, are hiding in a cave along the banks of the Arba. My one source says couriers are riding back and forth from this cave. I suspect he is receiving instructions from the cardinal and possible reinforcements. I have instructed my sources to intercept these couriers."

"We need written proof of the cardinal's instructions," said the *roi*. "Grand Master de Érail, bring me evidence of his machinations to replace what our blessed *Padre* Gabriel had removed from him. I want this nest of vipers crushed after we obtain enough evidence to convict the cardinal. This cunning snake has bitten me one too many times. *Don* Rodrigo, I want you to pack a sack of gold coins and buy every person from here to the Pyrénées who knows of de Tournay's whereabouts. Marcel de Tournay isn't where your sources say he is. He is too smart to stay in one place for long. I want those documents delivered to Grand Master Gilbért within a fortnight. Do you understand what I am asking?"

"*Si*, your *alteza*."

Don Rodrigo bowed his head as a sign of loyalty. *Roi* Alfonso grabbed a large leather sack, the size of my writing saddlebag, dropped it, which made a loud metal *clank* as it struck the stone floor. The *roi* reached down with both hands, lifted it, and then handed to *Don* Rodrigo. It was the largest sack of gold coins that I had ever seen.

The *roi* turned to Grand Master Gilbért. "Gilbért, tell me more about Cardinal Folquet's plans. What is he planning in my *royaume*? Please don't tell me he is selling my *royaume* to the order of St. John. Between your order and the Hospitalliers, I will have no lands left."

"He intends to start a holy crusade against the Cathars. Our commandery in Flanders says he has promised the nobles there all the Cathars' lands if they fight with him. All he needs is the blessing of the *Santo Père*."

"It is then apparent, Gilbért, he wants me to fight two crusades: the Moors and the Cathars. I have no fight with the Cathars. Many of them have sworn fealty to me. Why would you say this?" The *roi's* eyebrows rose with a questionable stare at Grand Master Gilbért and before he could answer, *Abad* Miguel spoke.

"My former pupil, you are too focused on what is below you and not above you. You are a wealthy and just *rey* and the people of Languedoc know this. Where would they go, if threatened? Once this happens, it will be the excuse for the cardinal and the northern nobles to invade your lands and declare you a heretic, and then your subjects would face interdiction. Your *reino* would be fighting the Moors, the Flanders nobles, the Holy *Père*, and then your nobles would seize the opportunity to appoint a new *rey*. Cardinal Folquet has many tentacles that can reach out to grab land and power. I have lost my upright twin *hermano*; I don't want my beloved pupil to succumb to the cardinal's evil spell. Am I correct in my summation, Gilbért?" *Abad* Miguel asked.

"*Si,* this is what I said earlier to the commandery members here at Zaragozza. I suspect that the *chevaliers* of St. John have been contacted by Cardinal Folquet; however, I have no definite proof."

Roi Alfonso sat in silence, stroking his auburn-colored beard in deep thought, then spoke.

"It's difficult for me to sit here and keep my composure. My emotions tell me to marshal my army, have you follow me with your Iberian Poor-Soldiers of Christ, and march on Toulouse, then ride toward the snake's den and capture the fiend. Strike before he tries to strike my *reino.* He's not fit to wear the holy red of a cardinal. I quite desire to put de Tournay on the rack and then behead him."

With an unexpected thud of his fist shaking the table in anger, his face flushed crimson, and, once again, he slammed his clenched fist on the table, rattling the gallery tray holding the *vin.*

"Gilbért, tell me more about the letter to the Holy *Padre* that *Padre* Gabriel was delivering to Rome." He crossed himself again and the anger drained from his face.

"My beloved *amigo* and *rey*, Cardinal Folquet, as archbishop of Toulouse, has stolen money from his church to finance his army. The Basilica of Saint-Sernin has no treasury. Cardinal Folquet has cheated the pilgrims of their money on the way to Santiago de Compostela, snaring them with his church's fake holy relics. Also, Cardinal Folquet has several mistresses and two *bâtard fils*. He's an expert at simony, by placing wealthy clerical members to help in his greedy evil political aims."

"What proof do you still have, Gilbért, of these charges?" *Roi* Alfonso asked.

"Before I left our commandery at Carcassonne, I entrusted a copy of my evidence with Commander Armound de Polignac. In secret, I told him that if anything was to happen to me, he was to deliver the letter to our entire order's grand master, Robert de Sablé. Now, you are one of the few people to know the whereabouts of this copy. I am at your mercy not to divulge this information to anyone else. Two courageous men have sacrificed their lives in trying to stop Cardinal Folquet. I am relying on everybody's trust in this room to keep this a secret."

This new fact made me somewhat confident in our fight against de Tournay and the cardinal. Grand Master Gilbért's new revelation continued to reinforce my strength in his stealth in dealing with evil adversaries. His new information prompted me to address *Don* Rodrigo and Grand Master Gilbért.

"*Don* Rodrigo, with your *alteza's* permission, could you travel to Carcassonne and obtain this evidence? I am sure Grand Master Gilbért will draft a letter of permission and seal it with his ring of authority, for nobody knows your connection to *Rey* Alfonso. At the same time, you will be gathering additional information on our evil adversaries. You can travel fast and be back at Zaragozza before Saint Stephen's Day."

I gazed at Grand Master Gilbért and *Roi* Alfonso for their approval, and both men nodded in unison. *Don* Rodrigo's face lit up with a cunning grin and spoke to his liege lord.

"Your *alteza*, may I have your permission to leave at once? My heart aches to see justice done."

"You have my permission to leave, but first let *Padre* Miguel say a prayer for your safe return and then sain you." We bowed our heads while *Abad* Miguel prayed.

After *Don* Rodrigo was sained, he grabbed the sack of gold coins, bowed to all of us, and stood to leave. *Roi* Alfonso rose, then moved to the corner bedpost, and removed the bed drapes closest to the stone wall, after which he placed his ring into a small indentation in one of the stone blocks. The wall behind the bed moved just enough for *Don* Rodrigo to squeeze through and disappear into the dark corridor. The *roi* turned and smiled in our direction as the stone wall swung back into place.

"The last Taifa *rey* of the Banu Hud dynasty had these devices installed for his safety and escape. I didn't find the hidden passages and chamber until I noticed small chiseled octagonal-shaped designs carved into the stone blocks. The legend that I heard said these were reminders of *Haram al-Sharif* or the Dome of the Rock. Nobody knew their true meaning, yet its design is too random to have a religious meaning. One day I was examining his old personal effects, long after he had died, and found an octagonal-shaped ring you see on my finger." He held up the emerald eight-sided gold ring for all to see. "Now, you're part of my secret; not even the *reina* knows of this place."

The *roi* turned and spoke, "I have been wondering, *Seigneur* Robert, why are you in truth with Grand Master Gilbért? It wasn't to come to this peninsula and sing your *chanson de geste*. Please, tell me, or should I ask Grand Master Gilbért?"

CHAPTER XXIX

I gazed at the grand master, suspecting he would give his approval, to which he nodded his agreement.

"We are in search of *le Sangraal* parchments," I replied, staring straight into the *roi's* light green eyes. "The first original set we have found, copied, and I think destroyed, though Cardinal Folquet may still have it, ready to use against the Holy *Padre*.

"I have heard many rumors of these so-called *Sangraal* parchments, just like the *trouvères* sing about the many *Santo Cálices*. They're just tales and gossip."

"You're wrong, my *amigo*," Grand Master Gilbért at once replied. "I discovered the first set of written parchments by Saint Joseph of Arimathea hidden in the Temple Mount of our headquarters. This is before Saladin conquered it. My deceased chaplain translated a little of the ancient manuscript. He authenticated the age and the author before he died a martyr.

"Several years ago, I brought it back from the Outremer and hid it at the abbey at Clairvaux. The parchments stayed there until Cardinal Folquet found out through his many spies about the possible contents of the book. At first, I believed he thought my order would use the book to gain power for ourselves. The cardinal, not wanting to miss a greedy opportunity, had the Curia declare the parchments heretical because of what Saint Joseph divulged about the initial set—"

"Why was the book declared heretical?" the *rey* interrupted in his hasty curiosity.

"Saint Joseph started the first organized Christian église years before Saint Peter and Saint James the Lesser, who were still in hiding from Caiaphas and the Roman authorities, started their église. According to *le Sangraal* parchments, our Lord and Savior bestowed on him special knowledge of numbers and the wisdom of *Rey* Solomon to start a New Jerusalem and Christian community. Saint Joseph was the first apostle to preach to both the Gentiles and the *Juifs*, just a few years after the crucifixion of Jesus.

"Where was this first official church? I don't know, yet. *Santo* Maria Magdalene and her visions have blessed *Seigneur* de Borron and me and helped lead us to the possible location of the second set. I uncovered a further clue in the Temple Mount that led me to a cave hideout of Saint Joseph of Arimathea. There, I believe, Saint Joseph finished an addition of the *Sangraal* manuscript and then hid it. They were later discovered by the first Emir ruler from Damascus, Tariq ibn Ziyad, who brought them to Toledo for translation. *Seigneur* de Borron has the *santo* ability to translate all of these ancient languages and the speed to make copies for our order to protect."

Roi Alfonso gulped a swallow from his silver cup. "If you have these special *santo* visions, *Seigneur* de Borron, why can't you just ask her where they are all hidden?"

"I can't just call her and she appears to me. *Santo* Maria Magdalene comes to me when she wills it. She has left it to me and the Poor-Soldiers of Christ to complete our God-given destiny. It's not our free will that spurs us on through many perils. It is in our motives and reactions to God's predestination that we are allowed some choice in what he has designed for us."

"Gilbért, now I see why you have enlisted this wise Burgundian *seigneur.* You and your men may be the tip of the spear in your quest, but *Seigneur* de Borron is the strong oak shank of your spear. However, *Seigneur Roberto*, you play a dangerous game with Cardinal Folquet. He will try to capture you, torture every vision out of you, and extract from your mind its meaning for his evil gain. After finishing with you, he will kill you and your body will never be unearthed."

"I know this already, your *alteza*, yet, as I said earlier, God has predestined me to help uncover his son's secret teachings. I have nothing to gain for money or power. All our small band seeks is the truth and nothing more."

"Grand Master Gilbért, it appears we have enough earthly evidence and the divine support of *Dios* and his *santos* to crush the cardinal. He has swallowed more than his stomach can hold and it will burst just as the traitor Judas spilled his intestines on the rocks. I have much faith in *Don* Rodrigo de Balaguer to help deliver the evidence to the *Santo Padre* in Rome. The guards will be doubled while you stay here and don't speak to anyone about this room and *Don* Rodrigo.

"If you travel outside of Zaragozza, let me know. *Seigneur Roberto*, see to it you are accompanied by the Poor-Soldiers of Christ at all times. There are traitors in our midst, and this makes it above all difficult when one of them could be from the Temple of Jerusalem. Now let's adjourn from this meeting and acquire some rest. Tomorrow is the first day of Advent and much rest is essential when fasting."

Roi Alfonso rose from his chair and moved toward the stone block wall next to his bedpost. Here he placed his ring in the same stone symbol, leaned his body weight against the stones, and the wall rotated inward. He motioned for us to follow, while he put his other hand to his lips indicating not to speak. We followed him toward a faint torchlight at the end of a narrow stone corridor. At several junctures in the stone passageway, it necessitated us to turn sideways to fit. Then I heard the steady dripping of water striking the stone floor along with the unpleasant scratching of rodent's feet crossing over my boot toes. The air was hard to breathe and smelled of mold. *How much farther would we travel in this corridor?*

Just then, the *roi* stopped, placed one eye at a peephole, and made the sign with his hand to stop. An oily smelling pitch torch appeared close to extinguishing itself, which was near a peephole. Again, the *roi* placed his ring in a stone block, and then a hidden exit door pivoted outward. He motioned for us to follow. Much to my relief, a gust of fresh air entered the secret passageway. To my surprise, we were outside the *château*. It was a remote section of the palace-fortress covered with dense scrubs.

The concealed exit was at the base of one of the drum-shaped towers. To my left, some distance away, was the stone causeway to the main entrance. The dark sky was moonless, and we blended in with the darkness, even with my white mantle and surcoat. *Roi* Alfonso whispered to follow him and Grand Master Gilbért. It was obvious the *roi* had been down this path many times, for one would have had to have the eyes of a cat to see in this ink-black night.

He led the way while I stumbled several times trying to keep up. *Roi* Alfonso was heading toward the torchlit portcullis of the main entrance. As he approached the main gate with our small band of followers, he shouted out, "Where is the sergeant of the guard?" From behind the portcullis came the *clinking* of chain mail, metal-tipped lances, and the thumping of soldiers' boots.

"Who goes there?" came a voice from the dark interior of the bailey and then another from the top of the tower crenels.

"It's your *rey*. Open at once! I have two men from the Temple of Jerusalem—a Levant *principi* and the *abad* from Huesca. Make haste or there will be hell to pay. No more discussion."

At once, from the dark interior of the bailey gave forth a metal *clanking* sound of iron chains being wrenched, followed by the thick wooden-beamed portcullis rising. The sergeant of the guard approached his *roi*, holding a lighted torch that gave off popping sounds as the black pitch ignited.

"Sire, I didn't know you were outside the palace. If I had known, a detailed escort would have accompanied you and your *amigos*. However, I see you have two *caballeros* from the Temple. Please, forgive my negligence."

"You need to be more vigilant, Sergeant, as well as observant. *Chevalier* de Tournay snuck into our banquet hall without my permission, and you didn't stop him. Under no circumstances will you let anybody into the palace grounds without my permission. I don't care if it's the *Santo Padre* from Rome. Do you understand, Sergeant?"

"*Si*, sire, not even the *Santo Padre* from Rome shall enter."

"For your punishment, you will clean all the garderobes for a fortnight, and this will be on your days not on duty. Do you understand, Sergeant?"

"*Si*, your *alteza*." The sergeant seemed relieved that the punishment wasn't more severe. *Roi* Alfonso turned, faced us, gave a wink, and grinned.

"Holy men of *Dios*, follow me to your quarters for some much-needed rest." At once, he grabbed the pitch torch from his sergeant and led us past the barbican entrance into the fortress interior. He turned and shouted one last order. "Sergeant, double the guards on the quarters of my *amigos* at once."

The bushy-bearded sergeant barked orders to the bailey guards to follow our small retinue. It felt pleasant knowing I would sleep well with extra guards to protect us. From the main entrance, we followed *Roi* Alfonso into the flickering torchlit bailey and proceeded along an ornate pillared cloister walkway. There, about halfway, he stopped, wished us good night, and gave further instructions to his palace guards. *Abad* Miguel, Grand Master Gilbért, and I continued to our rooms, knowing quite well we longed for sleep.

Grand Master Gilbért stopped before entering his room. "*Mes amis,* protect your backs tonight. We know Marcel de Tournay is still alive and out there close. I now leave to discuss with Muhammad what the *roi's* spymaster has told us. *Bonsoir, Abbé* Miguel and *Seigneur* Robert."

The final noise I heard was Grand Master Gilbért whispering Arabic to Muhammad at his door. I entered my quarters, and, to my surprise, there lay a sealed note on a wooden stand next to my bed. At once, my curiosity piqued, and I grabbed the note. I stood there staring at it, then sat on my bed, and little by little inhaled its vanilla-rose fragrance. With care, I broke the unfamiliar seal, put it near my flickering candle, and began reading its contents.

> *Dear Roberto,*
> *Are you still planning to travel with me and my retinue to inspect the vineyards at my estate? I understand that Abbé Jeremiah de Compostela, Commander Hugo Joffre, and Grand Master Gilbért are escorting us to the Rio Jalón and from there to their fortress at Calatayud. My château is located at Maluenda, less than a day's ride from there. Grand Master Gilbért said after his business at the Templar fortress at Calatayud, his moines would escort us to Maluenda. Chaplain Jeremiah says the weather ahead*

*appears favorable, clear, but cold. I know the
last thing you want to do is mount a horse,
yet the road is level, and the surrounding
hills still display some autumn leaves. The
trip shouldn't tire you if we leave before the
office of Prime. Meet us near the entrance of
Saint Martin's chapel and the palace barbican. I desire to see you tomorrow.
Helena*

After reading her note, my heart raced with anticipation, a sensation that I didn't want my mind to comprehend. Now, with regret that my letter didn't reach my *épouse*, Marie, this necessitated another letter to ease her possible concerns for me. Also, this would be an excellent diversion from my emotions for Helena. Yet why hadn't Grand Master Gilbért mentioned about going to his fortress at Calatayud? I suspected a possible traitor in our midst prompted him to do so.

The need for sleep conquered both my sense of anticipation and suspicion and pushed them from my thoughts. Right away, I shed my coif of chain mail, hauberk, and chausses. The last thing I remember before falling asleep was the rose petal smell of Helena's note, which I shoved out of my mind.

An unexpected pounding on my door aroused me from a deep sleep. My body hesitated to come out of its blissful cocoon. As I raised upward, my left shoulder felt tender and tight, but no pain.

"Lord Robert, it's Grand Master Gilbért, I must speak to you at once."

I slid out of bed, touching both of my warm feet on the cold hard stone floor. I moved toward the door, reaching for the metal bolt to unlatch it. At once, he squeezed through the edge of the opened door. It appeared my cohort was ready to ride, for his spurs scraped on the stone floor.

"I have several things to tell you," he said as he entered. "One is bad news, the other is more pleasant and should lift your spirits. I just heard the Holy Roman Emperor Frederick Barbarossa has died. *Roi* Alfonso told me after I left the chapel of Saint Martin. Emperor Frederick fell into a river in southeastern Anatolia and drown. He was leading over one hundred and fifty thousand men and was to meet *Roi* Richard I, *le Coeur de* Lion. Their combined forces were to annihilate Saladin's great army.

"Two rumors are coming out of the Levant. One, the Holy Roman Emperor dropped the Holy Spear of Christ, which caused him to fall off his horse trying to retrieve it, and two, *Roi* Richard won't reach the Levant until the winter is over. Some of my *chevaliers,* returning from our fortress at Acre, sent word that just five thousand of Emperor Frederick's men continued to the Levant and the rest returned home. This leaves *Roi* Richard not reaching the port of Acre until late spring. Saladin will now have time to rally both Sunni and Shia factions of his faith to challenge the Christian army.

"*Roi* Richard will marshal his forces in the Latin kingdom during the hot months of summer. None of this bodes well for our *frères* in Acre or any of our other fortifications. *Roi* Richard has his internal problems in England. The grand master of England has let our order know that Prince John, *Roi* Richard's *frère*, is fomenting trouble against him, which could affect the *roi's* stay in the Levant."

"Enough of this bad news. What does this have to do with our quest, other than the loss of the Holy Lance?" I retorted, while changing my clothes. "Let me hear some enjoyable news, for my heart longs to hear pleasant words."

"We are to travel to our fortress at Calatayud," Grand Master Gilbért revealed. "Chaplain Jeremiah has an extensive library there and thinks it may disclose the whereabouts of the second portion of the *Sangraal* parchments. In addition, we are to escort the *Princesse* Helena there and later to her *château* at Maluenda. For some unknown reason, she desires to check on her vineyard during December. The *princesse* is a woman who can be unpredictable, yet I fear she has a fondness for your troubadour skills. Be careful, *mon ami,* she is requesting your presence with her, and she could, without cause, hurt our holy quest. The *princesse* has several untrustworthy spies who could harm our cause. Her intentions are from God, yet her judgment is vulnerable, since her husband died at the Horns of Hattin.

"You need to finish dressing right away so we can leave before sunrise. Meet me at the chapel after Prime. Search for *Princesse* Helena, she will have members of the palace guard surrounding her."

I didn't say anything to Grand Master Gilbért about my note from Helena, for now I understood she wrote it using her vision of foresight. I found myself primping more than usual, applying a sweet-smelling ointment to my hair. Maybe he was right about her loneliness for male companionship, yet I felt the same for female companionship. I left the quarters of my room and strolled to the giant central courtyard, which still left me in awe with its intricate-carved filigree stone arches. Upon reaching the chapel, Helena greeted me.

"*Seigneur Roberto*, I see you chose to join our group. Our journey will rest you and what you see will inform you."

"*Oui*, but Grand Master Gilbért requested my presence."

Riders and courtier carriages were just moving shadows concealed by the ink-black night as Helena shouted for the palace guards to proceed. A thunderous noise rose from the horses' hooves thumping through the main gate. That signaled the Poor-Soldiers of Christ to gallop to the rear of the large entourage. I spurred my horse and galloped across the causeway into the shimmering sky of stars.

CHAPTER XXX

The early morning copper-colored sky was empty of any clouds, leaving the grass and soil covered with a thick mantle of ice crystals. Our royal retinue didn't converse until the warmth of the rising sun warmed our backs. My mind's thoughts weren't foggy from slumber but jumped with anxiety of what Marcel de Tournay might do next. It was a given evil he would try to thwart our holy quest for the next set of *Sangraal* parchments. Yet, more important, he had both the traits of a wolf and badger and could come at us from behind our backs and never tire or give up.

Up ahead I saw *Marquésa* Helena turn her horse and point him in our direction. Before I knew it, she stood alongside me on her snow-white palfrey horse. She wore a dark blue velvet-hooded cloak and matching colored dress. A small gold circlet encrusted with cut sapphire stones held her hair away from her face. The gold filigree clasp of her cloak came undone as she pulled up her reins to slow her horse. This exposed a small part of her chest that had a square bodice edged with pearls. Covering her long slender fingers were gray-colored kid gloves grasping the leather reins of her horse. She handled her horse like an experienced *chevalier*, better than some of the warrior-*moines*, I thought.

"*Seigneur Roberto*, what do these men from Toulouse want with you and Grand Master Gilbért?" she asked with her large bluish-gray eyes searching for an explanation. "It appears you're hiding something quite important they want, otherwise the archbishop of Toulouse wouldn't have sent his seneschal to serve a writ for Grand Master Gilbért's arrest. In particular, to confront two of the furthermost powerful men on the Iberian Peninsula."

"Marcel de Tournay is nothing but a poisonous snake hiding behind the red cassock of a far greater threat to Christendom," I replied. "Cardinal Folquet and his minions are the devil's disciples who wish us harm. I am afraid that is all I can say at this moment. Please, forgive me if it appears I don't trust you, but I have sworn an oath to God and Grand Master Gilbért not to reveal our quest."

I hoped my tenuous explanation would suffice, but I knew Helena may surmise otherwise, forcing me to change our conversation.

"Helena, we agreed to call each other by our Christian names and not by our titles. Let's enjoy our travel time together with a more pleasant conversation. Please, tell me about your *château* and vineyards at Maluenda. You are an unusual woman of business, and in my home country, such authority isn't allowed for a noblewoman. Where I live, Salic law says women lose their property title rights upon marriage. Did you not tell me you retained your land after your husband died?"

"*Oui*, and this land has been a balm of solace to me since my husband died, along with *Roi* Alfonso's trade alliances to sell the *vin*. The vineyard helps keep my mind busy, alert, and now I have an extended proud family of crofters."

Changing the subject had worked and I could see a pleasant smile form around her cheeks as she spoke of her beloved land. Also, the afternoon sun had warmed our conversation on matters of *vin* fermentation, the refurbishing of her *château*, and the personal lives of vineyard workers.

We had traveled about eight leagues when the River Jalón's rushing waters alerted us to its presence. From the river's edge, the road traveled in a southwestern direction. We followed the road until we came to a large range of hills that circled an expansive valley. On the southern utmost hill perched an enormous *château* facing the entire sandy-colored valley and the surrounding hills. Its appearance was quite formidable and covered the entire hilltop, which seemed like a small *montagne*. The sight of Fortress Calatayud gave me a sense of awe and relief knowing Marcel de Tournay hadn't attacked. This was further confirmed when Sergeants de Beziérs and de Hoult and Grand Master Gilbért came galloping up on their horses, declaring the way was clear up the steep hillside trail. Our horses snorted and wheezed as their heads pointed downward struggling up the last part of the trail. Muhammad shouted something in his native tongue, causing our horses' ears to point straight up, forcing their hooves to dig into the rocky soil that made a *clanking* sound on the rocks to gain further traction.

The *château's* presence was even larger, as we approached the square-shaped barbicans guarding a wooden causeway. The steep causeway narrowed, making me wonder if Helena's carriages would fit, yet to my surprise, the creaking wheels rolled across with ease. The base of the curtain walls, which surrounded the entire *château* were angled out, preventing a besieging army from mining under it. As we approached the portcullis, Grand Master Gilbért shouted *"non nobis Domine, non nobis,"* for the sergeant of the guard to let us enter. The guards didn't respond, leaving the portcullis gate closed, which drew the ire of the grand master. "This is your *Grand Patrón* Gilbért de Érail!" he hollered. "Raise the portcullis at once or you'll lose your habit!"

From the battlements, I saw several dark, green-colored tunic sergeants peeking out from behind the massive crenels to see who was threatening them. At once, several sergeants scurried to greet their grand master, which was followed by a creaking metal sound of the portcullis rising. The sergeant of the guard reached for the pommel of his sword and approached his leader, followed by several of his companions. They greeted him in unison. "*Pardón, su excelencia,* we were afraid it was a ruse to force us to open the gate. After the divine office of Nones, thirty *caballeros* dressed in white mantles appeared at our gate and tried to gain entrance. I became suspicious when their exposed saddle blanket edges had the design of the cross of Toulouse and a *fleur-de-lis*."

"Forgive me for my harshness to you, Sergeant. Your caution is commendable and prevented our ambush. No guard duty for you for a week."

"*Muchas gracias, Grand Patrón* de Érail; let me escort your retinue to their quarters."

The swarthy-faced, bear-shaped sergeant led us through the portcullis gate into a narrow passageway that bent at a sharp angle. Above my head, shafts of late evening light came from several murderer holes used to fire arrows or pour tar down on intruders. The bailey area was expansive and seemed to encompass the entire mountaintop. I surmised that this *château* was one of the biggest on the Iberian Peninsula. Grand Master Gilbért noticed my stare and spoke.

"I see by your steady gaze that our *château* isn't resembling the ones in your native Burgundy. Is this not so, Lord Robert?"

"*Oui*," I replied to his slight questioning grin.

"This *château* is one of the oldest Moor fortresses in Iberia and built by Amir Ayyub ben Habib. It stayed in Moorish hands for three hundred years, until *Roi* Alfonso the Battler conquered this part of Iberia. After he died, his estate gave it to our holy order, and we modified it to suit our purposes. See the many fighting pell posts in the distance? All our Iberian *frères* use them to hone their fighting skills. The posts are from the hardest oak woods we can find, and each member uses an oversized sword to practice his slashing skills. Behind the keep is a large area used for lance practice, which we'll use in the Levant."

"Grand Master Gilbért de Érail," Helena said, "you failed to mention the excellent scriptorium and library overseen by your savant chaplain, *Padre* Jeremiah Santiago de Compostela, and his scribes. I have from competent sources he is one of the smartest men on the continent." She glanced at the young *padre* behind her. Grand Master Gilbért grinned as we glanced at Chaplain Jeremiah's red face.

Abad Miguel stared in my direction with a smile of approval from the praise Helena bestowed upon the young *padre*. I suspected she knew who his *père* was, but out of friendship to Grand Master Gilbért, she kept it to herself.

Chaplain Jeremiah smiled at Helena. "*Muchas gracias,* your *alteza,* for the praise, but God wills it for me to help my *hermanos.* They come from the black darkness of ignorance to become learned men of the light."

We continued following the sergeant of the guard until we approached a gigantic keep. The larger tower of the keep was octagonal-shaped, and the smaller round and square towers were part of the stone curtain walls. These stone walls circled the keep, extending out some distance to form a large redoubt. Additional thick outer walls, which circled the hilltop, protected the keep along with a formidable third interior curtain wall protecting it too. I couldn't imagine these warrior-*moines* letting even Saladin, as Muhammad called him, and his great army of 200,000 men penetrate this well-built fortress.

We stopped in front of the main keep, while several young squires ran forth holding box-shaped wooden steps for us to dismount.

After I had dismounted, Helena asked, "*Seigneur* Robert, this dress makes it difficult to dismount from my saddle, would you please help?"

"*Oui,* it would be a privilege *Marquésa* Helena," I answered, as I grabbed her small waist and helped her out of the saddle. We met facing each other not more than a nose length from each other. Her bluish-gray-colored eyes stared into mine and our gazes seemed to freeze on each other's faces. Our trance-like stares ceased when Grand Master Gilbért told us to follow him to our quarters. We climbed spiral-shaped stone stairs that emanated a dank musty smell. Midway up the keep, we stopped at an entrance that had a large pattée cross on its lintel; from there we proceeded down a stone corridor with many doors. He directed us toward some doors at the end of the corridor, which had the same pattée cross carved into their wood.

"Lord Robert, this is your cell for the duration of our stay. *Padre* Jeremiah, *Abad* Miguel, and Muhammad will be two doors down, should you need anything. The marquésa will be on the top floor near the chapel. I must separate her from my men. Her guards will see to all her wishes and provide protection. We'll now rest before the Vespers service. There is a small chantry chapel next to the main chapel if you need to pray for the dead. The refectory hall is the next floor down and I'll see you there following Vespers. I am so glad to return to my old headquarter, but now I must attend to Templar business."

Afterward, Grand Master Gilbért accompanied the royal guards and Helena to the steps leading upward to her quarters. I pushed the heavy oak door, entered my small room, and surveyed its Spartan accommodations. It was the same size as the cell at Montpellier, yet room enough for a small straw mattress bed, with a writing table, a three-legged stool, and, to my surprise, a stone-carved dove akin to the one on the ceiling at Montpellier. It even had the same chiseled radiating lines from its head and pointed down toward the writing-table.

The singular difference was this room had more light coming through a larger arrow loop window. An arbalest crossbow would fit in the oversized opening. Next to the bed was a clay pitcher of water, some small towels, and a surcoat. This wasn't the Aljafería Palace, but a warrior-*moine's monastère* and one ready to do battle. I shuffled with languor toward my bed and fell forward onto the straw-filled mattress. At once, I slipped into a deep slumber, followed by a dancing scene of nightmares. The fitful dreams had visions of Marcel de Tournay holding my family for ransom, with the deceased Squire Hughes's voiceless face trying to warn me. The next fitful dream was Helena's staring gray eyes holding me paralyzed. The nightmares seemed to never end but kept repeating the same scenes until a loud thud aroused me from the hellish grin of de Tournay holding a knife to my youngest *fils'* throat.

"Lord de Borron, Vespers starts soon. I will be waiting for you outside the door."

The voice seemed unfamiliar to me, but just after clearing the nightmare from my head, I recognized it as *Padre* Jeremiah. Fear and anger still coursed through my veins as I put on my clean surcoat. Upon entering the corridor, the tall robust size of the grand master's illegitimate son still surprised me. He was several hands taller than his *père* and just as muscular to be a learned chaplain. He escorted me down the corridor until we reached some spiral-shaped steps. There he started a conversation about the loss of *Abad* Miguel's *frère* and then his ink-black eyes changed from that of sadness to curiosity.

"*Seigneur* de Borron, *Abad* Miguel has shown me the drawings from the *Iglesias* of San Pedro Viejo and San Juan de la Peña. These old clues were left for someone to retrieve. It's telling us we are on the right path to the next *Sangraal* parchments, yet you already know this. I believe at our library we might find the next *clave* or key to more information. After Compline, follow me to the scriptorium, but now let's proceed into the chapel to say our *Pater Nosters* and Glory Bes."

We entered the unadorned sanctuary, passed the crossing, and stood in front of the stalls. There began the opening versicle, a hymn, Psalm seventy, followed by readings from the Old Testament and the New Testament. During this time, my mind wandered back to the nightmare I just had. In my mind's eye, I could still see tears of fright rolling down both of my *fils'* cheeks, forcing me to clench my teeth and my fists with anger. Not until the singing of the Magnificent was my mind dislodged from the evil grin of de Tournay. Quiet laughter came over me for having such groundless fears, furthermore, Marie and my two *fils* were protected by one of Christendom's utmost fearless noble, my brother-in-law, the *Comte* Gautiér de Montbéliard. He and Grand Master Gilbért could fight anything or any persons the diabolical Cardinal Folquet might confront them with.

Padre Jeremiah requested we say thirteen *Pater Nosters* in the main chapel and the warrior-*moines* started the Lord's Prayer. Afterward, a sense of calm came over me as we gathered in the chantry chapel and started chanting for our deceased *frères*, benefactors, and departed relatives. After the completion of our ceremony, the sergeants and the *chevaliers* filed out in true martial fashion, followed by Grand Master Gilbért, Chaplain Jeremiah, and me.

A sudden squeaking noise from a side door to the chantry chapel caught my attention. Helena entered through the small apse door, after which she ambled toward the altar, and proceeded to kneel. As I proceeded under a stone-arched doorway, I noticed her fingers held a string of prayer beads as she faced the chancel. Her lips moved ever so slowly in prayer, with her eyes tightly shut in meditation. She didn't know I was there until she rose and lit a purple taper on a circular candelabrum. At once, there came a smile on her face as the candle glowed on her cheeks. She kept her smile, nodded, turned, and returned toward the chancel rail to continue praying. My heart raced from seeing her, however Grand Master Gilbért saw me pause, and with my eyes staring, he whispered his observations to me.

"Lord Robert, she is here to light the first purple candle of hope for the beginning of Advent. Besides, she prays each day at the Aljafería chantry chapel to honor her deceased *mari*. May Jesus the Christ protect his martyred soul and our departed *frères*." We both crossed ourselves.

His purposeful reminder to me of Helena's devotion to her late *mari* was for my benefit, which left me less elated and a signal I had an *épouse* and *fils* while furthering my guilt. As we marched out of the main chapel, the crowd of warrior-*moines* reminded me of numerous, white-feathered roosters exiting their tight-fitting coop.

After leaving the chapel, I followed *Abad* Miguel, Grand Master Gilbért, and his *fils* to the scriptorium. Not far from the chapel, we came to a double set of doors. There above the doors, embedded in the arch, was a stone-carved image of a large open book, and just below it was a stone relief of a pomegranate. One of the pages had the large Greek letter alpha and on the other side the Greek letter omega. The lintel above the door had the chiseled words, "Every word of the Lord written by a scribe is a wound inflicted on Satan."

The scriptorium and library were quite

befitting of any monastery of *moines*. To my right, upon entering, were individual desks, which consisted of sturdy dark-stained oak. Each desk had an inclined tabletop with a vellum parchment, written on with care by a quiet Templar *moine*. The late afternoon sun's rays cast its bright beams on each desk displaying different colors of illuminated artwork. Five greenish dark-robed copyists were sitting at their stations, while three of the *moines* were mixing colors of yellow, blue, and red. One scribe used a flat stone to smooth out the curls of each blank vellum parchment.

The Roman-vaulted scriptorium was as quiet as a forgotten cave; however, I could just hear the steady grinding sound of mortar and pestle making the various inks and colors. None of the *moines* saw us until one of them noticed *Abbé* Jeremiah. The copyist hopped off his stool, strolled forward, and embraced his superior.

"This is *Hermano* Carlos," Jeremiah said. "He is the *armarius,* my assistant, here at our scriptorium." I noticed the scribe's fingertips were colored with blues, reds, and black ink stains. I felt quite comfortable among the company of men who were writers like myself and had the same characteristically ink-stained fingertips.

"*Hermano* Carlos, I would like you to bring me two books from the cupboard. One is called *Timaeus* by Plato, the other is the apocrypha, called the First Book of Enoch."

The small *moine* scurried off like a black mouse in search of cheese, heading toward eight large cupboards filled with unrecognizable ancient tomes. He then grabbed two of the books, turned, and rushed back.

"These are excellent choices my precentor. I have read them several times this past year," commented the smiling diminutive-sized *moine* as he bowed his head. *Hermano* Carlos turned and then dashed to his long table, which held some unknown ingredients to make his various colored inks.

"Let's proceed to the warming room and discuss what I believe the clues are trying to tell us. Would you mind taking one of the books, *Seigneur* de Borron?" Chaplain Jeremiah asked.

"*Non*," I replied to his request as Gilbért, Miguel, and I exited the scriptorium. *Abbé* Jeremiah dawdled a moment to acknowledge his assistant, after which his long strides caught up with us and motioned for us to follow. I liked the sound of the "warming" room, for the scriptorium left me chilled. The book my hand held was as cold as a block of ice and the leather strap metal locking buckle seemed like an icicle against my forearm. I knew the Templar scribes were circumspect with their library and allowed no type of warming fire or flame to enter their scriptorium. Both were enemies to the great treasure of knowledge housed in the monastery fortress.

We continued downward on the spiral stairs

toward the cloister area. Once reaching the entrance, we strolled around the quadrangle until we reached a corner entrance. Through the late afternoon shadows, I saw a small lit torch, which exposed a dark enclosed corridor. *Abbé* Jeremiah grabbed the torch and we continued to follow him until we came to a large wooden door, bearing another carved *pattée* cross. He reached into his white robe, pulled out a large ring of keys, and searched for the proper one to unlock the door. As he opened the door, a gust of warm air struck my face, and we entered the room to see three blazing fireplaces burning three huge logs. In the center of the room stood a large table surrounded by six wooden stools. What might we find to aid us on our search for more parchments?

CHAPTER XXXI

My fellow *hermanos* in Christ, this is the room whereby we warm ourselves thrice. First the chopping of the wood, second building the fire, and third the best of all, drinking the fine Iberian *vino*," our chaplain said with a large grin.

"*Si*," we said in unison, as we each grabbed a stool to find our place around the table. Both large tomes were laid at the end of the table, after which the *bon abbé* grabbed a red-clay stone decanter and began to speak.

"First, before we drink, let me say a blessing, which Saint Joseph de Arimathea would have said over this *vino* grown in the *Marquésa* Helena's vineyard. *Barukh atah Adonai, Eloheinu Melekh ha-olam, borei p'riy ha-gafen.* Amen!"

There was an expression of bewilderment on my companions' faces, so I translated for the rest.

"He said, 'Blessed art thou, Lord, our God, King of the universe, who creates the fruits of the vine.' This blessing the Jews said at their *Seder* dinners, and Saint Joseph mentioned it numerous times in his writings."

"Speaking of *Santo* Joseph's writings, would you give me permission to bind your parchments into a book?" *Abbé* Jeremiah asked. "Traveling with bound parchments would make it easier to protect. I would like to illuminate your copy— what do you say, *Seigneur* de Borron?"

"It's a wonderful idea if Grand Master Gilbért agrees," I responded, gazing at Grand Master Gilbért for his nod of approval. When both men were close to each other, their physical features were so similar. Both had large hands with the same long-shaped fingers, except *Abbé* Jeremiah's fingers were ink-stained like mine. However, his *père's* nose was straighter, while the young chaplain's nose curved at the tip. His *fils'* ebony-colored eyes had the same ever-searching expression of his *père*, yet his was that of a savant in the quest of knowledge.

"Lord Robert, I have *non* objection if *Abbé* Jeremiah gathers the parchments into a book," came his verbal approval instead of a nod. "Let's discuss the words and symbols Saint Joseph is telling us. *Abbé* Jeremiah, has *Abad* Miguel briefed you on what we have discovered so far?"

"*Si, Su Excelencia* de Érail, the holy wheel at Huesca has eight spokes, as you well know, which correspond to the word *octave* spoken to *Santo* Joseph by our Lord, Jesus the Christ. I believe one of the meanings to the word *octave*, means eight steps or levels one must face. One of the definitions of the word *graal* means eight steps or levels in the human soul. Also, it's axiomatic, the Greek letters IXΘΥΣ, which originate from the lines of the wheel and those Greek letters form the word *fish*. The Greek letters themselves are an acronym for Jesus the Christ, God's son and Savior. Is this not so, *Abad* Miguel?"

"Si, *Padre* Jeremiah, and the image of the snake is telling us there is wisdom in what we seek. The coiled snake is a sign for the Greek pagan god Hermes, the messenger god. Lord Robert has told me the fish symbol is the sigil for *Santo* Joseph as the fisher king, which our Lord said he would be a fisher of men. The Greek letters between the spokes are alpha and omega, which is telling us we have a beginning and an end to our quest."

"In my teachings at the university, I have learned of a device called Gematria," *Abbé* Jeremiah said. "The Greeks and *Judios* say that all their letters have a numerical equivalent. Taking the twenty-four letters of the Greek alphabet and their assigned numerical values reveal some surprising results. For example, if you add up three number eights, you'll obtain the total of the Greek letter alphabet, twenty-four. If we add the Gematria value for the Greek letters for Jesus' name, IHΣOYΣ, we acquire the numerical sum of eight hundred and eighty-eight. The Gnostics called the sacredness of eight an *ogdoad,* which was their symbol for rebirth or renewal. Note, the baptismal font is eight-sided. And did you know that Maria de Magdalena and *Santo* Joseph de Arimathea are mentioned in eight chapters of the Gospels?"

We stared at one another in amazement at the breadth of this young man's mind, however, he continued with his facts on the significance of eight.

"The Saracens and the Moors use the eight-sided octagon design in their buildings and architecture. I know Grand Master Gilbért is familiar with *Haram al-Sharif* or the Dome of the Rock in Jerusalem, which has eight equal sides. I think there's a subtle or hidden message somewhere in these numerous symbols and they are telling us something we can't yet comprehend."

Abbé Jeremiah sat there in a moment of silence, his dark-colored eyes focusing upward toward his small round felt red cap. His intense concentration made his brow contort with heavy folds of skin, giving him the appearance of a mystic in the raptures of deep prayer. Each of us became awkward with his prolonged period of silence, yet the warming room seemed to emanate an anxious anticipation of what he was about to say.

"*Abad* Miguel," he at last replied, after breaking his trance. "Let me see the drawing from the cave at San Juan de la Peña."

The *abad* reached into his strapped satchel and handed it to him with care. He placed it on the table with a sense of reverence. His long fingers smoothed the curled edges as the learned chaplain gazed at its design.

"Aha!" he announced with a smile on his face. "It's a clue or clues I see." His eyes grew to the size of black walnuts. "If I hold a ruler and draw the same angles as the small star, we now have both a pentagram and a pentagon enclosed in the cinquefoil. This design or designs are telling us about the theory of sacred geometry. Have any of you heard of an ancient Greek by the name of Pythagoras?"

Both Grand Master Gilbért and I spoke at the same time. He and I agreed the sole ancient Greek story we knew was Homer and his epic tales of the Iliad and the Odyssey.

Abad Miguel cleared his throat. "My knowledge of sacred geometry is limited, but my understanding is Pythagoras believed the entire planet and the universe are composed of sacred numbers, which form all life and elements. This is seen in certain patterns in art, music, nature, and architecture."

"*Si*, you're correct, my reverend *padre*, and our greatest erudite *Santo* Isidore said, 'Remove the numbers in all things and everything perishes.' I see oneness with all things including God's way of communicating with us humble mortals. Our

Divine *Padre* is the greatest mathematician and architect of our infinite universe. He is leaving us clues to both our spiritual oneness with him and the material means to obtain this oneness.

"Pythagoras, Socrates, and above all Plato saw his true design for humankind. Pythagoras had many titles in ancient Greece, but quite memorable were his cognomens 'the Lover of Wisdom and the *Padre* of Musical Proportions,' hence the word *octave*. His geometric theorems were renowned in the ancient world, in particular one theorem that states in a right-angled triangle, the square of its hypotenuse side, which is the side opposite the right angle, is equal to the sum of the squares of the other two sides. He expressed this theorem with the letters and numbers a2+b2=c2."

At once, Chaplain Jeremiah reached for a quill from his leather satchel, along with a small piece of parchment, dipped the quill in a nearby clay inkpot, and began scribbling a design. He drew an odd-shaped triangle and three attached polygons, which didn't make any sense to me, yet he continued with his hypothesis.

"Our stonemason *hermanos* are quite familiar with this equation and use it in the construction of our *iglesias* and fortresses. Another equation that relates to our five-pointed star is the divine proportion. Pythagoras named it *phi* and he said each segment in our pentagram has the value of 1.61803, which this number is a divine proportion in the construction of all things, natural or humanmade."

I glanced at Grand Master Gilbért to observe a *père's* approval; however, to my surprise, his head bobbed with tiredness.

"Gilbért!" *Abad* Miguel hollered, wakening our dozing grand master. "What do you think of your chaplain's oral dissertation?"

At once, Grand Master Gilbért came out of his quick nap, glanced around with no embarrassment on his face, and to my surprise started speaking right where Chaplain Jeremiah's conversation ended.

"I don't see what history and mathematic equations have to do with finding the next section of the *Sangraal* book. We heard some of this information before at Huesca from *Abad* Miguel. *Abad* Miguel, is this not so?"

"*Si*, but let your chaplain continue, for I believe he will bring all this information together for a logical conclusion."

"Excuse me for my impetuousness, but the lack of time is even a greater enemy than Cardinal Folquet, please continue, Chaplain Jeremiah," stated Grand Master Gilbért.

"Before you continue, I have a question about Pythagoras," I said. "Where did he gain this special knowledge?

CHAPTER XXXII

Superb question, *Seigneur Roberto*. Please, let me explain. The ancient lore said the Egyptian pharaoh's priests taught him, which leads me to the Old Testament. Who were the people held in captivity for many years by the ancient Egyptians, and what important man was related to one of the pharaohs?"

"The Israelites and Moses, of course, many people know this, yet I still don't understand what this has to do with the pentagram star and a five-petal flower." I too felt my own impatience rising in my mind.

"Let me continue and I will soon answer your question," he replied with slight irritation in his voice.

"Pythagoras was thought to have written a book based on ancient Egyptian teachings. In his seminal treatise, he mentioned a five-pointed star that was holy to the pharaoh's priests, which they augured great kings would rule with the rising of this five-pointed star. Ancient Hebrew legends say *Rey* Solomon wore a signet ring embedded with a five-pointed star given to him by archangel *Santo* Miguel. He used his ring to harness demons, using them to help build the First Temple. There the tribes of Jacob housed the Ark of the Covenant.

"The Book of Enoch that you see on this table is the basis for the philosophy of Socrates, Plato, and his school to expound on the holiness of shapes, numbers, and sounds. Plato, in his book called *Timaeus*, states our creator is the grand architect of the infinite universe. Both codices are here on this table," he said, pointing at the thick tomes. "I believe these drawings are telling us *Santo* Joseph isn't just a writer and disciple, but an architect too!" He glanced at each one of us.

The young chaplain's words confused me, yet there was a kernel of logic in what he had just said. At once, the words returned to me about Moses and the two names of Bezalel and Oholiab, remembering these names from Saint Joseph's translated parchments.

I caught Jerimiah's eye. "Our Lord and Savior tells Saint Joseph to remember the deeds of Bezalel and Oholiab, but who were these men?" I hoped these names would help solve our conundrum and the whereabouts of the next parchments. The young chaplain's dark eyes enlarged, and a grin came over his face.

"*Seigneur Roberto*, you just added another link to our chain of knowledge about *Santo* Joseph. Bezalel and Oholiab were the God-directed architects of the First Tabernacle, where the Ark of the Covenant and God's presence lay. *Santo* Joseph is destined to build a new tabernacle to keep the *Santo Cáliz* of Jesus the Christ. Where, I don't know, yet I believe we'll find our answer in the sacred buildings in Toledo. Let me show you how you are the *clave* or key to finding the next set of parchments."

His long, ink-stained fingertips opened the ancient book and with a light touch found a section in the tome.

"Before you reveal additional information, let me place several more logs on the fire," Grand Master Gilbért said, as he stood from his stool. The brief break in our conversation gave me a chance to digest Chaplain Jeremiah's elucidation and try to understand how I was the key to unlock our next challenge. Grand Master Gilbért returned and the young chaplain continued.

"Plato says in this section that Pythagoras believes the 'elect' will know the true meaning of the words of the creator. What do you believe, *Seigneur Roberto*? His penetrating eyes searched mine for an opinion.

"*Oui*, I believe I am that elected one, however, I am just an instrument in God's divine plan to initiate his will. *Merci beaucoup, Abbé* Jeremiah, for your hypothesis. It's quite cogent. You have helped define several mysterious words and concepts Saint Joseph wrote in his parchments, to which I am quite grateful."

"I appreciate the compliment, but there's strength in our collective consciousness and this will prevail no matter what we may face in the future. God will never let us lose sight of this divine power, my *amigos*. Now, let me show you our next ancient tome, which is much older than our Grecian texts."

With great circumspection, he picked up the dusty book and placed its cracked leather covers in front of him. "This ancient tome contains words from the First Book of Enoch. Enoch was a prophet, patriarch, the son of Jared, and the great-grandfather of Noah. In Genesis, it's said he traversed the heavens with God, which no other prophet or patriarch can lay claim to!" Chaplain Jeremiah announced. "I believe *Santo* Joseph was the beneficiary of Enoch's God-given wisdom as he traveled with our creator. Let me share his *santo* wisdom, which was written down in Enoch's book."

With care, he unstrapped the bindings guarding the book. With his long fingers, he opened it.

"This book is a compilation of the apocrypha words and stories left out of our Bible. However, in chapter sixty-eight, verse one, Noah says, 'My great-grandfather Enoch gave me all the secrets in the book and in the parables, which had been given to him, and he put them together for me in words of the book of the parables.' God favored Enoch, and God sent his archangel Uriel to shine his light of knowledge and wisdom on Enoch. Some say there are two other divine books written by Enoch, all three telling of the beginning of mathematics, the written language, and predicting the coming of the Son of Man, our Lord and Savior. This augur was a millennium before the Old Testament prophets."

Grand Master Gilbért jumped up from his seat and asked if anybody would like some more *vino.* "Lord Robert, I see your cup is empty, would you like it refilled?"

"Just a modicum of the *vino,* please," I replied, as he poured me some of the ruby-red liquid. *Abad* Miguel motioned for his ex-student to pour him a full cup, after which he filled Chaplain Jeremiah's cup until it was replete with liquid.

"My chaplain needs another full cup, for I know he will reveal more information and we need not let his throat become dry," he said with a large grin identical to his *fils.*

I studied the book. "What is this barred cross, and the angels that are drawn alongside the words?" I pointed at the illuminated designs.

"It's a symbol saying these words came from one of the angels of presence; these were the angels who guarded God's throne. It's referencing the archangel Uriel, I surmise. The cross symbol came about some years after the crucifixion. Please, let me continue, for there is more pertinent information Enoch saw and predicted. Listen to this page about our Messiah."

His fingertips with reverence turned the crinkled pages until he came to a section where he or somebody had placed a purple and gold-colored strip of ribbon.

"Keep in mind, my fellow warriors in Christ, *Santo* Joseph was aware of this passage and may have used it in his ministry to convert *Judios* to Christianity. 'The righteous one will arise from his sleep; he will arise and travel in the paths of righteousness and all his path and his journey will be in piety and everlasting mercy.'

"Here is another passage, 'The Son of Man existed before the sun and stars were created, and he is to execute justice upon all sinners who oppress the righteous. For this end, there will be a resurrection of all Israel, a judgment in which the Son of Man will render to everyone according to his deeds.' Even our New Testament mentions Enoch in the Letters to Jude."

"*Si*, you're again correct, *Padre* Jeremiah," *Abad* Miguel added. "From Jude, verse fourteen, he said, 'Enoch, whose was the seventh generation from Adam, prophesized, saying, see the Lord is coming, with ten thousand of his angels, to execute judgment on all, and to convict everyone of all the deeds of ungodliness that they have committed in such a profane way, and of all the harsh things that sinners have spoken against him.' Judgment day is the warning to all humankind, not just to us, but the *Judios* and even to the house of Muhammad. The *Qur'an* says that the Judgment Day will come on a Friday because that was the day Adam was created and the day he was sent out of the Garden of Eden."

"What does the Second Coming and Judgment Day have to do with our search for the *Santo Cáliz* parchments?" Grand Master Gilbért interjected.

"Three things. First, Enoch predicted the coming of our Lord's birth before any of the prophets. Second, the mention of the archangels, Uriel, Michael, and Gabriel taking Enoch on a tour of the heavens. Third, God and Uriel revealed the mysteries of the stars, including the five-pointed star over Bethlehem and sacred geometry. The ancients have called Gabriel the 'Cup Bearer,' besides being the messenger of God.

"It's often painted with the archangel Uriel holding his opened hand with fire, similar to the hand-shaped amulet around your neck, *Seigneur Roberto*. His other hand holds a book, like the completed parchments we're searching for, which has the knowledge and wisdom of God. The light in his one hand lights the way for us to seek out the remaining parts of the *Sangraal* book.

At Huesca, the sacred wheel doesn't display the *Santos* Michael and Gabriel, but instead shows the *Santos* Gabriel and Uriel.

"All of my putative threads indicate that the next *Sangraal* parchments reside in a dark hidden location that the light of *Santo* Uriel will reveal. *Santo* Gabriel will show us the exact location; there the knowledge and wisdom of God will come forth. We now know that the next parchments exist in Toledo, which God, in his own time, will tell us."

I now surmised that Saint Joseph was not unlike both Moses and *Roi* Solomon of the Old Testament. Saint Joseph would teach the life and meaning of Jesus the Christ and build the New Jerusalem to house the *Sangraal* book and cup. There was no doubt in my mind the sacred parchments existed in the city of Toledo. It was just a matter of where they were located and preventing Cardinal Folquet from interfering.

"I have two sources in Toledo who may give us some directions to the parchments' whereabouts," Chaplain Jeremiah continued. "Each man is a learned scholar in his field of knowledge and well-respected throughout Iberia, Gaul, and Northern Africa. One is a *Judio*, and the other is a follower of Muhammad. Surprisingly, both are *amigos* and have written several treatises together. After Advent, let's plan on visiting them before we search for the next *Sangraal* parchments."

"You have enlightened us on a different picture of Saint Joseph, *Abbé* Jeremiah," I said. "Saint Joseph appears to have an even greater destiny than God and Jesus the Christ revealed. Now he will become an architect to a house of souls, a teacher of a holy book, and custodian to a Holy Cup. God's wonders never cease to amaze me."

The fire had dwindled some and the room became cooler, which seemed even more frigid as hail started plinking on the clay tile roof. This was our signal to adjourn for the divine office of Nones. I followed *Abbé* Jeremiah back to the scriptorium, while *Abad* Miguel and Grand Master Gilbért prepared for Nones. Upon approaching the entranceway, *Hermano* Carlos greeted us with a silent nod, and then he helped us carry the books back to their proper place.

"Did you find any new wisdom from God or see any new signs he gave you?" the *moine* asked. "All who read these books come back to our scriptorium with new insight into God's mysterious workings. The Prophet Enoch and both Greek men of letters, Pythagoras and Plato, have much to tell those who seek the hidden knowledge."

The *moine* waited for *Abbé* Jeremiah to dismiss him; however, his superior spoke to him in a hushed voice and requested him to follow us. After he replaced the books in the cupboard, at once he followed us out of the entrance. His small legs were running to keep pace with his precentor, and I could hear wheezing coming from the *moine*.

"Precentor . . . " came the gasping voice of Carlos, "please, slow down, I can't keep up."

"So sorry, my *armarius*, it's rude of me not to notice. Please, forgive me, I wasn't thinking. What *Seigneur Roberto* is about to show you will more than reward your physical efforts in following us."

The little *moine's* green eyes enlarged as he followed us to my cell. Once inside my room, with circumspection, I reached into the straw ticking of my bed and pulled out my saddlebags. After unfastening the leather straps, my hands slipped out the parchments with their dried oxen intestine covering.

"I see you protect your writings from moisture, *Seigneur Roberto*," Carlos said. "Where are the original parchments?" he asked.

"They have been either destroyed or used for an evil purpose; however, I was blessed in copying them before they were confiscated."

"Who wrote the original parchments, may I ask?" he inquired as he unrolled the first parchment.

I didn't answer right away but hesitated in giving him an answer. Could I trust him? After examining the first page, his round childlike face gazed up at me, searching for a reply. Glancing toward *Abbé* Jeremiah for approval, I continued my silence, leaving the *moine* vexed. *Abbé* Jeremiah gave his nod of approval and the words rolled off my lips. "It was written by *Santo* Joseph de Arimathea," I said. Once again, he asked me who wrote the parchments, not believing what he heard.

"*Santo* Joseph de Arimathea wrote the original parchments, which contained the never-before-seen words of our Lord and Savior." This time he heard my words with clarity, for he dropped to his knees, crossed himself, and cried out, "Merciful God, bless you for letting me hear your sacred words. I am your humble servant who will treat your *santo* words with utmost care." Once again, he crossed himself, after which he grabbed my hands and started kissing them. "Bless you, *Seigneur Roberto*, for surely you're in a state of grace given to you by *Jesu Cristo*." His moist lips made me uneasy, which forced me to raise him from his kneeling position.

"Please rise, *Hermano* Carlos, I am just a mortal man and nothing more. *Oui*, I have been blessed with special powers to read our Lord's words. Treat me no different than any of your fellow *hermanos*."

"Is there anything I can do to honor our *Santo* Joseph's sacred words?"

"*Oui* or *si*, there's one thing," I replied. "Don't divulge one word of what we have discussed, except to *Abad* Miguel, *Abbé* Jeremiah, or Grand Master Gilbért. Keep the parchments in your possession at all times, for righteous men have died trying to protect them. I will daily peruse your progress."

"I swear on the *Santo* Trinity not to speak a word of our meeting and just to the ones you have mentioned. I will hide the parchments in my cell, where I will bind and illuminate them in secret. Do you know your departure day, so I can complete the binding and illumination?"

"I suspect in about seven days, no later," I replied. "*Marquésa* Helena wants us to visit her vineyard and the *castile* at Maluenda."

"*Seigneur Roberto*, may I bid you *adieu* and start right away to work on the *santo* pages?"

"*Si*, and I wish you well in your sacred endeavor."

I opened the door, and he and Chaplain Jeremiah disappeared into the dark passageway. Their thumping sandals continued for a while as I sat down on my straw bed. I sensed no apprehension for my transcribed *Sangraal* parchments; however, my intuition told me to check each day on the small *moine's* progress. A safe easy emotional quietness came over me, yet it wasn't the same kind of relief of not riding for days in the saddle. My entire body eased into a euphoric state knowing the next seven days I had no concerns.

This left me with enjoyable conversation, studying, and the *Sangraal* parchments were now somebody else's responsibility. The free time would give me a chance to write to Marie and my *fils*, Henri and Brian. At Huesca, I had written my last letter and sent it with the *bon* martyred *moine*, Gabriel. I removed a small sheet of parchment from my saddlebag and began to compose a letter.

Mon Cher,

Please, forgive me for not writing sooner, but we have traveled a great distance on our way to Zaragozza. It's now Saint Nicholas Eve and the holy fast of Advent has already started. I am writing this letter at a château called Calatayud, in the Kingdom of Aragón. It is a fortress and scriptorium guarded by the Poor-Soldiers of Christ and larger than any château in Burgundy or all of Gaul. The Moors of Northern Africa built it during one of their conquests of Iberia.

I pray each day that you, Brian, and Henri are well and out of harm's way. How has staying with your frère been? I know the comte would like our quest and harmonize quite well with the Soldiers of Christ. Tell him his old ami, Gilbért de Érail, is now grand master of Provence, Montpellier, and all of Christian Iberia. This shouldn't surprise him, knowing Gilbért's reputation from their fighting days during the second crusade. Tell Gautiér to be vigilant with you and our fils' safety, for we have made some enemies on our holy quest. That's all I can say about the matter, but fear not, I am quite safe.

Next week we will leave for the Château Maluenda, which isn't far from here. Roi Alfonso's sister-in-law, Princesse

Helena, Marquise de Barcelona has a large estate encompassing many vineyards, which she wishes us to visit. From Maluenda, we will travel back to Zaragozza and stay there until the Epiphany of our Savior. Then it's on to our final destination of Toledo and then my return to Château Borron. May God protect you, Brian, and Henri, for my heart aches not being with you during Christ's Mass. Please continue praying for me, I must finish now.
Your affectueux mari,
Robert

I folded the paper, after which I dripped some red sealing wax on my missive, let it cool, and then embedded my signet ring into the spongy red wax. A great sense of sorrow came over me, causing my eyes to well up with tears that left me with blurry vision as I stared out an arrow loophole of my cell. My longing for Helena and its resulted guilt exacerbated my emotional state. I tried to focus on a vee formation of geese soaring in front of the *montagnes'* tooth-shaped tops. Yet, the ache of guilt and loneliness had already settled in the pit of my stomach. I remembered as a young child, far from home, the queasy homesickness of missing my parents.

My sudden funk ended with a soft knock on my cell door, followed by a woman's voice.

CHAPTER XXXIII

oberto, it's Helena, I wish to speak to you. Please open the door."

Her soft voice pulled me out of my lugubrious trance as I reached for the iron latch to my door. I opened it and saw two stunning women smiling at me to beckon them in. One was Helena and the other a smaller woman with a narrow waist and taut pulled-back black raven-colored hair. Her dark matching eyes stared at me with wide-eyed bewilderment.

"This is my primary lady-in-waiting," stated Helena. "Her name is Esperanza. Esperanza, this is *Seigneur Roberto* de Borron, Baron of Northern Burgundy."

"Bonjour, *Seigneur* Robert de Borron, it's a plea-sure to meet such a great writer, poet, and *trouvère*. I enjoyed the *chanson de geste* about *Chevalier* Percival. I haven't heard that ballad before."

"I see you speak my native language, *Dame*

Esperanza," I said, surprised to know another Iberian spoke like me.

"*Oui, mon* baron, *Princesse* Helena has taught me well." She glanced at her *princesse* for approval.

"*Roberto*, please come and stroll with us, for we're in need of conversation," Helena said. "There's a large visitor's parlor off the side of a small chapel where we can speak. It's out in the open and nobody will think the worse of us. Please come; it would make both of us quite happy."

I joined Helena and Esperanza in the stone hallway, and then locked my door. We proceeded down the dimly lit corridor, with each woman holding one of my arms. Oh, how the sweet smell of their perfume intoxicated me. To my surprise, the parlor was a short distance from my room and built similarly to the great halls in Northern Burgundy. There, in one corner, stood several large iron-made candle holders, positioned next to numerous padded chairs and one large wooden table. The opposite wall had a *crackling*-sounding stone-carved fireplace, with sufficient heat coming from it to warm the great hall. However, each woman pulled her silk shawl close to her long neck, as I seated each.

"What would you like to discuss, *Doña* Helena?"

"I heard *Père Supérieur* Miguel lost his twin blood *frère*. Is it true that brigands murdered him with their knives? What terrible news I hear anymore," Helena lamented. "Would you express my sorrow to him when you see him next?"

"*Oui*, I will," I replied, hoping not to reveal any further detail of his death.

"Did you know him well?" Helena continued with her questions.

"*Oui*, some, but not as long as Grand Master Gilbért, who knew him most of his life. *Père Supérieur* Miguel and *Frère* Gabriel tutored both the grand master and *Roi* Alfonso in their younger years, which I am surprised you didn't know." I knew she was probing me for information and hoping that I would give her something she didn't know. "He was a quite learned man and leader at the Huesca *abbaye* with a devotion to his faith that bordered on saintly. His absence will leave our lives with dolorous memories, yet an excellent example of our faith."

I crossed myself and thought of his martyred fate. Both women crossed themselves too; however, Helena reached down between her breasts, pulled out a small gold-chained crucifix, and put it up to her ruby-colored lips. Esperanza's eyes opened wide with surprise by the *marquésa's* behavior in front of a man, with her red-flushed face betraying her embarrassment. Helena eased the golden crucifix back between her breasts and gazed up at me after finishing her prayer.

"Lord *Roberto*," she continued. "Why would a poor learned *moine* be murdered by brigands? It doesn't make any sense," she stipulated. "I have heard rumors he was sent to the Holy *Père* to deliver some important papers. Is this true?" she demanded.

"I wish I could answer both of your questions, but that topic is quite sensitive, and Grand Master Gilbért may have the answers. That is all I can say of this, your *altesse*."

She didn't like my answer but pressed on with tidbits of information to try to force me to say more.

"My sources say he was carrying some documents incriminating Cardinal Folquet and Marcel de Tournay with fornicating with young servant girls, bearing their *bâtard* children, murder, heresy, and treason. I don't think this vile information will surprise the Holy *Père*, for some say, the Roman Curia holds him hostage. However, this isn't the first time a prince of the church has had immoral indiscretions. Yet, murder and treason are another matter."

After finishing her animated suppositions, she moved to the edge of her chair and gestured with her slender jewel-encrusted index finger, pointing it straight up. It seemed to me in her mind she was eliminating all insufficient probable causes for *Frère* Gabriel's demise.

It appeared she had used her several years of loneliness to her advantage, by sharpening her deductive reasoning skills, which also had increased her wealth.

She rose, strolled around the table, after which she turned her back to me and brushed her velveteen dress against my face. She stopped and then eased her fingers to raise the hem of her dress. This exposed two small black velveteen shoes and beige-colored silk hose, as both hands followed the contour of her calf. Upon reaching the lower part of her thigh, she grasped for a small, folded paper secured by a lace garter.

"This might help you and Grand Master Gilbért, yet I know neither one of you will tell me the truth," she said with a dimpled grin of accomplishment. "Just because I am a woman doesn't mean my gender can't be trusted and that I am inferior to men in intellect. Please read this testimony. I think you will be surprised." The tips of her fingers touched mine in handing me the letter. Her fixed gaze waited for me to read the letter, yet her blue-gray-eyed stare distracted me from the letter.

"Why are you not reading my letter, Lord *Roberto*?" she demanded.

"I am sorry. Please, forgive me, for I was distracted." I glanced at the document noticing two red wax seals broken on the letter. The bottom broken seal had a yellow ribbon running through it. On closer examination, the seal had the distinct ball-knobbed tipped cross of Toulouse embedded in it, which was the sigil of the *Comte* de Toulouse.

"This letter is from the *Comte* de Toulouse!" I blurted out without thinking or reading the contents of the letter.

"*Oui*, and you must read its contents. Please, continue; I think you will be enlightened." Another large grin formed on her angelic face, like that of a loved one giving a surprise gift to their *amant*. Her eyes moved back and forth, waiting with anticipation for me to complete the reading.

The beginning of the missive had the standard royal greetings about family and the *roi*, yet the second paragraph came right to the point. It accused Cardinal Folquet and his seneschal of murder, simony, malfeasance of his church office, graft, and the planned invasion of the *Royaume* de Aragón. The invasion would happen after the persecution of the Cathars, followed by the escapees fleeing to the safety of Aragón. I glanced up from the letter after reading the *comte's* same accusations, which were in our missing letter to the Holy *Père*. I sensed both my gaping mouth and wide eyes betrayed my face.

"I see you have read the pertinent paragraph of the letter. Continue, *mon ami*, there's more."

The third paragraph told of a spy in *Roi* Alfonso's midst. To my shock, it was *Don* Rodrigo de Balaguer, who was working for Cardinal Folquet as well as a traitor to the *roi*. A large lump formed in my throat and my head became dizzy with apprehension while realizing Helena saw my face drained of color.

"Is there something else disturbing in the *comte's* letter, *Roberto*?" she asked, raising her eyebrows in question.

"*Oui*, Helena, you have a traitor in the court of *Roi* Alfonso!"

"Oh, you must be reading the part about *Don* Rodrigo. Resume. You will be surprised again."

The next line said the *comte* uncovered a letter on him signed by the cardinal. The letter told *Don* Rodrigo to destroy the incriminating evidence against the cardinal, which Grand Master Gilbért had collected and left with the commander at Carcassonne. The *comte* said the letter bore the seal and signature of Cardinal Folquet. The *Comte* de Toulouse stated *Don* Rodrigo later met the hangman's noose upon his order with the help of Commander Polignac."

"How did you come about this letter, Helena, and does the *roi* know?" I asked, amazed at what she knew.

"He will know, and let's just say it was an old favor owed to my beloved *mari*, *Don* Pedro. Now it's paid, yet the *comte* is in a difficult position. Many of his subjects belong to the Cathar faith, including some of his nobles. The cardinal desires to declare the Cathars heretics and convince the Holy *Père* in Rome to declare a crusade against them. Hersey is just a ruse, so the cardinal can confiscate the land of *Comte* Raymond and his subjects. He knows that many will escape from Languedoc and cross over the Pyrénées to Aragón, which will give him an excuse to wage war against us. Now just you, my trusted lady-in-waiting Esperanza, and myself know of this letter."

To my surprise, included with the missive from the *comte,* was the actual letter written by Cardinal Folquet to *Don* Rodrigo de Balaguer, which helped assuage my fears.

"I see from the smile on your face, I have given you a prompt present before Epiphany." Helena smiled.

"*Oui,* not just for me, but one for Grand Master Gilbért and *Abbé* Miguel. But why give it to me instead of Grand Master Gilbért?"

"I know you are a gifted *chevalier* on a possible holy quest, and you listen to me with patience."

"Speaking for all of us, Helena, we are now in your debt and it's blithe news to my soul."

The completed letter and the new evidence against the cardinal left me shaking the letters with excitement. At once, I jumped up from my chair, then bowed to show my admiration to Helena, reached for her hand, and kissed it.

"*Merci beaucoup,* Robert, we're all in this battle together with God dictating his will or some of us succumbing to the devil's devices. Robert, God has bestowed on you a sacred quest and *oui,* indeed, I knew about the *Sangraal* parchments before you arrived at Zaragozza. Three crucial things I value in my life are loyalty, God's wisdom, and his love. You have shown your loyalty to me by your dedication to Grand Master Gilbért in keeping your quest a secret. God has shown his love for you in sharing his son's never-foretold words and his long-forgotten disciple. I'll use my royal God-given powers to obtain pertinent information. My power is just as efficient in cutting down the enemy as Grand Master Gilbért's sharp Damascus sword. Our *roi* isn't the lone person who knows of the old emir's secret corridor and room. Aljafería walls are like a sieve with many secrets flowing through them without anybody knowing it. You must not speak of important matters while here. I apologize for leading you on with my prying question, but it served a purpose."

"There's no need to apologize for your deception of ignorance, for you helped us more than you can imagine. Though this letter won't bring back the men who have died with me on our holy quest, it will help toward seeing Cardinal Folquet meet God's justice. Helena, help me not to see their faces in my dreams each night, for the fitful dreams have undermined my determination," I said, baring my soul.

"*Oui,* I too know of similar dreams that you speak of, for my late *mari's* face appears to me each night. The next morning when I wake up, my entire body aches and I cannot describe the pain. Most of the day, I still experience his warm presence next to me. Our Cathar *amis* believe that if you are blessed by their priests before you die, you may be reincarnated in another person and or time. I know this sounds blasphemous, yet there's a certain beauty of returning to another past time to seek out loved ones."

There was an awkward moment of silence as Helena bowed her head in dolorous contemplation, not saying another word. This powerful royal woman was a paradox to me in showing self-assurance, intellect, business acumen, leadership, astuteness, forthrightness, and reading my mind. However, at times she showed her vulnerability and loneliness, above all in her confessional voice and demeanor.

"*Roberto*, please, forgive my gloomy nature. I try to refrain from letting myself proceed with these fits of malaise. Can we meet again tomorrow at this same time? Maybe we can discuss less serious issues and you can tell me more about the people of Northern Burgundy. Would you escort Esperanza and me back to our rooms?"

"It would be a great pleasure to see both of you to your room." I helped Helena first with her chair, followed by Esperanza as she gave out a nervous laugh. All of a sudden both women grabbed each of my arms and held me tight as I proceeded down the stone passageway toward their room. Helena quickly released her grip and eased her warm fingers into mine holding my hand. Her vanilla-scented perfume caused me to swoon, coupled with Esperanza's rose petal-scented aroma. However, Esperanza's hands had a cold touch as she too slid her fingers into my palms.

"Esperanza, why is your hand so cold?" I asked, wondering if she might be unwell.

"Forgive me, for I am just a little nervous escorted by a famous *trouvère*. Lord *Roberto*, please, forgive my tension. I am just a servant helping my *princesse*."

"You are forgiven, *Dame* Esperanza, and don't fret about me. I am but a servant like you. May God bless us both as we follow his true design."

We climbed the circular set of stone steps. Both women and I reached the narrow entrance to the tower's corridor. To pass through the small opening, each of us drew closer so we could fit. Both women smiled at me as their firm breasts pressed against my chest. From there, I followed Helena single file up the steps as she hiked the hem of her scarlet and golden brocade dress to keep from tripping. This exposed her black velveteen-covered shoes and two firm sets of calves that tapered upward toward her knees. As we reached the next floor, both women squeezed my hands and we continued down the sparse candlelit corridor. The physical closeness, their perfume smells, along with their majestic beauty, made my heart race.

"Lord *Roberto*, you seem unsteady on your feet," Helena said with a voice of concern.

"It's nothing. I am just confused with the darkness." It was the first time in several months I felt the closeness of a woman, yet now it was two women. However, even more exciting, the warmth from their bodies made my manhood harden. At once, I became embarrassed, hoping both women wouldn't see the large bulge in my tunic. To my relief, the corridor was quite dark, which hid my noticeable male protuberance, making it more difficult to see their faces in the dim light. As we reached the entrance to their room, they hesitated before entering, whereupon I wished them both *bonsoir,* and, at last, they released their confident grips.

"*Mesdames,* have a *bon* night's sleep. We will conclude this conversation tomorrow and gain some more insight into Cardinal Folquet's machinations." Little by little, Helena started closing her door, with her eyes beckoning me into her room.

"Have a *bon* night's sleep, *Roberto,*" she said with a smile. "Will we meet at the same place and time tomorrow?"

"*Oui,*" I replied, but she had already closed the door.

Returning to my room, I felt happy. The loneliness was gone; however, not long after preparing for bed, my desirous guilt overcame me as I tried to sleep. The straw bed was comfortable, but the hardness of remorse soon replaced the bed's softness.

I don't know when I dozed off, but I awoke remembering in detail my fitful dream. In my dream, both the faces of Marie and Helena alternated in front of me, never ceasing in their sad expressions. I noticed the flame from my small table candle had burned to it brass rim, telling me dawn was near. I knew further sleep was futile, so I climbed out of my bed and dressed. Afterward,

I replaced my candle and proceeded once more to write in my personal journal.

Dawn's first light seemed long in its coming, forcing me to realize the sleep I had lost. The quill pen in my hand became unsteady, which caused me to make numerous mistakes. A rested clear mind I didn't have, so I stopped to seek out some food. Yet, before starting, the ever-present ringing of bells calling us to prayer and mass stopped me. Then I realized it was still Advent and fasting was in force, leaving my stomach growling and disappointed.

After mass, my hunger was unbearable, which left my mind with disjointed thoughts. I wasn't to meet Chaplain Jeremiah and Grand Master Gilbért until the completion of the office of Nones, which prompted me to find a diversion for my appetite. The voices from the bailey grounds drew my curiosity to investigate. This led me to some tower steps adjacent to the chapel. The steps descended to the main bailey entrance area, and I anticipated some distractions. Halfway down the tower, I met Sergeant de Hoult holding a small clay bowl of some unknown steaming liquid.

"*Bonjour*, Lord Robert, I see you're awake early. Did you sleep well last night?"

"*Non*, it was a terrible night on a great bed," I replied.

"I don't understand, Lord Robert," the battle-scarred sergeant said. "Is there anything I can do to help your sleepless night?"

"*Non*, I had a fitful dream that seemed to never end, and this is all I want to say. What's the dark liquid you have in your clay bowl?" I asked, hoping to change the direction of our conversation.

"Don't you remember? You drank it at the Aljafería Palace. The *Mudéjars* call it *qahwa* and one of the local Moors has a small stand set up near the fortress main gate. The Holy *Père* in Rome says it's permissible to drink during Advent and it helps stop my hunger pains. The vendor's name is Suleiman, and he charges a small fee for his drink. In addition, it keeps me quite alert in the morning and stays with me until we have a hardy meal at Compline."

"*Oui,* now I remember the drink and how alert it made me. *Merci beaucoup* for the information. Before exploring the *château* grounds, I want to meet this Suleiman and try his steaming elixir."

We parted company and I exited the tower entrance and to my surprise saw moisture from my breath. It was a cold December morning and near the portcullis, a small crowd of soldiers were gathered. The Moor was handing out steaming bowls of the *qahwa* drink to each man. The roasted nut fragrance drew me nearer to the strange-dressed Suleiman. He didn't wear the same style of clothes I had seen on the local Moors. Under his dark cape, he exposed a white samite tunic with a wide red sash that circled his waist. The exposed tips of his square-toed boots were a crimson color. Furthermore, he wore a black-colored turban draped across his mouth and chin, which left just a narrow slit for his coal black eyes. He was standing next to a brass cylinder covered with mysterious-shaped symbols made of copper. Near the bottom of the container was a small silver-colored spigot that he turned to fill up the steaming clay bowls of brew.

"Suleiman, *salaam alaikum*," I said, requiring his attention. He replied with, "*alaikum al salaam*," and handed me a bowl as he stared at me with his dark penetrating eyes while waiting for me to reach for some coins in my purse. While retrieving my coins, it occurred to me he seemed familiar. Upon handing him his money, I too stared at him, yet he turned his head and ignored my eyes. *Where have I seen this man before?* Putting the clay bowl up to my lips, the steam clouded my vision, making any further identification possible. At once, he turned his dark-caped back to me and in a hurry pushed his vendor's cart out of the main gate.

PART VIII

The Dove

CHAPTER XXXIV

Anno Domini 37
Arimathea

The next morning, the group of humble teach-ers prepared to leave Arimathea and travel to the nearby village of Lydda. There they would start preaching their *Maishiach's* holy words to the local people. Yoseph felt a little apprehension in doing this but knew the Holy Cup would give him confidence.

He had awakened by the loud braying of the camels. The travelers didn't break their fast, but at once they packed their humble belongings and started out on the morning road to Lydda. Eli's camels carried Yoseph's sister, little Enoch, Yosa, and Zechariah, while the rest of them traveled on foot. They arrived right before nightfall and located a suitable campsite next to a grove of date palms. A short distance away, they heard rushing water and all of them agreed this was an excellent place to stay.

"Yoseph, do you think this campground is sufficient while we stay in Lydda?" Philip asked, as he gazed around for strangers.

"Yes, it's perfect," Yoseph said, while glancing at Hebron for affirmation.

"I too agree since we have the highest ground around us."

Shimon the Zealot volunteered for the first watch of the night, while Martha and Miriam prepared a place for *kodesh* supper.

"Yoseph, I would like to speak to you in private," Nicodemus said, motioning Yoseph toward the edge of the campfire light.

"What is it you want to speak to me about?"

"How are we to protect ourselves and the new pupils who accept the words of our *Maishiach*? We have too many enemies—the Romans and the Jewish authorities—who want to kill us."

"Nicodemus, my friend, I know we shoulder a great responsibility and you're right, both groups could eradicate us before we have a chance to speak our Savior's words to the new brethren. But your fish-shaped signet ring will help us. It will give us the ability to proceed undetected."

"Yoseph, I am confused, what does my ring have to do with our protection?"

"You gave me the idea several days before the *Seder* dinner with Yeshua." Yoseph regarded his friend's vexed expression. "Let me show you." He grabbed a long leafless palm branch and drew an upside-down crescent-shaped line in the sandy dirt.

"Now observe your ring, it's part of the design in your ring. Now grab the palm branch stick and complete the design." Yoseph handed him the stick, Nicodemus glanced at his ring, and with care completed the bottom portion of the crescent line.

"It forms a fishlike image on my ring," he said.

"Yes, you're right, and now that we are fishers of men for Yeshua, this is our secret greeting among the unknown followers of the way. Tomorrow, we will teach this secret symbol to our new disciples. It will come to identify us as the true body of the *Maishiach*. Our new converts will teach it to their new students and the symbol will identify us throughout the ages."

"I like it, Yoseph. You have thought this out quite well, but what will we say about him as a man and the son of *El Shaddai?* In addition, how will we explain to the people of our old faith that he's *El Shaddai's* chosen son? You know that's blasphemy in the eyes of the sons of Abraham. Besides, they have heard of false *maishiachs* before.

"Let each teacher tell what they saw, heard, and felt while in the presence of Yeshua. We aren't here to have them memorize a long list of *mitzvot* or practice many ritual prayers." Yoseph stared at his friend. "It's late, now let's prepare our *kodesh* supper and see the many wonders he will give us."

They gathered around the campfire to celebrate another supper blessing. Each new member, who participated in the procession, was amazed as the supper unfolded. Smiles of wonder swelled on each passing member as they passed in front of him. Tonight, there wasn't any whispering sound, just a lone nightingale's steady chirping.

After the completion of the supper ceremony, each member returned to their blankets in the sand and fell asleep. Yoseph too succumbed to his own slumber, yet he awoke with a buzzing sound in his ears. Everyone else was fast asleep and not disturbed by what he heard, which now changed into raspy words. It wasn't his nephew's voice, but one he didn't recognize.

Right away, a glowing image started to form in front of him with hair whiter than a lamb's coat. Suspended from above his head was a pearl-encrusted diadem that threw out golden-white bolts of light. His feet never touched the ground but glided across the sandy soil. The apparition's appearance was like the two beings, which appeared to Yoseph four summers ago while in prison.

"Yoseph, I have been sent by the *tzaddik*, or the Righteous One, which you call the *Maishiach*, who sits on his throne of glory."

"What is your name, spirit?" Yoseph said, still not knowing if he was dreaming or awake.

"Some call me *Metatron*, or, in ancient days, I was called Enoch. Once in my human form, I was the great-grand *abba* to Noah, and I had a son called Methuselah. Your people know me as the seventh patriarch and once was a mortal man like you. My righteous life saw favor with *El Shaddai*, and he pulled me up to his abode. The *malachs*, Gabriel, Uriel, and Michael, showed me events of the future, taught me mathematics, astronomy, however, more important how to write words. Many millenniums ago, I saw the Son of Man and his messianic coming and he too was flesh like I once was. However, once more he will return as the *kodesh* spirit of final judgment, accompanied by his *malach*, Michael. On that day, solely known to *El Shaddai*, the Son of Man will judge all men and women, both alive and dead, according to their deeds in the Book of Life."

"Why are you telling me about this *kodesh malach*? It's not left up to me to judge others."

"Yes, that's true, but you are destined to build the First Tabernacle to preach the Son of Man's words and enclose the *kodesh* gifts he gave you. Yoseph, you will convert as many people to his way as there are the number of trees on this globe called earth. You will help fill his Kingdom of Heaven with his glory."

"How will I build a tabernacle? I haven't any money to construct a house for *El Shaddai* and his son. Observe my clothes, they're shredded rags, and I can't afford to travel and teach his words."

"Yoseph, do you remember where you were when your young nephew said, 'to whom much is given, much will be asked in return'?"

"Yes, I do remember. It was on the isle of the Celts, twenty-four summers ago."

"Also, do you remember, what your son, Alein Yosephe, offered you from the young Celtic king?"

"Yes, he offered some land in his kingdom; he called it the Isle of Mist."

"Search with your fellow teacher called Philip, for Philip will give you direction and purpose. Remember Philip's questions he asked about your travels when he spoke to you at the Mount of Olives, numerous springs ago. He searched both you and your son's mind concerning the people of the Celtic Isle. This isle and its people are now interwoven with your fate. Embrace them and plant your branch of the Tree of Life in their land, for here is the place of the New *Yerushalayim*. It's there the Son of Man will come once again, so prepare his cup of salvation to administer to his righteous men and women of this isle. If in need of reassurance, seek out my book, there you will find my wisdom to travel the road of salvation. The *Eyn Sof* has shown me that path and others who will seek this road after you're no more of this world.

"Yoseph, remember the Lord of Host is manifested in all numbers and the path to his heart is gathered in knowledge and wisdom. When young Enoch, your sister's son, becomes of age, he will have prophecy and see through the thin veil of time. At that moment, the end of your material life will be near; counsel him about the Son of Man and the Head of Days. Tell him of my words and remember what I say here for his future knowledge."

At once, he paused speaking, and his countenance grew as bright as the sun, then he continued.

"When I flew among the firmaments, I saw the mountain of God and the Tree of Life. The seventh mountain in the center of the mountains, higher than the rest, had a throne-shaped top. *Kodesh* Michael pointed at one tree more glorious than the rest, which encompassed the throne-shaped mountain. Here was planted the Tree of Life, and, oh, how its sweet spicy fragrance overpowered the other trees. Its blossoms never withered, and its leaves never fell. I learned the Tree of Life fruits were food for the pious and righteous elect and the *kodesh* tree would grow again in a holy place called the New *Yerushalayim.* There at the center of the world, judgment will be administered."

Without warning, his brilliant light dimmed, and he paused speaking. A moment later, his radiant light returned for a final word.

"Now, I must leave and travel back to the Son of Man and tell him you now understand where the New *Yerushalayim* shall be."

His brilliant image disappeared and all that remained were the twinkling lights of the stars. Yoseph didn't care if he had come to him in a dream or as a person, for now, he had some answers in where their ministry lay. He decided to keep this vision to himself.

The next day, they gathered their few humble belongings and prepared to leave for Lydda. After traveling down the large hill, they entered the small village about the time the inhabitants were breaking their fast. A blue haze of curling cooking smoke hovered over the small mud-brick homes. The village's greatest prominent structure was a limestone-carved Star of David above the entrance to a small synagogue. Every villager's head turned in their direction when they saw thirteen of them approach their communal well.

"Hello, strangers. I see you have traveled far," said a young man helping a woman fill a clay ewer of water.

"Yes, we have come far, and our journey's end is not yet in sight," Yoseph said, wondering if the young woman next to him was his wife. "Can we partake of some of your sweet water?" They nodded, but both the young man and the woman frowned with suspicion at them as they quenched their thirst.

"Where are you going?" the man asked Yoseph while gazing at the large satchel slung across his shoulder.

"Wherever *El Shaddai* will lead us," Yoseph replied.

"You appear to be people from the house of Abraham, for you called your supreme being *El Shaddai*. I am Greek by birth and so is my wife standing here. You may not want to continue speaking to us, for we are Gentiles. The two men and two women on the other side of the well are also from the house of Abraham."

Yoseph glanced over at the four of them and said, "*shalom*," but received no reply, just silent glares.

"They haven't spoken to us in the five summers we have lived here. Neither of these women will help treat my sick baby, although each is an expert in healing small children."

Until now, the young Greek man's wife hadn't said anything; however, she moved over to where the two women were standing and spat at their feet. At once, both women and the two men left mumbling and cursing at the Greek couple, saying they were swine eaters.

"What is your name, my friend?" Yoseph asked.

"I am called Georgeus, and my wife's name is Clotho."

"It's a pleasure to meet both of you, and I know my fellow teachers will agree the same. Your wife's name means spinner in Greek. Is that correct?" Clotho gave a small smile. "I predict you have two sisters named Lachesis and Atropos, who were once called Moerae sisters or the great fates." The grins grew larger on both their faces as Yoseph embraced them, along with the rest of the band.

"Your knowledge of Greek culture and language is superb, but please, don't worry that we are unclean because we are Gentiles," Georgeus said.

"Don't worry, my friends, our band of teachers refrain from following the strict rules of Temple law. Besides, we have many wondrous things to tell you and ask both of you to join us for supper tonight. What do you say?"

"We don't have enough food to contribute to the communal supper," Georgeus replied gazing toward Yoseph with a cherry-red face.

"That's fine, we ask just for a table to place our food and a private room."

The young man stared into his eyes, paused, and said nothing.

"Is that a problem?" Yoseph asked.

He glanced at his wife for agreement, which she right away gave a positive nod.

"No, it isn't a problem, and, yes, we do have a table and a secluded room."

"Well, it's then settled, Georgeus," Yoseph announced. "Which house is your home?"

"It's the one with ropes of hanging dates at the entrance. It's easy to find. However, I failed to ask your name, teacher; please forgive me for my rudeness."

"No forgiveness needed, my friend; you and your wife are worrying about your child's health.

My name is Yoseph of Arimathea, and we will return tonight and meet at your house when the first stars appear," Yoseph stated, as both Georgeus and Clotho carried the large clay water ewer toward their home.

They decided to visit the village that morning in groups of twos and threes. The women would seek out women with children, while several of the men would visit the shops, fields, and the remaining three of them would visit the synagogue. Yohanan led the way toward the small clay-domed structure, followed by Hebron and Yoseph. The synagogue was a short distance from the center of the village. The morning service of *Shakharit* was well underway with the chanting sound of high-pitched voices giving out a verse of praise.

To Yoseph's right, the shimmering glare of the *mikveh* waters caught his eyes as they approached the synagogue entrance. Two large stone columns, casting their shadows onto the red clay entrance steps, framed a large wooden door. They disrobed, then stepped in the *mikveh* bath, and cleansed their bodies. Afterward, they rushed drying with towels provided, dressed in the late morning sunlight, and then sauntered inside the already started service. Yoseph's eyes adjusted to the synagogue's shadowy interior, viewing a white mosaic stone floor in front of the *bimah*. The white floor revealed small images of blue, red, and green-colored sea creatures. The largest images were black-colored dolphins, which formed a large circle around the various sea creatures.

"Welcome, strangers," came a quiet voice from behind a stone pillar detecting their presence. "Have you traveled far to visit our humble synagogue?" A man stepped out from behind the pillar.

"Yes," Yoseph replied in a hushed voice. "We are in search of *El Shaddai's* goodness, and I believe it's a *Shabbat* service, but I am not sure."

"I see you and your friends have lost track of time," the man said with a wary glance at each one of them standing there. He handed all three them *tallits* to wear over their heads, and then six *teliffins* to wear on their heads and arms, then he directed them to the male section of the synagogue. As Yoseph sat down, to his left he saw an ornate designed *Mechitzah* embroidered curtain with pomegranate shapes, and each corner had a large King Solomon star seal that drew his eyes to them. It seemed odd that the poor people of this village had a far richer synagogue than he first thought. There were about thirty men and women sitting near the *bimah*.

"Since you appear the oldest of your fellow strangers," whispered the man to Yoseph, "would you like to be an *aliyah* for our service?"

His question caught Yoseph by surprise, for it was many summers ago he was so honored. However, this wasn't his purpose in coming there, that part of his life was over. All he wanted to do was speak the words and teachings of their *Maishiach*. He didn't answer him right away, leaving the man with a vexed expression.

"Yes, I will come up and do a blessing of the Torah," he replied, causing the man to relax. Hebron and Yohanan glanced in his direction with wondering eyes questioning Yoseph's reply. They had to sit down front, because of their late arrival, leaving him the closest to the *bimah* and the empty table where the scrolls would lie. He said nothing more as the priest and Levite finished their verses of praise. He adjusted his *tzitzit* knots to his head covering as the priest began the *Shema*. He faced the congregation and cried out, "*Sh'ma Yisrael Adonai Eloheinu Adonai Ecod. Barukh shem k'vod malkhuto l'olam va-ed.*"

Yoseph's mind began to wander after the second line of the *Shema*, with his eyes focused on the glare of the light coming from the brass hanging *ner tamid*. It seemed his mind was outside his body. However, he heard a reassuring whisper: it was the quiet voice of Yeshua speaking to him.

CHAPTER XXXV

Yoseph, my teacher, read from the books of the prophets, Jeremiah and Zechariah. Also, speak of what the patriarch Enoch has written and told you last night. Speak of my new covenant and why my human body died for the sins of humankind. You will awaken some of the souls of this congregation and help them slake their spiritual thirst, while others will accuse you of blasphemy. Fear not, my uncle, for I am with you right now."

His voice ended at once, just as the *Amidah*, or eighteen benedictions ended, causing Yoseph to refocus on the *bimah*. The priest edged toward the *Aron kodesh* or Ark, stopped in front of it, and with reverence separated the *parokhet* curtains.

By now, Hebron had figured out what the synagogue leader had wanted Yoseph to do and whispered a question.

"Yoseph, what are you going to read when called to the *bimah*?"

With a low voice, Yoseph replied, "From the Book of Enoch, for he spoke to me last night and told me what I must say." The cantor started to lead them in verses from the Book of Numbers. "Also, the words of our *Maishiach*, the prophets Jeremiah and Zechariah."

Both men glanced at him with bewilderment. However, each of them drew their attention toward the handheld covered Torah, which a man paraded with veneration in front of the faithful. Each member of the congregation touched the sacred scrolls with their prayer shawl as it came before them. The cantor said the *Shema* also, letting Yoseph's mind doubt his new faith, but the doubt was just fleeting. Today was his first official day of ministry and now his tongue would speak with the *Maishiach's* heart. The day his nephew's physical body died; his old faith ended.

Out of respect for the other's faith, he grabbed his tasseled prayer shawl corners and touched the *kodesh* scrolls of the law. By now, the cantor had completed the celebration of the Torah scrolls, returned to the *bimah*, climbed up the small set of steps, then placed the undressed scrolls on the table, and laid the *yad* or pointer next to the parchments. The unknown man was the cantor and the one who asked him to participate as an *aliyah*. He first called the son of the priest, who read a passage, followed with a blessing, then a second reading, and it too followed with another blessing. He called a second man, who was a Levite, and he also came forward and followed the same ritual.

"Yoseph," whispered Hebron, "are you sure you want to step up there?"

"Yes. *El Shaddai* will reveal his heart through my tongue."

"Yoseph, I fear for your name. If they know you have been banned from *Yerushalayim* and the Book of Life, you're in danger, my brother."

Yoseph whispered his thanks for Hebron's concern and readied himself for what he was about to preach.

"It's an honor to have the elder Yoseph of Arimathea to speak to us in our synagogue about the *kodesh* words of our *Adonai*," the cantor's voice boomed throughout the clay-domed house of *El Shaddai*.

Now everybody knew who he was, but his confidence kept him focused as he climbed up the steps to the *bimah*. With reverence, Yoseph picked up the *yad* and he began reading from Genesis.

"Then *Adonai, Eloheinu* said, 'see the man become like one of us, knowing good and evil, and now he might reach out his hand and grasp also from the Tree of Life, and eat, and live forever—therefore *Adonai, Eloheinu* sent him forth from the Garden of Eden, to till the ground from which he was removed.

He drove out man and woman; and at the east of the Garden of Eden, there he placed the archangel Uriel, and appeared a sword, flaming and turning to guard the way to the Tree of Life. My friends, I have located the Tree of Life and it's our *Maishiach!*" Yoseph exclaimed!

At once, there were wide-eyed expressions on the congregation's faces, followed with muted grumbling sounds of displeasure.

"Let me further tell you, brothers and sisters, what I have seen and heard!" Yoseph's loud voice caught their attention. "I have had a dream and the ancient prophet, Enoch, spoke to me. If you remember, he was a righteous man whose eyes *Eloheinu* opened and he had visions of heaven and its secrets. The Prophet Enoch saw a range of glorious mountains and on the seventh mountain, in the center, was a throne-shaped top. The archangel Michael tells Enoch there's a magnificent tree on top of the mountain circling the throne with the others. It is the Tree of Life, and its fruits and fragrance are quite superb.

"I have smelled and tasted the fruits from this *kodesh* tree, and its leaves never fall, its fruits never diminish, and this tree never withers. Those who eat from it will never die but have everlasting life. Its fruits shall be food for the elect and the *kodesh* tree will grow again to honor the Temple of the *Adonai,* our Eternal King. As told by Enoch, the Righteous One has risen from his sleep; he did travel among us showing the virtuous road before him. His path and journey were in piety and everlasting mercy. Those who follow his path and journey will have eternal life. We are the distant generation the Prophet Enoch speaks of in his travels with the archangels Uriel and Michael.

"I have seen, known, and touched the *Maishiach*, for he has shown me the way, and, my friends, I am here to teach you what he taught me. As Enoch wrote, 'He shall be a staff to the righteous whereupon they stay themselves and not fall. The Son of Man will be the guiding light of the Gentiles, the sons of Abraham, and the hope of those who are troubled of heart.'

"His love and miracles I have seen with my own eyes. He's here right now among us and my fellow teachers, Yohanan bar Zebedee and Hebron, will testify to seeing his wonders!"

Yoseph pointed at his fellow teachers. The congregation gazed at one another with surprise and then focused their attention back on Yoseph.

"What proof do you have that the *Maishiach* is here in this synagogue?" the cantor asked.

"Let me finish, my friend," Yoseph replied, seeing him shake his head with skepticism. He pointed the *yad* to a verse from the Book of Isaiah.

"Isaiah spoke about a child who would be born for us, a son is given to us. All authority will rest on his shoulders. We will call him a Wonderful Counselor, *El Shaddai*, Everlasting *Abba*, and

Prince of Peace. His authority shall grow without end, and there shall be ever-lasting peace for the throne of David and his kingdom. The Book of Isaiah further states what *Adonai's* covenant is with the Gentiles, 'For my house shall be called a house of prayer for all peoples. Thus, says *El Shaddai,* who gathers the outcast of *Yisrael.* I will gather others to them besides those already gathered.' Then he said, 'For I am about to create new heavens and a new earth; the former things shall not be remembered or come to mind. Yet, be glad and rejoice forever in what I am creating, for I am about to create a New *Yerushalayim.*'"

Yoseph with respectful hands used the spindles of the Torah scroll to unroll it, seeking with the *yad* pointer the Book of Zechariah. Everyone remained silent, staring at him.

"The Book of Zechariah speaks of a man with a measuring line in his hand. Zechariah has a vision, in which he asks, 'Where are you heading?' The man answers saying, 'To measure *Yerushalayim,* to see what is its width, and what is its length.' In this vision are two angels that speak to Zechariah and help him understand. One angel approached the man and said to him, 'Run,' he says to the young man, '*Yerushalayim* shall be inhabited like villages without walls.' Both prophets are auguring that a New *Yerushalayim* will come, and a new age will start. My friends, the *Maishiach* has commissioned me to build the

New *Yerushalayim* far from here. Herod's Temple and *Yerushalayim* will soon be swept away, and our way of life changed forever."

"You speak of blasphemy, Yoseph of Arimathea," charged the cantor. "You are a false prophet and nothing more!" he screamed to the congregation.

Glancing around, Yoseph saw a third of the members nod their heads in agreement and shake their fists. The rest looked disconcerted. Several had the stare of wonder in their eyes.

"Our *Maishiach* has placed all our sins on his back and then died for us so everyone who believes in him won't die, but have eternal life, just as the Tree of Life. Once I was a doubter like you and thought of him as my niece's son. However, his love and wisdom are boundless, and I have been ordained to help you seek eternal life. He who believes in him will obtain salvation and everlasting life, yet more important, you'll speak of his utmost lasting gift. He said to love your neighbor as much as yourself, whether that neighbor is Gentile, Roman, Samaritan, heathen, or any foreigner. I too have a young man in my midst who will help create a New *Yerushalayim*. I believe he is the one foretold by Zechariah to assist in building a new Temple. His name too is Zechariah."

"What you say is recorded in the Torah, but how do we know you and your people were sent by *El Shaddai?*" voiced one of the synagogue scribes sitting next to Hebron.

"Yes, I agree, what proof do you have other than testimony?" the synagogue priest protested. "You claim you're a new prophet and rabbi, but our people have heard about false prophets and *maishiachs* for the last nine hundred summers. Besides, I have heard the Sanhedrin tried you, threw you in prison, had your name stricken from the Book of Life, and banished from Palestine. Why should we believe you?"

With his truth about Yoseph revealed, the congregation buzzed with low conversations, and then they stopped and stared at him with the stillness of a *shiva* mourning ceremony. Right away, Yoseph had to give an answer and explain his prison confinement, but he knew his response wouldn't suffice, so he reached into his satchel, grabbed the *Kodesh* Cup, and then held it overhead.

CHAPTER XXXVI

ehold the cup of salvation that takes away the sins of many!" Yoseph shouted, with the cup's brilliant white light causing the synagogue members to place their arms over their eyes. Several congregation members fell to their knees, screaming from some unknown pain. Others clawed at their ears, while others covered them from an unheard sound. Several people emptied their stomachs on the stone floor and then started running toward the synagogue entrance. To Yoseph's surprise, fifteen people came forward with bent heads, drawn to the cup's shafts of light. Each held one hand above their eyes, using their feet to guide them toward the *bimah*. Not a word or cry was uttered as they approached Yoseph.

"I bare the cup of truth and all the wonders it will put forth," he said, as fifteen men and women were kneeling at his feet. "Please, rise, my friends, don't honor me, for I am just the *Maishiach's* messenger and teacher."

Yohanan and Hebron helped each stand up, as he slid the gleaming cup back into his satchel, extinguishing its shafts of light. One woman began to speak after her eyes adjusted to the dim light of the synagogue.

"Did this *Kodesh* Cup belong to the *Maishiach* you just spoke about?"

"Yes, and its shafts of light are passageways to *El Shaddai*, our *Abba*, and the *Shekhinah*, the moving spirit. Yeshua, my nephew, is the son of *El Shaddai*."

"How can this be?" the woman asked. "I was once told the coming *Maishiach* couldn't be from *El Shaddai*. That is considered blasphemous, and I thought he would come to us as a warrior-king."

"It's true, he is a warrior-king, but to the forces of evil. His army is in heaven and his soldiers are *malachs*; ready always to carry out his commands. He taught us to love one another and not hate. How can this not be from *El Shaddai*? Love and kindness to our brothers and sisters aren't blasphemous. He said we must honor his *Abba*, and no other, with all our love, praise, gratitude, and being. The second of my teacher's commandments, he told us to love one another as we love ourselves.

"I am just a humble teacher here today to show all of you the *Maishiach's* way. The two men next to me are teachers too. One is a scribe named Yohanan bar Zebedee, who traveled for two summers with our *Maishiach*, the other is my brother-in-law, Hebron."

Hebron and Yohanan acknowledged the small group, and then embraced each person.

"You must leave our synagogue at once!" shouted the synagogue leaders, who by now had recuperated from their pain. A knot of people had blocked the lone exit to leave. Yoseph could see wide-eyed fear in their eyes, yet they knew there was strength in a mob as they shook their fists in the air.

"You and your followers are possessed by demons!" screamed the priest. "We don't want a magus applying his evil tricks in our village. You used your nefarious cup to maim my congregation!" the priest further shouted. "You must leave this village, or I won't assume responsibility for what my members might do."

The priest and his fellow leaders edged forward, seeing there were just three of them, yet still fearful of the *Kodesh* Cup. One man had a long wooden staff, and another had a pitchfork. Behind the first two men, the glare of sunlight prevented Yoseph from seeing what the remaining men were holding as weapons.

"Yoseph, we appear trapped," Hebron whispered. "Let me challenge the front two with weapons. I outweigh each one by thirty stones, and you and Yohanan can handle the priest and the scribe. This will give you a chance to escape."

"We can help fight," came a reply from one of the men standing near Yoseph.

"No, my friend," Yoseph answered. "This is our fight, besides you're from this village and have a family to protect." At once, he whispered to Hebron and Yohanan. "I have a plan."

"Yoseph, what plan?" both questioned him at the same time.

"Wait and see," Yoseph replied. "I think you will be surprised."

Without notice, he grabbed the cup while he advanced toward the angry mob.

One man swore at him as he approached, and another holding a staff stared at the crowd to direct his remarks.

"These men, our Nazarenes, practice magic on all who come near. Before it's too late, let's seize them and run these evil swine out of our village."

The rest of the mob lined up behind him, paused for a moment, and then surged forward with the man holding the staff raising it to strike him. Hebron shouted for Yoseph to run, but Yoseph stood his ground. Just as the man lowered his weapon to crack his skull. Yoseph met his staff with his right hand holding the *Kodesh* Cup. It froze both the man and man's staff in midair, leaving him with a statue-like facial expression of horror. At once, he teetered backward, dropping his staff as he struck the stone floor. There he writhed back and forth with his mouth open while clutching his ears. The cup's golden shafts of light emanated a buzzing sound, not unlike a swarm of bees. However, it didn't affect Yoseph, Hebron, Yohanan, or their new followers. Other men in the rabble clutched their stomachs, bent downward retching clear liquid, and fell forward making gruesome guttural sounds.

"Yoseph, now is the time to escape," Hebron said, grabbing his free arm to push Yoseph over the squirming bodies. Yohanan stood behind Hebron as Yoseph stepped past the synagogue priest.

Once outside, his eyes focused on another mob forming with more villagers. There in front of the synagogue entrance stood twenty sets of dark eyes staring at them in bewilderment. They ran to one side of the crowd and headed toward the hillock and their camp. With care, Yoseph slipped the *Kodesh* Cup back into his satchel, while running up the hillock.

"Yoseph!" shouted Yohanan. "Look, there're more villagers waiting for us at the top of the hill." He pointed his hand toward the blinding noonday sun.

"I can't recognize the faces," Yoseph stated, praying Yohanan was wrong. "Hebron ... can you distinguish the faces?"

"It's our band of teachers," Hebron replied. "I see Miriam, her brother, and her sister standing near the date palm. The rest are rising to greet us."

Yoseph's heart was beating in his throat and knew he was near exhaustion as young Zechariah came running, holding his staff. Upon meeting, Yoseph fell to his knees and couldn't speak from exhaustion.

"Uncle Yoseph, is there trouble in the village?" the boy asked.

"We received a disagreeable reception in the synagogue this morning," Yoseph said, as young Zechariah handed him his staff. "Yet, I believe we may have established some followers."

Miriam approached him. "Yoseph, you're flushed; please come and rest." She handed him a clay cup of cool water. "Tell me, Yoseph, how did they receive you?"

"Our *Maishiach* and his *Kodesh* Cup drew numerous souls to his words. Also, the cup helped our escape from an uncontrollable mob of synagogue members. Miriam, gather the rest of the teachers, I want to hear their successes."

Yoseph sat down under the shade of the date palm and listened with wonder at the many successful results. Philip and Nicodemus told how well received they were from several Gentile homes. Lazarus and Thomas said the same, except without knowing, they visited the homes of some ardent sons of Abraham. Miriam spoke some great news about the women of the village, leading Yoseph to believe their *Maishiach* had blessed their undertaking.

"Yoseph, you haven't heard my worthy news," Enygeus added, standing in front of him with her hands on her hips. "Yosa and I have three mothers coming to our supper tonight wanting to hear Yeshua's words," she said with a large grin.

He sat there, against the date palm, with a cool breeze passing across his face, well knowing their small group of teachers had whetted the villagers' spiritual appetites for their *Maishiach's* words. However, he knew more of these violent encounters were waiting on the horizon, but now they had *El Shaddai's* confidence in them to prevail.

"Yoseph, do you see that small river to your right?" Philip asked, pointing toward the river.

"Yes, why?" he answered, while rising from his restful seat.

"We failed to baptize your son at Arimathea and now it's time to do it. What do you say, Alein?"

"Yes, I am ready," Alein replied, staring at the clear blue sky. "*Abba*, let's do it as soon as possible and not miss an opportunity, as we did at Arimathea."

"So be it," Yoseph replied. At once, they left the hillock and ambled down toward the river. When they reached the base of the hill, Yoseph's heart raced with anticipation. Yet, eight young women approached with their laundry baskets that distracted his happiness. Some were conversing, while others were singing unrecognizable songs. The men reached the river's edge first, while the women strolled toward the water.

Alein had disrobed, except for his loincloth, as he stepped into the rushing water. Philip waded in next to him and began to speak.

"Do you, Alein Yosephe bar Yoseph, repent of your past sins and promise to follow the *way* of Yeshua, our *Maishiach*?" He peered into Alein's eyes.

"Yes," he answered, as young Zechariah helped pour the clay ewer of water over Alein's head. All of a sudden, a white dove appeared and hovered over the four of them standing in the gushing river, followed by a brightly colored rainbow arching over both banks of the river. Yoseph searched the clear blue sky for rain, yet none was visible.

"Behold the lamb of *El Shaddai* who takes away the sins of the world!" Yoseph exclaimed, never doubting the miracles that their new faith bestowed.

A sudden buffeting wind accompanied them as they approached the muddy bank. The dove still hovered above the river. The eight women had stopped and gazed upward with opened mouths to see the rainbow above them. From Yoseph's viewpoint, they appeared like eight stone statues frozen in their footsteps. The sole movement Yoseph saw was the wind pressing the tall grass to the ground as Alein Yosephe trudged through the mud. His eyes were transfixed at the rainbow, and his face smiled with a soft serene grin.

"Strangers, what's happening?" shouted one of

the women on the opposite bank.

Soon as she finished her question, the dove and the rainbow vanished.

"Come tonight to the house of the Gentile man called Georgeus and I will explain!" Yoseph hollered across the small river. "Be there tonight and we'll share the bounty of our supper with all you."

"We aren't the children of Abraham!" one woman shouted. "You're from the *people of the book*. Is this not so?"

"Yes, it's true," he replied. "However, we have new teachings and ways to tell you. We have both men and women teachers who will speak of glorious new revelations. Do you know Georgeus and his wife, Clotho?"

"Yes, and I understand he has a quite sick baby, which your people don't want to help because they think we are unclean," she said in a scurrilous manner.

"Who has sent you and why should we trust you?" another woman asked.

It was apparent the disappearing white dove and the rainbow hadn't extinguished all their skepticism.

"First, I no longer follow the people of Abraham. I preach a new faith taught by one far greater than any mortal man before us. Come tonight and I will speak more about what he has taught us and who he is. I pray to see you tonight."

Once they reached the top of the hill, Alein's dark wavy hair was dry from the wind. He searched

Yoseph's eyes, and with a peaceful expression on his face spoke, "*Abba,* all the women will show up for supper tonight."

The setting sun fell behind some distant hills while they prepared to enter the village as three stars appeared. Rested from a late afternoon nap, all thirteen, baby Enoch in his mother's arms, and Zechariah started their descent down the hillock. Nicodemus had made a torch and their little band followed his lead as they approached the village. One after the other, the houses lit their many oil lamps, as if each room had captured a group of fireflies.

Georgeus's house was easy to find with the many ropes of dried dates covering the outside structure, but to Yoseph's surprise, he saw a large crowd of people milling around the front entrance. He recognized some of the women from the river, others from the *Shabbat* observance in the synagogue. When they saw them approach the entrance, the crowd cleared a path for them to enter and bowed their heads to greet them. After Yoseph's band had entered through the dark cloth covering the entrance, Georgeus and Clotho embraced each of them, yet he could see angst in their eyes.

"Rabbi Yoseph, I am glad you and your fellow teachers have arrived, but my wife and I fear some of these people, for several have shunned us or spoken ill about where we were born. I hope you and your teachers will protect us and our baby."

"Fear not, my friends, words can melt prejudices

just as easy as they can cause them. What we're about to say and show will protect your family like a suit of Roman armor."

A small wooden crib next to where Clotho was standing caught his attention. It held an ashen-colored infant, who lay motionless with its small dark eyes fixed on the ceiling of its home. As he moved closer to it to accommodate room for the rest of their band, the infant's eyes didn't move. At once, he feared the baby was dead, however, to his relief, its tiny chest heaved a slight upward moment. After a quick silent prayer of thanksgiving to *El Shaddai*, he directed his attention back to Georgeus.

"It's time to prepare for the supper of celebration as we agreed," Yoseph said, peering at Georgeus for affirmation. He nodded his approval.

"I haven't changed my mind Rabbi Yoseph, yet the thought did dwell in my mind for a while. Your kindness stayed with me all this afternoon and I felt in your debt to offer my home for your supper."

"Where is the table?" Yoseph inquired, not seeing it in the cramped room.

"Rabbi, it's in the next room, come and see."

He and Nicodemus followed Georgeus through another small cloth-covered entrance, which led into a bigger room. Against the back wall stood two long narrow tables butted against each other. Covering the tables were two plain flax woven cloths. Each were placed, at equal distances, with wooden trenchers and clay cups. On the floor were fifteen large straw-filled pillows arranged in proper fashion around the tables.

"Rabbi, it appears there isn't enough room and food to accommodate all our guests. What shall I do?" Georgeus wrung his hands, which held a white cleaning towel.

"Leave it to me, for our *Maishiach* will provide. You must have faith," Yoseph moved behind the tables and at the same time handed Nicodemus his large satchel.

"Nicodemus, see to it that our teachers have their *kodesh* objects and arrange them in proper order."

He left at once. The rest of their band seated themselves around the table and waited for the procession to begin.

"Rabbi, what do you want me to do with the overflow of village people who have come to see you and your teachers?" Georgeus asked.

"Have them come in and seat themselves, for we will start soon."

His departure was short, coming back with twenty-three people following him, which crowded themselves on Georgeus's dirt floor. Each person sat down in a quiet respectful manner, with Clotho sitting in front of Yoseph, trying to nurse her sick baby. His small lips tried to suck on his mother's nipple, but it was a futile effort. He still seemed quite listless, making Yoseph think he wouldn't live much longer.

After seated, the packed crowd spoke in a hushed manner, yet they sensed something was about to happen. Then the entire house became as quiet as a crypt, after which followed soft footfalls of the approaching procession. All the heads in the room turned to see who was coming, then focusing their eyes on Yohanan the writer as he entered the room. He held Yoseph's oil lamp in one hand and the *kodesh* parchments in the other. At once, the crowd stood, clearing a pathway for Yohanan and the others who were behind him. He moved past the table and placed the scrolls and oil lamp in front of Yoseph.

Next into the room came Nicodemus carrying the blood-tipped spear. Right away, there came combined sounds of *ahs* and *shrieks*. Then wide-eyed expressions of disbelief as the blood droplets rolled down the spear tip and disappeared before reaching the floor. He placed the spear in the corner and then seated himself at the supper table. Right behind him followed young Zechariah, holding his *abba's* execution sword above his head.

CHAPTER XXXVII

Behold the executioner's unjust sword!" Zechariah announced as he placed it next to the spear. With prudence, Hebron entered the room holding the salver. He placed it on the table in front of Yoseph, came around the table, and seated himself. Then came a long period of stillness; followed by a gliding shadow casting its female image on the wall. The image started moving with nimble arms held above its head, holding a black-shaped shadow of a chalice. As Miriam of Magdala entered the room radiating brilliant rays of light emanating from the chalice above her head.

The crowd was forced to bow their heads as the shafts of golden light touched their eyes. At last, she reached the supper table, stood before Yoseph, paused as he rose from his seat, and shouted,

"Behold the Lamb of *El Shaddai* who takes away the sins of many!" Several of their prospective students buried their faces against the dirt floor and begged for mercy. Many more tucked their heads in the crook of their elbows, trying to adjust their eyes to see. Miriam placed the radiating cup of light before Yoseph as its brilliance diminished.

"Our beloved Shepherd, the *Maishiach* is now present among us. Rejoice, my fellow students, for the salver sitting before me represents his broken body, which died on the Roman cross."

His pronouncement left several eyes of bewilderment on those who gazed at his face. At once, he reached for the salver and then raised it above his head, pausing for a moment, and lowered it with sections of flatbread stacked on top. The room at once filled with the smell of fresh-baked bread, causing each person present to give out an *ah* of delight.

He repeated the same procedures with the *Kodesh* Cup, but this time it exuded the colors of a rainbow. Yoseph lowered the cup and spoke, "The wine in our *Maishiach's* cup is his blood poured out from his crucifixion. Whoever drinks from his cup of salvation will have everlasting life."

After lowering it for all to see the cup replete with wine, one man shouted, "Rabbi, it's unclean to drink blood and it will make us sick."

"Don't worry, my friend, it tastes like wine, and his body tastes like bread; both have sustained me these many past summers. My teachers and I aren't cannibals, for both this blood and body are from *El Shaddai*. Come, friends, join us in the feast provided by our *Adonai*, and taste his *brit chadashah*. Your eyes and ears will be opened as never before, come up and sup with us and see what *El Shaddai* will reveal through his son. Come now and taste the goodness of our *Maishiach's* wisdom."

First, to come forth were Georgeus and Clotho, which prompted Yoseph to clasp the cup, while Miriam reached for the salver of bread, and they both strolled in front of the table to serve their feast. Georgeus and his wife tore off several pieces of the flatbread, little by little chewed the pieces, and Yoseph handed the *Kodesh* Cup for them to drink. At first, Georgeus was afraid to drink from the sacred glowing cup. Yoseph nodded to both, encouraging them to swallow a long draft of the garnet-colored liquid. At once, their wide round eyes spoke of the cup's ecstasy as they with still reverence returned to their seats. However, Clotho returned to sip another drink from the radiating cup.

"*Shalom aleichem*, my brother and sister, for letting us use your home for tonight's supper," Yoseph said, as their benefactors settled on the crowded floor.

The rest of their pupils ate and drank from their *Maishiach's* blessed supper and returned to their seats with a picture of awe growing across their faces. Several people came forth to verify the fullness of the cup and the completeness of the bread, telling others seated of the cup and salver's never-ending abundance. With their testimony, the rest of the crowd came forward and partook of the *Kodesh* Cup and the bread.

Afterward, the wind rushed through the room, spinning dust motes into the air with a low whisper of a voice becoming recognizable to Yoseph.

"Yoseph, you have done well here tonight. Now it's time to tell of my human life on earth," Yeshua's voice said, while caressing his ear.

Each person in the room turned their head trying to locate the voice, but it was futile. Then to everybody's surprise, a white dove appeared hovering over the cup and the salver. This sudden flapping bird apparition caused the crowd to buzz with amazement, followed by their raised arms of admirations.

One woman stood up and said, "Rabbi Yoseph, what is happening here? We want you to explain."

Another person rose, a village elder with his frizzled white hair and sagging wrinkles. He then spoke. "Yes, Rabbi, we want to know about this man who you call the *Maishiach*."

There was a resounding "yes" among all seated with their eyes focused on Yoseph to reply. By now, the white hovering dove had vanished, along with the bright shafts of light, leaving the room with small flickering flames from the oil lamps. The crowd continued shouting for Yoseph to tell them more about Yeshua's life and ministry before his death and resurrection.

"What I am about to tell you, my brothers, and sisters, it behooves you to listen and then go forth and tell others what I have told you. Some people will deny what you say, others will hate you, and some will try to kill you. Your new ministry isn't for the fainthearted, and I won't think less of you if you decide not to follow the *way* of our *Maishiach*. An evil heart won't endure in the cup's presence, for its radiant light will destroy that person. If you decide to join us, come to the river tomorrow at dawn. There we'll ask you to pledge your spiritual allegiance to *El Shaddai*, his son the *Maishiach*, and the *Kodesh Shekhinah* who led Moshe out of Egypt. Now with care, listen to what I am about to say."

Yoseph started at Yeshua's birth, told them of his relationship to him, their trip to the Isle of the Celts, his many miracles, and as a final point his crucifixion and resurrection. However, quite important, he spoke of Yeshua's new commandment to love one another, as they love themselves.

After he finished, the room was silent, not once did he detect a breath. All their faces were stonelike with wonder, and not an eyelash moved that Yoseph could see. He then spoke, freeing them from their frozen images.

"It's late, my friends, and we have an early day tomorrow; but before we leave, let me show you a symbol of your authority given to me from the *Maishiach*. This symbol will indicate to others who believe like us that we're all united in one new faith."

Yoseph grabbed a supper knife from the table, strolled to the back wall, and started cutting an outline of a large fish on the gray-colored clay wall.

"You will become fishers of men and women, and this is your symbol," Yoseph stated, as he finished the fish design with a tee-shaped sword running through the interior length of the fish symbol.

"Why the sword symbol, Rabbi Yoseph?" one woman asked.

"It's a symbol, for you who will become a defender of your faith against the evil ones who will try to destroy it. The design could be your fate, cut down for what you believe in, yet to rise again by the glory of the *Maishiach*. Now, let's proceed home and rest before preparing ourselves for tomorrow. *Shalom aleichem*, my fellow brothers and sisters."

The last of the visitors to leave was the village elder. His frizzy snow-white hair glistened in the lamplight as he approached the table.

"Rabbi, I have heard your name mentioned before tonight. Once, while in *Yerushalayim*, the market gossip said a rich man, who employed many workers, had all his lands, ships, and money confiscated by the High Priest Caiaphas, for burying his nephew in his family sepulcher. Also, the men in the marketplace said you were on the Sanhedrin council and once the richest man in the Mediterranean. How could this happen?"

"Yes, all of it's true. I am now penniless and a humble teacher, but remember, my friend, we may have to sacrifice other things besides our life and all our human possessions. We may have to leave family members as well. I have new riches beyond measure. They are the living, breathing words of *El Shaddai's* son, and no man or demon on earth can remove that precious gift from me. My power now comes from Yeshua, the *Maishiach*, not from my business wealth."

The old man said nothing more but turned to leave with a longing expression in his eyes to seek out more answers.

Georgeus started sweeping the dirt floor. "Rabbi Yoseph, I hoped you were pleased with our humble home and hospitality."

Before Yoseph could give his thanks, Clotho let out a piercing scream that caused him to flinch.

"My son is . . . dead!" she said with a crying stutter. "He isn't breathing, I beg you, Rabbi, please, help me!"

The poor baby's skin had turned from a pale white color to a light blue. Death was in the thralls of stealing him as one little arm lay motionless at the side of his tattered blanket.

At once, Yoseph fell on his knees and started praying his Lord's prayer, which leaped into his thoughts, still not remembering all of it at first. However, to his surprise, the words rolled off his lips, as if he was saying the words for him. Right away, the rest of their teachers fell on their knees and began saying the same prayer at different intervals.

When Yoseph finished, a gust of wind rushed through the room and whispered a voice. "Yoseph, tell the woman to suckle her child at once," came the recognized voice of Yeshua.

"Clotho, suckle your baby! Now!"

Tears streamed down her face. Her hands were wildly shaking and he feared she would drop her child at any moment. Miriam was the closest to her and moved with haste to aid her. Clotho gripped one hand, while Miriam steadied the baby and then Clotho reached into the top of her robe and pulled out a small breast. Clotho rubbed her nipple against the child's blue lips and squeezed out several small drops of what she thought would be milk.

But to Yoseph's amazement, the color of the liquid matched that of the *kodesh* wine. It seeped between the child's lips and disappeared, leaving the room with an agonizing moment of silence. His skin turned pink in color, his small arms started flailing with movement, and his mouth opened, screaming a loud cry. Clotho right away put him back to her breast.

"*Adonai,* be praised!" Yoseph yelled for all to hear, confirming another miracle from his *Maishiach* and his *Kodesh* Cup.

"My dearest Rabbi, bless you for saving my child from certain death," Clotho said, while wiping her eyes with her veil.

"It wasn't me who saved your child," Yoseph replied, "but our *Maishiach* and his cup you drank from tonight. I am just an instrument of his divine plan."

Clotho's face bore a large, dimpled smile of joy and the sweet tears of happiness had replaced those of sorrow. She kissed Yoseph on his cheek and followed with a large embrace while the baby continued to nurse.

"Rabbi, I thank you from my heart for saving my son." Georgeus reached for his son. He kissed him on his little tear-covered cheeks.

"Rabbi Yoseph, my wife and I would like to join you and your fellow teachers. I know we are still students and have much to learn."

"As I mentioned earlier, there may occur violence against us in the coming days. You heard about the synagogue elders threatening us today, this may happen in other synagogues and market squares where we travel." Yoseph hoped to test Georgeus's newfound faith.

"Yes, I've heard, but they treat us that way now, besides there is nothing to keep us in this village. Both my wife and I are Greek, and we can help and teach others like us. Over time, we could visit our relatives in Greece and preach the *Maishiach's* way, or as we would call him in our native tongue, *Christos.*"

"Let me discuss it with the other teachers and see what they say. In addition, I will pray to the *Maishiach* for guidance. You should discuss it further with your wife and both of you pray together for a positive outcome. It's late and your son needs more of his *amma's* milk."

"Again, thank you, Rabbi Yoseph, and you are welcome to sleep here tonight," Georgeus said, as he and his wife ambled to their private room.

They located a comfortable place on the dirt floor to sleep, yet Yoseph and several others couldn't sleep. Numerous events, in helping them grow their new faith, kept them excited with energy. Yoseph needed to write them down while they were still vivid in his head. Both his hands reached into his satchel and pulled out a parchment, a quill pen, and ink. He strolled over to the supper table, sat down, uncorked the clay bottle of ink, and started writing. The last time he had written anything was numerous days ago in front of the cave at Arimathea.

His writing hand sucked up his nervous energy and this was reflected in updating his copies and originals. Yoseph would use the copies to hide in the cave at Arimathea for his return someday or for others to find after he was no more of this earth. A surge of sublime confidence raced through his veins, guided by the way and Yeshua's voice.

"Yoseph, why are you not acquiring some rest?" Miriam asked.

"Yes, and your writing can wait until tomorrow." Yohanan also approached the table.

Both their eyes were wide and their movements quick like his, betraying their concern for him. "So, both of you can't sleep too." He smiled at them. "Let me follow you outside so I can loosen my writing hand and we can obtain some fresh air."

"Excellent idea, Yoseph." Miriam headed for the door.

He rose, strolled to the front of the table, met Yohanan there, and they both with caution stepped over all the sleeping bodies. Once, losing his balance, his foot stepped on Thomas, who didn't cry out but rolled over with eyes shaped like slits and spoke. "Yoseph, is that you?"

"Return to sleep, my good man. I am just obtaining some fresh air. Never mind me."

Once outside, the night air cooled Yoseph, and it further heightened his sense of resolve.

"Miriam and Yohanan, what would you think if we had Georgeus and Clotho join our band of teachers?"

Miriam replied first. "Yoseph, I think Yeshua would ask them to join him if he was here in human form. I see no problem with your request."

"I agree with Miriam," Yohanan said. "Yet Gentiles as teachers might be a problem in the synagogues. We faced some difficulties today and we were Jews. They aren't of our religious heritage or know what Yeshua preached and taught before his crucifixion. Is it a sound idea to divulge to them his family background and our ancestral history? Also, can we trust them?"

"Yes, we can trust them, and teaching them our heritage will make them quite flexible with all people in their preaching of the way," he said. "We must cast off the strict laws of our old faith and retain the best lessons Yeshua preached of the old religion as well as his new."

"Yoseph, I understand Yohanan's concerns, but I agree with you. They'll help us in our ministry, and with many of those in the synagogues who aren't happy with the high priest and the Pharisees. This was self-evident with the scribes, who are writing so many new laws and rules that crush us with restrictions. However, what I am quite concerned with is disagreement coming from Shimon bar Yona, not Shimon the Zealot, and Yeshua's brother."

Miriam shook her head. "He and Ya'akov won't approve of preaching to Gentiles, and neither will they approve of Gentile teachers. They don't trust the Gentiles and I understand why, for some of them are paid informants of the priests and scribes and this doesn't include the Roman informants. Besides, Shimon and Ya'akov's followers are being hunted down by one of Nicodemus's former students, Saul of Tarsus."

"We shouldn't fear any informant, because greed will always be used by the evil one for his nefarious purposes. Shimon is indecisive as usual, and his faith rises and falls like the sun. In due course, the light of the *Maishiach* will keep him focused and he will embrace all Gentiles one day. However, we must stay true to our *Maishiach's* preaching and include all nations, people, and heritages. We must lead by Yeshua's example, and I care less about Shimon's petty rules. He and Ya'akov bicker with each other over who should be the leader of Yeshua's legacy and fail to listen to the people's fears.

"Let's pray, my friends, and listen to what Yeshua says of Georgeus and Clotho's destiny."

The three of them knelt on the cool earth and prayed, which after a short moment a strong breeze arrived. The direction it came from was odd, for the wind shot straight down on their heads, forcing them to stare at the starry sky.

Then came a bodiless voice that said, "You have chosen wisely, so be it."

They turned to one another and smiled in wonder. A great sense of accomplishment came over Yoseph, and he knew their two new members would fulfill a spiritual destiny and continue Yeshua's ministry.

"Yoseph," Miriam whispered. "I see a dark shadow moving between the houses across from us."

"I too see the dark phantom," whispered Yohanan.

"Who goes there?" Yoseph shouted.

"It's me," came the quiet voice of Hebron.

"I thought you were asleep in Georgeus's house." He still didn't see Hebron's face.

"No, Yoseph, I couldn't sleep, so I used my time to scout around the village. Near the end of the village, there was a riderless camel. As I approached, a crouching dark outline of a man sprang out from between two houses and raced toward the camel. He jumped on the camel's back, used his stick to raise the beast, and before I could reach him, they were gone into the night. He was heading in the direction of Arimathea, but the darkness prevented me from seeing his face. However, he wore a sword, for its dark outline shown against his white tunic."

"Hebron, do you think this is the man who terrorized us back at the cave?" Yoseph asked.

"Yes, I believe it's him, yet our adversaries are still growing. We now have new ones from this village. I know you don't want to hear this, but I think we should leave as soon as possible."

"I agree with your judgment in the matters of our safety, yet we need at least six days of teaching, preaching, and the appointment of leaders for this village's converts."

Yoseph sucked in a deep breath. "They are cowards who don't show themselves in the daylight no matter where they originate. I'll let you pick a set of guards to protect us during the nights we stay here. You can tell them where to set up their best sentry points and then seek out any men with military experience. Now hurry and awake some men to help you until dawn arrives."

The three of them followed Hebron inside and acquired the sleeping places of the men he picked to patrol the village. Yoseph still couldn't sleep, now knowing maybe there was another possible stalker or the same one.

Dawn came too soon, as a distant cock crowed arousing them to awaken. Undisturbed, they left the village, not attracting much attention, and headed toward the river. The new followers were waiting for them at the riverbank with knotted groups of people holding oil lanterns. It was an overpowering sight, seeing forty glowing lanterns reflecting on the river's surface.

"Observe, Yoseph. There are about fifteen more people than yesterday," Nicodemus said, while pointing in the direction of the river. "It appears we have all gathered before the synagogue priest and the elders have awakened."

The golden shimmering reflection continued until they reached the riverbank. There the first rosy fingers of dawn appeared on the horizon, which started fading the river's golden color to replace it with shades of pink and orange.

They observed several large rocks to stand on, and then gave their testimony about Yeshua's life and his teachings. Yoseph spoke of his early boyhood adventures, how he made "fishers" of men and women, his new covenant, and the cup's gift of a sacred supper. Afterward, he grabbed his staff and drew a large crescent-shaped line in the soft sand to everyone's baffle-faced stares. Then he handed his staff to Nicodemus, who in turn drew another crescent-shaped line completing the shape of a fish.

Nicodemus gazed at the crowd. "This is your symbol as a follower of the *Maishiach* from Galilee. Greet each brother and sister you meet with half of this symbol. If he or she completes this *kodesh* symbol, you will know they're a follower of the way. If they don't complete the design, tell them what you have heard from our teacher here today and the days that will follow." Nicodemus completed his portion of testimony and teachings.

After all their teachers had spoken, the large crowd of postulants lined up single file at the edge of the riverbank. The act of baptisms filled the rest of the afternoon, until about the third watch when they finished.

"Yoseph, observe!" Miriam cried out while pointing toward the hilltop of their camp. Hovering above the date palm trees was a large ball of rotating fire, which issued forth a hot gust of wind. The flaming sphere crept toward the ground, halted, and then issued forth a thunderous voice from its rotating flames.

"Yoseph of Arimathea, you and your fellow teachers have done well, my beloved rabbi." The voice stated in a roaring crackling sound. At once, the entire crowd of new followers gasped a collective shriek. Then the crowd fell on their stomachs in fear. Yoseph too, along with his fellow teachers, fell to the wet ground in prostrate reverence as their faces and bodies kissed the soft wet sand.

To Yoseph's satisfaction, their group of postulants grew each day and so did their *kodesh* supper guests. On the last day of their stay, all their fellow teachers had a meeting to appoint village teachers. The vetting process lasted the entire day, which was composed of praying, verbal discussions, and final determinations. They assembled their swelling group of village followers at the riverbank and announced their decisions. The new teaching elders were composed of men, women, and the old.

The appointed head of the village elders was the frizzy white-haired man Yoseph had met earlier. His name was Yitzhak, whom his fellow new teachers elected. All of Yoseph's close companion teachers, including himself, were embraced by the village's new teachers with final farewells. Yoseph's band gathered their few belongings and started on the road toward *Yoppa* with Georgeus, Clotho, and their baby, now named after Yoseph.

There were many smiles of elation and accomplishment on their faces as they ambled down the dusty road to their next destination, yet Yoseph sensed unseen eyes observing them from afar, which somewhat robbed him of his elation. Would they reach the *Yoppa* port without danger, or would evil raise its monstrous head?

GLOSSARY

Latin Terms

Cantos—major division in poem or song
Chantry—chapel for an endowment for a priest or priests to celebrate mass for the deceased
Chasuble—a sleeveless outer vestment worn by a priest when celebrating mass
Cognomens—nicknames used by ancient Greeks and Romans
Deus Vult—God's will
Gladius—Roman sword used by a legionnaire
Greaves—Roman soldier metal shin guards
League—unit of measure equaling three miles
Logos—divine reason implicit in the cosmos (holy words)
Magus—ancient seer from the east
Non nobis Domine, non nobis, sed nomini tuo da gloriam—Not unto us, O Lord, not unto us, but to thy name give glory (Psalm 115:1, KJV) —Knights Templar battle cry
Pater Noster—Lord's Prayer
Pax vobiscum—peace be with you
Rota Romana—an ecclesiastical court of Rome (papal court)
Sub Rosa—happening or done in secret
Templi omnium hominum pacis—father of the temple of peace of men

Iberian (Spanish) Terms

Abad—abbot
Abadia—abbey
Abuelo—grandfather

Altesse—noble woman (highness)
Alteza—high king
Atención—attention
Bandido—bandit
Bastardos—bastards
Beticos—a Gypsy (Romany) tribe in Iberia
Bienvenido—welcome
Caballero—gentleman or knight
Castille—county or kingdom in Iberia
Castillo—castle
Clave—key
Conde—count
Condesa—countess
Diable—characteristics of the devil
Doña—lady
Don—gentleman
El Rey de Reys—the King of Kings
Esposa—wife
Excelencia—excellency
Gadjes—term for yokel or bumpkin
Gitano—Gypsy
Gran Patrón—great leader
Herari—Gypsy tribe in Iberia
Hermano—brother
Hija—daughter
Hijo—son
Iglesia—church
Judios—Jewish people
Klass—glass
Madre—mother
Marquésa—marquess, female royal title
Marqués—marquis, royal title
Monasterio—monastery
Monje—monk

Mozarabs—name of Christians living in Muslim Iberia and their architecture before the Muslim conquest
Muchacho—young boy
Muchas gracias—thank you much
Mudéjar—Iberian Muslims
Princesa—princess
Principe—prince
Reina—queen
Reino—kingdom
Rey—king
Santo Cáliz—holy chalice
Santo Verdad—holy truth
Seguir mi—follow me
Seis—six
Señoras—ladies
Senoritas—young ladies
Señor—mister
Su excelencia—your excellency
Taza de Christo—Cup of Christ
Zorro—fox
Zuda—former Mudéjar fortress in Aragón

Medieval Terms

Arbalest—large and stronger crossbow
Archivolt—a religious ornamental molding on an arched entrance to a Christian church
Armarius—monk librarian at a monastery scriptorium
Bartizan—an overhanging, wall-mounted turret projecting from a wall of a castle
Biggen—head covering with cloth straps, sometimes called an arming cap
Center of the earth—another name of Jerusalem
Chausses—chain mail armor to protect the legs

Clerestory—medieval church architecture of a series of high-arched, stained-glass windows

Dame—a lady, wife of a knight, or a female knight

Entremets—a light dishes of food served between courses

Fripperies—ostentatious dressing

Gambeson—a padded defensive jacket worn with or without armor

Garderobes—castle or medieval toilets

Gematria—an alphanumeric code of assigning numerical values to names, words, or phrases according to its letters

Graal—another name for the Holy Grail, or the word can mean measurement

Labarum cross—Christian military standard cross displaying the Greek letters *chi* and *rho* for Christ

March—medieval word for borderland

Menhir—large monolithic tapered stones of religious significance

Merlon—a solid stone or brick, toothlike section of a castle battlement

Pell post—sword-practicing posts of thick hardwood

Reliquary—a container of holy relics usually shaped like a miniature golden church, hand, or head

Sain—make the sign of the cross or bless

Seneschal—top administrator or steward in a noble or religious household

Siege perilous—in Arthurian legend, it is a vacant seat at the Round Table reserved by Merlin for the perfect knight to obtain the Holy Grail

Solteties—medieval, small, designed cakes served at meals

Transept—either one of two parts of a church forming the design of arms of a cross

Trushul—a trident or divine symbol

Viand—food

Visigoths—ruled Iberia (Spain) from the AD fifth century until overthrown by the Muslim Moors in 711

Jewish and Aramaic Terms

Abba—father
Adonai—our Lord
Amidah—Jewish prayer blessing
Amma—mother
Ben or *bar*—son of
Bet din—judgment hall or religious court
Bimah—podium or platform in a synagogue from which the Torah and Prophets are read
Birkat ha-mazon—the prayer blessing for food after the meal
Brit chadashah—new covenant
Chokmah—meaning wisdom or one of the sefirot for wisdom in the mystical Jewish Kabbalah
El Shaddai—The Almighty
Eloheinu—meaning our God, which is used in the Jewish Shema
Eyn Sof—meaning the endless one or infinity before creation, Kabbalistic in nature
Hashkiveinu—the second blessing following the Shema
Kabod—halo or bright light
Kavanah—direction, intention, or purpose
Kodesh—holy
Maishiach—anointed one (The Messiah)
Malach—angel
Mathetes—student or disciple of a learned teacher
Mechitzah—synagogue partition separating men from women
Metatron—the name of the Prophet Enoch after his transformation to the highest angel
Mezuzah—Hebrew sacred doorpost with selected

Torah verses
Mikveh—ritual baths
Mitzvot—the 613 commandments by God
Ner tamid—the lamp that burns perpetually in a Jewish synagogue
Ogdoad—an early Gnostic term meaning eight divine beings, including their consorts
Omein—amen or so be it
Parokhet—a screen hanging in front of the Torah Ark as a partition
Pesach—Jewish Passover
Ruah—spiritual wind or holy breath
Seder—order for Passover service
Shabbat—Jewish Sabbath
Shakharit—morning Jewish prayer
Shalom aleichem—peace be with you
Shalom bayit—peace of the home
Shekhinah—the presence of God in the world or the dwelling place of God
Shema—"Hear, O Israel, the Lord is our God, the Lord is One! Blessed is the name of His glorious kingdom for ever and ever," prayer recited twice a day by Jews
Sheol—hell or burning pit
Shiva—the seven-day period of formalized mourning by the immediatefamily of a deceased Jew
Teliffin—worn leather prayer boxes attached to the forehead and arms
Tzaddik—a righteous or saintly person in the Jewish faith
Ya'akov—name for James
Yad—hand-shaped pointer used to read Jewish scriptures from the Torah
Yehudah—Judea
Yerushalayim—Jerusalem
Yisrael—Israel

Frankish Gaul Terms

Abbaye—abbey
Abbé—priest (father)
Adieu—goodbye
Affectueux—loving
Amant—lover
Ami—friend
Arrêter—stop
Baphomet—a saint or saints, possibly John the Baptizer and John the Evangelist
Baron—another nobility title for lord
Bâtard—bastard
Bienvenu—welcome
Bon—good
Bon ami—good friend
Bonjour—hello
Bonsoir—good evening
Cabochons—gems polished but not faceted
Chanson de geste—a medieval historical romance in French verse, typically one of conquest or bravery
Chevalier—knight
Chevauchées—raids
Coeur—heart
Comte—count (title)
Duc—duke
Église—church
Épouse—wife
Fils—son or sons (des fils)
Frère—brother
Garçon—young boy
Gonfanier—Knights Templar battle flag standard bearer
Juif—Jewish man
Juive—Jewish woman

Languedoc—geographical region located in southern Gaul (France) along the Mediterranean coast
Le Sangraal—the Cup of Christ (the Holy Grail)
Mari—husband
Mère—mother
Mes amis—my friends
Mesdames—ladies
Moine—monk
Mon bon—my dear
Monsieur—mister
Montagne(s)—mountain or mountains
Oubliette—dirty basement prison
Père Supérieur—superior father (pope)
Père—father
Princesse—princess
Provence—geographical region in southwestern Gaul (France) facing the Mediterranean
Raison de être—reason for being
Reine—the queen
Roi—king
Royaume—kingdom
Santo Père—holy father
Seigneur—lord (title)
Soeur—sister
Très bien—very good
Trouvère—poet/singer
Vin—wine

Muslim Terms

Alaikum al salaam—I return the peace unto you
Allah akbar or Allahu akbar—God is great or greatest
Allah—God
Baraq—Prophet Muhammad's mare horse
Hamsa—amulet to ward off the evil eye

Mujahid—a Muslim who fights for his faith
Sadiq—honest friend
Salaam alaikum—peace be upon you
Salat—a ritual prayer by a Muslim

Medieval Terms

Aketon—long quilt-padded shirt covered with chain mail
Apse—rounded alcove behind a church altar
Bailey—castle courtyard
Barbican—gateway or outer works defending a drawbridge
Beauséant—piebald-colored flag of the Knights Templar
Coif—hood of chain mail
Keep—heavily fortified tower in the interior of a castle
Nave—central part of a church
Portcullis—heavy wooden-grilled gate that can be raised and lowered
Quarrel—thick metal tip of a crossbow arrow
Refectory—common hall where monks eat
Romany—Gypsies
Sacristy—room in a church where sacred vestments and vessels are kept
Saint Michaelmas—holy feast day celebrated on September 29
Sally port—small hidden door to a fortress
Tympanum—area of a church between the lintel of a doorway and the arch above it. May have biblical scenes carved in this area

Lord Robert de Borron and Saint Joseph of Arimathea's quest is continued in *The Tree of Life* with the help of research and long-forgotten legends coming from the mysterious land of Iberia. Not much is recognized today of the Holy Grail on this ancient diverse peninsula. For some period of time, there was a historical lull in the conflict of the three Abrahamic faiths. During the year (1190) of *The Tree of Life*, each Iberian religious community contributed to the advancement of the human condition (science, math, medicine, diplomacy, and an ever-increasing merchant middle class).

The Holy Grail and Saint Joseph of Arimathea's writings give subtle clues and not-so-subtle clues to the whereabouts of the Cup of Christ and the first organized Christian church. Old Greek symbols, similar to the slightly altered Constantine (chi-rho), and the Saint Ambrose cross propel Lord Robert into the interior of Iberia. In 1190, Spain was composed of numerous Christian kingdoms and Moorish sultanates. Both the Moorish cities and the Christian monasteries were great repositories of long-forgotten knowledge. Christian monks, Moorish scholars, and intellectual Jewish religious leaders were the librarians and copyists of the medieval era.

Books during this time were rare and expensive to reproduce. They were highly protected and hidden from view.

The greatly known Christian religious pilgrim trail, El Camino Santiago de Compostela, wasn't the only holy route in Iberia. Little is recorded of the Spanish Holy Grail trail, which started in the Iberian city of Puerto del Palo in the north and traversed San Juan de la Peña, San Pedro el Viejo at Huesca (this book's Part III illustration), Zaragozza, Teruel, and finally ending at the Valencia Cathedral in Spain. Here today resides a red agate cup purported to be the Holy Grail. Spanish legend says an Iberian Roman soldier brought the cup from Rome to Spain (AD third century) for safety, on the instructions of Saint Lawrence (Lorenzo), because it was about to be destroyed by the Roman emperor. In 2006, Pope Benedict XIII celebrated mass using this cup. Author and historian Dr. Karen Ralls said it best in her 2012 book, *The Templars and the Grail: Knights of the Quest*, "There are as many holy grails as there are grail seekers."

In *The Tree of Life*, I used a more historical Jewish influence in the second book of the Cup of Christ and the Forgotten Disciple series. The esoteric kabbala and the Old Testament prophet Enoch and his apocryphal books were used as a foundation of secret knowledge to help Lord Robert locate the diaphanous Cup of Christ, Saint

Joseph's parchments, and the whereabouts of the first organized Christian church. Enoch, a descendant of Seth (Adam and Eve's third son) and great-grandfather to Noah, left books to help Noah build the ark. The books also revealed the secrets of the Jewish mystical kabbala. Noah said, "My great-grandfather Enoch gave me the teaching of all the secrets in the book in the Parables, which had been given to him, and he put them together for me in the words of the book of Parables" (S.N. Strutt, *Enoch Insights*, 162).

In addition, I used the fictitious son (Templar chaplain Jeremiah Santiago de Compostela) of Grand Master Gilbért de Érail as a scholastic character to help move the grail quest forward. Jeremiah's helpful intellectual insight helps Lord Robert interpret his writings from Saint Joseph of Arimathea. Jeremiah, as a Templar chaplain, would be privy to religious symbolism and languages. The chaplain's dissertation on geometric polygons, Pythagoras, the sacred numbers five (penta) and eight (octa), and gematria (letters representing number codes) leads the reader to the three eights (which add up to twenty-four letters of the Greek alphabet and Jesus the Christ's name in Greek).

Eight was the number of humans on Noah's ark and also the number of sides of the Dome of the Rock in Jerusalem. Jewish males are circumcised eight days after they are born. The eight women of Pleiades were turned into stars to serve as guideposts. Eight types of furniture were in the first Jewish Temple. King David was the eighth son of his father Jesse. The octagram star is a gnostic symbol of creation. The Feast of Tabernacles lasts eight days. Both the Holy of Holies in the Tabernacle and the first Jewish Temple were shaped like a cube (2x2x2 = 8). The geometric shape of the vesica piscis (also called the vessel of the fish) is designed like a numerical eight. Eliyah performed eight miracles. The old Celtic calendar had eight spokes or seasons. In the Book of Revelation, the New Jerusalem is described as a cube. The Muslim Kaaba at Mecca is in the shape of a cube.

Legends say that King Solomon had a powerful five-pointed star ring he used to harness demons to build the First Temple to house the Ark of the Covenant. Every measurement in the old Jewish tabernacle was a multiple of five. According to Pythagoras, the pentagram (the star length segment points) has a divine proportion, which ancient Egyptian and Greek builders used. It is called phi with a ratio of 1.61803. Later used by operative Masons, the early Templars used it for their fortresses, castles, and churches. There are five virtues of knighthood. The Bethlehem star was five-pointed, and this star design represented the five wounds of Christ and the five joys of Mary, mother of Jesus.

Plato, in his book *Timaeus*, declares that the creator is the grand architect of the infinite universe. Pythagoras said the number five typified light. To the Masons, it represents the five virtues or points of fellowship. There were five polished stones prepared to use in David's sling against Goliath. The ancient sigil for Jerusalem was a five-pointed star. To the Muslims, it represents the Five Pillars of Islam. Also, to the ancient Greeks, the pentagram represented the star of Hermes (lighting the way). The number five is a prime number.

The following books are excellent reading sources, if the reader is interested in reference materials for *The Tree of Life.*

The Books of Enoch by Joseph B. Lumpkin
Dictionary of Symbols by Carl G. Liungman
The Dimensions of Paradise by John Michell
The Lost Pillars of Enoch by Tobias Churton
Sacred Symbols by Clare Gibson
The Secret Language of Symbols by David Fontana

I hope readers have enjoyed the second book, *The Tree of Life,* in the Cup of Christ and the Forgotten Disciple series and will look forward to the next book in this trilogy.

The New Jerusalem

The third book in The Cup of Christ series finds Joseph of Arimathea as a teacher and new rabbi. He now has additional followers and fellow teachers of the words of his late great nephew Rabbi Yeshua ben Yoseph. His teaching forces him to leave Palestine and travel to new mysterious lands of Gaul and Albion. There he and his band of teachers are confronted by ancient Druids, a serial killer, and the Roman authorities.

Thank you for reading the second book in my
trilogy series and please sign up
for my newsletter
at my web page for book discounts.
jackmholt.com

Jack Holt

can often be found researching the forgotten people of history's mysteries. He attended Purdue University, has coauthored several local history books after retiring from banking and has traveled extensively in the British Isles. Jack is a long-time member and past prior of SMOTJ GP USA (Knights Templar) and lives in Indiana with his wife. Please visit him at his website www.jackmholt.com

9 781735 528359